T0246637

MONSTERS

MONSTERS

Mary Shelley's
FRANKENSTEIN AND MATHILDA

Edited and with an Introduction by Claire Millikin Raymond

2LP CLASSICS

FLORIDA ■ NEW YORK
www.2leafpress.org

P.O. Box 4378
Grand Central Station
New York, New York 10163-4378
editor@2leafpress.org
www.2leafpress.org

2LEAF PRESS INC. is a
nonprofit 501(c)(3) organization that promotes
multicultural literature and literacy.
Stephanie Ann Agosto, Executive Director
www.2lpinc.org

Copyright © 2018 Claire Millikin Raymond
Shelley, Mary Wollstonecraft.
Frankenstein, Or, The Modern Prometheus,
the 1831 text.

Shelley, Mary Wollstonecraft. *Mathilda,*
the 1959 text of Elizabeth Nitchie.

Edited by: Claire Millikin Raymond
Cover art: Dé-Jon Graves.
Layout and design: Gabrielle David

Library of Congress Control Number: 201793101

ISBN-13: 978-1-940939-70-4 (Paperback)
ISBN-13: 978-1-940939-84-1 (eBook)

10   9   8   7   6   5   4   3   2   1

Published in the United States of America

First Edition | First Printing

2Leaf Press trade distribution is handled by University of Chicago Press / Chicago Distribution Center (www.press.uchicago.edu) 773.702.7010. Titles are also available for corporate, premium, and special sales. Please direct inquiries to the UCP Sales Department, 773.702.7248.

All rights reserved. No part of this publication may be reproduced, stored in a retrieval system, or transmitted in any form or by any means electronic, mechanical, photocopied, recorded or otherwise without written permission from 2Leaf Press, Inc., except in the case of brief quotations embodied in critical reviews and certain other noncommercial uses permitted by copyright law. For permission requests, contact the publisher at editor@2leafpress.org.

In Memoriam
Meena Alexander
(1951-2018)

AUTHOR'S NOTE ON THE 1831 EDITION

AS FAR BACK AS 1988 Anne K. Mellor made the persuasive case that Mary Shelley's original 1818 edition of *Frankenstein* should be the touchstone of all study of this novel. Since then, scholarly consensus largely has concurred with Professor Mellor, that in the 1818 edition we see the "real" Frankenstein. I present here the 1831 edition not in disagreement with the value of the 1818 edition of Frankenstein but rather to offer interested readers an opportunity to read the novel as Mary Shelley edited it for the 1831 edition. At this time, she was in her early thirties and her influential and revered husband was deceased. In other words, the 1831 edition reflects editorial decisions that Mary Shelley made as a still youthful, but now fully autonomous adult reflecting on her novel. For this reason, there is room for both the 1818 and 1831 versions to be read. The purpose of scholarship, and the benefit of reading Mary Shelley's work in general, is not to create dogmatic camps of value but rather to read as much of Shelley's own writing with its reflection of her changing thinking over time, as we possibly can. In that spirit, I present here Shelley's 1831 edition of *Frankenstein*. ◂

—Claire Millikin Raymond

CONTENTS

NAMING MARY SHELLEY'S MONSTERS

I N THIS BICENTENNIAL YEAR of the publication of Mary Wollstonecraft Shelley's novel *Frankenstein; or, the Modern Prometheus,* it is time to turn and face our monsters. Monstrous political, economic, and environmental forces attend us in the twenty-first century. Displaced and dispossessed persons are tragically emblematic of the second decade of the twenty-first century. The hubris and abuses of patriarchy, exposed in public discourses such as the #MeToo movement, and expressed when children are torn from their asylum-seeking parents at the United States border, emblematize our era. The corrupting and painful legacy of colonialism, with racism a deeply unresolved aspect of our political world, shapes the twenty-first century. A list of our century's woes would be incomplete without mention of global warming: scientifically engendered industrial processes, such as combustion engines and coal-fired power plants, have generated climate shifts that threaten the planet. Our intertwining of human identity with machines—through social media, online search engines, and the like—may be a step toward a society in which artificial intelligence (AI) dominates. While many in the world suffer hunger and poverty, American billionaires seek the capacity to live forever by attempting to invent ways to replace their failing bodily systems with computer parts.[1] Eerily, uncannily, Mary Shelley's works, *Frankenstein; or, the Modern Prometheus* (1818) and *Mathilda* (written in 1819-20, published in 1959) predict these cultural cleavages and tragedies. A very young woman when she created these works, Shelley came to see herself as a Cassandra figure, who saw disasters on the horizon that others could not see and therefore did not heed.[2]

Mary Shelley was the daughter of the feminist philosopher Mary Wollstone-craft.[3] Although her mother did not live to see it, as a teenager Shelley created in *Frankenstein* a myth of modern identity that reaches beyond any other work of Romanticism (the literary period and style in which Shelley wrote) in its impact on the cultural imagination. Literary scholars know the work of Mary Shelley's husband, the poet Percy Bysshe Shelley; philosophers and historians know the work of her mother, Mary Wollstonecraft, and father, William Godwin. But virtually anyone who reads or watches movies or looks at comic books knows some version of Mary Shelley's *Frankenstein:* the story of a monster cobbled together from corpses, brought to life by a kind of galvanism.[4] *Frankenstein* is not the name of the monster but the name of the monster's creator: Victor Frankenstein, an aristocratic scientist. The unnamed monster's capacity to symbolize the lost, the exile, the outcast, the motherless, the estranged—and also the terrifying effects of violent hubris that casts out the vulnerable and the needy—makes him a figure for the modern condition. The twinned figure of Victor Franken-stein and his "monster" forms a character that calls out with the force of myth. Arguably this story is the most consistent myth of modernity, if to be modern is to be estranged from communal identity, to know the curse of isolated striving; if to be modern is to be a hybrid, as Victor Frankenstein and his monster are in their conjoined identities.

In this volume, that brings together Mary Shelley's youthful novel *Franken-stein* (first published in 1818) with her almost equally youthful novella *Mathilda* (written in 1819-20, but unpublished until the mid-twentieth century), I eluci-date the monstrous themes that unify these works. What makes *Frankenstein* so disturbingly similar to Shelley's slightly later story of father-daughter incest, told in the eponymous novella *Mathilda?* The theme of the outcast, the one outside societal bounds, the theme of the father whose hubris and desire condemns his child to endless suffering and isolation, echoes in both these works. Mary Shelley's youth, her gender, her motherless condition, her precarious social position—as a teenager, she was mistress to the already married Percy Shelley—placed her in a position of vulnerability, or wound-ability, and she responded to this difficulty by creating literary works, *Frankenstein* and *Mathilda,* that plumb the depths of social ostracism, familial loss, the haunted and haunting terrain of embodied identity, and the strain of violence stemming from the Enlightenment (Age of Reason) credo of human perfectibility. Daughter of philosophers, Mary Shelley probed the fallibility of absolute faith in human rationality. Her early works show that the belief in human perfectibility and triumphant rationality can itself act as a lure, with unchecked pride drawing her characters toward catastrophe, monstrosity, and living death, not despite but because they limn Enlightenment ideals.

Teenage Rebel

MARY WOLLSTONECRAFT SHELLEY was born to Mary Wollstonecraft, a philosopher and early feminist, and William Godwin, a philosopher and novelist, in 1797. Her parents were luminaries of the intellectual world and Mary Shelley manifests, in her two earliest works, a hinge between Enlightenment thought, with its belief in reason and human perfectibility, and Romanticism, with its emphasis on emotion, the self, and the natural world as mirror to the self's soul. Her own origin story is immediately marked by tragedy, as Wollstonecraft died shortly after giving birth to the infant Mary, her second child. Mary Shelley, then, knew her mother only by reading her mother's books—the 1792 feminist classic, *A Vindication of the Rights of Woman,* prime among them—and by visiting her mother's grave. [5] She was a motherless girl. This sense of being lost, and of having lost the one great love—her mother—that could support her intellectually and spiritually perhaps led to young Mary Wollstonecraft Godwin's decision, when she was not yet seventeen years old, to fall into a sexual relationship with a married man, the poet Percy Bysshe Shelley. She and the poet fled England and lived together, not married but most definitely in a carnal relationship, for nearly three years, in Europe.

After the suicide of Percy Shelley's first wife, Mary and Percy married, in 1816. [6] Hence, very early on Mary Shelley went from being a motherless daughter to being a figure of scandal: mistress to a married man whose pregnant wife then committed suicide. During this time, still a teenager, Mary became pregnant and gave birth to a premature child who died weeks after being born. The events of Mary Shelley's early life—her infancy and her teens—to an unusual degree were characterized by loss and violence, by precariousness and risk. These themes permeate her early work. Even so, *Frankenstein* and *Mathilda* transcend biography. *Frankenstein* and *Mathilda* present bone-rattling symbolic narratives and figures, engaging themes of mortality, ethics, good and evil that preeminently question the ethos of techno-modernity melded to patriarchal power. Should fathers have complete power over their children's lives? Mary Shelley raises this question in her works. Should scientific progress take precedence over all other aspects of human culture and society? Mary Shelley's works raise this question fervently. Shelley creates typographies of the monstrous in fictional realms that chart the risks of male dominated techno-modernity. To trace the centrality of the monster, the monstrous, in these works, I turn first to a discussion of *Frankenstein.*

The Abortion

AS MUCH AS THE NOVEL *Frankenstein* is about a monster, or a monstrous creation, it is about a creator: a scientist, a father. The novel is subtitled to point our attention to this creator: "The Modern Prometheus." In classical mythology Prometheus, a Titan, is the figure who risks taking on the power of the Olympian gods: in Greek myth, Prometheus not only steals fire from the gods, he creates mankind from clay.[7] In Shelley's novel, Victor Frankenstein takes the power over life and death that has belonged to the gods (or to those forces of origin, inception, ignition, degeneration, descent, ascent, loss, and redemption, that we often gloss by the term "gods"). Frankenstein, out of corpses, creates a living creature. By titling her novel to point to the monster's creator, Shelley emphasizes that her work is not primarily about the sins of the monster but rather those of his father/creator. *Frankenstein* is a story of parenting, of birth, of the pain and trauma of being a child of a father whose selfishness overwhelms his ability to act ethically.

Strikingly, Frankenstein calls his monster an "abortion," (a term that in the early nineteenth century had a different meaning than it does now), conveying a feeling of insuperable tragedy, grief, and violence. Frankenstein calling his monster an abortion references a child born too early to survive. (Only in twentieth-century parlance has the term come to stand for a procedure to terminate pregnancy.) Frankenstein's monster, unlike other abortions, survives, but only as a figure of living death. His body is composed of corpses and the galvanism that vivifies him does not entirely take.[8] Though galvanized into life, the creature is never unified into a recognizable human figure. He remains a figure outside of any social group, an outcast from all human social worlds.

Monster, etymologically, means "to show," hence a monster is something that reveals, that is revelatory. Mary Shelley's monster, in *Frankenstein*, is the embodied form that shows the monstrousness of his father/creator, or rather the monstrousness of the interlocking systems of overwhelming faith in science, without ethical parameters, and of male dominance. Although the monster ultimately behaves violently, Shelley's novel suggests that his violence is the result of an intolerable wound, the blow of his father not loving him, the pain of his father's shame and disavowal of his progeny, and the monster's utter and complete rejection by human beings who show themselves to be selfish and shallow in response to his attempts to befriend them. The monster is not the biological progeny of Frankenstein, but in this novel what has meaning is the psychological and social dynamic of the parent-child bond. A betrayal at the root of that bond causes the monster's ultimately violent behavior; this wound is deepened because all the other human beings the monster encounters are little better than Victor Frankenstein in their ethics. They see the monster's strange face and body, and they reject him. They do not consider that he might have within him kindness, love, intelligence. Interestingly, one might say the monster qualifies as a genius. He teaches himself language and reads literature extraordinarily quickly. He survives by teaching himself to speak, read, interpret. No one helps him. When he confronts Frankenstein, he speaks as eloquently as the poet John Milton, not only because Shelley borrows heavily from Milton's *Paradise Lost* in framing the monster's speech, but also because she intends the monster to be perceived by readers as eloquent, luminously brilliant. Hence, his suffering moves us.

The monster, then, is a showing or revelation of his creator's overweening pride and the shallowness of regard and abiding self-interest that governs other human beings. Even the beautiful De Lacey family turns on the monster as viciously as peasants. Creating his monster, Victor Frankenstein commits acts that, in the early nineteenth-century, would have been considered degrading, violative of the dead: he manipulates and mutilates corpses, he seizes the power over life and death that had traditionally been seen as the power of deities. In the early nineteenth-century, the idea of pride as a deadly sin was also still prominent in the cultural imagination.[9] Overly full of himself, full of zeal for his own capacity, Victor behaves as an extreme fusion of an ideal Enlightenment man and Romantic visionary, betraying the flaws in these ideologies.

Even as passion drives Victor's quest, the monster's creator is absolutely faithful to the scientific method. He uses rational thought to achieve his desired goal. In this very exemplification of Enlightenment ideals, Frankenstein reveals the underlying monstrosity of a total belief in the power of rational and scientific thought ungrounded in ethical, moral, and community parameters. Shelley's book is not anti-science, but it does look at the underside of the modern consciousness emerging in her era, with its turn toward absolute reverence for technology and science as immutable, sacrosanct truths. With acutance, clarity of focus, Mary Shelley shows how the Enlightenment ideal—the man of reason, the man of science, the man of technology—can create monstrosity. She shows that absolute faith in our human rationality and perfection, extrapolation to the extreme of Enlightenment belief, creates monstrosity because it strips away the capacity to critique oneself. In particular, it denudes us of the capacity to see ourselves as part of a larger human community. Victor Frankenstein creates a living being but gives insufficient thought to how this "Other" will feel, think, and survive.[10] Frankenstein thinks only of himself, his own triumphant scientific act, while he is creating the monster. He turns away from community, ignores everyone, and lives only according to the dictates of his desire to triumph through science. His urge to bring to life a creature whom he has created from dead parts uncannily, eerily, mimics childbearing but it is childbearing without love or concern for the child.

As a teenager, Mary Shelley gave birth to a premature daughter who died soon after being born.[11] Shelley dreamed that she was able to bring her baby back to life by warming it, and one may see that this desire to bring the dead back to life is transformed, in Frankenstein, from a tender urge to an act of monstrous selfishness. What could be the vehicle of this conceptual transformation? It is worth noting that as a teenager Shelley was surrounded by and expected to admire (and apparently did admire), intellectually prominent and gifted men, notably her husband Percy Bysshe Shelley, the poet George Gordon Lord Byron, and last but definitely not least, her father, William Godwin. The childbed death of her mother left Shelley without a living feminist protector and mentor. It is hardly credible that Mary Shelley's teenage pregnancies were a sign of Percy Shelley's serious interest in her intellectual potential. When Shelley grafts the maternal role onto the male character Frankenstein (who creates and brings forth the monster), she sharply emphasizes masculine hubris and selfish desire for control of the other. The monster's longing for a parent who values and loves him is so naked and palpable in the novel: one ties it to Mary Shelley's insuperable pain in losing her mother who, for her, stood as an ideal of feminist championing of the rights of women. When her mother died in childbirth, Mary Shelley did not simply lose a mother, she lost her best hope for a female intellectual mentor. But this loss then extends to Shelley's interpretation of the death of her first child, shortly after birth. Through childbirth she connects to her mother, and it is a painful connection wrought through the parallel deaths of Shelley's mother, in childbirth, and her own first daughter, shortly after being born.

One may link Frankenstein's monster's longing for a parent who values and nurtures him, to the discussion in Mary Wollstonecraft's late eighteenth-century novel, *Maria: Or, the Wrongs of Woman* (1798), of the tortured subject position of the motherless daughter.[12] In *Maria,* Wollstonecraft forcefully argues that a motherless daughter is a girl of whom the world will take advantage. In creating a monster who has only a father, Mary Shelley not only limns her own situation, a motherless daughter, but also connects, intertextually, with her mother's work. In so doing, Shelley ingeniously reflects something haunting about patriarchy, the way that patriarchy denudes mothers of real social power, making children vulnerable to the—sometimes—monstrous desires of fathers.

"I...love you"

HERE, THEN, IS THE MOST salient link between *Frankenstein* and *Mathilda:* the horror of the child who has only a father. What is so fascinating about Shelley's obsession with this predicament is not whether it reflects her own life. (Was Godwin incestuously attracted to his daughter? There is no contemporary evidence of such.)[13] Rather, it reflects her brilliantly intuitive understanding that patriarchy and male power work by destroying female agency and authority. The motherless child recurs as a figure of horror in both *Frankenstein* and *Mathilda*. The horror is not simply a motherless child, per se, but that the fathers—Victor Frankenstein and Mathilda's father, who goes unnamed in the novella—attach to their progeny with monstrous and deeply selfish desire.

Frankenstein experiments with the body of his "child," his creature, to see if he alone of all men can bring the dead back to life, while Mathilda's father fantasizes himself as the romantic/sexual partner of his young daughter. It is very interesting to me that scholarly discussions of *Mathilda* suggest that it is the daughter who incestuously desires the father, in this novella.[14] I believe such interpretations reflect just how difficult it is for our culture, even now, to dissect and critique the power of the father because a careful reading of *Mathilda* makes clear that the father is the aggressor in this story. He is an adult, his daughter a teen. By reading *Frankenstein* and *Mathilda* together, we see that Victor Frankenstein and Mathilda's father are parallel, paternal figures whose desires are monstrous. These monstrous desires, in each case, create a child who is a figure of living death. Mathilda is a victim of her father's incestuous desire for her. The monster is a victim of his creator's desire for scientific supremacy. *Frankenstein* and *Mathilda,* then, are palimpsest stories, imbricated and interwoven through symbolic parsing of the toxic capacity of a father's selfish "love" or "passion" in a patriarchal society.

The idea that a father could be a villain who destroys his child is uncomfortable even now because we retain the skeletal structure of patriarchy. Hence, my claim, (in a book published twelve years ago called *The Posthumous Voice in Women's Writing)* that Shelley's *Mathilda* delineates a daughter's trauma from being incestuously desired by her father, was interpreted as a difficult and angry argument, described as "retaliatory." This reception shocked me because, as a young woman writing that book, I thought that our society had evolved to the place where we would be able to critique the abuse of patriarchy that is incest. But, before the #MeToo movement, this was not so.

The Living Dead

THE VULNERABILITIES OF MATHILDA and the monster are paramount in both works. As young progeny, they lack social, financial, and cultural power and hence lack the means to defend themselves or establish themselves apart from their abusive parents. Frankenstein's monster, of course, could not refuse to be brought to life. He awakens and is faced with a nightmare that is his own embodiment, utterly without protection in the world. It is precisely his innocence in this event of his own creation that the monster poignantly brings before Frankenstein when he begs his father/creator to treat him with respect and love. Equally so, Mathilda, the young daughter in Shelley's subsequent novella, did not cause her father to desire her. She is not seduced by her father, rather she is forced by him to accept his monstrous longing. Orphaned as an infant after her mother's death and father's defection, Mathilda has longed for parental care, but when her father returns to her life, he offers her not paternal care but rather an eroticized love that eviscerates Mathilda's understandable desire for a happy family life.

Frankenstein's monster becomes the living dead because he is a figure of revivified corpses; Mathilda becomes the living dead because her story is told through the trope, or "turn," of the dead speaker. Throughout Shelley's novella, the narrator Mathilda is speaking to us from the boundary of death, on her deathbed. This horrific fact is played down in Shelley's novella *Mathilda*, just as the horror of the monster's living death is played up in *Frankenstein*. But it is important to notice that both works turn on the dramatic engine of a central character who embodies the living dead.

Mary Shelley's depiction of an incest victim, in *Mathilda,* implies that the daughter does not survive being incestuously desired by her father. Instead, she is killed by her father's violent love and tells her story from the vantage of the living-dead. Monstrously, she is able to tell her story despite her double death (initially she fakes her own death, but by the time she narrates the story she is actually dying). Like Frankenstein's monster, Mathilda is both alive and dead. Now, this state, the living dead, is an obvious trope (or turn) of horror fiction and horror movies and television. But it goes deeper: in the young teen, Mathilda, as in the character of Frankenstein's monster, Mary Shelley creates figures that have experienced what sociologist Orlando Patterson calls "social death."[15] Social death means that you are alive but are seen by the society in which you live as inhuman, unloved, unwanted, and—in particular—unfathered. The way that Patterson defines social death is specifically the unfathered, that is, the person whose father does not (or cannot) protect him or her, the father who does not offer social protection as status to his child. Obviously, this is a way of seeing that presumes a society in which male power is paramount. In Mary Shelley's time and place, male power was paramount, written into the laws of England. Patterson argues that a person becomes the living dead, a living human being whose social status is that of nonbeing, when he or she is blocked from inheriting social position, prestige, protection, and meaning, from his or her father. For Patterson, this person is seen by others as a "non-né," that is, a "never-born." Physically, the socially dead person is alive. He or she may even be young and physically healthy. But, socially, he or she is perceived by others as having no power, no prestige, no political rights.

Social death is the condition of Frankenstein's monster and also the condition of Mathilda, the incested daughter. As the daughter whose father incestuously desires her, Mathilda becomes a person who (already without a mother) has no father because incest destroys the fundamental structure of parental care. The daughter whose father desires her sexually loses her social status as a child protected by her father and instead takes on the social status of the fatherless because her father, far from sheltering and nurturing her, violates and makes use of her. Mathilda's father comes to see his daughter as a potential lover, someone with whom to engage in romantic relations. She hence becomes something other than his daughter — socially — in the sense that she is no longer socially protected by him or by his name but instead is victimized by him. Victor Frankenstein sees his monster not as progeny he should protect and nurture, but as an abomination that reveals his (Frankenstein's) own embodied lust, pride, and sinfulness. In a striking chiasmus (crossing) Victor Frankenstein's monster has no name, and Mathilda's father has no name. A nameless horror crosses through these two novels, but I will give it a name: it is the horror of corrupt paternity.

Outcasts

TWO OF THE MOST IMPORTANT STRANDS of scholarship on Mary Shelley's *Frankenstein* have been feminist scholarship and post-colonial scholarship. These strands of analysis are entwined, insofar as both pursue an understanding of Shelley's novel as a critique of Euro-patriarchal domination. I will briefly gloss feminist and post-colonial interpretations of Shelley's work, but also encourage the interested reader to pursue the suggestions for further reading that close this volume. With regards to *Mathilda,* I discuss briefly the concept of the "abject text" that scholar Tilotamma Rajan very usefully develops in her reading of the work. For, indeed, *Mathilda* remained unpublished for one hundred forty years after Mary Shelley wrote it. Arguably, *Mathilda* was deemed unpublishable in the early nineteenth-century, because of its scandalously realistic depiction of incest.

(Incest as a theme was popular in Romantic literature, but *Mathilda* removes incest from fanciful symbolic representation into the realm of a harsh and disturbing realism). Shelley's father, the prominent intellectual William Godwin, forbad her to publish the novella; he called it disgusting. Mary Shelley did not publish it during her lifetime not simply because her father refused to return the manuscript to her, but also because her handling of the incest theme was out of step with her contemporaries.[16] Her husband, Percy Shelley, and friend, George Gordon Lord Byron, had both published works with incest themes, but these works lack the distressing and unpalatable psychological realism—and uncanny insight into incest—that typifies Shelley's *Mathilda*.

The textual abject, as Rajan develops the concept, indicates a text (such as Mary Shelley's novella, *Mathilda*), that seems intended by its creator to not be published or rather to not be publishable.[17] This is a fascinating concept to bring to bear on Shelley's *Frankenstein,* in that Frankenstein's monster is something of a textual abject himself (while the novel, *Frankenstein,* was quickly published and sold well from the beginning). The term "abject" means that which is cast out, outcast, that which cannot be accepted into the body politic, society, or, even that which cannot be accepted by the human body (vomitus is an abject substance, for example). *Mathilda,* the novella, is a "textual abject" because it was written in a manner that Mary Shelley perhaps knew would make it unpublishable. While incest was a popular theme of Romantic poetry, Mary Shelley's non-fanciful, psychologically wrenching depiction of the incested daughter's suffering brought her work *Mathilda* into the realm of a kind of realism. Shelley's novella is not in the Realist tradition, but it is more psychologically realistic than other Romantic renditions of incest. This shift into a more psychologically intense terrain rendered the subject of incest shocking and, in the opinion of her father and sometime publisher, William Godwin, disgusting. Shelley's decision to send to her father a manuscript that she asks him to publish, and which describes in vivid detail an incestuous father, borders on the bizarre. If she wanted to make public a description of a father who incestuously abuses his young daughter, why did she send this text to her father, asking him to publish it? It seems a guaranteed way to not have the novella published. Perhaps Shelley had mixed feelings about exposing her knowledge of the devastating psychological impact of incest. The abject thought is that idea which cannot be brought into the circle of acceptable knowledge.

It is not the monstrous embodiment of the daughter that Mary Shelley brings forward in *Mathilda* but the nightmarish social position of the feminine: the daughter has no protection against her father's incestuous desire for her because her father is placed, by a patriarchal society, as her protector. What do you do when your protector violates you? Where can you go and be safe? In *Frankenstein,* a similar conundrum faces the monster: his creator does not love him and refuses to shelter and sustain him, and yet all the monster has is his creator. However, unlike the daughter Mathilda, the monster has a very large, masculine body. Strikingly, he uses this large, masculine body to punish his creator/father in ways that are beyond the reach of Mathilda, but very well might be part of the fantasy of an incested daughter — a fantasy of being physically large and strong enough to punish her abuser.

Between Men

FRANKENSTEIN ALSO PLUMBS THE HORROR of embodiment, in particular the horror of encompassing life and death in one body. In this sense, it pertains to the experience of pregnancy that ends not with a live, healthy birth but with a stillborn child. Of course, Mary Shelley, at a very young age, experienced something like a life-death boundary event, when her premature infant, and first child, died a few weeks after birth.

It is not that Shelley, in creating monsters, writes female embodiment as monstrous: *Frankenstein's* monster is not a signifier for the idea that the female body is monstrous. No. However, being female means that one may encounter the experience of pregnancy and that experience can, unfortunately, sometimes lead to miscarriage, stillbirth, or birth of an unhealthy child who cannot survive. In this sense, it is peculiarly female (not feminine which is a social performative category) to experience this uncanny boundary state of death-in-life, miscarriage or stillbirth, the child that is born dead or incapable of survival. The trajectory of late twentieth-century feminism has been to negate the idea that female embodiment is different from male embodiment.[18] There is obviously a very liberating quality to this argument: indeed, if we strive to define female embodiment in the abstract we find that it is almost impossible to do. There is no single experience, trait, or quality that unifies and defines all women (woman being shorthand for human beings born with XX chromosomes, but of course not all people defined as women actually have XX chromosomes). Not all women get pregnant, so pregnancy certainly does not define being female. On the other hand, in the aggregate, many women do experience pregnancy (and XY men never do). Mary Shelley experienced pregnancy, early and often. By the time her husband died when she was twenty-four years old, she had been pregnant five times, seen three of her children die, and had a nearly fatal hemorrhage following a miscarriage. The oppressive sense of the burden of the material, physical, mortal world that makes *Frankenstein* a novel of horror, as well as sci-fi, can certainly be connected to the differential experience of sex, or rather the effect of sex, that pregnant women undergo. The "filthy workshop" of Victor Frankenstein is an easy metaphor for sex, and the monster himself becomes the damaged and scandalized body resultant upon the onanistic "workshop" of *Frankenstein,* the novel.

In particular, it is important to be aware of the social position that Mary Shelley, as a young woman, inhabited. During her lifetime, England followed the law of coverture, whereby a married woman could not own property in her own right, and also — significantly for a writer — could not own a copyright to her own work. It would belong to her husband. It is true that Mary Shelley had not yet married Percy when she bore her first child by him, and when she wrote *Frankenstein;* yet her position as Percy's mistress was hardly empowering. Because of this liaison, Mary Shelley was never fully accepted into proper society, not even years after Percy's death. Moreover, at the time of writing *Frankenstein,* she was a very young woman, aspiring to be a writer, in the company of two established and famous male writers, George Gordon Lord Byron and Percy Bysshe Shelley. Knowing that her mother, Mary Wollstonecraft, had written significant and important books surely influenced Mary Shelley's sense of her own capacity to write.

Even so, as a teenager who had scant publications, Shelley was trying to prove herself as a writer in the company of older and successful male writers. Unlike other nineteenth-century women writers, say, Jane Austen, Charlotte Bronte, or Emily Dickinson, Mary Shelley did not have privacy in which to develop her gift or, if you prefer, craft. She had to do so while surrounded by and perhaps engulfed by her lover's and then husband's success and his self-regard. The emphasis that *Frankenstein* and *Mathilda* place on gendered power differentials may emerge from Shelley's own experience as a very young woman pressed into the company of older, successful, male writers even as she began to fight for her own voice.

Creating Race

FRANKENSTEIN'S MONSTER IS PROTEAN; he stands for many forms of trouble, grief, and haunting. Any viable interpretation of *Frankenstein,* and of *Mathilda,* has to reflect the multiple layers of cultural symbolic at work in the texts. These are not books with one meaning; instead they are multifarious. Frankenstein's monster is described as physically different from other human beings, so much so that his appearance prevents him from being able to move into any human society. In this, the monster is like and unlike Mathilda, who looks like a pretty young girl but carries an invisible monstrous secret, and because of her secret cannot be part of society. Some post-colonial critics have suggested that Shelley makes of her monster a figure for the plight of the colonized, and this line of analysis warrants mention.[19] For Shelley was writing after two hundred years of aggressive European colonization of the Americas and also writing just before the British Empire began an extraordinary expansion of its domain. The violence of colonialism was unquestionably part of her nation and her world.

In my brief discussion here, I write about a few ways that *Frankenstein* radically (for its time) perhaps presents an empathetic view of the position of the colonized. Critical race theory scholars have discussed the idea that Mary Shelley's monster, in *Frankenstein,* is a racially marked figure, a colonized subject, a source of simultaneous fascination and racist disgust to Europeans.[20] Shelley writes *Frankenstein* in the early nineteenth-century, after centuries of aggressive European colonization efforts in the Americas, Asia, Africa. To be sure, the novel *Frankenstein* is ambivalent in its embrace of the point of view of the colonized subject. Shelley's novel edges into expressing racist sentiment — disgust and horror at the embodiment of the "Other," with the monster as a figure for human "Other" — but also, paradoxically, the novel supports an understanding of the humanity, intellectual brilliance, and the deeply unjust suffering of the colonized subject.[21] The reader, then, should bear in mind that Shelley's novel is somewhat ambivalent on this ground. Even as I will argue that Frankenstein empathetically presents the subjectivity and personhood of the ostracized subject, that can stand symbolically for the colonized subject, the novel can also be interpreted as presenting a disturbingly racist paradigm in which the monster stands for the idea of the colonized subject having an inhuman, freakish, embodiment, an embodiment that cannot safely be brought into the center and that must be kept, forcibly, at the periphery.

On this razor's edge, I suggest that Shelley draws a cue of her depiction of the monster from early nineteenth-century (that is contemporary with Mary Shelley) European descriptions of indigenous Americans. In particular, the description of the monster's hair seems to draw from colonizing European descriptions of indigenous Americans. The ideology driving the visceral and violent colonization of the Americas was the broadly held cultural belief, among Europeans, that indigenous Americans were physically, mentally, and culturally, inferior, that they could be killed without guilt to clear the American continent for colonization. [22] Shelley, in key ways, subverts this racist ideological stance in *Frankenstein.*

If we follow the metaphoric arc of the novel, we see that Frankenstein's monster is literally made by the overweening, hubristic actions of a European, Enlightenment scientist-scholar. Here, Shelley compactly expresses, through metaphor, the arguments ultimately made by twentieth century theorists Theodor

Adorno and Michel Foucault that the Enlightenment carried with it a violence, a willingness to see those who are different from the dominant group as outside human perfectibility, in contrast to the supposed perfection of the European, "rational" man.[23] Hence, Frankenstein's monster is created by European hubris and cruelty. The monster is not monstrous in comparison to Europeans (which would be the racist way to interpret the novel *Frankenstein*). Rather, he is constructed as a monster by Europeans. Only the racist gaze creates the belief in the monstrous "Other." In Shelley's novel, this gaze, as construct, is figural, an embodied symbol, with the monster standing for the history of European colonization of the Americas, and parts of Africa and Asia, a history in which the ideology of the racially aberrant "Other" was created and fomented, causing horrific suffering for many colonized peoples. In this sense, Shelley's novel reveals not the monstrousness of those who have been colonized but rather instead the monstrousness of the process of colonization, the extreme and horrific violence by which European peoples displaced, killed, denigrated, and attempted to destroy the cultures, religions, and identities of non-Europeans. The concept of race as a cudgel by which to dispossess millions of people not of European descent, arguably, echoes in the monster's story and fate. The monster is conceptually materialized by Victor Frankenstein as Frankenstein's possession, and then he is articulated by Frankenstein as the antithesis of the human—even as the monster's evident intelligence and desire for community indicates that he is very much a human being.

While *Frankenstein* draws some educative parallel between the monster, as outcast, and an "Arabian" daughter, Safie, who is also depicted as an "Other" to Western culture, giving legitimacy to the kind of post-colonial gloss of the novel that I note above, *Mathilda* does not on its surface appear to contest or even engage ideologies of race and empire. Even so, one may see that in the intimate frame of *Mathilda,* the idea of the monstrous violence of the European father who violates others is drawn. Mathilda's father is described as a man who cannot contain his passions, cannot contain himself, and his incontinence expresses itself in geographically. After the death of his wife, he travels ceaselessly, making the world his own, becoming a one-man force of empire, as it were. His urge is to colonize, to exert his will across geographic and also human terrain. The traveling father at last returns to his adolescent daughter Mathilda only to tell her he has become incestuously attracted to her. This sequence, then, suggests a monstrousness both in his desire to assert his presence in cultures and countries that are not his own and in his desire to assert his sexual presence over his daughter. The idea of the outsider, the person whom Euro-patriarchy casts as a monstrous "Other," an outsider, then, is a key theme in both *Frankenstein* and *Mathilda.*

The incestuously harmed daughter in *Mathilda* is not depicted as a racial other, but then, neither is Frankenstein's monster: the monster is cobbled together from corpses of Europeans, European people and animals. Hence, both "monster" figures, the incested daughter and the revivified corpse, are "monstrous" through social mechanisms, rendered outcasts by the acts of others. They are not born monsters but become monstrous through the acts of European men who at the surface appear to be exceedingly cultured, intelligent, rational, and representative of the best of European society. Shelley's implicit understanding of the way that European forces of colonization, during the seventeenth-, eighteenth-, and nineteenth-centuries, created a conceptual "Other" so as to attain social power and dominance is exhibited in her empathic handling of her monsters. As I have noted, Shelley's novel *Frankenstein; or, The Modern Prometheus,* and her novella *Mathilda,* have the strength of being multifaceted works. Hence, to suggest that the works straightforwardly purport a single political point of view would be a mistake. What they do reveal is the deep fissure between the hubris and self-congratulatory force of Euro-patriarchal power and the harms caused by Euro-patriarchy. Shelley's works make clear the way that the outcast, the "monstrous" Other, is created through the acts of European men in power; men who seem to be rational, scientific, well-educated, and intelligent, men on whose social power no real checks are exerted.

Even as Frankenstein displays the problem of the father's hubris, with Victor Frankenstein playing the father to the creature he makes from corpses and brings back to life with galvanism, *Mathilda* goes further, suggesting that the father's sins against his child are not accidental but have to do with his desire specifically in regards to her. *Frankenstein* has a focus on the scientific while *Mathilda* derives its intellectual subtext from a critique of the Western Christian (Catholic) belief in purgatory. When Mary Shelley first drafted the novella *Mathilda,* she developed the manuscript from her mother's incomplete draft, *The Cave of Fancy.* Shelley initially wrote the daughter Mathilda's narrative as being spoken in purgatory, that is, in the place where the Catholic religion believes those who have sinned but can be purified of their sins go after death. In revising the novella, Shelley placed Mathilda, the narrator, in a metaphorical rather than literal purgatory: she is dying, young, and will never have the chance to live her life because her father's incestuous desire for her has, from the outset, negated her capacity for social existence.

AI

THERE ARE SOME PARALLELS between Shelley's critique of an absolute faith in science and our situation in the twenty-first century. It is fascinating to note that in the early twenty-first century one of the founders and chief theorists for Google (the online search engine named for the number googol, or near-infinity), claimed that the real goal of Google is to lead the way to artificial intelligence that will be superior to the human brain and take over most of the functions of our brains.[24] This AI (artificial intelligence) would ultimately be capable of being placed in our brains, so suggest some of the founders of Google. One of Google's masterminds goes so far as to argue that, through computer science developing AI, we will no longer die but instead will extend our lives by taking on computer parts, becoming actual cyborgs. Ultimately, the goal of this Google mastermind is to "reverse engineer the human brain."[25] That phrase, unequivocally, evokes Mary Shelley's *Frankenstein*. In it inheres the belief that human life can be modulated, replicated, extended, and ultimately created, through engineering. The belief—expressed by some founders of Google—in the capacity of science to solve all human problems, the largest problem being mortality, is entirely contiguous with the mindset of Mary Shelley's Victor Frankenstein. Victor is an engineer of the highest order. This mindset in which one is incapable of stepping outside oneself and critiquing one's own urges extends from Victor Frankenstein (a fictional character, of course) to some of the men who shaped and continue to shape the Internet and our world today.[26]

The characteristic of an increasing interest in developing scientific knowledge typifies the eighteenth- and nineteenth-centuries, signifying a fundamental break, or shift, in patterns of thought and belief.[27] The Enlightenment ushers in a belief in the capacity of rational thought to perfect mankind and save us from all ills. Absolute faith in science in this era ultimately became part and participle of a major cultural shift in the West and we still, in the twenty-first century, live in that age that has absolute faith in scientific progress and the credo of science.[28] In this sense, we live an extension of key aspects of Enlightenment dogma. This comment is not to claim that no aspect of Enlightenment thought is beneficial or, well, enlightened but rather to note the intellectual lineage from Descartes, Locke, Hume, and Smith to the problematically unchallenged idea of techno-logical ascendency with which we now live.

Victor Frankenstein's desire to undo death is programmatic and very much an engineer's approach to "solving" mortality. Methodically, Frankenstein gathers parts of corpses, methodically—that is using the scientific method—Frankenstein harnesses something akin to galvanism to bring the energy of life back into the form built of human corpses. Likewise, Google's founders' vision for artificial intelligence as a way to undo human mortality and, while they are at it, the need for human brains, is methodical, scientific, urged forward by the "progress" of machines. The wish of these specific engineers for machines that can create a network of knowledge that will surpass human beings and thereby solve all the world's problems—including mortality— eerily echoes Frankenstein's urge to solve death by drawing on science to re-engineer the human.

The flaw in such thinking is that most problems human beings encounter remain unresolved not due to our collective lack of knowledge or lack of intelligence; rather, they are unresolved because of ethical, moral, faults in our society, and in ourselves. We human beings create our hells by taking from each other that which should not be taken, and that pattern is unlikely to be solved by machines. Of course, mortality is ultimately part of being human, but the way we experience mortality is profoundly affected and inflected by our actions toward each other. Many causes of death, such as starvation, war, depression, violence, environmental degradation, which in turns can lead to cancer and to some infectious diseases, follow from human beings' violations of each other. Mary Shelley figures precisely this angle in *Frankenstein*. She is concerned to show how scientific progress without ethical self-critique loses the capacity to improve human lives.

Far from failing as a scientist, Frankenstein is in fact successful in his creation of his monster: he brings the dead to life. His monster is intelligent, tall, and strong, a superman of a sort. And yet, Frankenstein in ethical terms utterly fails in his creation of the monster: the creature destroys those whom Frankenstein loves, and in turn the creature is himself tormented by the aching and inappeasable psychic wound inflicted by his creator. He haunts Frankenstein endlessly, fusing his fate with his creator's. The creation of his monster destroys Victor Frankenstein's happiness, destroys his beloved, his best friend, all that he holds dear. The monster destroys, very precisely, the human identity of Victor Frankenstein: his family and friends, his sense of himself as honorable and useful. Shelley ends her novel ambiguously, leaving open the possibility that the monster may destroy much more than just those people beloved by Frankenstein. The monster's destructive potential may be endless. If one reads across the arc of Shelley's career, indeed, one sees that her work *The Last Man* (1826) is a novel that envisions the end of human society, albeit through a plague rather than a monster.

Inasmuch as *Mathilda* positions its narration between life and death, with early drafts of Mathilda placing the novel's eponymous narrator in purgatory, Mathilda tells her story from an unbearable edge of being outcast not only from human society but even from the separate worlds of the living and the dead. Neither dead nor alive, neither forgiven nor unforgivable, the resolution, for Mathilda, is to find her place really among the dead. As we conclude *Mathilda,* we know the narrator will die, and her story will be carried only by Woodville, who will be saved from incestuous contamination precisely because Mathilda only confesses her incest secret by positioning its release to occur after she is dead. By contrast, one reads a tense lack of resolution in *Frankenstein*.

If we think of the two works as engaging intertwined concerns, we see that the resolution for the horrific moral, ethical, transgressions that Victor Frankenstein and Mathilda's father commit is death. Not only the death of the violators but also the deaths of those who are violated. Mathilda's death acts as the resolution to both the novella *Mathilda* and also, arguably, it is a resolution to the novel *Frankenstein*. For just as Victor Frankenstein's refusal of mortality causes him to create the monster, Mathilda's deep acceptance of mortality resolves both her father's sin— and perhaps also that of Victor Frankenstein. Certainly, Shelley expresses a depressive view of the world and the future in these works. And yet, she also struggles to assert a human frame, which includes mortality as part of the moral world, in the face of the outsize desires of Victor Frankenstein and Mathilda's father. Much as the father's incestuous desire for his daughter enacts a refusal, on the level of concept, to accept mortality and the passage of time—asserting a desire to conflate generational separation rather than respect generational difference—so also Victor Frankenstein's urge to create his monster is instigated in part by Victor's mother's death, which causes Victor unresolved pain. Hence, the monster's creation is fueled by a desire to refuse to acquiesce to the passing of generations.

Monsters

WHO, THEN, ARE THE "monsters" in *Frankenstein* and *Mathilda?* Are the incestuously abused daughter and the unloved, revivified creature the monsters? Figures to kill or jail so that we can sleep tight at night? Or are they signs that extend from and point to indict the patriarchal forces that created them as figures of living death? Mary Shelley brings before us, in her works *Frankenstein* and *Mathilda,* painfully clear depictions of the ways that overwhelming social power and prestige, in those incapable of self-critique, create monstrosity. Victor Frankenstein's creation, like the incestuously desired daughter Mathilda, has no possible social realm in which to become a person well-regarded and respected by others. All vistas are foreclosed for Frankenstein's creature and for Mathilda. This condition of death-in-life is caused by the creators/fathers of Shelley's youthful novel and novella. The monstrous impetus to take absolute control of another human being, whether that be a person one creates through science or a child who is one's biological progeny, Mary Shelley radically ascribes to patterns of

European patriarchy. Hauntingly, her works have been interpreted as expositions of embodied female monstrosity or narratives of female desire when, in fact, they expose—giving the formal and symbolic shape of—the ethical horror of rational European men, men of science, who are unable to see themselves as equal to, and not above, other human beings. ◀

— Claire Millikin Raymond
Charlottesville, Virginia, August 2018

WORKS CITED

1. Franklin Foer, *World Without Mind: The Existential Threat of Big Tech* (New York: Penguin, 2017), 46.

2. Audrey Fisch, Anne K. Mellor, Esther H. Schor, eds., *The Other Mary Shelley: Beyond Frankenstein* (New York: Oxford University Press, 1993), 15; *see also,* Anne K. Mellor, *Mary Shelley: Her Life, Her Fiction, Her Monsters* (New York: Routledge, 1988); Betty J. Bennett and Stuart Curran, eds. *Mary Shelley in Her Times* (Baltimore, MD: John Hopkins University Press, 2000).

3. Charlotte Gordon, *Romantic Outlaws: The Extraordinary Lives of Mary Wollstonecraft and Mary Shelley* (New York: Random House, 2016), xv.

4. Harold Bloom, *The Ringers in the Tower: Studies in the Romantic Tradition* (Chicago and London: University of Chicago Press, 1971), 119-129; *see also,* Mario Praz, *The Romantic Agony* [1933], trans. Angus Davidson (Oxford: Oxford University Press, 1951; 1970), 116; Jerrold E. Hogle "Romantic Contexts" in *The Cambridge Companion to Frankenstein,* ed. Andrew Smith (Cambridge: Cambridge University Press, 2016), 41-55.

5. Miriam Brody, ed. *Mary Wollstonecraft, A Vindication of the Rights of Woman* (New York: Penguin, 2004).

6. James Bieri, *Percy Bysshe Shelley: A Biography* (Baltimore: Johns Hopkins University Press, 2008).

7. H. J. Rose, *A Handbook of Greek Mythology* (New York: E.P. Dutton, 1959), 54-56.

8. Sharon Ruston, "The Science of Life and Death in Mary Shelley's Frankenstein" The British Library, Discovering Literature: Romantics & Victorians (2014), https://www.bl.uk/romantics-and-victorians/articles/the-science-of-life-and-death-in-mary-shelleys-frankenstein. Accessed February 2, 2018.

9. John Holmes and Sharon Ruston, *The Routledge Research Companion to Nineteenth-Century British Literature and Science* (London: Routledge, 2017).

10. Edward Said, *Orientalism* (New York: Vintage, 1979).

11. Miranda Seymour, *Mary Shelley* (New York: Grove Press, 2002).

12. Mary Wollstonecraft, *Maria: Or, the Wrongs of Woman* (New York: W. W. Norton, 1975).

13. Had Mary Shelley lived in our century, her youthful pregnancy might have been interpreted as part of the sexual 'acting out' that sometimes afflicts survivors of paternal sexual attention. However, across centuries diagnostic speculation is unreliable. *See,* Penelope Trickett, Jennie Noll, Frank Putnam "The Impact of Sexual Abuse on Female Development," *Development and Psychopathology* 23, no 2 (May 2011): 243-276.

14. Gordon, *Romantic Outlaws,* 325. *See also,* Margaret Davenport Garrett, "Writing and Re-Writing Incest in Mary Shelley's *Mathilda,*" *Keats-Shelley Journal,* 45 (1996): 44-60; Kathleen A. Miller. ""The Remembrance Haunts Me Like a Crime": Narrative Control, the Dramatic, and the Female Gothic, in Mary Wollstonecraft Shelley's *Mathilda.*" *Tulsa Studies in Women's Literature* 27, no. 2 (2008): 291-30, https://muse.jhu.edu/. Accessed January 20, 2019, 291-308.

15. Orlando Patterson, *Slavery and Social Death: A Comparative Study* (Cambridge, MA: Harvard University Press, 1982).

16. *See,* Gordon, *Romantic Outlaws,* p. 326, Gordon suggests that Shelley could have taken *Mathilda* to another publisher after her father rejected it. But Shelley's novella is sufficiently outside the bounds of other Romantic depictions of incest as to make it a text out of step with Shelley's time, not just with her father.

17. Tilottama Rajan, "Mary Shelley's *Mathilda:* Melancholy and the political economy of Romanticism," *Studies, in the Novel,* 26, no. 1/2 (1994): 43-68.

18. Judith Butler, *Gender Trouble: Feminism and the Subversion of Identity* (New York: Routledge, 1990).

19. Gayatri Chakravorty Spivak "Three Women's Texts and a Critique of Imperialism" *Critical Inquiry,* 12:1 (Autumn 1985): 235-61.

20. H.L. Malchow, "Frankenstein's Monster and Images of Race in Nineteenth-Century Britain" *Past & Present No. 139* (May, 1993): 90-130; Allan Lloyd Smith, "This Thing of Darkness: Racial Discourse in Mary Shelley's Frankenstein," *Gothic Studies,* 6, no 2 (2004): 208-222.

21. Said, *Orientalism*, 92-112.

22. Tzvetan Todorov, *The Conquest of America: The Question of the Other* (University of Oklahoma Press, 1999).

23. Theodor Adorno and Max Horkheimer, *The Dialectic of Enlightenment* (Stanford University Press, 2007).

24. Foer, *World Without Mind,* 36-39.

25. Donna Soti-Morretini, "Reverse Engineering the Human: Artificial Intelligence and Acting Theory," *Connection Science,* 29, no 1 (2017): 64-76.

26. This desire to use human ingenuity to forestall mortality, to be sure, is not uniquely modern. The emperor Ying Zheng, in 210 BCE ordered his advisors, the scholars of his day, to create an elixir that would permanently forestall his death. The advisors fed him quicksilver pills, mercury, and the emperor died of mercury poisoning brought on by his quest to become immortal. *See,* Mark Edward Lewis, *The Early Chinese Empires: Qin and Han* (Harvard at the Belknap Press, 2010).

27. J. D. Bernal "Science, Industry and Society in the Nineteenth-Century," *Centaurus,* 3, no. 1 (1953): 138-165.

28. Michel Foucault, *The Order of Things: An Archeology of the Human Sciences* (New York: Vintage, 1994).

Frankenstein
Or
The Modern Prometheus

INTRODUCTION

T HE PUBLISHERS OF THE STANDARD NOVELS, in selecting "Frankenstein" for one of their series, expressed a wish that I should furnish them with some account of the origin of the story. I am the more willing to comply, because I shall thus give a general answer to the question, so frequently asked me—"How I, then a young girl, came to think of, and to dilate upon, so very hideous an idea?" It is true that I am very averse to bringing myself forward in print; but as my account will only appear as an appendage to a former production, and as it will be confined to such topics as have connection with my authorship alone, I can scarcely accuse myself of a personal intrusion.

It is not singular that, as the daughter of two persons of distinguished literary celebrity, I should very early in life have thought of writing. As a child I scribbled; and my favourite pastime, during the hours given me for recreation, was to "write stories." Still I had a dearer pleasure than this, which was the formation of castles in the air—the indulging in waking dreams—the following up trains of thought, which had for their subject the formation of a succession of imaginary incidents. My dreams were at once more fantastic and agreeable than my writings. In the latter I was a close imitator—rather doing as others had done, than putting down the suggestions of my own mind. What I wrote was intended at least for one other eye—my childhood's companion and friend; but my dreams were all my own; I accounted for them to nobody; they were my refuge when annoyed—my dearest pleasure when free.

I lived principally in the country as a girl, and passed a considerable time in Scotland. I made occasional visits to the more picturesque parts; but my habitual residence was on the blank and dreary northern shores of the Tay, near Dundee. Blank and dreary on retrospection I call them; they were not so to me then. They were the eyry of freedom, and the pleasant region where unheeded I could commune with the creatures of my fancy. I wrote then—but in a most common-place style. It was beneath the trees of the grounds belonging to our house, or on the bleak sides of the woodless mountains near, that my true compositions, the airy flights of my imagination, were born and fostered. I did not make myself the heroine of my tales. Life appeared to me too common-place an affair as regarded myself. I could not figure to myself that romantic woes or wonderful events would ever be my lot; but I was not confined to my own identity, and I could people the hours with creations far more interesting to me at that age, than my own sensations.

After this my life became busier, and reality stood in place of fiction. My husband, however, was from the first, very anxious that I should prove myself worthy of my parentage, and enrol myself on the page of fame. He was for ever inciting me to obtain literary reputation, which even on my own part I cared for then, though since I have become infinitely indifferent to it. At this time he desired that I should write, not so much with the idea that I could produce any thing worthy of notice, but that he might himself judge how far I possessed the promise of better things hereafter. Still I did nothing. Travelling, and the cares of a family, occupied my time; and study, in the way of reading, or improving my ideas in communication with his far more cultivated mind, was all of literary employment that engaged my attention.

In the summer of 1816, we visited Switzerland, and became the neighbours of Lord Byron. At first we spent our pleasant hours on the lake, or wandering on its shores; and Lord Byron, who was writing the third canto of Childe Harold, was the only one among us who put his thoughts upon paper. These, as he brought them successively to us, clothed in all the light and harmony of poetry, seemed to stamp as divine the glories of heaven and earth, whose influences we partook with him.

But it proved a wet, ungenial summer, and incessant rain often confined us for days to the house. Some volumes of ghost stories, translated from the German into French, fell into our hands. There was the History of the Inconstant Lover, who, when he thought to clasp the bride to whom he had pledged his vows, found himself in the arms of the pale ghost of her whom he had deserted. There was the tale of the sinful founder of his race, whose miserable doom it was to bestow the kiss of death on all the younger sons of his fated house, just when they reached the age of promise. His gigantic, shadowy form, clothed like the ghost in Hamlet, in complete armour, but with the beaver up, was seen at midnight, by the moon's fitful beams, to advance slowly along the gloomy avenue. The shape was lost beneath the shadow of the castle walls; but soon a gate swung back, a step was heard, the door of the chamber opened, and he advanced to the couch of the blooming youths, cradled in healthy sleep. Eternal sorrow sat upon his face as he bent down and kissed the forehead of the boys, who from that hour withered like flowers snapt upon the stalk. I have not seen these stories since then; but their incidents are as fresh in my mind as if I had read them yesterday.

"We will each write a ghost story," said Lord Byron; and his proposition was acceded to. There were four of us. The noble author began a tale, a fragment of which he printed at the end of his poem of Mazeppa. Shelley, more apt to embody ideas and sentiments in the radiance of brilliant imagery, commenced one founded on the experiences of his early life. Poor Polidori had some terrible idea about a skull-headed lady, who was so punished for peeping through a key-hole—what to see I forget—something very shocking and wrong of course; but when she was reduced to a worse condition than the renowned Tom of Coventry, he did not know what to do with her, and was obliged to despatch her to the tomb of the Capulets, the only place for which she was fitted. The illustrious poets also, annoyed by the platitude of prose, speedily relinquished the uncongenial task.

I busied myself to think of a story, —a story to rival those which had excited us to this task. One which would speak to the mysterious fears of our nature, and awaken thrilling horror—one to make the reader dread to look round, to curdle the blood, and quicken the beatings of the heart. If I did not accomplish these things, my ghost story would be unworthy of its name. I thought and pondered—vainly. I felt that blank incapability of invention which is the greatest misery of authorship, when dull Nothing replies to our anxious invocations. Have you thought of a story? I was asked each morning, and each morning I was forced to reply with a mortifying negative.

Every thing must have a beginning, to speak in Sanchean phrase; and that beginning must be linked to something that went before. The Hindoos give the world an elephant to support it, but they make the elephant stand upon a tortoise. Invention, it must be humbly admitted, does not consist in creating out of void, but out of chaos; the materials must, in the first place, be afforded: it can give form to dark, shapeless substances, but cannot bring into being the substance itself. In all matters of discovery and invention, even of those that appertain to the imagination, we are continually reminded of the story of Columbus and his egg. Invention consists in the capacity of seizing on the capabilities of a subject, and in the power of moulding and fashioning ideas suggested to it.

Many and long were the conversations between Lord Byron and Shelley, to which I was a devout but nearly silent listener. During one of these, various philosophical doctrines were discussed, and among others the nature of the principle of life, and whether there was any probability of its ever being discovered and communicated. They talked of the experiments of Dr. Darwin, (I speak not of what the Doctor really did, or said that he did, but, as more to my purpose, of what was then spoken of as having been done by him,) who preserved a piece of vermicelli in a glass case, till by some extraordinary means it began to move with voluntary motion. Not thus, after all, would life be given. Perhaps a corpse would be re-animated; galvanism had given token of such things: perhaps the component parts of a creature might be manufactured, brought together, and endued with vital warmth.

Night waned upon this talk, and even the witching hour had gone by, before we retired to rest. When I placed my head on my pillow, I did not sleep, nor could I be said to think. My imagination, unbidden, possessed and guided me, gifting the successive images that arose in my mind with a vividness far beyond the usual bounds of reverie. I saw—with shut eyes, but acute mental vision, —I saw the pale student of unhallowed arts kneeling beside the thing he had put together. I saw the hideous phantasm of a man stretched out, and then, on the working of some powerful engine, show signs of life, and stir with an uneasy, half vital motion. Frightful must it be; for supremely frightful would be the effect of any human endeavour to mock the stupendous mechanism of the Creator of the world. His success would terrify the artist; he would rush away from his odious handywork, horror-stricken. He would hope that, left to itself, the slight spark of life which he had communicated would fade; that this thing, which had received such imperfect animation, would subside into dead matter; and he might sleep in the belief that the silence of the grave would quench for ever the transient existence of the hideous corpse which he had looked upon as the cradle of life. He sleeps; but he is awakened; he opens his eyes; behold the horrid thing stands at his bedside, opening his curtains, and looking on him with yellow, watery, but speculative eyes.

I opened mine in terror. The idea so possessed my mind, that a thrill of fear ran through me, and I wished to exchange the ghastly image of my fancy for the realities around. I see them still; the very room, the dark parquet, the closed shutters, with the moonlight struggling through, and the sense I had that the glassy lake and white high Alps were beyond. I could not so easily get rid of my hideous phantom; still it haunted me. I must try to think of something else. I recurred to my ghost story, my tiresome unlucky ghost story! O! if I could only contrive one which would frighten my reader as I myself had been frightened that night!

Swift as light and as cheering was the idea that broke in upon me. "I have found it! What terrified me will terrify others; and I need only describe the spectre which had haunted my midnight pillow." On the morrow I announced that I had thought of a story. I began that day with the words, It was on a dreary night of November , making only a transcript of the grim terrors of my waking dream.

At first I thought but of a few pages of a short tale; but Shelley urged me to develope the idea at greater length. I certainly did not owe the suggestion of one incident, nor scarcely of one train of feeling, to my husband, and yet but for his incitement, it would never have taken the form in which it was presented. From this declaration I must except the preface. As far as I can recollect, it was entirely written by him.

And now, once again, I bid my hideous progeny go forth and prosper. I have an affection for it, for it was the offspring of happy days, when death and grief were but words, which found no true echo in my heart. Its several pages speak of many a walk, many a drive, and many a conversation, when I was not alone; and my companion was one who, in this world, I shall never see more. But this is for myself; my readers have nothing to do with these associations.

I will add but one word as to the alterations I have made. They are principally those of style. I have changed no portion of the story, nor introduced any new ideas or circumstances. I have mended the language where it was so bald as to interfere with the interest of the narrative; and these changes occur almost exclusively in the beginning of the first volume. Throughout they are entirely confined to such parts as are mere adjuncts to the story, leaving the core and substance of it untouched. ◄

— M. W. S.
London, October 15, 1831[1]

---

1.   Following the lead of James O'Rourke, we present here the edition of *Frankenstein* that Mary Shelley edited herself, several years after the death of her husband, the poet Percy Bysshe Shelley. In developing the 1818 novel, Percy appears to have helped the then teenage Mary to edit the novel. While his edits were surely appreciated by a very young Mary Shelley, Percy did not, as some have claimed, write *Frankenstein*. Please see, James O'Rourke, The "1831 Introduction and Revisions to 'Frankenstein:' Mary Shelley Dictates Her Legacy" *Studies in Romanticism* Vol. 38, No. 3 (Fall, 1999), pp. 365-385.

THE LETTERS

Letter 1

St. Petersburgh, Dec. 11th, 17—
To Mrs. Saville, England

YOU WILL REJOICE TO HEAR that no disaster has accompanied the commencement of an enterprise which you have regarded with such evil forebodings. I arrived here yesterday, and my first task is to assure my dear sister of my welfare and increasing confidence in the success of my undertaking.[1]

I am already far north of London, and as I walk in the streets of Petersburgh, I feel a cold northern breeze play upon my cheeks, which braces my nerves and fills me with delight. Do you understand this feeling? This breeze, which has travelled from the regions towards which I am advancing, gives me a foretaste of those icy climes. Inspirited by this wind of promise, my daydreams become more fervent and vivid. I try in vain to be persuaded that the pole is the seat of frost and desolation; it ever presents itself to my imagination as the region of beauty and delight. There, Margaret, the sun is forever visible, its broad disk just skirting the horizon and diffusing a perpetual splendour. There — for with your leave, my sister, I will put some trust in preceding navigators — there snow and frost are banished; and, sailing over a calm sea, we may be wafted to a land surpassing in wonders and in beauty every region hitherto discovered on the habitable globe. Its productions and features may be without example, as the phenomena of the heavenly bodies undoubtedly are in those undiscovered solitudes. What may not be expected in a country of eternal light? I may there discover the wondrous power which attracts the needle and may regulate a thousand celestial observations that require only this voyage to render their seeming eccentricities consistent forever. I shall satiate my ardent curiosity with the sight of a part of the world never before visited, and may tread a land never before imprinted by the foot of man. These are my enticements, and they are sufficient to conquer all fear of danger or death and to induce me to commence this laborious voyage with the joy a child feels when he embarks in a little boat, with his holiday mates, on an expedition of discovery up his native river. But supposing all these conjectures to be false, you cannot contest the inestimable benefit which I shall confer on all mankind, to the last generation, by discovering a passage near the pole to those countries, to reach which at present so many months are requisite; or by ascertaining the secret of the magnet, which, if at all possible, can only be effected by an undertaking such as mine.

These reflections have dispelled the agitation with which I began my letter, and I feel my heart glow with an enthusiasm which elevates me to heaven, for nothing contributes so much to tranquillize the mind as a steady purpose—a point on which the soul may fix its intellectual eye. This expedition has been the favourite dream of my early years. I have read with ardour the accounts of the various voyages which have been made in the prospect of arriving at the North Pacific Ocean through the seas which surround the pole. You may remember that a history of all the voyages made for purposes of discovery composed the whole of our good Uncle Thomas' library. My education was neglected, yet I was passionately fond of reading. These volumes were my study day and night, and my familiarity with them increased that regret which I had felt, as a child, on learning that my father's dying injunction had forbidden my uncle to allow me to embark in a seafaring life.

These visions faded when I perused, for the first time, those poets whose effusions entranced my soul and lifted it to heaven. I also became a poet and for one year lived in a paradise of my own creation; I imagined that I also might obtain a niche in the temple where the names of Homer and Shakespeare are consecrated. You are well acquainted with my failure and how heavily I bore the disappointment. But just at that time I inherited the fortune of my cousin, and my thoughts were turned into the channel of their earlier bent.

Six years have passed since I resolved on my present undertaking. I can, even now, remember the hour from which I dedicated myself to this great enterprise. I commenced by inuring my body to hardship. I accompanied the whale-fishers on several expeditions to the North Sea; I voluntarily endured cold, famine, thirst, and want of sleep; I often worked harder than the common sailors during the day and devoted my nights to the study of mathematics, the theory of medicine, and those branches of physical science from which a naval adventurer might derive the greatest practical advantage. Twice I actually hired myself as an under-mate in a Greenland whaler, and acquitted myself to admiration. I must own I felt a little proud when my captain offered me the second dignity in the vessel and entreated me to remain with the greatest earnestness, so valuable did he consider my services. And now, dear Margaret, do I not deserve to accomplish some great purpose? My life might have been passed in ease and luxury, but I preferred glory to every enticement that wealth placed in my path. Oh, that some encouraging voice would answer in the affirmative! My courage and my resolution is firm; but my hopes fluctuate, and my spirits are often depressed. I am about to proceed on a long and difficult voyage, the emergencies of which will demand all my fortitude: I am required not only to raise the spirits of others, but sometimes to sustain my own, when theirs are failing.

This is the most favourable period for travelling in Russia. They fly quickly over the snow in their sledges; the motion is pleasant, and, in my opinion, far more agreeable than that of an English stagecoach. The cold is not excessive, if you are wrapped in furs—a dress which I have already adopted, for there is a great difference between walking the deck and remaining seated motionless for hours, when no exercise prevents the blood from actually freezing in your veins. I have no ambition to lose my life on the post-road between St. Petersburgh and Archangel. I shall depart for the latter town in a fortnight or three weeks; and my intention is to hire a ship there, which can easily be done by paying the insurance for the owner, and to engage as many sailors as I think necessary among those who are accustomed to the whale-fishing. I do not intend to sail until the month of June; and when shall I return? Ah, dear sister, how can I answer this question? If I succeed, many, many months, perhaps years, will pass before you and I may meet. If I fail, you will see me again soon, or never. Farewell, my dear, excellent Margaret. Heaven shower down blessings on you, and save me, that I may again and again testify my gratitude for all your love and kindness.

Your affectionate brother, R. Walton

Letter 2

Archangel, 28th March, 17—
To Mrs. Saville, England

HOW SLOWLY THE TIME PASSES HERE, encompassed as I am by frost and snow! Yet a second step is taken towards my enterprise. I have hired a vessel and am occupied in collecting my sailors; those whom I have already engaged appear to be men on whom I can depend and are certainly possessed of dauntless courage.

But I have one want which I have never yet been able to satisfy, and the absence of the object of which I now feel as a most severe evil, I have no friend, Margaret: when I am glowing with the enthusiasm of success, there will be none to participate my joy; if I am assailed by disappointment, no one will endeavour to sustain me in dejection. I shall commit my thoughts to paper, it is true; but that is a poor medium for the communication of feeling. I desire the company of a man who could sympathize with me, whose eyes would reply to mine. You may deem me romantic, my dear sister, but I bitterly feel the want of a friend. I have no one near me, gentle yet courageous, possessed of a cultivated as well as of a capacious mind, whose tastes are like my own, to approve or amend my plans. How would such a friend repair the faults of your poor brother! I am too ardent in execution and too impatient of difficulties. But it is a still greater evil to me that I am self-educated: for the first fourteen years of my life I ran wild on a common and read nothing but our Uncle Thomas' books of voyages. At that age I became acquainted with the celebrated poets of our own country; but it was only when it had ceased to be in my power to derive its most important benefits from such a conviction that I perceived the necessity of becoming acquainted with more languages than that of my native country. Now I am twenty-eight and am in reality more illiterate than many schoolboys of fifteen. It is true that I have thought more and that my daydreams are more extended and magnificent, but they want (as the painters call it) KEEPING; and I greatly need a friend who would have sense enough not to despise me as romantic, and affection enough for me to endeavour to regulate my mind. Well, these are useless complaints; I shall certainly find no friend on the wide ocean, nor even here in Archangel, among merchants and seamen. Yet some feelings, unallied to the dross of human nature, beat even in these rugged bosoms. My lieutenant, for instance, is a man of wonderful courage and enterprise; he is madly desirous of glory, or rather, to word my phrase more characteristically, of advancement in his profession. He is an Englishman, and in the midst of national and professional prejudices, unsoftened by cultivation, retains some of the noblest endowments of humanity. I first became acquainted with him on board a whale vessel; finding that he was unemployed in this city, I easily engaged him to assist in my enterprise. The master is a person of an excellent disposition and is remarkable in the ship for his gentleness and the mildness of his discipline. This circumstance, added to his well-known integrity and dauntless courage, made me very desirous to engage him. A youth passed in solitude, my best years spent under your gentle and feminine fosterage, has so refined the groundwork of my character that I cannot overcome an intense distaste to the usual brutality exercised on board ship: I have never believed it to be necessary, and when I heard of a mariner equally noted for his kindliness of heart and the respect and obedience paid to him by his crew, I felt myself peculiarly fortunate in being able to secure his services. I heard of him first in rather a romantic manner, from a lady who owes to him the happiness of her life. This, briefly, is his story. Some years ago he loved a young Russian lady of moderate fortune, and having amassed a considerable sum in prize-money, the father of the girl consented to the match. He saw his mistress once before the destined ceremony; but she was bathed in tears, and throwing herself at his feet, entreated him to spare her, confessing at the same time that she loved another, but that he was poor, and that her father would never consent to the union. My generous friend reassured the suppliant, and on being informed of the name of her lover, instantly abandoned his pursuit. He had already bought a farm with his money, on which he had designed to pass the remainder of his life; but he bestowed the whole on his rival, together with the remains of his prize-money to purchase stock, and then himself solicited the young woman's father to consent to her marriage with her lover. But the old man decidedly refused, thinking himself bound in honour to my friend, who, when he found the father inexorable, quitted his country, nor returned until he heard that his former mistress was married according to her inclinations. "What a noble fellow!" you will exclaim. He is so; but then he is wholly uneducated: he is as silent as a Turk, and a kind of ignorant carelessness attends him, which, while it renders his conduct the more astonishing, detracts from the interest and sympathy which otherwise he would command.

Yet do not suppose, because I complain a little or because I can conceive a consolation for my toils which I may never know, that I am wavering in my resolutions. Those are as fixed as fate, and my voyage is only now delayed until the weather shall permit my embarkation. The winter has been dreadfully severe, but the spring promises well, and it is considered as a remarkably early season, so that perhaps I may sail sooner than I expected. I shall do nothing rashly: you know me sufficiently to confide in my prudence and considerateness whenever the safety of others is committed to my care.

I cannot describe to you my sensations on the near prospect of my undertaking. It is impossible to communicate to you a conception of the trembling sensation, half pleasurable and half fearful, with which I am preparing to depart. I am going to unexplored regions, to "the land of mist and snow," but I shall kill no albatross; therefore do not be alarmed for my safety or if I should come back to you as worn and woeful as the "Ancient Mariner." You will smile at my allusion, but I will disclose a secret. I have often attributed my attachment to, my passionate enthusiasm for, the dangerous mysteries of ocean to that production of the most imaginative of modern poets. There is something at work in my soul which I do not understand. I am practically industrious—painstaking, a workman to execute with perseverance and labour—but besides this there is a love for the marvellous, a belief in the marvellous, intertwined in all my projects, which hurries me out of the common pathways of men, even to the wild sea and unvisited regions I am about to explore. But to return to dearer considerations. Shall I meet you again, after having traversed immense seas, and returned by the most southern cape of Africa or America? I dare not expect such success, yet I cannot bear to look on the reverse of the picture. Continue for the present to write to me by every opportunity: I may receive your letters on some occasions when I need them most to support my spirits. I love you very tenderly. Remember me with affection, should you never hear from me again.[2]

Your affectionate brother, Robert Walton

Letter 3

July 7th, 17—
To Mrs. Saville, England

MY DEAR SISTER,

I write a few lines in haste to say that I am safe—and well advanced on my voyage. This letter will reach England by a merchantman now on its homeward voyage from Archangel; more fortunate than I, who may not see my native land, perhaps, for many years. I am, however, in good spirits: my men are bold and apparently firm of purpose, nor do the floating sheets of ice that continually pass us, indicating the dangers of the region towards which we are advancing, appear to dismay them. We have already reached a very high latitude; but it is the height of summer, and although not so warm as in England, the southern gales, which blow us speedily towards those shores which I so ardently desire to attain, breathe a degree of renovating warmth which I had not expected.

No incidents have hitherto befallen us that would make a figure in a letter. One or two stiff gales and the springing of a leak are accidents which experienced navigators scarcely remember to record, and I shall be well content if nothing worse happen to us during our voyage.

Adieu, my dear Margaret. Be assured that for my own sake, as well as yours, I will not rashly encounter danger. I will be cool, persevering, and prudent.

But success SHALL crown my endeavours. Wherefore not? Thus far I have gone, tracing a secure way over the pathless seas, the very stars themselves being witnesses and testimonies of my triumph. Why not still proceed over the untamed yet obedient element? What can stop the determined heart and resolved will of man?

My swelling heart involuntarily pours itself out thus. But I must finish. Heaven bless my beloved sister!

R.W.

Letter 4

August 5th, 17—
To Mrs. Saville, England

SO STRANGE AN ACCIDENT has happened to us that I cannot forbear recording it, although it is very probable that you will see me before these papers can come into your possession.

Last Monday (July 31st) we were nearly surrounded by ice, which closed in the ship on all sides, scarcely leaving her the sea-room in which she floated. Our situation was somewhat dangerous, especially as we were compassed round by a very thick fog. We accordingly lay to, hoping that some change would take place in the atmosphere and weather.

About two o'clock the mist cleared away, and we beheld, stretched out in every direction, vast and irregular plains of ice, which seemed to have no end. Some of my comrades groaned, and my own mind began to grow watchful with anxious thoughts, when a strange sight suddenly attracted our attention and diverted our solicitude from our own situation. We perceived a low carriage, fixed on a sledge and drawn by dogs, pass on towards the north, at the distance of half a mile; a being which had the shape of a man, but apparently of gigantic stature, sat in the sledge and guided the dogs. We watched the rapid progress of the traveller with our telescopes until he was lost among the distant inequalities of the ice. This appearance excited our unqualified wonder. We were, as we believed, many hundred miles from any land; but this apparition seemed to denote that it was not, in reality, so distant as we had supposed. Shut in, however, by ice, it was impossible to follow his track, which we had observed with the greatest attention. About two hours after this occurrence we heard the ground sea, and before night the ice broke and freed our ship. We, however, lay to until the morning, fearing to encounter in the dark those large loose masses which float about after the breaking up of the ice. I profited of this time to rest for a few hours.

In the morning, however, as soon as it was light, I went upon deck and found all the sailors busy on one side of the vessel, apparently talking to someone in the sea. It was, in fact, a sledge, like that we had seen before, which had drifted towards us in the night on a large fragment of ice. Only one dog remained alive; but there was a human being within it whom the sailors were persuading to enter the vessel. He was not, as the other traveller seemed to be, a savage inhabitant of some undiscovered island, but a European. When I appeared on deck the master said, "Here is our captain, and he will not allow you to perish on the open sea."

On perceiving me, the stranger addressed me in English, although with a foreign accent. "Before I come on board your vessel," said he, "will you have the kindness to inform me whither you are bound?"

You may conceive my astonishment on hearing such a question addressed to me from a man on the brink of destruction and to whom I should have supposed that my vessel would have been a resource which he would not have exchanged for the most precious wealth the earth can afford. I replied, however, that we were on a voyage of discovery towards the northern pole.

Upon hearing this he appeared satisfied and consented to come on board. Good God! Margaret, if you had seen the man who thus capitulated for his safety, your surprise would have been boundless. His limbs were nearly frozen, and his body dreadfully emaciated by fatigue and suffering. I never saw a man in so wretched a condition. We attempted to carry him into the cabin, but as soon as he had quitted the fresh air he fainted. We accordingly brought him back to the deck and restored him to animation by rubbing him with brandy and forcing him to swallow a small quantity. As soon as he showed signs of life we wrapped him up in blankets and placed him near the chimney of the kitchen stove. By slow degrees he recovered and ate a little soup, which restored him wonderfully.

Two days passed in this manner before he was able to speak, and I often feared that his sufferings had deprived him of understanding. When he had in some measure recovered, I removed him to my own cabin and attended on him as much as my duty would permit. I never saw a more interesting creature: his eyes have generally an expression of wildness, and even madness, but there are moments when, if anyone performs an act of kindness towards him or does him any the most trifling service, his whole countenance is lighted up, as it were, with a beam of benevolence and sweetness that I never saw equalled. But he is generally melancholy and despairing, and sometimes he gnashes his teeth, as if impatient of the weight of woes that oppresses him.

When my guest was a little recovered I had great trouble to keep off the men, who wished to ask him a thousand questions; but I would not allow him to be tormented by their idle curiosity, in a state of body and mind whose restoration evidently depended upon entire repose. Once, however, the lieutenant asked why he had come so far upon the ice in so strange a vehicle.

His countenance instantly assumed an aspect of the deepest gloom, and he replied, "To seek one who fled from me."

"And did the man whom you pursued travel in the same fashion?"

"Yes."

"Then I fancy we have seen him, for the day before we picked you up we saw some dogs drawing a sledge, with a man in it, across the ice."

This aroused the stranger's attention, and he asked a multitude of questions concerning the route which the demon, as he called him, had pursued. Soon after, when he was alone with me, he said, "I have, doubtless, excited your curiosity, as well as that of these good people; but you are too considerate to make inquiries."

"Certainly; it would indeed be very impertinent and inhuman in me to trouble you with any inquisitiveness of mine."

"And yet you rescued me from a strange and perilous situation; you have benevolently restored me to life."

Soon after this he inquired if I thought that the breaking up of the ice had destroyed the other sledge. I replied that I could not answer with any degree of certainty, for the ice had not broken until near midnight, and the traveller might have arrived at a place of safety before that time; but of this I could not judge. From this time a new spirit of life animated the decaying frame of the stranger. He manifested the greatest eagerness to be upon deck to watch for the sledge which had before appeared; but I have persuaded him to remain in the cabin, for he is far too weak to sustain the rawness of the atmosphere. I have promised that someone should watch for him and give him instant notice if any new object should appear in sight.

Such is my journal of what relates to this strange occurrence up to the present day. The stranger has gradually improved in health but is very silent and appears uneasy when anyone except myself enters his cabin. Yet his manners are so conciliating and gentle that the sailors are all interested in him, although they have had very little communication with him. For my own part, I begin to love him as a brother, and his constant and deep grief fills me with sympathy and compassion. He must have been a noble creature in his better days, being even now in wreck so attractive and amiable. I said in one of my letters, my dear Margaret, that I should find no friend on the wide ocean; yet I have found a man who, before his spirit had been broken by misery, I should have been happy to have possessed as the brother of my heart.

I shall continue my journal concerning the stranger at intervals, should I have any fresh incidents to record.

August 13th, 17—

MY AFFECTION FOR MY GUEST increases every day. He excites at once my admiration and my pity to an astonishing degree. How can I see so noble a creature destroyed by misery without feeling the most poignant grief? He is so gentle, yet so wise; his mind is so cultivated, and when he speaks, although his words are culled with the choicest art, yet they flow with rapidity and unparalleled eloquence. He is now much recovered from his illness and is continually on the deck, apparently watching for the sledge that preceded his own. Yet, although unhappy, he is not so utterly occupied by his own misery but that he interests himself deeply in the projects of others. He has frequently conversed with me on mine, which I have communicated to him without disguise. He entered attentively into all my arguments in favour of my eventual success and into every minute detail of the measures I had taken to secure it. I was easily led by the sympathy which he evinced to use the language of my heart, to give utterance to the burning ardour of my soul and to say, with all the fervour that warmed me, how gladly I would sacrifice my fortune, my existence, my every hope, to the furtherance of my enterprise. One man's life or death were but a small price to pay for the acquirement of the knowledge which I sought, for the dominion I should acquire and transmit over the elemental foes of our race. As I spoke, a dark gloom spread over my listener's countenance. At first I perceived that he tried to suppress his emotion; he placed his hands before his eyes, and my voice quivered and failed me as I beheld tears trickle fast from between his fingers; a groan burst from his heaving breast. I paused; at length he spoke, in broken accents: "Unhappy man! Do you share my madness? Have you drunk also of the intoxicating draught? Hear me; let me reveal my tale, and you will dash the cup from your lips!"[3]

Such words, you may imagine, strongly excited my curiosity; but the paroxysm of grief that had seized the stranger overcame his weakened powers, and many hours of repose and tranquil conversation were necessary to restore his composure. Having conquered the violence of his feelings, he appeared to despise himself for being the slave of passion; and quelling the dark tyranny of despair, he led me again to converse concerning myself personally. He asked me the history of my earlier years. The tale was quickly told, but it awakened various trains of reflection. I spoke of my desire of finding a friend, of my thirst for a more intimate sympathy with a fellow mind than had ever fallen to my lot, and expressed my conviction that a man could boast of little happiness who did not enjoy this blessing. "I agree with you," replied the stranger; "we are unfashioned creatures, but half made up, if one wiser, better, dearer than ourselves — such a friend ought to be — do not lend his aid to perfectionate our weak and faulty natures. I once had a friend, the most noble of human creatures, and am entitled, therefore, to judge respecting friendship. You have hope, and the world before you, and have no cause for despair. But I — I have lost everything and cannot begin life anew."

As he said this his countenance became expressive of a calm, settled grief that touched me to the heart. But he was silent and presently retired to his cabin.

Even broken in spirit as he is, no one can feel more deeply than he does the beauties of nature. The starry sky, the sea, and every sight afforded by these wonderful regions seem still to have the power of elevating his soul from earth. Such a man has a double existence: he may suffer misery and be overwhelmed by disappointments, yet when he has retired into himself, he will be like a celestial spirit that has a halo around him, within whose circle no grief or folly ventures.

Will you smile at the enthusiasm I express concerning this divine wanderer? You would not if you saw him. You have been tutored and refined by books and retirement from the world, and you are therefore somewhat fastidious; but this only renders you the more fit to appreciate the extraordinary merits of this wonderful man. Sometimes I have endeavoured to discover what quality it is which he possesses that elevates him so immeasurably above any other person I ever knew. I believe it to be an intuitive discernment, a quick but never-failing power of judgment, a penetration into the causes of things, unequalled for clearness and precision; add to this a facility of expression and a voice whose varied intonations are soul-subduing music.

August 19, 17—

YESTERDAY THE STRANGER said to me, "You may easily perceive, Captain Walton, that I have suffered great and unparalleled misfortunes. I had determined at one time that the memory of these evils should die with me, but you have won me to alter my determination. You seek for knowledge and wisdom, as I once did; and I ardently hope that the gratification of your wishes may not be a serpent to sting you, as mine has been. I do not know that the relation of my disasters will be useful to you; yet, when I reflect that you are pursuing the same course, exposing yourself to the same dangers which have rendered me what I am, I imagine that you may deduce an apt moral from my tale, one that may direct you if you succeed in your undertaking and console you in case of failure. Prepare to hear of occurrences which are usually deemed marvellous. Were we among the tamer scenes of nature I might fear to encounter your unbelief, perhaps your ridicule; but many things will appear possible in these wild and mysterious regions which would provoke the laughter of those unacquainted with the ever-varied powers of nature; nor can I doubt but that my tale conveys in its series internal evidence of the truth of the events of which it is composed."

You may easily imagine that I was much gratified by the offered communication, yet I could not endure that he should renew his grief by a recital of his misfortunes. I felt the greatest eagerness to hear the promised narrative, partly from curiosity and partly from a strong desire to ameliorate his fate if it were in my power. I expressed these feelings in my answer.

"I thank you," he replied, "for your sympathy, but it is useless; my fate is nearly fulfilled. I wait but for one event, and then I shall repose in peace. I understand your feeling," continued he, perceiving that I wished to interrupt him; "but you are mistaken, my friend, if thus you will allow me to name you; nothing can alter my destiny; listen to my history, and you will perceive how irrevocably it is determined."

He then told me that he would commence his narrative the next day when I should be at leisure. This promise drew from me the warmest thanks. I have resolved every night, when I am not imperatively occupied by my duties, to record, as nearly as possible in his own words, what he has related during the day. If I should be engaged, I will at least make notes. This manuscript will doubtless afford you the greatest pleasure; but to me, who know him, and who hear it from his own lips — with what interest and sympathy shall I read it in some future day! Even now, as I commence my task, his full-toned voice swells in my ears; his lustrous eyes dwell on me with all their melancholy sweetness; I see his thin hand raised in animation, while the lineaments of his face are irradiated by the soul within.

Strange and harrowing must be his story, frightful the storm which embraced the gallant vessel on its course and wrecked it — thus! ◄

THE LETTERS
Annotations

1.   The book you are holding contains the 1831 edition of Mary Shelley's novel, *Frankenstein; or, the Modern Prometheus,* and the 1959 edition of her novella, *Mathilda.* For the 1831 edition of Frankenstein, Mary Shelley revised her novel, originally published in 1818. Her novella *Mathilda,* however, was not published in Shelley's lifetime but instead edited and brought out by scholar Elizabeth Nitchie in 1959. I have not edited the editions given above, but rather in the notes that follow offer commentary on these texts. *Frankenstein* and *Mathilda* are Mary Shelley's earliest adult works and — as it happens — her best-known works. Shelley went on to publish several more novels and many short stories. Her later works include *The Last Man, Valperga, Lodore,* and *Falkner.* However, her two earliest works, *Frankenstein* and *Mathilda,* stand in conversation with each other, so much so that it seems to me impossible to understand either *Frankenstein* or *Mathilda* without reading them both, pulling through the many discursive, thematic, and symbolic threads that join them. My notes, then, reflect this interpretation of the works as twin texts.

Mary Shelley begins *Frankenstein* in epistolary style, using the literary conceit to suggest that we are reading personal letters rather than a novel. Her choice here connects *Frankenstein* stylistically to Johann Wolfgang von Goethe's 1774 novel *The Sorrows of Young Werther,* which also employs the epistolary style. Both novels present the theme of a brilliant young man who faces a triangulated love situation, a situation which causes his ruin. However, whereas Goethe's fatal love triangle is exactly that, Shelley reduplicates the triangle so that Victor Frankenstein, Elizabeth, Frankenstein's monster, and the monster's half-formed mate that Frankenstein tears apart before completion, form a chiasmus — a crossing — wherein Victor, the monster, and Elizabeth make up one triangle, and Victor, the monster, and the monster's aborted mate make up a second triangle. The monster and Victor also are paired with each female character, by turns, creating intertwined love triangles: Victor creates the female monster and then tears her apart, while his male monster visits Victor's betrothed, Elizabeth, on her wedding night and in her wedding bed kills her. These triangles are especially intertwined if we follow the queer theory argument that Victor and his monster are bound together homoerotically. By such a reading it is not that the monster is jealous of Victor's happiness with a woman because he, the monster, lacks a woman as rather that the monster, in killing Victor's bride, expresses the erotic desires that bind him and Victor together. The theme of the brilliant young man searching for the meaning of the soul and unable to find solace, in any case, clearly extends from Goethe's 1774 novel into Shelley's 1818 (revised 1831) novel. Beginning her novel with the epistolary style that she subsequently drops, Shelley signifies that Goethe's *The Sorrows of Young Werther* is a text on which she is commenting in her novel. She claims her place as a Romantic writer by alluding to Goethe's foundational text. But Shelley takes the Romantic notion of the passionately searching young man and gives it a brilliantly insolvable form that is all her own.

The first "letter" in *Frankenstein* establishes the oscillating tension that enlivens Shelley's entire novel: the reader is brought in, intimately connected with the novel as if looking over the shoulder of Walton's sister, and yet the domestic ease and comfort that seems always almost offered in the novel is forever jerked away by horrific events that upend the hope for quiet domesticity. Peace and tranquility are always out of reach for Walton and for Frankenstein. Possibly only Walton's sister has it, and we never meet her. Also observe that this sister, the recipient of the letters, bears the same initials as Mary Wollstonecraft Shelley, suggesting that the narrative, while utterly male-dominated on its surface, is actually conveyed by a woman. It is M. W. S. who delivers the novel to us, the readers.

2. The staging of this initial part of the novel in the farthest north, with explorer Robert Walton seeking his fame and success not in the realm of the mind — he tried and failed to become a poet — but in the realm of geography, shows Shelley's adroit fusing of the Romantic idea of the soulful *quest* with the contemporaneous European goal of *conquest*. Walton writes, "Success SHALL crown my endeavors," indicating precisely the European concept of geographical space as territory to be conquered. Walton is not seeking to conquer a specific people, but he thinks that the landscape he is exploring is uninhabited. In point of fact, indigenous peoples have long inhabited the farthest north, the terrain that Walton explores. Aleuts, Yenets (or, Enets), Inuit, Kereks, Kets, Nenets, and Saami, for example, have inhabited the far north for millennia. The idea of *terra nullius,* or *nobody's land,* is a product of the ideology that conceives geography as conquest, rather than a reflection of geographical places actually not inhabited.

3. Walton describes Victor Frankenstein in exalted terms, stating that Franken-stein possesses qualities that elevate "him so immeasurably above any other person" whom Walton has ever known. Thus, Shelley presents the story of Victor Frankenstein as one told — since Walton conveys to his reader that we will now read the story in Victor Frankenstein's own words — by a man of extraordinary intellectual brilliance and noble character. At the same time, Walton also describes Frankenstein as "wrecked." Within this gulf, between the golden brilliance of what Walton believes to be Frankenstein's natural gifts and the destroyed person that Frankenstein is when he meets Walton, is the whole of the narrative about to be told. Shelley does not, then, overtly suggest that Victor Frankenstein brought about his own ruin. Rather, she subtly suggests that perhaps this very structure of thought that would elevate one man, or one type of man, over and above all other creatures is precisely the problem. *Frankenstein* is presented as the epitome of both the Romantic visionary, the poet/seer, and also the Enlightenment man of science and reason. Neither of these tropes of exclusivity and mythic personal genius, Shelley's narrative makes clear, are realistic, fair, just, and useful to human society. While she seems, by her narrative's descriptions of Frankenstein, to accede to Romantic and Enlightenment tropes of the man of genius, in the active structure of her narrative, Mary Shelley precisely tears apart these beliefs in male, and European exceptionalism. ◄

CHAPTER 1

I AM BY BIRTH A GENEVESE, and my family is one of the most distinguished of that republic. My ancestors had been for many years counsellors and syndics, and my father had filled several public situations with honour and reputation. He was respected by all who knew him for his integrity and indefatigable attention to public business. He passed his younger days perpetually occupied by the affairs of his country; a variety of circumstances had prevented his marrying early, nor was it until the decline of life that he became a husband and the father of a family.

As the circumstances of his marriage illustrate his character, I cannot refrain from relating them. One of his most intimate friends was a merchant who, from a flourishing state, fell, through numerous mischances, into poverty. This man, whose name was Beaufort, was of a proud and unbending disposition and could not bear to live in poverty and oblivion in the same country where he had formerly been distinguished for his rank and magnificence. Having paid his debts, therefore, in the most honourable manner, he retreated with his daughter to the town of Lucerne, where he lived unknown and in wretchedness. My father loved Beaufort with the truest friendship and was deeply grieved by his retreat in these unfortunate circumstances. He bitterly deplored the false pride which led his friend to a conduct so little worthy of the affection that united them. He lost no time in endeavouring to seek him out, with the hope of persuading him to begin the world again through his credit and assistance.

Beaufort had taken effectual measures to conceal himself, and it was ten months before my father discovered his abode. Overjoyed at this discovery, he hastened to the house, which was situated in a mean street near the Reuss. But when he entered, misery and despair alone welcomed him. Beaufort had saved but a very small sum of money from the wreck of his fortunes, but it was sufficient to provide him with sustenance for some months, and in the meantime he hoped to procure some respectable employment in a merchant's house. The interval was, consequently, spent in inaction; his grief only became more deep and rankling when he had leisure for reflection, and at length it took so fast hold of his mind that at the end of three months he lay on a bed of sickness, incapable of any exertion.

His daughter attended him with the greatest tenderness, but she saw with despair that their little fund was rapidly decreasing and that there was no other prospect of support. But Caroline Beaufort possessed a mind of an uncommon mould, and her courage rose to support her in her adversity. She procured plain work; she plaited straw and by various means contrived to earn a pittance scarcely sufficient to support life.

Several months passed in this manner. Her father grew worse; her time was more entirely occupied in attending him; her means of subsistence decreased; and in the tenth month her father died in her arms, leaving her an orphan and a beggar. This last blow overcame her, and she knelt by Beaufort's coffin weeping bitterly, when my father entered the chamber. He came like a protecting spirit to the poor girl, who committed herself to his care; and after the interment of his friend he conducted her to Geneva and placed her under the protection of a relation. Two years after this event Caroline became his wife.

There was a considerable difference between the ages of my parents, but this circumstance seemed to unite them only closer in bonds of devoted affection. There was a sense of justice in my father's upright mind which rendered it necessary that he should approve highly to love strongly. Perhaps during former years he had suffered from the late-discovered unworthiness of one beloved and so was disposed to set a greater value on tried worth. There was a show of gratitude and worship in his attachment to my mother, differing wholly from the doting fondness of age, for it was inspired by reverence for her virtues and a desire to be the means of, in some degree, recompensing her for the sorrows she had endured, but which gave inexpressible grace to his behaviour to her. Everything was made to yield to her wishes and her convenience. He strove to shelter her, as a fair exotic is sheltered by the gardener, from every rougher wind and to surround her with all that could tend to excite pleasurable emotion in her soft and benevolent mind. Her health, and even the tranquillity of her hitherto constant spirit, had been shaken by what she had gone through. During the two years that had elapsed previous to their marriage my father had gradually relinquished all his public functions; and immediately after their union they sought the pleasant climate of Italy, and the change of scene and interest attendant on a tour through that land of wonders, as a restorative for her weakened frame.

From Italy they visited Germany and France. I, their eldest child, was born at Naples, and as an infant accompanied them in their rambles. I remained for several years their only child. Much as they were attached to each other, they seemed to draw inexhaustible stores of affection from a very mine of love to bestow them upon me. My mother's tender caresses and my father's smile of benevolent pleasure while regarding me are my first recollections. I was their plaything and their idol, and something better — their child, the innocent and helpless creature bestowed on them by heaven, whom to bring up to good, and whose future lot it was in their hands to direct to happiness or misery, according as they fulfilled their duties towards me. With this deep consciousness of what they owed towards the being to which they had given life, added to the active spirit of tenderness that animated both, it may be imagined that while during every hour of my infant life I received a lesson of patience, of charity, and of self-control, I was so guided by a silken cord that all seemed but one train of enjoyment to me. For a long time I was their only care. My mother had much desired to have a daughter, but I continued their single offspring. When I was about five years old, while making an excursion beyond the frontiers of Italy, they passed a week on the shores of the Lake of Como. Their benevolent disposition often made them enter the cottages of the poor. This, to my mother, was more than a duty; it was a necessity, a passion — remembering what she had suffered, and how she had been relieved — for her to act in her turn the guardian angel to the afflicted. During one of their walks a poor cot in the foldings of a vale attracted their notice as being singularly disconsolate, while the number of half-clothed children gathered about it spoke of penury in its worst shape. One day, when my father had gone by himself to Milan, my mother, accompanied by me, visited this abode. She found a peasant and his wife, hard working, bent down by care and labour, distributing a scanty meal to five hungry babes. Among these there was one which attracted my mother far above all the rest. She appeared of a different stock. The four others were dark-eyed, hardy little vagrants; this child was thin and very fair. Her hair was the brightest living gold, and despite the poverty of her clothing, seemed to set a crown of distinction on her head. Her brow was clear and ample, her blue eyes cloudless, and her lips and the moulding of her face so expressive of sensibility and sweetness that none could behold her without looking on her as of a distinct species, a being heaven-sent, and bearing a celestial stamp in all her features. The peasant woman, perceiving that my mother fixed eyes of wonder and admiration on this lovely girl, eagerly communicated her history. She was not her child, but the daughter of a Milanese nobleman. Her mother was a German and had died on giving her birth. The infant had been placed with these good people to nurse: they were better off then. They had not been long married, and their eldest child was but just born. The father of their charge was one of those Italians nursed in the memory of the antique glory of Italy—one among the schiavi ognor frementi, who exerted himself to obtain the liberty of his country. He became the victim of its weakness. Whether he had died or still lingered in the dungeons of Austria was not known. His property was confiscated; his child became an orphan and a beggar. She continued with her foster parents and bloomed in their rude abode, fairer than a garden rose among dark-leaved brambles. When my father returned from Milan, he found playing with me in the hall of our villa a child fairer than pictured cherub—a creature who seemed to shed radiance from her looks and whose form and motions were lighter than the chamois of the hills. The apparition was soon explained. With his permission my mother prevailed on her rustic guardians to yield their charge to her. They were fond of the sweet orphan. Her presence had seemed a blessing to them, but it would be unfair to her to keep her in poverty and want when Providence afforded her such powerful protection. They consulted their village priest, and the result was that Elizabeth Lavenza became the inmate of my parents' house—my more than sister—the beautiful and adored companion of all my occupations and my pleasures.[1]

Everyone loved Elizabeth. The passionate and almost reverential attachment with which all regarded her became, while I shared it, my pride and my delight. On the evening previous to her being brought to my home, my mother had said playfully, "I have a pretty present for my Victor—tomorrow he shall have it." And when, on the morrow, she presented Elizabeth to me as her promised gift, I, with childish seriousness, interpreted her words literally and looked upon Elizabeth as mine—mine to protect, love, and cherish. All praises bestowed on her I received as made to a possession of my own. We called each other familiarly by the name of cousin. No word, no expression could body forth the kind of relation in which she stood to me—my more than sister, since till death she was to be mine only. ◀

CHAPTER 1
Annotations

1. The theme of rising and falling fortunes in capitalism, that Shelley describes in the Beaufort family, picks up on shifts in the eighteenth- and nineteenth-centuries as European social structures of nobility were giving way to new forces of capitalism and industrialization. Frankenstein's mother, Caroline, and his bride-to-be, Elizabeth, are victims of their families' loss of wealth and status. And yet both Caroline and Elizabeth are described as inherently noble or aristocratic. As we will see as the novel progresses, a similar fate awaits the De Lacey family. This theme of commerce entwined with politics, as a force that quickly destroys and ruins family fortunes, plays out beneath the surface, structuring the narrative of *Frankenstein*. The fungibility (the quality of being exchangeable) between the role of daughter, sister, and wife, is also to be noted here, as Caroline is first cared for as a child and then married to Frankenstein's father, while Elizabeth is brought into the Frankenstein family as a sister to the children but then becomes betrothed to Victor. Here is an inherently incestuous structure by which young women become a form of capital: Elizabeth is actually described as a "gift" for Victor. As the narrative progresses, this incestuous structure is fatal to these women. Importantly, there is a clear link between the assumption in the social world of the novel that impoverished young women are possessions of the wealthy males who take them in and Victor Frankenstein's assumption that it is morally acceptable for him to create and "possess" his own creature, the monster. In this way, Mary Shelley subtly shows us that the social world in which women are possessed by men is a monstrous social world. Out of fidelity to Mary Shelley, throughout this book her original spelling has been retained except in those cases where the sense of the sentence might be lost without correction. ◄

CHAPTER 2

W E WERE BROUGHT UP TOGETHER; there was not quite a year difference in our ages. I need not say that we were strangers to any species of disunion or dispute. Harmony was the soul of our companionship, and the diversity and contrast that subsisted in our characters drew us nearer together. Elizabeth was of a calmer and more concentrated disposition; but, with all my ardour, I was capable of a more intense application and was more deeply smitten with the thirst for knowledge. She busied herself with following the aerial creations of the poets; and in the majestic and wondrous scenes which surrounded our Swiss home — the sublime shapes of the mountains, the changes of the seasons, tempest and calm, the silence of winter, and the life and turbulence of our Alpine summers — she found ample scope for admiration and delight. While my companion contemplated with a serious and satisfied spirit the magnificent appearances of things, I delighted in investigating their causes. The world was to me a secret which I desired to divine. Curiosity, earnest research to learn the hidden laws of nature, gladness akin to rapture, as they were unfolded to me, are among the earliest sensations I can remember.

On the birth of a second son, my junior by seven years, my parents gave up entirely their wandering life and fixed themselves in their native country. We possessed a house in Geneva, and a *campagne* on Belrive, the eastern shore of the lake, at the distance of rather more than a league from the city. We resided principally in the latter, and the lives of my parents were passed in considerable seclusion. It was my temper to avoid a crowd and to attach myself fervently to a few. I was indifferent, therefore, to my school-fellows in general; but I united myself in the bonds of the closest friendship to one among them. Henry Clerval was the son of a merchant of Geneva. He was a boy of singular talent and fancy. He loved enterprise, hardship, and even danger for its own sake. He was deeply read in books of chivalry and romance. He composed heroic songs and began to write many a tale of enchantment and knightly adventure. He tried to make us act plays and to enter into masquerades, in which the characters were drawn from the heroes of Roncesvalles, of the Round Table of King Arthur, and the chivalrous train who shed their blood to redeem the holy sepulchre from the hands of the infidels.

No human being could have passed a happier childhood than myself. My parents were possessed by the very spirit of kindness and indulgence. We felt that they were not the tyrants to rule our lot according to their caprice, but the agents and creators of all the many delights which we enjoyed. When I mingled with other families I distinctly discerned how peculiarly fortunate my lot was, and gratitude assisted the development of filial love.

My temper was sometimes violent, and my passions vehement; but by some law in my temperature they were turned not towards childish pursuits but to an eager desire to learn, and not to learn all things indiscriminately. I confess that neither the structure of languages, nor the code of governments, nor the politics of various states possessed attractions for me. It was the secrets of heaven and earth that I desired to learn; and whether it was the outward substance of things or the inner spirit of nature and the mysterious soul of man that occupied me, still my inquiries were directed to the metaphysical, or in its highest sense, the physical secrets of the world.

Meanwhile Clerval occupied himself, so to speak, with the moral relations of things. The busy stage of life, the virtues of heroes, and the actions of men were his theme; and his hope and his dream was to become one among those whose names are recorded in story as the gallant and adventurous benefactors of our species. The saintly soul of Elizabeth shone like a shrine-dedicated lamp in our peaceful home. Her sympathy was ours; her smile, her soft voice, the sweet glance of her celestial eyes, were ever there to bless and animate us. She was the living spirit of love to soften and attract; I might have become sullen in my study, rough through the ardour of my nature, but that she was there to subdue me to a semblance of her own gentleness. And Clerval—could aught ill entrench on the noble spirit of Clerval? Yet he might not have been so perfectly humane, so thoughtful in his generosity, so full of kindness and tenderness amidst his passion for adventurous exploit, had she not unfolded to him the real loveliness of beneficence and made the doing good the end and aim of his soaring ambition.

I feel exquisite pleasure in dwelling on the recollections of childhood, before misfortune had tainted my mind and changed its bright visions of extensive usefulness into gloomy and narrow reflections upon self. Besides, in drawing the picture of my early days, I also record those events which led, by insensible steps, to my after tale of misery, for when I would account to myself for the birth of that passion which afterwards ruled my destiny I find it arise, like a mountain river, from ignoble and almost forgotten sources; but, swelling as it proceeded, it became the torrent which, in its course, has swept away all my hopes and joys. Natural philosophy is the genius that has regulated my fate; I desire, therefore, in this narration, to state those facts which led to my predilection for that science. When I was thirteen years of age we all went on a party of pleasure to the baths near Thonon; the inclemency of the weather obliged us to remain a day confined to the inn. In this house I chanced to find a volume of the works of Cornelius Agrippa. I opened it with apathy; the theory which he attempts to demonstrate and the wonderful facts which he relates soon changed this feeling into enthusiasm. A new light seemed to dawn upon my mind, and bounding with joy, I communicated my discovery to my father. My father looked carelessly at the title page of my book and said, "Ah! Cornelius Agrippa! My dear Victor, do not waste your time upon this; it is sad trash."[1]

If, instead of this remark, my father had taken the pains to explain to me that the principles of Agrippa had been entirely exploded and that a modern system of science had been introduced which possessed much greater powers than the ancient, because the powers of the latter were chimerical, while those of the former were real and practical, under such circumstances I should certainly have thrown Agrippa aside and have contented my imagination, warmed as it was, by returning with greater ardour to my former studies. It is even possible that the train of my ideas would never have received the fatal impulse that led to my ruin. But the cursory glance my father had taken of my volume by no means assured me that he was acquainted with its contents, and I continued to read with the greatest avidity. When I returned home my first care was to procure the whole works of this author, and afterwards of Paracelsus and Albertus Magnus. I read and studied the wild fancies of these writers with delight; they appeared to me treasures known to few besides myself. I have described myself as always having been imbued with a fervent longing to penetrate the secrets of nature. In spite of the intense labour and wonderful discoveries of modern philosophers, I always came from my studies discontented and unsatisfied. Sir Isaac Newton is said to have avowed that he felt like a child picking up shells beside the great and unexplored ocean of truth. Those of his successors in each branch of natural philosophy with whom I was acquainted appeared even to my boy's apprehensions as tyros engaged in the same pursuit.

The untaught peasant beheld the elements around him and was acquainted with their practical uses. The most learned philosopher knew little more. He had partially unveiled the face of Nature, but her immortal lineaments were still a wonder and a mystery. He might dissect, anatomize, and give names; but, not to speak of a final cause, causes in their secondary and tertiary grades were utterly unknown to him. I had gazed upon the fortifications and impediments that seemed to keep human beings from entering the citadel of nature, and rashly and ignorantly I had repined.

But here were books, and here were men who had penetrated deeper and knew more. I took their word for all that they averred, and I became their disciple. It may appear strange that such should arise in the eighteenth century; but while I followed the routine of education in the schools of Geneva, I was, to a great degree, self-taught with regard to my favourite studies. My father was not scientific, and I was left to struggle with a child's blindness, added to a student's thirst for knowledge. Under the guidance of my new preceptors I entered with the greatest diligence into the search of the philosopher's stone and the elixir of life; but the latter soon obtained my undivided attention. Wealth was an inferior object, but what glory would attend the discovery if I could banish disease from the human frame and render man invulnerable to any but a violent death! Nor were these my only visions. The raising of ghosts or devils was a promise liberally accorded by my favourite authors, the fulfilment of which I most eagerly sought; and if my incantations were always unsuccessful, I attributed the failure rather to my own inexperience and mistake than to a want of skill or fidelity in my instructors. And thus for a time I was occupied by exploded systems, mingling, like an unadept, a thousand contradictory theories and floundering desperately in a very slough of multifarious knowledge, guided by an ardent imagination and childish reasoning, till an accident again changed the current of my ideas. When I was about fifteen years old we had retired to our house near Belrive, when we witnessed a most violent and terrible thunderstorm. It advanced from behind the mountains of Jura, and the thunder burst at once with frightful loudness from various quarters of the heavens. I remained, while the storm lasted, watching its progress with curiosity and delight. As I stood at the door, on a sudden I beheld a stream of fire issue from an old and beautiful oak which stood about twenty yards from our house; and so soon as the dazzling light vanished, the oak had disappeared, and nothing remained but a blasted stump. When we visited it the next morning, we found the tree shattered in a singular manner. It was not splintered by the shock, but entirely reduced to thin ribbons of wood. I never beheld anything so utterly destroyed.

Before this I was not unacquainted with the more obvious laws of electricity. On this occasion a man of great research in natural philosophy was with us, and excited by this catastrophe, he entered on the explanation of a theory which he had formed on the subject of electricity and galvanism, which was at once new and astonishing to me. All that he said threw greatly into the shade Cornelius Agrippa, Albertus Magnus, and Paracelsus, the lords of my imagination; but by some fatality the overthrow of these men disinclined me to pursue my accustomed studies. It seemed to me as if nothing would or could ever be known. All that had so long engaged my attention suddenly grew despicable. By one of those caprices of the mind which we are perhaps most subject to in early youth, I at once gave up my former occupations, set down natural history and all its progeny as a deformed and abortive creation, and entertained the greatest disdain for a would-be science which could never even step within the threshold of real knowledge. In this mood of mind I betook myself to the mathematics and the branches of study appertaining to that science as being built upon secure foundations, and so worthy of my consideration.

Thus strangely are our souls constructed, and by such slight ligaments are we bound to prosperity or ruin. When I look back, it seems to me as if this almost miraculous change of inclination and will was the immediate suggestion of the guardian angel of my life—the last effort made by the spirit of preservation to avert the storm that was even then hanging in the stars and ready to envelop me. Her victory was announced by an unusual tranquillity and gladness of soul which followed the relinquishing of my ancient and latterly tormenting studies. It was thus that I was to be taught to associate evil with their prosecution, happiness with their disregard.

It was a strong effort of the spirit of good, but it was ineffectual. Destiny was too potent, and her immutable laws had decreed my utter and terrible destruction. ◄

CHAPTER 2
Annotations

1. In this paragraph, Mary Shelley conveys the arc of Victor's ruin. The narrative emphasizes on the one hand the Romantic belief in the innocence and purity of what the child sees and knows. Hence, Victor's childhood is described as pristine, without blemish, and this faith in the value of the child's original experience precisely correlates with Romantic ideology. But Shelley turns the tables on this belief system — even as she writes within it — by having Victor state that from *within* his pristine childhood emerged the seeds of his destruction. Victor, here, suggests flaws in the Romantic belief in the purity and transcendence of childhood. He states that his destruction was set in motion by factors and forces already present in his idyllic childhood. The shift is set decisively at the onset of puberty: at the age of thirteen, Victor discovers the writings of the ancient alchemist Agrippa and it is to these writings, and to his father's failure to protect him from them, that Victor attributes his own ruin (that is, his decision to create the monster). Yes, the Frankenstein patriarch says to Victor that Agrippa is "sad trash" but he does not stop his son from exploring it. There is a way in which this scene — the newly pubertal boy reading "trash" and the father not stopping him — is clandestinely erotic. As if Victor stumbled on pornography and his father allowed it. That said, the main import of Victor's comment here is that by being pulled away from observation of external daily world, and being pulled into obsessive regard for and interest in the interior, secret sphere of what makes the world, Victor loses his soul. It is a striking thought, implying not a disconnection but an ulterior continuity between the goals and souls of ancient alchemists and modern scientists. ◄

CHAPTER 3

WHEN I HAD ATTAINED THE AGE of seventeen my parents resolved that I should become a student at the university of Ingolstadt. I had hitherto attended the schools of Geneva, but my father thought it necessary for the completion of my education that I should be made acquainted with other customs than those of my native country. My departure was therefore fixed at an early date, but before the day resolved upon could arrive, the first misfortune of my life occurred—an omen, as it were, of my future misery. Elizabeth had caught the scarlet fever; her illness was severe, and she was in the greatest danger. During her illness many arguments had been urged to persuade my mother to refrain from attending upon her. She had at first yielded to our entreaties, but when she heard that the life of her favourite was menaced, she could no longer control her anxiety. She attended her sickbed; her watchful attentions triumphed over the malignity of the distemper—Elizabeth was saved, but the consequences of this imprudence were fatal to her preserver. On the third day my mother sickened; her fever was accompanied by the most alarming symptoms, and the looks of her medical attendants prognosticated the worst event. On her deathbed the fortitude and benignity of this best of women did not desert her. She joined the hands of Elizabeth and myself. "My children," she said, "my firmest hopes of future happiness were placed on the prospect of your union. This expectation will now be the consolation of your father. Elizabeth, my love, you must supply my place to my younger children. Alas! I regret that I am taken from you; and, happy and beloved as I have been, is it not hard to quit you all? But these are not thoughts befitting me; I will endeavour to resign myself cheerfully to death and will indulge a hope of meeting you in another world."

She died calmly, and her countenance expressed affection even in death. I need not describe the feelings of those whose dearest ties are rent by that most irreparable evil, the void that presents itself to the soul, and the despair that is exhibited on the countenance. It is so long before the mind can persuade itself that she whom we saw every day and whose very existence appeared a part of our own can have departed forever — that the brightness of a beloved eye can have been extinguished and the sound of a voice so familiar and dear to the ear can be hushed, never more to be heard. These are the reflections of the first days; but when the lapse of time proves the reality of the evil, then the actual bitterness of grief commences. Yet from whom has not that rude hand rent away some dear connection? And why should I describe a sorrow which all have felt, and must feel? The time at length arrives when grief is rather an indulgence than a necessity; and the smile that plays upon the lips, although it may be deemed a sacrilege, is not banished. My mother was dead, but we had still duties which we ought to perform; we must continue our course with the rest and learn to think ourselves fortunate whilst one remains whom the spoiler has not seized.

My departure for Ingolstadt, which had been deferred by these events, was now again determined upon. I obtained from my father a respite of some weeks. It appeared to me sacrilege so soon to leave the repose, akin to death, of the house of mourning and to rush into the thick of life. I was new to sorrow, but it did not the less alarm me. I was unwilling to quit the sight of those that remained to me, and above all, I desired to see my sweet Elizabeth in some degree consoled.

She indeed veiled her grief and strove to act the comforter to us all. She looked steadily on life and assumed its duties with courage and zeal. She devoted herself to those whom she had been taught to call her uncle and cousins. Never was she so enchanting as at this time, when she recalled the sunshine of her smiles and spent them upon us. She forgot even her own regret in her endeavours to make us forget.

The day of my departure at length arrived. Clerval spent the last evening with us. He had endeavoured to persuade his father to permit him to accompany me and to become my fellow student, but in vain. His father was a narrow-minded trader and saw idleness and ruin in the aspirations and ambition of his son. Henry deeply felt the misfortune of being debarred from a liberal education. He said little, but when he spoke I read in his kindling eye and in his animated glance a restrained but firm resolve not to be chained to the miserable details of commerce.

We sat late. We could not tear ourselves away from each other nor persuade ourselves to say the word "Farewell!" It was said, and we retired under the pretence of seeking repose, each fancying that the other was deceived; but when at morning's dawn I descended to the carriage which was to convey me away, they were all there—my father again to bless me, Clerval to press my hand once more, my Elizabeth to renew her entreaties that I would write often and to bestow the last feminine attentions on her playmate and friend.

I threw myself into the chaise that was to convey me away and indulged in the most melancholy reflections. I, who had ever been surrounded by amiable companions, continually engaged in endeavouring to bestow mutual pleasure—I was now alone. In the university whither I was going I must form my own friends and be my own protector. My life had hitherto been remarkably secluded and domestic, and this had given me invincible repugnance to new countenances. I loved my brothers, Elizabeth, and Clerval; these were "old familiar faces," but I believed myself totally unfitted for the company of strangers. Such were my reflections as I commenced my journey; but as I proceeded, my spirits and hopes rose. I ardently desired the acquisition of knowledge. I had often, when at home, thought it hard to remain during my youth cooped up in one place and had longed to enter the world and take my station among other human beings. Now my desires were complied with, and it would, indeed, have been folly to repent.

I had sufficient leisure for these and many other reflections during my journey to Ingolstadt, which was long and fatiguing. At length the high white steeple of the town met my eyes. I alighted and was conducted to my solitary apartment to spend the evening as I pleased.

The next morning I delivered my letters of introduction and paid a visit to some of the principal professors. Chance—or rather the evil influence, the Angel of Destruction, which asserted omnipotent sway over me from the moment I turned my reluctant steps from my father's door—led me first to M. Krempe, professor of natural philosophy. He was an uncouth man, but deeply imbued in the secrets of his science. He asked me several questions concerning my progress in the different branches of science appertaining to natural philosophy. I replied carelessly, and partly in contempt, mentioned the names of my alchemists as the principal authors I had studied. The professor stared. "Have you," he said, "really spent your time in studying such nonsense?"

I replied in the affirmative. "Every minute," continued M. Krempe with warmth, "every instant that you have wasted on those books is utterly and entirely lost. You have burdened your memory with exploded systems and useless names. Good God! In what desert land have you lived, where no one was kind enough to inform you that these fancies which you have so greedily imbibed are a thousand years old and as musty as they are ancient? I little expected, in this enlightened and scientific age, to find a disciple of Albertus Magnus and Paracelsus. My dear sir, you must begin your studies entirely anew."

So saying, he stepped aside and wrote down a list of several books treating of natural philosophy which he desired me to procure, and dismissed me after mentioning that in the beginning of the following week he intended to commence a course of lectures upon natural philosophy in its general relations, and that M. Waldman, a fellow professor, would lecture upon chemistry the alternate days that he omitted.

I returned home not disappointed, for I have said that I had long considered those authors useless whom the professor reprobated; but I returned not at all the more inclined to recur to these studies in any shape. M. Krempe was a little squat man with a gruff voice and a repulsive countenance; the teacher, therefore, did not prepossess me in favour of his pursuits. In rather a too philosophical and connected a strain, perhaps, I have given an account of the conclusions I had come to concerning them in my early years. As a child I had not been content with the results promised by the modern professors of natural science. With a confusion of ideas only to be accounted for by my extreme youth and my want of a guide on such matters, I had retrod the steps of knowledge along the paths of time and exchanged the discoveries of recent inquirers for the dreams of forgotten alchemists. Besides, I had a contempt for the uses of modern natural philosophy. It was very different when the masters of the science sought immortality and power; such views, although futile, were grand; but now the scene was changed. The ambition of the inquirer seemed to limit itself to the annihilation of those visions on which my interest in science was chiefly founded. I was required to exchange chimeras of boundless grandeur for realities of little worth.

Such were my reflections during the first two or three days of my residence at Ingolstadt, which were chiefly spent in becoming acquainted with the localities and the principal residents in my new abode. But as the ensuing week commenced, I thought of the information which M. Krempe had given me concerning the lectures. And although I could not consent to go and hear that little conceited fellow deliver sentences out of a pulpit, I recollected what he had said of M. Waldman, whom I had never seen, as he had hitherto been out of town.

Partly from curiosity and partly from idleness, I went into the lecturing room, which M. Waldman entered shortly after. This professor was very unlike his colleague. He appeared about fifty years of age, but with an aspect expressive of the greatest benevolence; a few grey hairs covered his temples, but those at the back of his head were nearly black. His person was short but remarkably erect and his voice the sweetest I had ever heard. He began his lecture by a recapitulation of the history of chemistry and the various improvements made by different men of learning, pronouncing with fervour the names of the most distinguished discoverers. He then took a cursory view of the present state of the science and explained many of its elementary terms. After having made a few preparatory experiments, he concluded with a panegyric upon modern chemistry, the terms of which I shall never forget: "The ancient teachers of this science," said he, "promised impossibilities and performed nothing. The modern masters promise very little; they know that metals cannot be transmuted and that the elixir of life is a chimera but these philosophers, whose hands seem only made to dabble in dirt, and their eyes to pore over the microscope or crucible, have indeed performed miracles. They penetrate into the recesses of nature and show how she works in her hiding-places. They ascend into the heavens; they have discovered how the blood circulates, and the nature of the air we breathe. They have acquired new and almost unlimited powers; they can command the thunders of heaven, mimic the earthquake, and even mock the invisible world with its own shadows."

Such were the professor's words—rather let me say such the words of the fate—enounced to destroy me. As he went on I felt as if my soul were grappling with a palpable enemy; one by one the various keys were touched which formed the mechanism of my being; chord after chord was sounded, and soon my mind was filled with one thought, one conception, one purpose. So much has been done, exclaimed the soul of Frankenstein—more, far more, will I achieve; treading in the steps already marked, I will pioneer a new way, explore unknown powers, and unfold to the world the deepest mysteries of creation.

I closed not my eyes that night. My internal being was in a state of insurrection and turmoil; I felt that order would thence arise, but I had no power to produce it. By degrees, after the morning's dawn, sleep came. I awoke, and my yesternight's thoughts were as a dream. There only remained a resolution to return to my ancient studies and to devote myself to a science for which I believed myself to possess a natural talent. On the same day I paid M. Waldman a visit. His manners in private were even more mild and attractive than in public, for there was a certain dignity in his mien during his lecture which in his own house was replaced by the greatest affability and kindness. I gave him pretty nearly the same account of my former pursuits as I had given to his fellow professor. He heard with attention the little narration concerning my studies and smiled at the names of Cornelius Agrippa and Paracelsus, but without the contempt that M. Krempe had exhibited. He said that "These were men to whose indefatigable zeal modern philosophers were indebted for most of the foundations of their knowledge. They had left to us, as an easier task, to give new names and arrange in connected classifications the facts which they in a great degree had been the instruments of bringing to light. The labours of men of genius, however erroneously directed, scarcely ever fail in ultimately turning to the solid advantage of mankind." I listened to his statement, which was delivered without any presumption or affectation, and then added that his lecture had removed my prejudices against modern chemists; I expressed myself in measured terms, with the modesty and deference due from a youth to his instructor, without letting escape (inexperience in life would have made me ashamed) any of the enthusiasm which stimulated my intended labours. I requested his advice concerning the books I ought to procure.

"I am happy," said M. Waldman, "to have gained a disciple; and if your application equals your ability, I have no doubt of your success. Chemistry is that branch of natural philosophy in which the greatest improvements have been and may be made; it is on that account that I have made it my peculiar study; but at the same time, I have not neglected the other branches of science. A man would make but a very sorry chemist if he attended to that department of human knowledge alone. If your wish is to become really a man of science and not merely a petty experimentalist, I should advise you to apply to every branch of natural philosophy, including mathematics." He then took me into his laboratory and explained to me the uses of his various machines, instructing me as to what I ought to procure and promising me the use of his own when I should have advanced far enough in the science not to derange their mechanism. He also gave me the list of books which I had requested, and I took my leave.

Thus ended a day memorable to me; it decided my future destiny. ◀

CHAPTER 4

FROM THIS DAY NATURAL PHILOSOPHY, and particularly chemistry, in the most comprehensive sense of the term, became nearly my sole occupation. I read with ardour those works, so full of genius and discrimination, which modern inquirers have written on these subjects. I attended the lectures and cultivated the acquaintance of the men of science of the university, and I found even in M. Krempe a great deal of sound sense and real information, combined, it is true, with a repulsive physiognomy and manners, but not on that account the less valuable. In M. Waldman I found a true friend. His gentleness was never tinged by dogmatism, and his instructions were given with an air of frankness and good nature that banished every idea of pedantry. In a thousand ways he smoothed for me the path of knowledge and made the most abstruse inquiries clear and facile to my apprehension. My application was at first fluctuating and uncertain; it gained strength as I proceeded and soon became so ardent and eager that the stars often disappeared in the light of morning whilst I was yet engaged in my laboratory.

As I applied so closely, it may be easily conceived that my progress was rapid. My ardour was indeed the astonishment of the students, and my proficiency that of the masters. Professor Krempe often asked me, with a sly smile, how Cornelius Agrippa went on, whilst M. Waldman expressed the most heartfelt exultation in my progress. Two years passed in this manner, during which I paid no visit to Geneva, but was engaged, heart and soul, in the pursuit of some discoveries which I hoped to make. None but those who have experienced them can conceive of the enticements of science. In other studies you go as far as others have gone before you, and there is nothing more to know; but in a scientific pursuit there is continual food for discovery and wonder. A mind of moderate capacity which closely pursues one study must infallibly arrive at great proficiency in that study; and I, who continually sought the attainment of one object of pursuit and was solely wrapped up in this, improved so rapidly that at the end of two years I made some discoveries in the improvement of some chemical instruments, which procured me great esteem and admiration at the university. When I had arrived at this point and had become as well acquainted with the theory and practice of natural philosophy as depended on the lessons of any of the professors at Ingolstadt, my residence there being no longer conducive to my improvements, I thought of returning to my friends and my native town, when an incident happened that protracted my stay.

One of the phenomena which had peculiarly attracted my attention was the structure of the human frame, and, indeed, any animal endued with life. Whence, I often asked myself, did the principle of life proceed? It was a bold question, and one which has ever been considered as a mystery; yet with how many things are we upon the brink of becoming acquainted, if cowardice or carelessness did not restrain our inquiries. I revolved these circumstances in my mind and determined thenceforth to apply myself more particularly to those branches of natural philosophy which relate to physiology. Unless I had been animated by an almost supernatural enthusiasm, my application to this study would have been irksome and almost intolerable. To examine the causes of life, we must first have recourse to death. I became acquainted with the science of anatomy, but this was not sufficient; I must also observe the natural decay and corruption of the human body. In my education my father had taken the greatest precautions that my mind should be impressed with no supernatural horrors. I do not ever remember to have trembled at a tale of superstition or to have feared the apparition of a spirit. Darkness had no effect upon my fancy, and a churchyard was to me merely the receptacle of bodies deprived of life, which, from being the seat of beauty and strength, had become food for the worm. Now I was led to examine the cause and progress of this decay and forced to spend days and nights in vaults and charnel-houses. My attention was fixed upon every object the most insupportable to the delicacy of the human feelings. I saw how the fine form of man was degraded and wasted; I beheld the corruption of death succeed to the blooming cheek of life; I saw how the worm inherited the wonders of the eye and brain. I paused, examining and analysing all the minutiae of causation, as exemplified in the change from life to death, and death to life, until from the midst of this darkness a sudden light broke in upon me—a light so brilliant and wondrous, yet so simple, that while I became dizzy with the immensity of the prospect which it illustrated, I was surprised that among so many men of genius who had directed their inquiries towards the same science, that I alone should be reserved to discover so astonishing a secret.

Remember, I am not recording the vision of a madman. The sun does not more certainly shine in the heavens than that which I now affirm is true. Some miracle might have produced it, yet the stages of the discovery were distinct and probable. After days and nights of incredible labour and fatigue, I succeeded in discovering the cause of generation and life; nay, more, I became myself capable of bestowing animation upon lifeless matter.

The astonishment which I had at first experienced on this discovery soon gave place to delight and rapture. After so much time spent in painful labour, to arrive at once at the summit of my desires was the most gratifying consummation of my toils. But this discovery was so great and overwhelming that all the steps by which I had been progressively led to it were obliterated, and I beheld only the result. What had been the study and desire of the wisest men since the creation of the world was now within my grasp. Not that, like a magic scene, it all opened upon me at once: the information I had obtained was of a nature rather to direct my endeavours so soon as I should point them towards the object of my search than to exhibit that object already accomplished. I was like the Arabian who had been buried with the dead and found a passage to life, aided only by one glimmering and seemingly ineffectual light.

I see by your eagerness and the wonder and hope which your eyes express, my friend, that you expect to be informed of the secret with which I am acquainted; that cannot be; listen patiently until the end of my story, and you will easily perceive why I am reserved upon that subject. I will not lead you on, unguarded and ardent as I then was, to your destruction and infallible misery. Learn from me, if not by my precepts, at least by my example, how dangerous is the acquirement of knowledge and how much happier that man is who believes his native town to be the world, than he who aspires to become greater than his nature will allow.

When I found so astonishing a power placed within my hands, I hesitated a long time concerning the manner in which I should employ it. Although I possessed the capacity of bestowing animation, yet to prepare a frame for the reception of it, with all its intricacies of fibres, muscles, and veins, still remained a work of inconceivable difficulty and labour. I doubted at first whether I should attempt the creation of a being like myself, or one of simpler organization; but my imagination was too much exalted by my first success to permit me to doubt of my ability to give life to an animal as complex and wonderful as man. The materials at present within my command hardly appeared adequate to so arduous an undertaking, but I doubted not that I should ultimately succeed. I prepared myself for a multitude of reverses; my operations might be incessantly baffled, and at last my work be imperfect, yet when I considered the improvement which every day takes place in science and mechanics, I was encouraged to hope my present attempts would at least lay the foundations of future success. Nor could I consider the magnitude and complexity of my plan as any argument of its impracticability. It was with these feelings that I began the creation of a human being. As the minuteness of the parts formed a great hindrance to my speed, I resolved, contrary to my first intention, to make the being of a gigantic stature, that is to say, about eight feet in height, and proportionably large. After having formed this determination and having spent some months in successfully collecting and arranging my materials, I began.

No one can conceive the variety of feelings which bore me onwards, like a hurricane, in the first enthusiasm of success. Life and death appeared to me ideal bounds, which I should first break through, and pour a torrent of light into our dark world. A new species would bless me as its creator and source; many happy and excellent natures would owe their being to me. No father could claim the gratitude of his child so completely as I should deserve theirs. Pursuing these reflections, I thought that if I could bestow animation upon lifeless matter, I might in process of time (although I now found it impossible) renew life where death had apparently devoted the body to corruption.[1]

These thoughts supported my spirits, while I pursued my undertaking with unremitting ardour. My cheek had grown pale with study, and my person had become emaciated with confinement. Sometimes, on the very brink of certainty, I failed; yet still I clung to the hope which the next day or the next hour might realize. One secret which I alone possessed was the hope to which I had dedicated myself; and the moon gazed on my midnight labours, while, with unrelaxed and breathless eagerness, I pursued nature to her hiding-places. Who shall conceive the horrors of my secret toil as I dabbled among the unhallowed damps of the grave or tortured the living animal to animate the lifeless clay? My limbs now tremble, and my eyes swim with the remembrance; but then a resistless and almost frantic impulse urged me forward; I seemed to have lost all soul or sensation but for this one pursuit. It was indeed but a passing trance, that only made me feel with renewed acuteness so soon as, the unnatural stimulus ceasing to operate, I had returned to my old habits. I collected bones from charnel-houses and disturbed, with profane fingers, the tremendous secrets of the human frame. In a solitary chamber, or rather cell, at the top of the house, and separated from all the other apartments by a gallery and staircase, I kept my workshop of filthy creation; my eyeballs were starting from their sockets in attending to the details of my employment. The dissecting room and the slaughter-house furnished many of my materials; and often did my human nature turn with loathing from my occupation, whilst, still urged on by an eagerness which perpetually increased, I brought my work near to a conclusion.

The summer months passed while I was thus engaged, heart and soul, in one pursuit. It was a most beautiful season; never did the fields bestow a more plentiful harvest or the vines yield a more luxuriant vintage, but my eyes were insensible to the charms of nature. And the same feelings which made me neglect the scenes around me caused me also to forget those friends who were so many miles absent, and whom I had not seen for so long a time. I knew my silence disquieted them, and I well remembered the words of my father: "I know that while you are pleased with yourself you will think of us with affection, and we shall hear regularly from you. You must pardon me if I regard any interruption in your correspondence as a proof that your other duties are equally neglected."

I knew well therefore what would be my father's feelings, but I could not tear my thoughts from my employment, loathsome in itself, but which had taken an irresistible hold of my imagination. I wished, as it were, to procrastinate all that related to my feelings of affection until the great object, which swallowed up every habit of my nature, should be completed.

I then thought that my father would be unjust if he ascribed my neglect to vice or faultiness on my part, but I am now convinced that he was justified in conceiving that I should not be altogether free from blame. A human being in perfection ought always to preserve a calm and peaceful mind and never to allow passion or a transitory desire to disturb his tranquillity. I do not think that the pursuit of knowledge is an exception to this rule. If the study to which you apply yourself has a tendency to weaken your affections and to destroy your taste for those simple pleasures in which no alloy can possibly mix, then that study is certainly unlawful, that is to say, not befitting the human mind. If this rule were always observed; if no man allowed any pursuit whatsoever to interfere with the tranquillity of his domestic affections, Greece had not been enslaved, Caesar would have spared his country, America would have been discovered more gradually, and the empires of Mexico and Peru had not been destroyed.

But I forget that I am moralizing in the most interesting part of my tale, and your looks remind me to proceed. My father made no reproach in his letters and only took notice of my silence by inquiring into my occupations more particularly than before. Winter, spring, and summer passed away during my labours; but I did not watch the blossom or the expanding leaves — sights which before always yielded me supreme delight — so deeply was I engrossed in my occupation. The leaves of that year had withered before my work drew near to a close, and now every day showed me more plainly how well I had succeeded. But my enthusiasm was checked by my anxiety, and I appeared rather like one doomed by slavery to toil in the mines, or any other unwholesome trade than an artist occupied by his favourite employment. Every night I was oppressed by a slow fever, and I became nervous to a most painful degree; the fall of a leaf startled me, and I shunned my fellow creatures as if I had been guilty of a crime. Sometimes I grew alarmed at the wreck I perceived that I had become; the energy of my purpose alone sustained me: my labours would soon end, and I believed that exercise and amusement would then drive away incipient disease; and I promised myself both of these when my creation should be complete. ◄

CHAPTER 4
Annotations

1. Frankenstein describes scientific discovery as comparable to poetic or artistic inspiration. Mary Shelley was not a scientist, nor did she receive a formal education comparable to that of well-born men of her time, and yet she was intellectually curious and avidly read about the advancements in science of her era. What is remarkable about the language of the passages describing Victor's attraction to science, and chemistry in particular, is the oscillation between pleasure and horror. Prof. Krempe is described as grotesque, Prof. Waldman as heroic and yet there is a suggestion that, beneath the surface, these men are the same. Victor's pleasure in studying science also has a violent torque—he describes science as "penetrating" the "hiding places" of nature, a kind of hunt, or even a rape. Having discovered the secret of the generative source of life—which of course cannot be distilled to one source—Frankenstein has penetrated deeper than anyone into nature's hiding places. From this knowledge, he begins to build a giant human being. He gives no reason whatsoever for this decision to create a new creature: why not use his discovery to bring back the very recently dead? But in contrast to Christ who, according to the New Testament revives Tabitha and Lazarus just at the brink of death, Frankenstein wants his own creation. He longs to be owner of a human being who belongs to no one else.

   In describing this desire, Mary Shelley brilliantly fuses the tendency toward male dominance of science—summed as the urge to penetrate nature's recesses—and the practice of enslavement, the urge to own and control another human being. It is interesting that, as I write these notes in early 2018, a new Google product is being marketed as an artificial intelligence "personal assistant" that will do anything its owner commands. In Mary Shelley's day, slavery was still legal in in the British Empire (it was outlawed only in 1833). Hence we may see in her writing of Victor Frankenstein a subtle critique of slave-owners and their lust to own and command entirely another human being as one's own. ◄

CHAPTER 5

T WAS ON A DREARY NIGHT of November that I beheld the accomplishment of my toils. With an anxiety that almost amounted to agony, I collected the instruments of life around me, that I might infuse a spark of being into the lifeless thing that lay at my feet. It was already one in the morning; the rain pattered dismally against the panes, and my candle was nearly burnt out, when, by the glimmer of the half-extinguished light, I saw the dull yellow eye of the creature open; it breathed hard, and a convulsive motion agitated its limbs.

How can I describe my emotions at this catastrophe, or how delineate the wretch whom with such infinite pains and care I had endeavoured to form? His limbs were in proportion, and I had selected his features as beautiful. Beautiful! Great God! His yellow skin scarcely covered the work of muscles and arteries beneath; his hair was of a lustrous black, and flowing; his teeth of a pearly whiteness; but these luxuriances only formed a more horrid contrast with his watery eyes, that seemed almost of the same colour as the dun-white sockets in which they were set, his shrivelled complexion and straight black lips.[1]

The different accidents of life are not so changeable as the feelings of human nature. I had worked hard for nearly two years, for the sole purpose of infusing life into an inanimate body. For this I had deprived myself of rest and health. I had desired it with an ardour that far exceeded moderation; but now that I had finished, the beauty of the dream vanished, and breathless horror and disgust filled my heart. Unable to endure the aspect of the being I had created, I rushed out of the room and continued a long time traversing my bed-chamber, unable to compose my mind to sleep. At length lassitude succeeded to the tumult I had before endured, and I threw myself on the bed in my clothes, endeavouring to seek a few moments of forgetfulness. But it was in vain; I slept, indeed, but I was disturbed by the wildest dreams. I thought I saw Elizabeth, in the bloom of health, walking in the streets of Ingolstadt. Delighted and surprised, I embraced her, but as I imprinted the first kiss on her lips, they became livid with the hue of death; her features appeared to change, and I thought that I held the corpse of my dead mother in my arms; a shroud enveloped her form, and I saw the grave-worms crawling in the folds of the flannel. I started from my sleep with horror; a cold dew covered my forehead, my teeth chattered, and every limb became convulsed; when, by the dim and yellow light of the moon, as it forced its way through the window shutters, I beheld the wretch — the miserable monster whom I had created. He held up the curtain of the bed; and his eyes, if eyes they may be called, were fixed on me. His jaws opened, and he muttered some inarticulate sounds, while a grin wrinkled his cheeks. He might have spoken, but I did not hear; one hand was stretched out, seemingly to detain me, but I escaped and rushed downstairs. I took refuge in the courtyard belonging to the house which I inhabited, where I remained during the rest of the night, walking up and down in the greatest agitation, listening attentively, catching and fearing each sound as if it were to announce the approach of the demoniacal corpse to which I had so miserably given life.[2]

Oh! No mortal could support the horror of that countenance. A mummy again endued with animation could not be so hideous as that wretch. I had gazed on him while unfinished; he was ugly then, but when those muscles and joints were rendered capable of motion, it became a thing such as even Dante could not have conceived.

I passed the night wretchedly. Sometimes my pulse beat so quickly and hardly that I felt the palpitation of every artery; at others, I nearly sank to the ground through languor and extreme weakness. Mingled with this horror, I felt the bitterness of disappointment; dreams that had been my food and pleasant rest for so long a space were now become a hell to me; and the change was so rapid, the overthrow so complete!

Morning, dismal and wet, at length dawned and discovered to my sleepless and aching eyes the church of Ingolstadt, its white steeple and clock, which indicated the sixth hour. The porter opened the gates of the court, which had that night been my asylum, and I issued into the streets, pacing them with quick steps, as if I sought to avoid the wretch whom I feared every turning of the street would present to my view. I did not dare return to the apartment which I inhabited, but felt impelled to hurry on, although drenched by the rain which poured from a black and comfortless sky.

I continued walking in this manner for some time, endeavouring by bodily exercise to ease the load that weighed upon my mind. I traversed the streets without any clear conception of where I was or what I was doing. My heart palpitated in the sickness of fear, and I hurried on with irregular steps, not daring to look about me:

> Like one who, on a lonely road,
> Doth walk in fear and dread,
> And, having once turned round, walks on,
> And turns no more his head;
> Because he knows a frightful fiend
> Doth close behind him tread.
> Coleridge's "Ancient Mariner."

Continuing thus, I came at length opposite to the inn at which the various diligences and carriages usually stopped. Here I paused, I knew not why; but I remained some minutes with my eyes fixed on a coach that was coming towards me from the other end of the street. As it drew nearer I observed that it was the Swiss diligence; it stopped just where I was standing, and on the door being opened, I perceived Henry Clerval, who, on seeing me, instantly sprung out. "My dear Frankenstein," exclaimed he, "how glad I am to see you! How fortunate that you should be here at the very moment of my alighting!"

Nothing could equal my delight on seeing Clerval; his presence brought back to my thoughts my father, Elizabeth, and all those scenes of home so dear to my recollection. I grasped his hand, and in a moment forgot my horror and misfortune; I felt suddenly, and for the first time during many months, calm and serene joy. I welcomed my friend, therefore, in the most cordial manner, and we walked towards my college. Clerval continued talking for some time about our mutual friends and his own good fortune in being permitted to come to Ingolstadt. "You may easily believe," said he, "how great was the difficulty to persuade my father that all necessary knowledge was not comprised in the noble art of book-keeping; and, indeed, I believe I left him incredulous to the last, for his constant answer to my unwearied entreaties was the same as that of the Dutch schoolmaster in *The Vicar of Wakefield*: 'I have ten thousand florins a year without Greek, I eat heartily without Greek.' But his affection for me at length overcame his dislike of learning, and he has permitted me to undertake a voyage of discovery to the land of knowledge."

"It gives me the greatest delight to see you; but tell me how you left my father, brothers, and Elizabeth."

"Very well, and very happy, only a little uneasy that they hear from you so seldom. By the by, I mean to lecture you a little upon their account myself. But, my dear Frankenstein," continued he, stopping short and gazing full in my face, "I did not before remark how very ill you appear; so thin and pale; you look as if you had been watching for several nights."

"You have guessed right; I have lately been so deeply engaged in one occupation that I have not allowed myself sufficient rest, as you see; but I hope, I sincerely hope, that all these employments are now at an end and that I am at length free."

I trembled excessively; I could not endure to think of, and far less to allude to, the occurrences of the preceding night. I walked with a quick pace, and we soon arrived at my college. I then reflected, and the thought made me shiver, that the creature whom I had left in my apartment might still be there, alive and walking about. I dreaded to behold this monster, but I feared still more that Henry should see him. Entreating him, therefore, to remain a few minutes at the bottom of the stairs, I darted up towards my own room. My hand was already on the lock of the door before I recollected myself. I then paused, and a cold shivering came over me. I threw the door forcibly open, as children are accustomed to do when they expect a spectre to stand in waiting for them on the other side; but nothing appeared. I stepped fearfully in: the apartment was empty, and my bedroom was also freed from its hideous guest. I could hardly believe that so great a good fortune could have befallen me, but when I became assured that my enemy had indeed fled, I clapped my hands for joy and ran down to Clerval.

We ascended into my room, and the servant presently brought breakfast; but I was unable to contain myself. It was not joy only that possessed me; I felt my flesh tingle with excess of sensitiveness, and my pulse beat rapidly. I was unable to remain for a single instant in the same place; I jumped over the chairs, clapped my hands, and laughed aloud. Clerval at first attributed my unusual spirits to joy on his arrival, but when he observed me more attentively, he saw a wildness in my eyes for which he could not account, and my loud, unrestrained, heartless laughter frightened and astonished him.

"My dear Victor," cried he, "what, for God's sake, is the matter? Do not laugh in that manner. How ill you are! What is the cause of all this?"

"Do not ask me," cried I, putting my hands before my eyes, for I thought I saw the dreaded spectre glide into the room; "HE can tell. Oh, save me! Save me!" I imagined that the monster seized me; I struggled furiously and fell down in a fit.

Poor Clerval! What must have been his feelings? A meeting, which he anticipated with such joy, so strangely turned to bitterness. But I was not the witness of his grief, for I was lifeless and did not recover my senses for a long, long time.

This was the commencement of a nervous fever which confined me for several months. During all that time Henry was my only nurse. I afterwards learned that, knowing my father's advanced age and unfitness for so long a journey, and how wretched my sickness would make Elizabeth, he spared them this grief by concealing the extent of my disorder. He knew that I could not have a more kind and attentive nurse than himself; and, firm in the hope he felt of my recovery, he did not doubt that, instead of doing harm, he performed the kindest action that he could towards them.

But I was in reality very ill, and surely nothing but the unbounded and unremitting attentions of my friend could have restored me to life. The form of the monster on whom I had bestowed existence was forever before my eyes, and I raved incessantly concerning him. Doubtless my words surprised Henry; he at first believed them to be the wanderings of my disturbed imagination, but the pertinacity with which I continually recurred to the same subject persuaded him that my disorder indeed owed its origin to some uncommon and terrible event.

By very slow degrees, and with frequent relapses that alarmed and grieved my friend, I recovered. I remember the first time I became capable of observing outward objects with any kind of pleasure, I perceived that the fallen leaves had disappeared and that the young buds were shooting forth from the trees that shaded my window. It was a divine spring, and the season contributed greatly to my convalescence. I felt also sentiments of joy and affection revive in my bosom; my gloom disappeared, and in a short time I became as cheerful as before I was attacked by the fatal passion.

"Dearest Clerval," exclaimed I, "how kind, how very good you are to me. This whole winter, instead of being spent in study, as you promised yourself, has been consumed in my sick room. How shall I ever repay you? I feel the greatest remorse for the disappointment of which I have been the occasion, but you will forgive me."

"You will repay me entirely if you do not discompose yourself, but get well as fast as you can; and since you appear in such good spirits, I may speak to you on one subject, may I not?"

I trembled. One subject! What could it be? Could he allude to an object on whom I dared not even think? "Compose yourself," said Clerval, who observed my change of colour, "I will not mention it if it agitates you; but your father and cousin would be very happy if they received a letter from you in your own handwriting. They hardly know how ill you have been and are uneasy at your long silence."

"Is that all, my dear Henry? How could you suppose that my first thought would not fly towards those dear, dear friends whom I love and who are so deserving of my love?"

"If this is your present temper, my friend, you will perhaps be glad to see a letter that has been lying here some days for you; it is from your cousin, I believe." ◄

CHAPTER 5
Annotations

1. Frankenstein has discovered the elixir of life, but this discovery paradoxically places him with the dead: charnel houses and slaughter houses. Victor himself becomes deathlike as her pursues his creation: he grows pale and emaciated, he breaks off communication with his family and friends, and he loses touch with the natural world, which acts as a touchstone of the soul throughout *Frankenstein* and *Mathilda*. Creating his monster, Victor Frankenstein shuns other human beings as if "guilty of a crime." The tension that runs throughout this novel is the question of whether he is indeed a criminal, who knowing the consequences acted for evil or, on the contrary, an innocent young man violated by the failure of paternal figures — his father and Professor Waldman — to protect him from his own passion. The phrase "filthy workshop" that describes Frankenstein's laboratory sounds very nearly a double entendre for onanism. Mary Shelley, thus, succinctly suggests that some aspects of scientific experimentation are masturbatory in the sense that they are not taken on to produce communal good but for the solipsistic pleasure of the scientist. In contrast to scientific pursuits which are capable of destroying the soul, Shelley consistently depicts the natural world — left to its own devices and unmolested by men — as a balm to the soul and also, significantly, a litmus test of the extent of depravity and loss suffered. As Frankenstein is drawn further into suffering after the creation of the monster, he becomes persistently unable to draw comfort, strength, and inspiration from nature. This is the Romantic version of the person who has sealed a pact with the devil and becomes unable to take comfort from the Christian church. For Romanticism, nature is the source of sacred truth and meaning.

2. Mary Shelley's description of the monster's 'birth' is uncannily connected to the experience of childbirth in the early nineteenth century. Bear in mind Mary Shelley's own birth: her mother, the philosopher Mary Wollstonecraft, delivered the baby daughter in good health but was then in effect killed by the attending male physician who apparently inserted his bare hands into Wollstonecraft so as to pull out the afterbirth. By this gesture, he introduced infection that led to sepsis and death. Childbirth was a dangerous venture in this era, when natural childbirth with an attending midwife, which is relatively safe, was being replaced by birth attended by a male doctor. Barbara

Ehrenreich and Deirdre English write eloquently about this cultural shift in *Witches, Midwives, and Nurses* (1972). As masculinized science pushed its way into the realms of traditional healers including midwives, unfortunate health consequences unfolded for women in the West. Mary Shelley uncannily reflects this problem in her monstrous birth scenario. Here, the monster is born without a mother; women have been entirely pushed out of the birth scene.

Elements of Shelley's delivery of a premature infant daughter who did not long survive are likely also reflected in the description of the late night scene of the monster's birth. Frankenstein's belief that the monster he created is inhumanly hideous flies in the face of the sentimental attachment we assume a mother will have for her newborn. Shelley is making several points here with the concision of a nightmare: that the sentimentality thrown across maternity does an injustice to women's actual experience of giving birth; that scientific 'progress' carries with it a toxic dose of masculine domination. Also, Shelley brings in, here, problematic tropes of racism. As I discuss in my Introduction to this volume, Shelley walks a line wherein she can be interpreted as radically critiquing systems of masculine domination that become entrenched in modernity under the guise of science, but also Shelley vacillates between critiquing and participating in the racist xenophobia that arises as Britain and other Western nations violently colonize the Americas, and parts of Asia and Africa. The monster is described in terms that may suggest a racist typology of Otherness, even as the description also suggests that the monster's difference is fabricated by Victor Frankenstein — that he literally creates the Otherness of the monster. My suggestion is that *Frankenstein* read in connection with *Mathilda* allows us to understand Shelley, in these early texts, finding her way to an understanding of the harms of colonization and racism that is intuitive, and radical, a perception largely not pursued in her later works. ◄

CHAPTER 6

C LERVAL THEN PUT the following letter into my hands. It was from my own Elizabeth:

"My dearest Cousin,

"You have been ill, very ill, and even the constant letters of dear kind Henry are not sufficient to reassure me on your account. You are forbidden to write — to hold a pen; yet one word from you, dear Victor, is necessary to calm our apprehensions. For a long time I have thought that each post would bring this line, and my persuasions have restrained my uncle from undertaking a journey to Ingolstadt. I have prevented his encountering the inconveniences and perhaps dangers of so long a journey, yet how often have I regretted not being able to perform it myself! I figure to myself that the task of attending on your sickbed has devolved on some mercenary old nurse, who could never guess your wishes nor minister to them with the care and affection of your poor cousin. Yet that is over now: Clerval writes that indeed you are getting better. I eagerly hope that you will confirm this intelligence soon in your own handwriting.

"Get well — and return to us. You will find a happy, cheerful home and friends who love you dearly. Your father's health is vigorous, and he asks but to see you, but to be assured that you are well; and not a care will ever cloud his benevolent countenance. How pleased you would be to remark the improvement of our Ernest! He is now sixteen and full of activity and spirit. He is desirous to be a true Swiss and to enter into foreign service, but we cannot part with him, at least until his elder brother returns to us. My uncle is not pleased with the idea of a military career in a distant country, but Ernest never had your powers of application. He looks upon study as an odious fetter; his time is spent in the open air, climbing the hills or rowing on the lake. I fear that he will become an idler unless we yield the point and permit him to enter on the profession which he has selected.

"Little alteration, except the growth of our dear children, has taken place since you left us. The blue lake and snow-clad mountains — they never change; and I think our placid home and our contented hearts are regulated by the same immutable laws. My trifling occupations take up my time and amuse me, and I am rewarded for any exertions by seeing none but happy, kind faces around me. Since you left us, but one change has taken place in our little household. Do you remember on what occasion Justine Moritz entered our family? Probably you do not; I will relate her history, therefore in a few words. Madame Moritz, her mother, was a widow with four children, of whom Justine was the third. This girl had always been the favourite of her father, but through a strange perversity, her mother could not endure her, and after the death of M. Moritz, treated her very ill. My aunt observed this, and when Justine was twelve years of age, prevailed on her mother to allow her to live at our house. The republican institutions of our country have produced simpler and happier manners than those which prevail in the great monarchies that surround it. Hence there is less distinction between the several classes of its inhabitants; and the lower orders, being neither so poor nor so despised, their manners are more refined and moral. A servant in Geneva does not mean the same thing as a servant in France and England. Justine, thus received in our family, learned the duties of a servant, a condition which, in our fortunate country, does not include the idea of ignorance and a sacrifice of the dignity of a human being.

"Justine, you may remember, was a great favourite of yours; and I recollect you once remarked that if you were in an ill humour, one glance from Justine could dissipate it, for the same reason that Ariosto gives concerning the beauty of Angelica — she looked so frank-hearted and happy. My aunt conceived a great attachment for her, by which she was induced to give her an education superior to that which she had at first intended. This benefit was fully repaid; Justine was the most grateful little creature in the world: I do not mean that she made any professions I never heard one pass her lips, but you could see by her eyes that she almost adored her protectress. Although her disposition was gay and in many respects inconsiderate, yet she paid the greatest attention to every gesture of my aunt. She thought her the model of all excellence and endeavoured to imitate her phraseology and manners, so that even now she often reminds me of her.

"When my dearest aunt died every one was too much occupied in their own grief to notice poor Justine, who had attended her during her illness with the most anxious affection. Poor Justine was very ill; but other trials were reserved for her.

"One by one, her brothers and sister died; and her mother, with the exception of her neglected daughter, was left childless. The conscience of the woman was troubled; she began to think that the deaths of her favourites was a judgement from heaven to chastise her partiality. She was a Roman Catholic; and I believe her confessor confirmed the idea which she had conceived. Accordingly, a few months after your departure for Ingolstadt, Justine was called home by her repentant mother. Poor girl! She wept when she quitted our house; she was much altered since the death of my aunt; grief had given softness and a winning mildness to her manners, which had before been remarkable for vivacity. Nor was her residence at her mother's house of a nature to restore her gaiety. The poor woman was very vacillating in her repentance. She sometimes begged Justine to forgive her unkindness, but much oftener accused her of having caused the deaths of her brothers and sister. Perpetual fretting at length threw Madame Moritz into a decline, which at first increased her irritability, but she is now at peace for ever. She died on the first approach of cold weather, at the beginning of this last winter. Justine has just returned to us; and I assure you I love her tenderly. She is very clever and gentle, and extremely pretty; as I mentioned before, her mien and her expression continually remind me of my dear aunt.

"I must say also a few words to you, my dear cousin, of little darling William. I wish you could see him; he is very tall of his age, with sweet laughing blue eyes, dark eyelashes, and curling hair. When he smiles, two little dimples appear on each cheek, which are rosy with health. He has already had one or two little WIVES, but Louisa Biron is his favourite, a pretty little girl of five years of age.

"Now, dear Victor, I dare say you wish to be indulged in a little gossip concerning the good people of Geneva. The pretty Miss Mansfield has already received the congratulatory visits on her approaching marriage with a young Englishman, John Melbourne, Esq. Her ugly sister, Manon, married M. Duvillard, the rich banker, last autumn. Your favourite schoolfellow, Louis Manoir, has suffered several misfortunes since the departure of Clerval from Geneva. But he has already recovered his spirits, and is reported to be on the point of marrying a lively pretty Frenchwoman, Madame Tavernier. She is a widow, and much older than Manoir; but she is very much admired, and a favourite with everybody.

"I have written myself into better spirits, dear cousin; but my anxiety returns upon me as I conclude. Write, dearest Victor,—one line—one word will be a blessing to us. Ten thousand thanks to Henry for his kindness, his affection, and his many letters; we are sincerely grateful. Adieu! my cousin; take care of your self; and, I entreat you, write!

"Elizabeth Lavenza"
"Geneva, March 18, 17 —."

"Dear, dear Elizabeth!" I exclaimed, when I had read her letter: "I will write instantly and relieve them from the anxiety they must feel." I wrote, and this exertion greatly fatigued me; but my convalescence had commenced, and proceeded regularly. In another fortnight I was able to leave my chamber.

One of my first duties on my recovery was to introduce Clerval to the several professors of the university. In doing this, I underwent a kind of rough usage, ill befitting the wounds that my mind had sustained. Ever since the fatal night, the end of my labours, and the beginning of my misfortunes, I had conceived a violent antipathy even to the name of natural philosophy. When I was otherwise quite restored to health, the sight of a chemical instrument would renew all the agony of my nervous symptoms. Henry saw this, and had removed all my apparatus from my view. He had also changed my apartment; for he perceived that I had acquired a dislike for the room which had previously been my laboratory. But these cares of Clerval were made of no avail when I visited the professors. M. Waldman inflicted torture when he praised, with kindness and warmth, the astonishing progress I had made in the sciences. He soon perceived that I disliked the subject; but not guessing the real cause, he attributed my feelings to modesty, and changed the subject from my improvement, to the science itself, with a desire, as I evidently saw, of drawing me out. What could I do? He meant to please, and he tormented me. I felt as if he had placed carefully, one by one, in my view those instruments which were to be afterwards used in putting me to a slow and cruel death. I writhed under his words, yet dared not exhibit the pain I felt. Clerval, whose eyes and feelings were always quick in discerning the sensations of others, declined the subject, alleging, in excuse, his total ignorance; and the conversation took a more general turn. I thanked my friend from my heart, but I did not speak. I saw plainly that he was surprised, but he never attempted to draw my secret from me; and although I loved him with a mixture of affection and reverence that knew no bounds, yet I could never persuade myself to confide in him that event which was so often present to my recollection, but which I feared the detail to another would only impress more deeply.

M. Krempe was not equally docile; and in my condition at that time, of almost insupportable sensitiveness, his harsh blunt encomiums gave me even more pain than the benevolent approbation of M. Waldman. "D — n the fellow!"

cried he; "why, M. Clerval, I assure you he has outstript us all. Ay, stare if you please; but it is nevertheless true. A youngster who, but a few years ago, believed in Cornelius Agrippa as firmly as in the gospel, has now set himself at the head of the university; and if he is not soon pulled down, we shall all be out of countenance. — Ay, ay," continued he, observing my face expressive of suffering, "M. Frankenstein is modest; an excellent quality in a young man. Young men should be diffident of themselves, you know, M. Clerval: I was myself when young; but that wears out in a very short time."

M. Krempe had now commenced an eulogy on himself, which happily turned the conversation from a subject that was so annoying to me.

Clerval had never sympathized in my tastes for natural science; and his literary pursuits differed wholly from those which had occupied me. He came to the university with the design of making himself complete master of the oriental languages, and thus he should open a field for the plan of life he had marked out for himself. Resolved to pursue no inglorious career, he turned his eyes toward the East, as affording scope for his spirit of enterprise. The Persian, Arabic, and Sanskrit languages engaged his attention, and I was easily induced to enter on the same studies. Idleness had ever been irksome to me, and now that I wished to fly from reflection, and hated my former studies, I felt great relief in being the fellow-pupil with my friend, and found not only instruction but consolation in the works of the orientalists. I did not, like him, attempt a critical knowledge of their dialects, for I did not contemplate making any other use of them than temporary amusement. I read merely to understand their meaning, and they well repaid my labours. Their melancholy is soothing, and their joy elevating, to a degree I never experienced in studying the authors of any other country. When you read their writings, life appears to consist in a warm sun and a garden of roses, — in the smiles and frowns of a fair enemy, and the fire that consumes your own heart. How different from the manly and heroical poetry of Greece and Rome!

Summer passed away in these occupations, and my return to Geneva was fixed for the latter end of autumn; but being delayed by several accidents, winter and snow arrived, the roads were deemed impassable, and my journey was retarded until the ensuing spring. I felt this delay very bitterly; for I longed to see my native town and my beloved friends. My return had only been delayed so long, from an unwillingness to leave Clerval in a strange place, before he had become acquainted with any of its inhabitants. The winter, however, was spent cheerfully; and although the spring was uncommonly late, when it came its beauty compensated for its dilatoriness.

The month of May had already commenced, and I expected the letter daily which was to fix the date of my departure, when Henry proposed a pedestrian tour in the environs of Ingolstadt, that I might bid a personal farewell to the country I had so long inhabited. I acceded with pleasure to this proposition: I was fond of exercise, and Clerval had always been my favourite companion in the ramble of this nature that I had taken among the scenes of my native country.

We passed a fortnight in these perambulations: my health and spirits had long been restored, and they gained additional strength from the salubrious air I breathed, the natural incidents of our progress, and the conversation of my friend. Study had before secluded me from the intercourse of my fellow-creatures, and rendered me unsocial; but Clerval called forth the better feelings of my heart; he again taught me to love the aspect of nature, and the cheerful faces of children. Excellent friend! how sincerely you did love me, and endeavour to elevate my mind until it was on a level with your own. A selfish pursuit had cramped and narrowed me, until your gentleness and affection warmed and opened my senses; I became the same happy creature who, a few years ago, loved and beloved by all, had no sorrow or care. When happy, inanimate nature had the power of bestowing on me the most delightful sensations. A serene sky and verdant fields filled me with ecstasy. The present season was indeed divine; the flowers of spring bloomed in the hedges, while those of summer were already in bud. I was undisturbed by thoughts which during the preceding year had pressed upon me, notwithstanding my endeavours to throw them off, with an invincible burden.

Henry rejoiced in my gaiety, and sincerely sympathised in my feelings: he exerted himself to amuse me, while he expressed the sensations that filled his soul. The resources of his mind on this occasion were truly astonishing: his conversation was full of imagination; and very often, in imitation of the Persian and Arabic writers, he invented tales of wonderful fancy and passion. At other times he repeated my favourite poems, or drew me out into arguments, which he supported with great ingenuity. We returned to our college on a Sunday afternoon: the peasants were dancing, and every one we met appeared gay and happy. My own spirits were high, and I bounded along with feelings of unbridled joy and hilarity. ◀

CHAPTER 7

O N MY RETURN, I found the following letter from my father: —
"My dear Victor,

"You have probably waited impatiently for a letter to fix the date of your return to us; and I was at first tempted to write only a few lines, merely mentioning the day on which I should expect you. But that would be a cruel kindness, and I dare not do it. What would be your surprise, my son, when you expected a happy and glad welcome, to behold, on the contrary, tears and wretchedness? And how, Victor, can I relate our misfortune? Absence cannot have rendered you callous to our joys and griefs; and how shall I inflict pain on my long absent son? I wish to prepare you for the woeful news, but I know it is impossible; even now your eye skims over the page to seek the words which are to convey to you the horrible tidings.

"William is dead! — that sweet child, whose smiles delighted and warmed my heart, who was so gentle, yet so gay! Victor, he is murdered!

"I will not attempt to console you; but will simply relate the circumstances of the transaction.

"Last Thursday (May 7th), I, my niece, and your two brothers, went to walk in Plainpalais. The evening was warm and serene, and we prolonged our walk farther than usual. It was already dusk before we thought of returning; and then we discovered that William and Ernest, who had gone on before, were not to be found. We accordingly rested on a seat until they should return. Presently

Ernest came, and enquired if we had seen his brother; he said, that he had been playing with him, that William had run away to hide himself, and that he vainly sought for him, and afterwards waited for a long time, but that he did not return.

"This account rather alarmed us, and we continued to search for him until night fell, when Elizabeth conjectured that he might have returned to the house. He was not there. We returned again, with torches; for I could not rest, when I thought that my sweet boy had lost himself, and was exposed to all the damps and dews of night; Elizabeth also suffered extreme anguish. About five in the morning I discovered my lovely boy, whom the night before I had seen blooming and active in health, stretched on the grass livid and motionless; the print of the murder's finger was on his neck.

"He was conveyed home, and the anguish that was visible in my countenance betrayed the secret to Elizabeth. She was very earnest to see the corpse. At first I attempted to prevent her but she persisted, and entering the room where it lay, hastily examined the neck of the victim, and clasping her hands exclaimed, 'O God! I have murdered my darling child!'

"She fainted, and was restored with extreme difficulty. When she again lived, it was only to weep and sigh. She told me, that that same evening William had teased her to let him wear a very valuable miniature that she possessed of your mother. This picture is gone, and was doubtless the temptation which urged the murderer to the deed. We have no trace of him at present, although our exertions to discover him are unremitted; but they will not restore my beloved William!

"Come, dearest Victor; you alone can console Elizabeth. She weeps continually, and accuses herself unjustly as the cause of his death; her words pierce my heart. We are all unhappy; but will not that be an additional motive for you, my son, to return and be our comforter? Your dear mother! Alas, Victor! I now say, Thank God she did not live to witness the cruel, miserable death of her youngest darling!

"Come, Victor; not brooding thoughts of vengeance against the assassin, but with feelings of peace and gentleness, that will heal, instead of festering, the wounds of our minds. Enter the house of mourning, my friend, but with kindness and affection for those who love you, and not with hatred for your enemies.

"Your affectionate and afflicted father,

"Alphonse Frankenstein.

"Geneva, May 12th, 17 — ."

Clerval, who had watched my countenance as I read this letter, was surprised to observe the despair that succeeded the joy I at first expressed on receiving new from my friends. I threw the letter on the table, and covered my face with my hands.

"My dear Frankenstein," exclaimed Henry, when he perceived me weep with bitterness, "are you always to be unhappy? My dear friend, what has happened?"

I motioned him to take up the letter, while I walked up and down the room in the extremest agitation. Tears also gushed from the eyes of Clerval, as he read the account of my misfortune.

"I can offer you no consolation, my friend," said he; "your disaster is irreparable. What do you intend to do?"

"To go instantly to Geneva: come with me, Henry, to order the horses."

During our walk, Clerval endeavoured to say a few words of consolation; he could only express his heartfelt sympathy. "Poor William!" said he, "dear lovely child, he now sleeps with his angel mother! Who that had seen him bright and joyous in his young beauty, but must weep over his untimely loss! To die so miserably; to feel the murderer's grasp! How much more a murdered that could destroy radiant innocence! Poor little fellow! one only consolation have we; his friends mourn and weep, but he is at rest. The pang is over, his sufferings are at an end for ever. A sod covers his gentle form, and he knows no pain. He can no longer be a subject for pity; we must reserve that for his miserable survivors."

Clerval spoke thus as we hurried through the streets; the words impressed themselves on my mind and I remembered them afterwards in solitude. But now, as soon as the horses arrived, I hurried into a cabriolet, and bade farewell to my friend.

My journey was very melancholy. At first I wished to hurry on, for I longed to console and sympathise with my loved and sorrowing friends; but when I drew near my native town, I slackened my progress. I could hardly sustain the multitude of feelings that crowded into my mind. I passed through scenes familiar to my youth, but which I had not seen for nearly six years. How altered every thing might be during that time! One sudden and desolating change had taken place; but a thousand little circumstances might have by degrees worked other alterations, which, although they were done more tranquilly, might not be the less decisive. Fear overcame me; I dared no advance, dreading a thousand nameless evils that made me tremble, although I was unable to define them. I remained two days at Lausanne, in this painful state of mind. I contemplated the lake: the waters were placid; all around was calm; and the snowy mountains, 'the palaces of nature,' were not changed. By degrees the calm and heavenly scene restored me, and I continued my journey towards Geneva.

The road ran by the side of the lake, which became narrower as I approached my native town. I discovered more distinctly the black sides of Jura, and the bright summit of Mont Blanc. I wept like a child. "Dear mountains! my own beautiful lake! how do you welcome your wanderer? Your summits are clear; the sky and lake are blue and placid. Is this to prognosticate peace, or to mock at my unhappiness?"

I fear, my friend, that I shall render myself tedious by dwelling on these preliminary circumstances; but they were days of comparative happiness, and I think of them with pleasure. My country, my beloved country! who but a native can tell the delight I took in again beholding thy streams, thy mountains, and, more than all, thy lovely lake!

Yet, as I drew nearer home, grief and fear again overcame me. Night also closed around; and when I could hardly see the dark mountains, I felt still more gloomily. The picture appeared a vast and dim scene of evil, and I foresaw obscurely that I was destined to become the most wretched of human beings. Alas! I prophesied truly, and failed only in one single circumstance, that in all the misery I imagined and dreaded, I did not conceive the hundredth part of the anguish I was destined to endure. It was completely dark when I arrived in the environs of Geneva; the gates of the town were already shut; and I was obliged to pass the night at Secheron, a village at the distance of half a league from the city. The sky was serene; and, as I was unable to rest, I resolved to visit the spot where my poor William had been murdered. As I could not pass through the town, I was obliged to cross the lake in a boat to arrive at Plainpalais. During this short voyage I saw the lightning playing on the summit of Mont Blanc in the most beautiful figures. The storm appeared to approach rapidly, and, on landing, I ascended a low hill, that I might observe its progress. It advanced; the heavens were clouded, and I soon felt the rain coming slowly in large drops, but its violence quickly increased.[1]

I quitted my seat, and walked on, although the darkness and storm increased every minute, and the thunder burst with a terrific crash over my head. It was echoed from Saleve, the Juras, and the Alps of Savoy; vivid flashes of lightning dazzled my eyes, illuminating the lake, making it appear like a vast sheet of fire; then for an instant every thing seemed of a pitchy darkness, until the eye recovered itself from the preceding flash. The storm, as is often the case in Switzerland, appeared at once in various parts of the heavens. The most violent storm hung exactly north of the town, over the part of the lake which lies between the promontory of Belrive and the village of Copet. Another storm enlightened Jura with faint flashes; and another darkened and sometimes disclosed the Mole, a peaked mountain to the east of the lake.

While I watched the tempest, so beautiful yet terrific, I wandered on with a hasty step. This noble war in the sky elevated my spirits; I clasped my hands, and exclaimed aloud, "William, dear angel! this is thy funeral, this thy dirge!" As

I said these words, I perceived in the gloom a figure which stole from behind a clump of trees near me; I stood fixed, gazing intently: I could not be mistaken. A flash of lightning illuminated the object, and discovered its shape plainly to me; its gigantic stature, and the deformity of its aspect more hideous than belongs to humanity, instantly informed me that it was the wretch, the filthy daemon, to whom I had given life. What did he there? Could he be (I shuddered at the conception) the murderer of my brother? No sooner did that idea cross my imagination, than I became convinced of its truth; my teeth chattered, and I was forced to lean against a tree for support. The figure passed me quickly, and I lost it in the gloom.

Nothing in human shape could have destroyed the fair child. HE was the murderer! I could not doubt it. The mere presence of the idea was an irresistible proof of the fact. I thought of pursuing the devil; but it would have been in vain, for another flash discovered him to me hanging among the rocks of the nearly perpendicular ascent of Mont Saleve, a hill that bounds Plainpalais on the south. He soon reached the summit, and disappeared.

I remained motionless. The thunder ceased; but the rain still continued, and the scene was enveloped in an impenetrable darkness. I revolved in my mind the events which I had until now sought to forget: the whole train of my progress toward the creation; the appearance of the works of my own hands at my bedside; its departure. Two years had now nearly elapsed since the night on which he first received life; and was this his first crime? Alas! I had turned loose into the world a depraved wretch, whose delight was in carnage and misery; had he not murdered my brother?

No one can conceive the anguish I suffered during the remainder of the night, which I spent, cold and wet, in the open air. But I did not feel the inconvenience of the weather; my imagination was busy in scenes of evil and despair. I considered the being whom I had cast among mankind, and endowed with the will and power to effect purposes of horror, such as the deed which he had now done, nearly in the light of my own vampire, my own spirit let loose from the grave, and forced to destroy all that was dear to me.

Day dawned; and I directed my steps towards the town. The gates were open, and I hastened to my father's house. My first thought was to discover what I knew of the murderer, and cause instant pursuit to be made. But I paused when I reflected on the story that I had to tell. A being whom I myself had formed, and endued with life, had met me at midnight among the precipices of an inaccessible mountain. I remembered also the nervous fever with which I had been seized just at the time that I dated my creation, and which would give an air of delirium to a tale otherwise so utterly improbable. I well knew that if any other had communicated such a relation to me, I should have looked upon it as the ravings of insanity. Besides, the strange nature of the animal would elude all pursuit, even if I were so far credited as to persuade my relatives to commence it. And then of what use would be pursuit? Who could arrest a creature capable of scaling the overhanging sides of Mont Saleve? These reflections determined me, and I resolved to remain silent.

It was about five in the morning when I entered my father's house. I told the servants not to disturb the family, and went into the library to attend their usual hour of rising.

Six years had elapsed, passed in a dream but for one indelible trace, and I stood in the same place where I had last embraced my father before my departure for Ingolstadt. Beloved and venerable parent! He still remained to me. I gazed on the picture of my mother, which stood over the mantel-piece. It was an historical subject, painted at my father's desire, and represented Caroline Beaufort in an agony of despair, kneeling by the coffin of her dead father. Her garb was rustic, and her cheek pale; but there was an air of dignity and beauty, that hardly permitted the sentiment of pity. Below this picture was a miniature of William; and my tears flowed when I looked upon it. While I was thus engaged, Ernest entered: he had heard me arrive, and hastened to welcome me: "Welcome, my dearest Victor," said he. "Ah! I wish you had come three months ago, and then you would have found us all joyous and delighted. You come to us now to share a misery which nothing can alleviate; yet your presence will, I hope, revive our father, who seems sinking under his misfortune; and your persuasions will induce poor Elizabeth to cease her vain and tormenting self-accusations.—Poor William! he was our darling and our pride!"

Tears, unrestrained, fell from my brother's eyes; a sense of mortal agony crept over my frame. Before, I had only imagined the wretchedness of my desolated home; the reality came on me as a new, and a not less terrible, disaster. I tried to calm Ernest; I enquired more minutely concerning my father, and here I named my cousin.

"She most of all," said Ernest, "requires consolation; she accused herself of having caused the death of my brother, and that made her very wretched. But since the murderer has been discovered—"

"The murderer discovered! Good God! how can that be? who could attempt to pursue him? It is impossible; one might as well try to overtake the winds, or confine a mountain-stream with a straw. I saw him too; he was free last night!"

"I do not know what you mean," replied my brother, in accents of wonder, "but to us the discovery we have made completes our misery. No one would believe it at first; and even now Elizabeth will not be convinced, notwithstanding all the evidence. Indeed, who would credit that Justine Moritz, who was so amiable, and fond of all the family, could suddenly become so capable of so frightful, so appalling a crime?"

"Justine Moritz! Poor, poor girl, is she the accused? But it is wrongfully; every one knows that; no one believes it, surely, Ernest?"

"No one did at first; but several circumstances came out, that have almost forced conviction upon us; and her own behaviour has been so confused, as to add to the evidence of facts a weight that, I fear, leaves no hope for doubt. But she will be tried today, and you will then hear all."

He then related that, the morning on which the murder of poor William had been discovered, Justine had been taken ill, and confined to her bed for several days. During this interval, one of the servants, happening to examine the apparel she had worn on the night of the murder, had discovered in her pocket the picture of my mother, which had been judged to be the temptation of the murderer. The servant instantly showed it to one of the others, who, without saying a word to any of the family, went to a magistrate; and, upon their deposition, Justine was apprehended. On being charged with the fact, the poor girl confirmed the suspicion in a great measure by her extreme confusion of manner.

This was a strange tale, but it did not shake my faith; and I replied earnestly, "You are all mistaken; I know the murderer. Justine, poor, good Justine, is innocent."

At that instant my father entered. I saw unhappiness deeply impressed on his countenance, but he endeavoured to welcome me cheerfully; and, after we had exchanged our mournful greeting, would have introduced some other topic than that of our disaster, had not Ernest exclaimed, "Good God, papa! Victor says that he knows who was the murderer of poor William."

"We do also, unfortunately," replied my father, "for indeed I had rather have been for ever ignorant than have discovered so much depravity and ungratitude in one I valued so highly."

"My dear father, you are mistaken; Justine is innocent."

"If she is, God forbid that she should suffer as guilty. She is to be tried today, and I hope, I sincerely hope, that she will be acquitted."

This speech calmed me. I was firmly convinced in my own mind that Justine, and indeed every human being, was guiltless of this murder. I had no fear, therefore, that any circumstantial evidence could be brought forward strong enough to convict her. My tale was not one to announce publicly; its astounding horror would be looked upon as madness by the vulgar. Did any one indeed exist, except I, the creator, who would believe, unless his senses convinced him, in the existence of the living monument of presumption and rash ignorance which I had let loose upon the world?

We were soon joined by Elizabeth. Time had altered her since I last beheld her; it had endowed her with loveliness surpassing the beauty of her childish years. There was the same candour, the same vivacity, but it was allied to an expression more full of sensibility and intellect. She welcomed me with the greatest affection. "Your arrival, my dear cousin," said she, "fills me with hope. You perhaps will find some means to justify my poor guiltless Justine. Alas! who is safe, if she be convicted of crime? I rely on her innocence as certainly as I do upon my own. Our misfortune is doubly hard to us; we have not only lost that lovely darling boy, but this poor girl, whom I sincerely love, is to be torn away by even a worse fate. If she is condemned, I never shall know joy more. But she will not, I am sure she will not; and then I shall be happy again, even after the sad death of my little William."

"She is innocent, my Elizabeth," said I, "and that shall be proved; fear nothing, but let your spirits be cheered by the assurance of her acquittal."

"How kind and generous you are! every one else believes in her guilt, and that made me wretched, for I knew that it was impossible: and to see every one else prejudiced in so deadly a manner rendered me hopeless and despairing." She wept.

"Dearest niece," said my father, "dry your tears. If she is, as you believe, innocent, rely on the justice of our laws, and the activity with which I shall prevent the slightest shadow of partiality." ◄

CHAPTER 7
Annotations

1. After the traumatic vivification of his monster, Victor's friend Henry Clerval's appearance, just at the moment of direst need, saves Frankenstein's life. Clerval represents all the qualities Victor lacks: he is selfless, empathic, kind, not overreaching. He stands as a model figure and also is doomed, as we will learn, to be killed because Victor Frankenstein created a monster *and* because Clerval subsequently saves Victor's life. This tension between Clerval and Frankenstein presents a larger question that Mary Shelley poses about what kind of masculinity the new world order — run by scientists, industrialists, and colonizers — values. Henry Clerval is a sacrificial character no less than Elizabeth. Clerval is punished because of Victor Frankenstein's selfishness and ambition; Clerval is also punished as the result of his own kindness and fidelity. Shelley draws connections between one person's 'private' behavior (that is, Victor Frankenstein creating a monster), and the widespread effects of his actions. Victor's desire for immortality through science destroys everyone he loves. But before that destruction, Henry Clerval, the epitome of friendship's goodness, saves Victor Frankenstein's life.

   With the death of innocent William, Victor's youngest brother, our understanding that Victor's actions are going to have ruinous consequences takes hold. When Henry Clerval learns of the death, he bluntly tells Victor that for such catastrophic events there is no consolation. This is precisely where Mary Shelley's novel begins to tighten its claim on an uncanny moral symmetry. Victor has acted selfishly, with solipsism and vanity, he has put away from himself the mitigating influences of forces such as family, the arts, religion, friendship, and romantic love, and above all he has rejected the sovereignty of the natural world. Having become so wholly a man of science, Victor has become a demon even as he regrets his earlier actions. Here, the novel echoes Goethe's *Faust*, which in turn echoes traditional Western European myths of the man who sells his soul to the devil for worldly gain. But what Shelley makes new, in this reworking of the old, is the double erasure of a religious frame of reference and also — strikingly — the removal of a moment when Victor (in the Faustus position) makes a clear decision to sign a pact with the devil. Victor, hauntingly, never seems to have understood what he was doing, in an holistic moral sense. This is the modern turn of Shelley's myth for our age: that we can make a pact with the devil not by deciding consciously to do so, but instead through blind obedience to cultural codes, such as that of masculinist science, and its extreme self-involvement. Victor turns, decisively, from any community-oriented activity ever deeper inward as he works to create his monster. He does not strive for personal ascendency through an explicit pact with the devil. Instead, Shelley delineates how the overweening force of self-promotion and self-regard is tantamount to befriending a demon.

Of further note: Mont Blanc, in this passage, is an important landmark. It signifies the Romantic ideal of the sublime. And yet, Mont Blanc does not save Frankenstein. He has gone beyond the recuperative effects of the aesthetic sublime. His home does not comfort him, natural beauty does not comfort him, he is outside the reach of these comforts because he turned from them in his self-absorbed pursuit of scientific accomplishment. ◄

CHAPTER 8

W̲E PASSED A FEW SAD HOURS until eleven o'clock, when the trial was to commence. My father and the rest of the family being obliged to attend as witnesses, I accompanied them to the court. During the whole of this wretched mockery of justice I suffered living torture. It was to be decided whether the result of my curiosity and lawless devices would cause the death of two of my fellow beings: one a smiling babe full of innocence and joy, the other far more dreadfully murdered, with every aggravation of infamy that could make the murder memorable in horror. Justine also was a girl of merit and possessed qualities which promised to render her life happy; now all was to be obliterated in an ignominious grave, and I the cause! A thousand times rather would I have confessed myself guilty of the crime ascribed to Justine, but I was absent when it was committed, and such a declaration would have been considered as the ravings of a madman and would not have exculpated her who suffered through me.

The appearance of Justine was calm. She was dressed in mourning, and her countenance, always engaging, was rendered, by the solemnity of her feelings, exquisitely beautiful. Yet she appeared confident in innocence and did not tremble, although gazed on and execrated by thousands, for all the kindness which her beauty might otherwise have excited was obliterated in the minds of the spectators by the imagination of the enormity she was supposed to have committed. She was tranquil, yet her tranquillity was evidently constrained; and as her confusion had before been adduced as a proof of her guilt, she worked up her mind to an appearance of courage. When she entered the court she threw her eyes round it and quickly discovered where we were seated. A tear seemed to dim her eye when she saw us, but she quickly recovered herself, and a look of sorrowful affection seemed to attest her utter guiltlessness.

The trial began, and after the advocate against her had stated the charge, several witnesses were called. Several strange facts combined against her, which might have staggered anyone who had not such proof of her innocence as I had. She had been out the whole of the night on which the murder had been committed and towards morning had been perceived by a market-woman not far from the spot where the body of the murdered child had been afterwards found. The woman asked her what she did there, but she looked very strangely and only returned a confused and unintelligible answer. She returned to the house about eight o'clock, and when one inquired where she had passed the night, she replied that she had been looking for the child and demanded earnestly if anything had been heard concerning him. When shown the body, she fell into violent hysterics and kept her bed for several days. The picture was then produced which the servant had found in her pocket; and when Elizabeth, in a faltering voice, proved that it was the same which, an hour before the child had been missed, she had placed round his neck, a murmur of horror and indignation filled the court.

Justine was called on for her defence. As the trial had proceeded, her countenance had altered. Surprise, horror, and misery were strongly expressed. Sometimes she struggled with her tears, but when she was desired to plead, she collected her powers and spoke in an audible although variable voice.

"God knows," she said, "how entirely I am innocent. But I do not pretend that my protestations should acquit me; I rest my innocence on a plain and simple explanation of the facts which have been adduced against me, and I hope the character I have always borne will incline my judges to a favourable interpretation where any circumstance appears doubtful or suspicious."

She then related that, by the permission of Elizabeth, she had passed the evening of the night on which the murder had been committed at the house of an aunt at Chene, a village situated at about a league from Geneva. On her return, at about nine o'clock, she met a man who asked her if she had seen anything of the child who was lost. She was alarmed by this account and passed several hours in looking for him, when the gates of Geneva were shut, and she was forced to remain several hours of the night in a barn belonging to a cottage, being unwilling to call up the inhabitants, to whom she was well known. Most of the night she spent here watching; towards morning she believed that she slept for a few minutes; some steps disturbed her, and she awoke. It was dawn, and she quitted her asylum, that she might again endeavour to find my brother. If she had gone near the spot where his body lay, it was without her knowledge.

That she had been bewildered when questioned by the market-woman was not surprising, since she had passed a sleepless night and the fate of poor William was yet uncertain. Concerning the picture she could give no account.

"I know," continued the unhappy victim, "how heavily and fatally this one circumstance weighs against me, but I have no power of explaining it; and when I have expressed my utter ignorance, I am only left to conjecture concerning the probabilities by which it might have been placed in my pocket. But here also I am checked. I believe that I have no enemy on earth, and none surely would have been so wicked as to destroy me wantonly. Did the murderer place it there? I know of no opportunity afforded him for so doing; or, if I had, why should he have stolen the jewel, to part with it again so soon?

"I commit my cause to the justice of my judges, yet I see no room for hope. I beg permission to have a few witnesses examined concerning my character, and if their testimony shall not overweigh my supposed guilt, I must be condemned, although I would pledge my salvation on my innocence."

Several witnesses were called who had known her for many years, and they spoke well of her; but fear and hatred of the crime of which they supposed her guilty rendered them timorous and unwilling to come forward. Elizabeth saw even this last resource, her excellent dispositions and irreproachable conduct, about to fail the accused, when, although violently agitated, she desired permission to address the court.

"I am," said she, "the cousin of the unhappy child who was murdered, or rather his sister, for I was educated by and have lived with his parents ever since and even long before his birth. It may therefore be judged indecent in me to come forward on this occasion, but when I see a fellow creature about to perish through the cowardice of her pretended friends, I wish to be allowed to speak, that I may say what I know of her character. I am well acquainted with the accused. I have lived in the same house with her, at one time for five and at another for nearly two years. During all that period she appeared to me the most amiable and benevolent of human creatures. She nursed Madame Frankenstein, my aunt, in her last illness, with the greatest affection and care and afterwards attended her own mother during a tedious illness, in a manner that excited the admiration of all who knew her, after which she again lived in my uncle's house, where she was beloved by all the family. She was warmly attached to the child who is now dead and acted towards him like a most affectionate mother. For my own part, I do not hesitate to say that, notwithstanding all the evidence produced against her, I believe and rely on her perfect innocence. She had no temptation for such an action; as to the bauble on which the chief proof rests, if she had earnestly desired it, I should have willingly given it to her, so much do I esteem and value her."

A murmur of approbation followed Elizabeth's simple and powerful appeal, but it was excited by her generous interference, and not in favour of poor Justine, on whom the public indignation was turned with renewed violence, charging her with the blackest ingratitude. She herself wept as Elizabeth spoke, but she did not answer. My own agitation and anguish was extreme during the whole trial. I believed in her innocence; I knew it. Could the demon who had (I did not for a minute doubt) murdered my brother also in his hellish sport have betrayed the innocent to death and ignominy? I could not sustain the horror of my situation, and when I perceived that the popular voice and the countenances of the judges had already condemned my unhappy victim, I rushed out of the court in agony. The tortures of the accused did not equal mine; she was sustained by innocence, but the fangs of remorse tore my bosom and would not forgo their hold.

I passed a night of unmingled wretchedness. In the morning I went to the court; my lips and throat were parched. I dared not ask the fatal question, but I was known, and the officer guessed the cause of my visit. The ballots had been thrown; they were all black, and Justine was condemned.

I cannot pretend to describe what I then felt. I had before experienced sensations of horror, and I have endeavoured to bestow upon them adequate expressions, but words cannot convey an idea of the heart-sickening despair that I then endured. The person to whom I addressed myself added that Justine had already confessed her guilt. "That evidence," he observed, "was hardly required in so glaring a case, but I am glad of it, and, indeed, none of our judges like to condemn a criminal upon circumstantial evidence, be it ever so decisive."

This was strange and unexpected intelligence; what could it mean? Had my eyes deceived me? And was I really as mad as the whole world would believe me to be if I disclosed the object of my suspicions? I hastened to return home, and Elizabeth eagerly demanded the result.

"My cousin," replied I, "it is decided as you may have expected; all judges had rather that ten innocent should suffer than that one guilty should escape. But she has confessed."

This was a dire blow to poor Elizabeth, who had relied with firmness upon Justine's innocence. "Alas!" said she. "How shall I ever again believe in human goodness? Justine, whom I loved and esteemed as my sister, how could she put on those smiles of innocence only to betray? Her mild eyes seemed incapable of any severity or guile, and yet she has committed a murder."

Soon after we heard that the poor victim had expressed a desire to see my cousin. My father wished her not to go but said that he left it to her own judgment and feelings to decide. "Yes," said Elizabeth, "I will go, although she is guilty; and you, Victor, shall accompany me; I cannot go alone." The idea of this visit was torture to me, yet I could not refuse. We entered the gloomy prison chamber and beheld Justine sitting on some straw at the farther end; her hands were manacled, and her head rested on her knees. She rose on seeing us enter, and when we were left alone with her, she threw herself at the feet of Elizabeth, weeping bitterly. My cousin wept also.

"Oh, Justine!" said she. "Why did you rob me of my last consolation? I relied on your innocence, and although I was then very wretched, I was not so miserable as I am now."

"And do you also believe that I am so very, very wicked? Do you also join with my enemies to crush me, to condemn me as a murderer?" Her voice was suffocated with sobs.

"Rise, my poor girl," said Elizabeth; "why do you kneel, if you are innocent? I am not one of your enemies, I believed you guiltless, notwithstanding every evidence, until I heard that you had yourself declared your guilt. That report, you say, is false; and be assured, dear Justine, that nothing can shake my confidence in you for a moment, but your own confession."

"I did confess, but I confessed a lie. I confessed, that I might obtain absolution; but now that falsehood lies heavier at my heart than all my other sins. The God of heaven forgive me! Ever since I was condemned, my confessor has besieged me; he threatened and menaced, until I almost began to think that I was the monster that he said I was. He threatened excommunication and hell fire in my last moments if I continued obdurate. Dear lady, I had none to support me; all looked on me as a wretch doomed to ignominy and perdition. What could I do? In an evil hour I subscribed to a lie; and now only am I truly miserable."

She paused, weeping, and then continued, "I thought with horror, my sweet lady, that you should believe your Justine, whom your blessed aunt had so highly honoured, and whom you loved, was a creature capable of a crime which none but the devil himself could have perpetrated. Dear William! dearest blessed child! I soon shall see you again in heaven, where we shall all be happy; and that consoles me, going as I am to suffer ignominy and death."

"Oh, Justine! Forgive me for having for one moment distrusted you. Why did you confess? But do not mourn, dear girl. Do not fear. I will proclaim, I will prove your innocence. I will melt the stony hearts of your enemies by my tears and prayers. You shall not die! You, my playfellow, my companion, my sister, perish on the scaffold! No! No! I never could survive so horrible a misfortune."

Justine shook her head mournfully. "I do not fear to die," she said; "that pang is past. God raises my weakness and gives me courage to endure the worst. I leave a sad and bitter world; and if you remember me and think of me as of one unjustly condemned, I am resigned to the fate awaiting me. Learn from me, dear lady, to submit in patience to the will of heaven!"

During this conversation I had retired to a corner of the prison room, where I could conceal the horrid anguish that possessed me. Despair! Who dared talk of that? The poor victim, who on the morrow was to pass the awful boundary between life and death, felt not, as I did, such deep and bitter agony. I gnashed my teeth and ground them together, uttering a groan that came from my inmost soul. Justine started. When she saw who it was, she approached me and said, "Dear sir, you are very kind to visit me; you, I hope, do not believe that I am guilty?"

I could not answer. "No, Justine," said Elizabeth; "he is more convinced of your innocence than I was, for even when he heard that you had confessed, he did not credit it."

"I truly thank him. In these last moments I feel the sincerest gratitude towards those who think of me with kindness. How sweet is the affection of others to such a wretch as I am! It removes more than half my misfortune, and I feel as if I could die in peace now that my innocence is acknowledged by you, dear lady, and your cousin."

Thus the poor sufferer tried to comfort others and herself. She indeed gained the resignation she desired. But I, the true murderer, felt the never-dying worm alive in my bosom, which allowed of no hope or consolation. Elizabeth also wept and was unhappy, but hers also was the misery of innocence, which, like a cloud that passes over the fair moon, for a while hides but cannot tarnish its brightness. Anguish and despair had penetrated into the core of my heart; I bore a hell within me which nothing could extinguish. We stayed several hours with Justine, and it was with great difficulty that Elizabeth could tear herself away. "I wish," cried she, "that I were to die with you; I cannot live in this world of misery."

Justine assumed an air of cheerfulness, while she with difficulty repressed her bitter tears. She embraced Elizabeth and said in a voice of half-suppressed emotion, "Farewell, sweet lady, dearest Elizabeth, my beloved and only friend; may heaven, in its bounty, bless and preserve you; may this be the last misfortune that you will ever suffer! Live, and be happy, and make others so."

And on the morrow Justine died. Elizabeth's heart-rending eloquence failed to move the judges from their settled conviction in the criminality of the saintly sufferer. My passionate and indignant appeals were lost upon them. And when I received their cold answers and heard the harsh, unfeeling reasoning of these men, my purposed avowal died away on my lips. Thus I might proclaim myself a madman, but not revoke the sentence passed upon my wretched victim. She perished on the scaffold as a murderess!

From the tortures of my own heart, I turned to contemplate the deep and voiceless grief of my Elizabeth. This also was my doing! And my father's woe, and the desolation of that late so smiling home all was the work of my thrice-accursed hands! Ye weep, unhappy ones, but these are not your last tears! Again shall you raise the funeral wail, and the sound of your lamentations shall again and again be heard! Frankenstein, your son, your kinsman, your early, much-loved friend; he who would spend each vital drop of blood for your sakes, who has no thought nor sense of joy except as it is mirrored also in your dear countenances, who would fill the air with blessings and spend his life in serving you — he bids you weep, to shed countless tears; happy beyond his hopes, if thus inexorable fate be satisfied, and if the destruction pause before the peace of the grave have succeeded to your sad torments!

Thus spoke my prophetic soul, as, torn by remorse, horror, and despair, I beheld those I loved spend vain sorrow upon the graves of William and Justine, the first hapless victims to my unhallowed arts. ◄

CHAPTER 9

NOTHING IS MORE PAINFUL to the human mind than, after the feelings have been worked up by a quick succession of events, the dead calmness of inaction and certainty which follows and deprives the soul both of hope and fear. Justine died, she rested, and I was alive. The blood flowed freely in my veins, but a weight of despair and remorse pressed on my heart which nothing could remove. Sleep fled from my eyes; I wandered like an evil spirit, for I had committed deeds of mischief beyond description horrible, and more, much more (I persuaded myself) was yet behind. Yet my heart overflowed with kindness and the love of virtue. I had begun life with benevolent intentions and thirsted for the moment when I should put them in practice and make myself useful to my fellow beings. Now all was blasted; instead of that serenity of conscience which allowed me to look back upon the past with self-satisfaction, and from thence to gather promise of new hopes, I was seized by remorse and the sense of guilt, which hurried me away to a hell of intense tortures such as no language can describe.

This state of mind preyed upon my health, which had perhaps never entirely recovered from the first shock it had sustained. I shunned the face of man; all sound of joy or complacency was torture to me; solitude was my only consolation—deep, dark, deathlike solitude.

My father observed with pain the alteration perceptible in my disposition and habits and endeavoured by arguments deduced from the feelings of his serene conscience and guiltless life to inspire me with fortitude and awaken in me the courage to dispel the dark cloud which brooded over me. "Do you think, Victor," said he, "that I do not suffer also? No one could love a child more than I loved your brother"—tears came into his eyes as he spoke—"but is it not a duty to the survivors that we should refrain from augmenting their unhappiness by an appearance of immoderate grief? It is also a duty owed to yourself, for excessive sorrow prevents improvement or enjoyment, or even the discharge of daily usefulness, without which no man is fit for society."

This advice, although good, was totally inapplicable to my case; I should have been the first to hide my grief and console my friends if remorse had not mingled its bitterness, and terror its alarm, with my other sensations. Now I could only answer my father with a look of despair and endeavour to hide myself from his view.[1]

About this time we retired to our house at Belrive. This change was particularly agreeable to me. The shutting of the gates regularly at ten o'clock and the impossibility of remaining on the lake after that hour had rendered our residence within the walls of Geneva very irksome to me. I was now free. Often, after the rest of the family had retired for the night, I took the boat and passed many hours upon the water. Sometimes, with my sails set, I was carried by the wind; and sometimes, after rowing into the middle of the lake, I left the boat to pursue its own course and gave way to my own miserable reflections. I was often tempted, when all was at peace around me, and I the only unquiet thing that wandered restless in a scene so beautiful and heavenly—if I except some bat, or the frogs, whose harsh and interrupted croaking was heard only when I approached the shore—often, I say, I was tempted to plunge into the silent lake, that the waters might close over me and my calamities forever. But I was restrained, when I thought of the heroic and suffering Elizabeth, whom I tenderly loved, and whose existence was bound up in mine. I thought also of my father and surviving brother; should I by my base desertion leave them exposed and unprotected to the malice of the fiend whom I had let loose among them?

At these moments I wept bitterly and wished that peace would revisit my mind only that I might afford them consolation and happiness. But that could not be. Remorse extinguished every hope. I had been the author of unalterable evils, and I lived in daily fear lest the monster whom I had created should perpetrate some new wickedness. I had an obscure feeling that all was not over and that he would still commit some signal crime, which by its enormity should almost efface the recollection of the past. There was always scope for fear so long as anything I loved remained behind. My abhorrence of this fiend cannot be conceived. When I thought of him I gnashed my teeth, my eyes became inflamed, and I ardently wished to extinguish that life which I had so thoughtlessly bestowed. When I reflected on his crimes and malice, my hatred and revenge burst all bounds of moderation. I would have made a pilgrimage to the highest peak of the Andes, could I when there have precipitated him to their base. I wished to see him again, that I might wreak the utmost extent of abhorrence on his head and avenge the deaths of William and Justine. Our house was the house of mourning. My father's health was deeply shaken by the horror of the recent events. Elizabeth was sad and desponding; she no longer took delight in her ordinary occupations; all pleasure seemed to her sacrilege toward the dead; eternal woe and tears she then thought was the just tribute she should pay to innocence so blasted and destroyed. She was no longer that happy creature who in earlier youth wandered with me on the banks of the lake and talked with ecstasy of our future prospects. The first of those sorrows which are sent to wean us from the earth had visited her, and its dimming influence quenched her dearest smiles.

"When I reflect, my dear cousin," said she, "on the miserable death of Justine Moritz, I no longer see the world and its works as they before appeared to me. Before, I looked upon the accounts of vice and injustice that I read in books or heard from others as tales of ancient days or imaginary evils; at least they were remote and more familiar to reason than to the imagination; but now misery has come home, and men appear to me as monsters thirsting for each other's blood.[2] Yet I am certainly unjust. Everybody believed that poor girl to be guilty; and if she could have committed the crime for which she suffered, assuredly she would have been the most depraved of human creatures. For the sake of a few jewels, to have murdered the son of her benefactor and friend, a child whom she had nursed from its birth, and appeared to love as if it had been her own! I could not consent to the death of any human being, but certainly I should have thought such a creature unfit to remain in the society of men. But she was innocent. I know, I feel she was innocent; you are of the same opinion, and that confirms me. Alas! Victor, when falsehood can look so like the truth, who can assure themselves of certain happiness? I feel as if I were walking on the edge of a precipice, towards which thousands are crowding and endeavouring to plunge me into the abyss. William and Justine were assassinated, and the murderer escapes; he walks about the world free, and perhaps respected. But even if I were condemned to suffer on the scaffold for the same crimes, I would not change places with such a wretch."

I listened to this discourse with the extremest agony. I, not in deed, but in effect, was the true murderer. Elizabeth read my anguish in my countenance, and kindly taking my hand, said, "My dearest friend, you must calm yourself. These events have affected me, God knows how deeply; but I am not so wretched as you are. There is an expression of despair, and sometimes of revenge, in your countenance that makes me tremble. Dear Victor, banish these dark passions.

Remember the friends around you, who centre all their hopes in you. Have we lost the power of rendering you happy? Ah! While we love, while we are true to each other, here in this land of peace and beauty, your native country, we may reap every tranquil blessing—what can disturb our peace?"

And could not such words from her whom I fondly prized before every other gift of fortune suffice to chase away the fiend that lurked in my heart? Even as she spoke I drew near to her, as if in terror, lest at that very moment the destroyer had been near to rob me of her.

Thus not the tenderness of friendship, nor the beauty of earth, nor of heaven, could redeem my soul from woe; the very accents of love were ineffectual. I was encompassed by a cloud which no beneficial influence could penetrate. The wounded deer dragging its fainting limbs to some untrodden brake, there to gaze upon the arrow which had pierced it, and to die, was but a type of me.

Sometimes I could cope with the sullen despair that overwhelmed me, but sometimes the whirlwind passions of my soul drove me to seek, by bodily exercise and by change of place, some relief from my intolerable sensations. It was during an access of this kind that I suddenly left my home, and bending my steps towards the near Alpine valleys, sought in the magnificence, the eternity of such scenes, to forget myself and my ephemeral, because human, sorrows. My wanderings were directed towards the valley of Chamounix. I had visited it frequently during my boyhood. Six years had passed since then: I was a wreck, but nought had changed in those savage and enduring scenes.

I performed the first part of my journey on horseback. I afterwards hired a mule, as the more sure-footed and least liable to receive injury on these rugged roads. The weather was fine; it was about the middle of the month of August, nearly two months after the death of Justine, that miserable epoch from which I dated all my woe. The weight upon my spirit was sensibly lightened as I plunged yet deeper in the ravine of Arve. The immense mountains and precipices that overhung me on every side, the sound of the river raging among the rocks, and the dashing of the waterfalls around spoke of a power mighty as Omnipotence—and I ceased to fear or to bend before any being less almighty than that which had created and ruled the elements, here displayed in their most terrific guise. Still, as I ascended higher, the valley assumed a more magnificent and astonishing character. Ruined castles hanging on the precipices of piny mountains, the impetuous Arve, and cottages every here and there peeping forth from among the trees formed a scene of singular beauty. But it was augmented and rendered sublime by the mighty Alps, whose white and shining pyramids and domes towered above all, as belonging to another earth, the habitations of another race of beings.

I passed the bridge of Pelissier, where the ravine, which the river forms, opened before me, and I began to ascend the mountain that overhangs it. Soon after, I entered the valley of Chamounix. This valley is more wonderful and sublime, but not so beautiful and picturesque as that of Servox, through which I had just passed. The high and snowy mountains were its immediate boundaries, but I saw no more ruined castles and fertile fields. Immense glaciers approached the road; I heard the rumbling thunder of the falling avalanche and marked the smoke of its passage. Mont Blanc, the supreme and magnificent Mont Blanc, raised itself from the surrounding aiguilles, and its tremendous dome overlooked the valley.

A tingling long-lost sense of pleasure often came across me during this journey. Some turn in the road, some new object suddenly perceived and recognized, reminded me of days gone by, and were associated with the lighthearted gaiety of boyhood. The very winds whispered in soothing accents, and maternal Nature bade me weep no more. Then again the kindly influence ceased to act—I found myself fettered again to grief and indulging in all the misery of reflection. Then I spurred on my animal, striving so to forget the world, my fears, and more than all, myself—or, in a more desperate fashion, I alighted and threw myself on the grass, weighed down by horror and despair.

At length I arrived at the village of Chamounix. Exhaustion succeeded to the extreme fatigue both of body and of mind which I had endured. For a short space of time I remained at the window watching the pallid lightnings that played above Mont Blanc and listening to the rushing of the Arve, which pursued its noisy way beneath. The same lulling sounds acted as a lullaby to my too keen sensations; when I placed my head upon my pillow, sleep crept over me; I felt it as it came and blessed the giver of oblivion. ◀

CHAPTER 9
Annotations

1. The monster kills little William to punish Victor and while this slaughter of the innocent (and much has been made of the fact that Shelley's son was called William, her father also named William) is shocking, the perverse twist of the murder is the monster's trick to frame Justine Moritz. Justine, the Frankenstein family's servant/adopted child, is then killed by capital punishment for a crime she did not commit. Justine's name, cognate with "justice," suggests the turn of injustice that takes over Frankenstein's family as the result of his creation of the monster. The miniature portrait painted of Caroline, Victor and William's mother, becomes a central trope in the monster's framing of the murder, for he places the miniature in Justine's pocket, that had been placed earlier around William's neck. The aching loss of a mother, or a parent who loves and cares for him, is the monster's original trauma, and by framing Justine he signifies to Frankenstein his motive for what is in effect a double murder of William and Justine. He kills them because he himself lacks a parent with Caroline's gentle, selfless, devotion.

   Notably, Victor Frankenstein is the only person with clear knowledge of Justine's innocence, and yet despite that he knows she is going to be put to death, Victor holds his tongue out of fear that he will be considered a madman if he tells his story. He proclaims her innocent but does not really say why he considers her innocent. Here, we see Victor's continued habit of self-protection- and self-absorption. He sees himself—his public reputation—as more important that Justine's life. One could say that Victor's fear of his tale not being believed is part of his nightmare: that he cannot expiate his crime because none will believe him. But it is still worth noting that *he does not try* to expiate his crime through confession of the whole truth, even when he sees that Justine is going to be killed for the crime he knows full well she did not commit.

2. Mary Shelley gives Elizabeth a worldview that seems to express Shelley's own. Elizabeth says: "Men appear as monsters thirsting for each other's blood." *Frankenstein* and *Mathilda* express a Gothic, haunted, and tragic worldview. That said, this passage directly implicates Victor. He is the real murderer in the sense that he created the monster who kills William and Justine. Victor on the one hand acknowledges, to himself, his own guilt, calling himself

guilty as the "true murderer," but he also blames the monster for "crimes and malice," and of course Victor does not confess to Elizabeth his own true role in causing her suffering. He does not tell the truth, hiding behind the excuse that the truth is too bizarre, that it will do no good to tell the truth. Shelley presents his choice here as an extension of his earlier decision to create the monster: hubris, a belief that he knows more than others, and is therefore not required to adhere to moral codes to which others adhere. ◄

CHAPTER 10

SPENT THE FOLLOWING DAY roaming through the valley. I stood beside the sources of the Arveiron, which take their rise in a glacier, that with slow pace is advancing down from the summit of the hills to barricade the valley. The abrupt sides of vast mountains were before me; the icy wall of the glacier overhung me; a few shattered pines were scattered around; and the solemn silence of this glorious presence-chamber of imperial nature was broken only by the brawling waves or the fall of some vast fragment, the thunder sound of the avalanche or the cracking, reverberated along the mountains, of the accumulated ice, which, through the silent working of immutable laws, was ever and anon rent and torn, as if it had been but a plaything in their hands. These sublime and magnificent scenes afforded me the greatest consolation that I was capable of receiving. They elevated me from all littleness of feeling, and although they did not remove my grief, they subdued and tranquillized it. In some degree, also, they diverted my mind from the thoughts over which it had brooded for the last month. I retired to rest at night; my slumbers, as it were, waited on and ministered to by the assemblance of grand shapes which I had contemplated during the day. They congregated round me; the unstained snowy mountain-top, the glittering pinnacle, the pine woods, and ragged bare ravine, the eagle, soaring amidst the clouds — they all gathered round me and bade me be at peace.

Where had they fled when the next morning I awoke? All of soul-inspiriting fled with sleep, and dark melancholy clouded every thought. The rain was pouring in torrents, and thick mists hid the summits of the mountains, so that

I even saw not the faces of those mighty friends. Still I would penetrate their misty veil and seek them in their cloudy retreats. What were rain and storm to me? My mule was brought to the door, and I resolved to ascend to the summit of Montanvert. I remembered the effect that the view of the tremendous and ever-moving glacier had produced upon my mind when I first saw it. It had then filled me with a sublime ecstasy that gave wings to the soul and allowed it to soar from the obscure world to light and joy. The sight of the awful and majestic in nature had indeed always the effect of solemnizing my mind and causing me to forget the passing cares of life. I determined to go without a guide, for I was well acquainted with the path, and the presence of another would destroy the solitary grandeur of the scene.

The ascent is precipitous, but the path is cut into continual and short windings, which enable you to surmount the perpendicularity of the mountain. It is a scene terrifically desolate. In a thousand spots the traces of the winter avalanche may be perceived, where trees lie broken and strewed on the ground, some entirely destroyed, others bent, leaning upon the jutting rocks of the mountain or transversely upon other trees. The path, as you ascend higher, is intersected by ravines of snow, down which stones continually roll from above; one of them is particularly dangerous, as the slightest sound, such as even speaking in a loud voice, produces a concussion of air sufficient to draw destruction upon the head of the speaker. The pines are not tall or luxuriant, but they are sombre and add an air of severity to the scene. I looked on the valley beneath; vast mists were rising from the rivers which ran through it and curling in thick wreaths around the opposite mountains, whose summits were hid in the uniform clouds, while rain poured from the dark sky and added to the melancholy impression I received from the objects around me. Alas! Why does man boast of sensibilities superior to those apparent in the brute; it only renders them more necessary beings. If our impulses were confined to hunger, thirst, and desire, we might be nearly free; but now we are moved by every wind that blows and a chance word or scene that that word may convey to us.

> We rest; a dream has power to poison sleep.
>   We rise; one wand'ring thought pollutes the day.
> We feel, conceive, or reason; laugh or weep,
>   Embrace fond woe, or cast our cares away;
> It is the same: for, be it joy or sorrow,
>   The path of its departure still is free.
> Man's yesterday may ne'er be like his morrow;
>   Nought may endure but mutability!

It was nearly noon when I arrived at the top of the ascent. For some time I sat upon the rock that overlooks the sea of ice. A mist covered both that and the surrounding mountains. Presently a breeze dissipated the cloud, and I descended upon the glacier. The surface is very uneven, rising like the waves of a troubled sea, descending low, and interspersed by rifts that sink deep. The field of ice is almost a league in width, but I spent nearly two hours in crossing it. The opposite mountain is a bare perpendicular rock. From the side where I now stood Montanvert was exactly opposite, at the distance of a league; and above it rose Mont Blanc, in awful majesty. I remained in a recess of the rock, gazing on this wonderful and stupendous scene. The sea, or rather the vast river of ice, wound among its dependent mountains, whose aerial summits hung over its recesses. Their icy and glittering peaks shone in the sunlight over the clouds. My heart, which was before sorrowful, now swelled with something like joy; I exclaimed, "Wandering spirits, if indeed ye wander, and do not rest in your narrow beds, allow me this faint happiness, or take me, as your companion, away from the joys of life."[1]

As I said this I suddenly beheld the figure of a man, at some distance, advancing towards me with superhuman speed. He bounded over the crevices in the ice, among which I had walked with caution; his stature, also, as he approached, seemed to exceed that of man. I was troubled; a mist came over my eyes, and I felt a faintness seize me, but I was quickly restored by the cold gale of the mountains. I perceived, as the shape came nearer (sight tremendous and abhorred!) that it was the wretch whom I had created. I trembled with rage and horror, resolving to wait his approach and then close with him in mortal combat. He approached; his countenance bespoke bitter anguish, combined with disdain and malignity, while its unearthly ugliness rendered it almost too horrible for human eyes. But I scarcely observed this; rage and hatred had at first deprived me of utterance, and I recovered only to overwhelm him with words expressive of furious detestation and contempt.

"Devil," I exclaimed, "do you dare approach me? And do not you fear the fierce vengeance of my arm wreaked on your miserable head? Begone, vile insect! Or rather, stay, that I may trample you to dust! And, oh! That I could, with the extinction of your miserable existence, restore those victims whom you have so diabolically murdered!"

"I expected this reception," said the daemon. "All men hate the wretched; how, then, must I be hated, who am miserable beyond all living things! Yet you, my creator, detest and spurn me, thy creature, to whom thou art bound by ties only dissoluble by the annihilation of one of us. You purpose to kill me. How dare you sport thus with life? Do your duty towards me, and I will do mine towards you and the rest of mankind. If you will comply with my conditions, I will leave them and you at peace; but if you refuse, I will glut the maw of death, until it be satiated with the blood of your remaining friends."

"Abhorred monster! Fiend that thou art! The tortures of hell are too mild a vengeance for thy crimes. Wretched devil! You reproach me with your creation, come on, then, that I may extinguish the spark which I so negligently bestowed."

My rage was without bounds; I sprang on him, impelled by all the feelings which can arm one being against the existence of another.

He easily eluded me and said,

"Be calm! I entreat you to hear me before you give vent to your hatred on my devoted head. Have I not suffered enough, that you seek to increase my misery? Life, although it may only be an accumulation of anguish, is dear to me, and I will defend it. Remember, thou hast made me more powerful than thyself; my height is superior to thine, my joints more supple. But I will not be tempted to set myself in opposition to thee. I am thy creature, and I will be even mild and docile to my natural lord and king if thou wilt also perform thy part, the which thou owest me. Oh, Frankenstein, be not equitable to every other and trample upon me alone, to whom thy justice, and even thy clemency and affection, is most due. Remember that I am thy creature; I ought to be thy Adam, but I am rather the fallen angel, whom thou drivest from joy for no misdeed. Everywhere I see bliss, from which I alone am irrevocably excluded. I was benevolent and good; misery made me a fiend. Make me happy, and I shall again be virtuous."

"Begone! I will not hear you. There can be no community between you and me; we are enemies. Begone, or let us try our strength in a fight, in which one must fall."

"How can I move thee? Will no entreaties cause thee to turn a favourable eye upon thy creature, who implores thy goodness and compassion? Believe me, Frankenstein, I was benevolent; my soul glowed with love and humanity; but am I not alone, miserably alone? You, my creator, abhor me; what hope can I gather from your fellow creatures, who owe me nothing? They spurn and hate me. The desert mountains and dreary glaciers are my refuge. I have wandered here many days; the caves of ice, which I only do not fear, are a dwelling to me, and the only one which man does not grudge. These bleak skies I hail, for they are kinder to me than your fellow beings. If the multitude of mankind knew of my existence, they would do as you do, and arm themselves for my destruction. Shall I not then hate them who abhor me? I will keep no terms with my enemies. I am miserable, and they shall share my wretchedness. Yet it is in your power to recompense me, and deliver them from an evil which it only remains for you to make so great, that not only you and your family, but thousands of others, shall be swallowed up in the whirlwinds of its rage. Let your compassion be moved, and do not disdain me. Listen to my tale; when you have heard that, abandon or commiserate me, as you shall judge that I deserve. But hear me. The guilty are allowed, by human laws, bloody as they are, to speak in their own defence before they are condemned. Listen to me, Frankenstein. You accuse me of murder, and yet you would, with a satisfied conscience, destroy your own creature. Oh, praise the eternal justice of man! Yet I ask you not to spare me; listen to me, and then, if you can, and if you will, destroy the work of your hands."

"Why do you call to my remembrance," I rejoined, "circumstances of which I shudder to reflect, that I have been the miserable origin and author? Cursed be the day, abhorred devil, in which you first saw light! Cursed (although I curse myself) be the hands that formed you! You have made me wretched beyond expression. You have left me no power to consider whether I am just to you or not. Begone! Relieve me from the sight of your detested form."

"Thus I relieve thee, my creator," he said, and placed his hated hands before my eyes, which I flung from me with violence; "thus I take from thee a sight which you abhor. Still thou canst listen to me and grant me thy compassion. By the virtues that I once possessed, I demand this from you. Hear my tale; it is long and strange, and the temperature of this place is not fitting to your fine sensations; come to the hut upon the mountain. The sun is yet high in the heavens; before it descends to hide itself behind your snowy precipices and illuminate another world, you will have heard my story and can decide. On you it rests, whether I quit forever the neighbourhood of man and lead a harmless life, or become the scourge of your fellow creatures and the author of your own speedy ruin."

As he said this he led the way across the ice; I followed. My heart was full, and I did not answer him, but as I proceeded, I weighed the various arguments that he had used and determined at least to listen to his tale. I was partly urged by curiosity, and compassion confirmed my resolution. I had hitherto supposed him to be the murderer of my brother, and I eagerly sought a confirmation or denial of this opinion. For the first time, also, I felt what the duties of a creator towards his creature were, and that I ought to render him happy before I complained of his wickedness. These motives urged me to comply with his demand. We crossed the ice, therefore, and ascended the opposite rock. The air was cold, and the rain again began to descend; we entered the hut, the fiend with an air of exultation, I with a heavy heart and depressed spirits. But I consented to listen, and seating myself by the fire which my odious companion had lighted, he thus began his tale.[2] ◄

CHAPTER 10
Annotations

1. Victor seeks to escape the effects of his actions by wandering the world. He specifically seeks out Mont Blanc and Montanvert (Mer de Glace), seeking to renew his soul through communion with the natural sublime for which these mountains stand as symbols. However, the monster finds him there: the monster stalks him and approaches Victor in the holy of holies of the Romantic sublime, Mont Blanc. In their conversation, Shelley's novel echoes John Milton's *Paradise Lost*, with the monster playing the role of Lucifer. But unlike *Paradise Lost*, Shelley draws both her characters—both Victor and his creation—as mired in wrong-doing. They are both the fallen angel. Victor is not very much like God. Instead, he has usurped the role of the divinity in trying to overmaster the natural world. Victor calls his creation a "devil" but he shares absolutely in the blame for the monster's actions. The monster explains eloquently that the experience of being abhorred and shunned by all human beings, most importantly by his father-creator, has turned him to violence. Whether we find his argument persuasive depends on what we think about parenting, and the responsibility of parents, writ large, to nurture and shelter their progeny. Victor repeatedly refers to his own father as venerable, and yet he has little enough to do with him. Victor himself is a failed—fallen—parent, who hated his creation from the moment of his 'birth' and refuses to shelter or nurture him. Shelley, here, makes the radical argument that the way we raise our children creates their nature—that children are not born evil or good but become moral subjects through the process of being cared for and educated. Sadly, this lesson is still very pressing and resonant, as I write early in the summer of 2018, when children and infants seeking asylum in the United States are treated as *de facto* criminals, locked up without warrant. Shelley's emphasis on parenting, in describing the monster's unloved plight, also reflects the emphasis in Enlightenment thought, in particular that of Jean-Jacques Rousseau and Shelley's own mother, Mary Wollstonecraft, on education as the key to human benevolence. The monster is very much a trope, if wildly exaggerated, stemming from Rousseau's argument that we are shaped profoundly by our education. The monster's fate proves that parental abuse, neglect, and lack of care can destroy the child.

2. Mary Shelley's decision to give the monster a brilliant, eloquent, compelling, and sympathetic, testimony is the master-stroke of the novel. Without the

monster's testimony, the novel is a nightmare. But the monster is utterly real: he speaks and has thoughts, emotions, intelligence, and a history. He is not just Frankenstein's creation but also is an individual of great intelligence and sensitivity. The story the monster tells is heartbreaking. He describes being defenseless, alone, outcast, alienated. The monster sees human beings unadorned. Even as human beings react to the monster with horror only because of the way he looks, he also sees them (us!) without the cover of societal and cultural niceties: he sees that human beings can be brutally unkind to outsiders, to those deemed different. Ironically, he would agree with Elizabeth's claim that human beings are "monsters."

Shelley here also, whether purposely and specifically or generally in response to events and trends of her era, illuminates the cruelty of colonization. In her era, as Western powers invade the Americas, parts of Asia and Africa, the same pattern plays out: indigenous peoples are called savages and barbaric by precisely those Europeans who are committing acts of extreme violence against indigenous peoples. Shelley's monster is in some ways comparable, in position, to indigenous peoples being colonized.

To be sure, indigenous peoples are definitely not literally created by Western colonizers. But there is a clear sense in which colonization creates an "Other" to the Western subject — this thesis is beautifully laid out in Edward Said's *Orientalism* and Gayatri Spivak applies the thesis to Frankenstein. This negative act of creation that is colonization instates a group of people who are profoundly disempowered through a mythico-socio-economic structure founded on self-serving Western beliefs in the inferiority of non-Westerners. This myth of the ethnic Other is violent, immoral, and erroneous, and it is notable that Mary Shelley's monster speaks truth when he describes the barbarism of so-called civilized people in their violent and merciless behavior toward him. The monster speaks eloquently, moreover, for anyone who has been accused of barbarism when they themselves have been the victim of violence that originates with their accusers.

It is interesting, also, to compare the monster's predicament with that of an abused child. For so often it is the case that children brutally abused by their parents become adults who are themselves capable of violence. This is the monster's trajectory precisely; and we can look ahead and compare it to Mathilda's situation, the other abused-child character from the pen of a very young Mary Shelley. ◀

CHAPTER 11

I T IS WITH CONSIDERABLE DIFFICULTY that I remember the original era of my being; all the events of that period appear confused and indistinct. A strange multiplicity of sensations seized me, and I saw, felt, heard, and smelt at the same time; and it was, indeed, a long time before I learned to distinguish between the operations of my various senses. By degrees, I remember, a stronger light pressed upon my nerves, so that I was obliged to shut my eyes. Darkness then came over me and troubled me, but hardly had I felt this when, by opening my eyes, as I now suppose, the light poured in upon me again. I walked and, I believe, descended, but I presently found a great alteration in my sensations. Before, dark and opaque bodies had surrounded me, impervious to my touch or sight; but I now found that I could wander on at liberty, with no obstacles which I could not either surmount or avoid. The light became more and more oppressive to me, and the heat wearying me as I walked, I sought a place where I could receive shade. This was the forest near Ingolstadt; and here I lay by the side of a brook resting from my fatigue, until I felt tormented by hunger and thirst. This roused me from my nearly dormant state, and I ate some berries which I found hanging on the trees or lying on the ground. I slaked my thirst at the brook, and then lying down, was overcome by sleep.

"It was dark when I awoke; I felt cold also, and half frightened, as it were, instinctively, finding myself so desolate. Before I had quitted your apartment, on a sensation of cold, I had covered myself with some clothes, but these were insufficient to secure me from the dews of night. I was a poor, helpless, miserable wretch; I knew, and could distinguish, nothing; but feeling pain invade me on all sides, I sat down and wept.

"Soon a gentle light stole over the heavens and gave me a sensation of pleasure. I started up and beheld a radiant form rise from among the trees. [The moon] I gazed with a kind of wonder. It moved slowly, but it enlightened my path, and I again went out in search of berries. I was still cold when under one of the trees I found a huge cloak, with which I covered myself, and sat down upon the ground. No distinct ideas occupied my mind; all was confused. I felt light, and hunger, and thirst, and darkness; innumerable sounds rang in my ears, and on all sides various scents saluted me; the only object that I could distinguish was the bright moon, and I fixed my eyes on that with pleasure.

"Several changes of day and night passed, and the orb of night had greatly lessened, when I began to distinguish my sensations from each other. I gradually saw plainly the clear stream that supplied me with drink and the trees that shaded me with their foliage. I was delighted when I first discovered that a pleasant sound, which often saluted my ears, proceeded from the throats of the little winged animals who had often intercepted the light from my eyes. I began also to observe, with greater accuracy, the forms that surrounded me and to perceive the boundaries of the radiant roof of light which canopied me. Sometimes I tried to imitate the pleasant songs of the birds but was unable. Sometimes I wished to express my sensations in my own mode, but the uncouth and inarticulate sounds which broke from me frightened me into silence again.

"The moon had disappeared from the night, and again, with a lessened form, showed itself, while I still remained in the forest. My sensations had by this time become distinct, and my mind received every day additional ideas. My eyes became accustomed to the light and to perceive objects in their right forms; I distinguished the insect from the herb, and by degrees, one herb from another. I found that the sparrow uttered none but harsh notes, whilst those of the blackbird and thrush were sweet and enticing.

"One day, when I was oppressed by cold, I found a fire which had been left by some wandering beggars, and was overcome with delight at the warmth I experienced from it. In my joy I thrust my hand into the live embers, but quickly drew it out again with a cry of pain. How strange, I thought, that the same cause should produce such opposite effects! I examined the materials of the fire, and to my joy found it to be composed of wood. I quickly collected some branches, but they were wet and would not burn. I was pained at this and sat still watching the operation of the fire. The wet wood which I had placed near the heat dried and itself became inflamed. I reflected on this, and by touching the various branches, I discovered the cause and busied myself in collecting a great quantity of wood, that I might dry it and have a plentiful supply of fire. When night came on and brought sleep with it, I was in the greatest fear lest my fire should be extinguished. I covered it carefully with dry wood and leaves and placed wet branches upon it; and then, spreading my cloak, I lay on the ground and sank into sleep.

"It was morning when I awoke, and my first care was to visit the fire. I uncovered it, and a gentle breeze quickly fanned it into a flame. I observed this also and contrived a fan of branches, which roused the embers when they were nearly extinguished. When night came again I found, with pleasure, that the fire gave light as well as heat and that the discovery of this element was useful to me in my food, for I found some of the offals that the travellers had left had been roasted, and tasted much more savoury than the berries I gathered from the trees. I tried, therefore, to dress my food in the same manner, placing it on the live embers. I found that the berries were spoiled by this operation, and the nuts and roots much improved.

"Food, however, became scarce, and I often spent the whole day searching in vain for a few acorns to assuage the pangs of hunger. When I found this, I resolved to quit the place that I had hitherto inhabited, to seek for one where the few wants I experienced would be more easily satisfied. In this emigration I exceedingly lamented the loss of the fire which I had obtained through accident and knew not how to reproduce it. I gave several hours to the serious consideration of this difficulty, but I was obliged to relinquish all attempt to supply it, and wrapping myself up in my cloak, I struck across the wood towards the setting sun. I passed three days in these rambles and at length discovered the open country. A great fall of snow had taken place the night before, and the fields were of one uniform white; the appearance was disconsolate, and I found my feet chilled by the cold damp substance that covered the ground.

"It was about seven in the morning, and I longed to obtain food and shelter; at length I perceived a small hut, on a rising ground, which had doubtless been built for the convenience of some shepherd. This was a new sight to me, and I examined the structure with great curiosity. Finding the door open, I entered. An old man sat in it, near a fire, over which he was preparing his breakfast. He turned on hearing a noise, and perceiving me, shrieked loudly, and quitting the hut, ran across the fields with a speed of which his debilitated form hardly appeared capable. His appearance, different from any I had ever before seen, and his flight somewhat surprised me. But I was enchanted by the appearance of the hut; here the snow and rain could not penetrate; the ground was dry; and it presented to me then as exquisite and divine a retreat as Pandemonium appeared to the demons of hell after their sufferings in the lake of fire. I greedily devoured the remnants of the shepherd's breakfast, which consisted of bread, cheese, milk, and wine; the latter, however, I did not like. Then, overcome by fatigue, I lay down among some straw and fell asleep.

"It was noon when I awoke, and allured by the warmth of the sun, which shone brightly on the white ground, I determined to recommence my travels; and, depositing the remains of the peasant's breakfast in a wallet I found, I proceeded across the fields for several hours, until at sunset I arrived at a village. How miraculous did this appear! The huts, the neater cottages, and stately houses engaged my admiration by turns. The vegetables in the gardens, the milk and cheese that I saw placed at the windows of some of the cottages, allured my appetite. One of the best of these I entered, but I had hardly placed my foot within the door before the children shrieked, and one of the women fainted. The whole village was roused; some fled, some attacked me, until, grievously bruised by stones and many other kinds of missile weapons, I escaped to the open country and fearfully took refuge in a low hovel, quite bare, and making a wretched appearance after the palaces I had beheld in the village. This hovel however, joined a cottage of a neat and pleasant appearance, but after my late dearly bought experience, I dared not enter it. My place of refuge was constructed of wood, but so low that I could with difficulty sit upright in it. No wood, however, was placed on the earth, which formed the floor, but it was dry; and although the wind entered it by innumerable chinks, I found it an agreeable asylum from the snow and rain.

"Here, then, I retreated and lay down happy to have found a shelter, however miserable, from the inclemency of the season, and still more from the barbarity of man. As soon as morning dawned I crept from my kennel, that I might view the adjacent cottage and discover if I could remain in the habitation I had found. It was situated against the back of the cottage and surrounded on the sides which were exposed by a pig sty and a clear pool of water. One part was open, and by that I had crept in; but now I covered every crevice by which I might be perceived with stones and wood, yet in such a manner that I might move them on occasion to pass out; all the light I enjoyed came through the sty, and that was sufficient for me.

"Having thus arranged my dwelling and carpeted it with clean straw, I retired, for I saw the figure of a man at a distance, and I remembered too well my treatment the night before to trust myself in his power. I had first, however, provided for my sustenance for that day by a loaf of coarse bread, which I purloined, and a cup with which I could drink more conveniently than from my hand of the pure water which flowed by my retreat. The floor was a little raised, so that it was kept perfectly dry, and by its vicinity to the chimney of the cottage it was tolerably warm.

"Being thus provided, I resolved to reside in this hovel until something should occur which might alter my determination. It was indeed a paradise compared to the bleak forest, my former residence, the rain-dropping branches, and dank earth. I ate my breakfast with pleasure and was about to remove a plank to procure myself a little water when I heard a step, and looking through a small chink, I beheld a young creature, with a pail on her head, passing before my hovel. The girl was young and of gentle demeanour, unlike what I have since found cottagers and farmhouse servants to be. Yet she was meanly dressed, a coarse blue petticoat and a linen jacket being her only garb; her fair hair was plaited but not adorned: she looked patient yet sad. I lost sight of her, and in about a quarter of an hour she returned bearing the pail, which was now partly filled with milk. As she walked along, seemingly incommoded by the burden, a young man met her, whose countenance expressed a deeper despondence. Uttering a few sounds with an air of melancholy, he took the pail from her head and bore it to the cottage himself. She followed, and they disappeared. Presently I saw the young man again, with some tools in his hand, cross the field behind the cottage; and the girl was also busied, sometimes in the house and sometimes in the yard.

"On examining my dwelling, I found that one of the windows of the cottage had formerly occupied a part of it, but the panes had been filled up with wood. In one of these was a small and almost imperceptible chink through which the eye could just penetrate. Through this crevice a small room was visible, whitewashed and clean but very bare of furniture. In one corner, near a small fire, sat an old man, leaning his head on his hands in a disconsolate attitude. The young girl was occupied in arranging the cottage; but presently she took something out of a drawer, which employed her hands, and she sat down beside the old man, who, taking up an instrument, began to play and to produce sounds sweeter than the voice of the thrush or the nightingale. It was a lovely sight, even to me, poor wretch who had never beheld aught beautiful before. The silver hair and benevolent countenance of the aged cottager won my reverence, while the gentle manners of the girl enticed my love. He played a sweet mournful air which I perceived drew tears from the eyes of his amiable companion, of which the old man took no notice, until she sobbed audibly; he then pronounced a few sounds, and the fair creature, leaving her work, knelt at his feet. He raised her and smiled with such kindness and affection that I felt sensations of a peculiar and overpowering nature; they were a mixture of pain and pleasure, such as I had never before experienced, either from hunger or cold, warmth or food; and I withdrew from the window, unable to bear these emotions.

"Soon after this the young man returned, bearing on his shoulders a load of wood. The girl met him at the door, helped to relieve him of his burden, and taking some of the fuel into the cottage, placed it on the fire; then she and the youth went apart into a nook of the cottage, and he showed her a large loaf and a piece of cheese. She seemed pleased and went into the garden for some roots and plants, which she placed in water, and then upon the fire. She afterwards continued her work, whilst the young man went into the garden and appeared busily employed in digging and pulling up roots. After he had been employed thus about an hour, the young woman joined him and they entered the cottage together.

"The old man had, in the meantime, been pensive, but on the appearance of his companions he assumed a more cheerful air, and they sat down to eat. The meal was quickly dispatched. The young woman was again occupied in arranging the cottage, the old man walked before the cottage in the sun for a few minutes, leaning on the arm of the youth. Nothing could exceed in beauty the contrast between these two excellent creatures. One was old, with silver hairs and a countenance beaming with benevolence and love; the younger was slight and graceful in his figure, and his features were moulded with the finest symmetry, yet his eyes and attitude expressed the utmost sadness and despondency. The old man returned to the cottage, and the youth, with tools different from those he had used in the morning, directed his steps across the fields.

"Night quickly shut in, but to my extreme wonder, I found that the cottagers had a means of prolonging light by the use of tapers, and was delighted to find that the setting of the sun did not put an end to the pleasure I experienced in watching my human neighbours. In the evening the young girl and her companion were employed in various occupations which I did not understand; and the old man again took up the instrument which produced the divine sounds that had enchanted me in the morning. So soon as he had finished, the youth began, not to play, but to utter sounds that were monotonous, and neither resembling the harmony of the old man's instrument nor the songs of the birds; I since found that he read aloud, but at that time I knew nothing of the science of words or letters.

"The family, after having been thus occupied for a short time, extinguished their lights and retired, as I conjectured, to rest." ◄

CHAPTER 12

LAY ON MY STRAW, but I could not sleep. I thought of the occurrences of the day. What chiefly struck me was the gentle manners of these people, and I longed to join them, but dared not. I remembered too well the treatment I had suffered the night before from the barbarous villagers, and resolved, whatever course of conduct I might hereafter think it right to pursue, that for the present I would remain quietly in my hovel, watching and endeavouring to discover the motives which influenced their actions.

"The cottagers arose the next morning before the sun. The young woman arranged the cottage and prepared the food, and the youth departed after the first meal.

"This day was passed in the same routine as that which preceded it. The young man was constantly employed out of doors, and the girl in various laborious occupations within. The old man, whom I soon perceived to be blind, employed his leisure hours on his instrument or in contemplation. Nothing could exceed the love and respect which the younger cottagers exhibited towards their venerable companion. They performed towards him every little office of affection and duty with gentleness, and he rewarded them by his benevolent smiles.

"They were not entirely happy. The young man and his companion often went apart and appeared to weep. I saw no cause for their unhappiness, but I was deeply affected by it. If such lovely creatures were miserable, it was less strange that I, an imperfect and solitary being, should be wretched. Yet why were these gentle beings unhappy? They possessed a delightful house (for such it was in my eyes) and every luxury; they had a fire to warm them when chill and delicious viands when hungry; they were dressed in excellent clothes; and, still more, they enjoyed one another's company and speech, interchanging each day looks of affection and kindness. What did their tears imply? Did they really express pain? I was at first unable to solve these questions, but perpetual attention and time explained to me many appearances which were at first enigmatic.

"A considerable period elapsed before I discovered one of the causes of the uneasiness of this amiable family: it was poverty, and they suffered that evil in a very distressing degree. Their nourishment consisted entirely of the vegetables of their garden and the milk of one cow, which gave very little during the winter, when its masters could scarcely procure food to support it. They often, I believe, suffered the pangs of hunger very poignantly, especially the two younger cottagers, for several times they placed food before the old man when they reserved none for themselves.

"This trait of kindness moved me sensibly. I had been accustomed, during the night, to steal a part of their store for my own consumption, but when I found that in doing this I inflicted pain on the cottagers, I abstained and satisfied myself with berries, nuts, and roots which I gathered from a neighbouring wood.

"I discovered also another means through which I was enabled to assist their labours. I found that the youth spent a great part of each day in collecting wood for the family fire, and during the night I often took his tools, the use of which I quickly discovered, and brought home firing sufficient for the consumption of several days.

"I remember, the first time that I did this, the young woman, when she opened the door in the morning, appeared greatly astonished on seeing a great pile of wood on the outside. She uttered some words in a loud voice, and the youth joined her, who also expressed surprise. I observed, with pleasure, that he did not go to the forest that day, but spent it in repairing the cottage and cultivating the garden.

"By degrees I made a discovery of still greater moment. I found that these people possessed a method of communicating their experience and feelings to one another by articulate sounds. I perceived that the words they spoke sometimes produced pleasure or pain, smiles or sadness, in the minds and countenances of the hearers. This was indeed a godlike science, and I ardently desired to become acquainted with it. But I was baffled in every attempt I made for this purpose. Their pronunciation was quick, and the words they uttered, not having any apparent connection with visible objects, I was unable to discover any clue by which I could unravel the mystery of their reference. By great application, however, and after having remained during the space of several revolutions of the moon in my hovel, I discovered the names that were given to some of the most familiar objects of discourse; I learned and applied the words, 'fire,' 'milk,' 'bread,' and 'wood.' I learned also the names of the cottagers themselves. The youth and his companion had each of them several names, but the old man had only one, which was 'father.' The girl was called 'sister' or 'Agatha,' and the youth 'Felix,' 'brother,' or 'son.' I cannot describe the delight I felt when I learned the ideas appropriated to each of these sounds and was able to pronounce them. I distinguished several other words without being able as yet to understand or apply them, such as 'good,' 'dearest,' 'unhappy.'

"I spent the winter in this manner. The gentle manners and beauty of the cottagers greatly endeared them to me; when they were unhappy, I felt depressed; when they rejoiced, I sympathized in their joys. I saw few human beings besides them, and if any other happened to enter the cottage, their harsh manners and rude gait only enhanced to me the superior accomplishments of my friends. The old man, I could perceive, often endeavoured to encourage his children, as sometimes I found that he called them, to cast off their melancholy. He would talk in a cheerful accent, with an expression of goodness that bestowed pleasure even upon me. Agatha listened with respect, her eyes sometimes filled with tears, which she endeavoured to wipe away unperceived; but I generally found that her countenance and tone were more cheerful after having listened to the exhortations of her father. It was not thus with Felix. He was always the saddest of the group, and even to my unpractised senses, he appeared to have suffered more deeply than his friends. But if his countenance was more sorrowful, his voice was more cheerful than that of his sister, especially when he addressed the old man.

"I could mention innumerable instances which, although slight, marked the dispositions of these amiable cottagers. In the midst of poverty and want, Felix carried with pleasure to his sister the first little white flower that peeped out from beneath the snowy ground. Early in the morning, before she had risen, he cleared away the snow that obstructed her path to the milk-house, drew water from the well, and brought the wood from the outhouse, where, to his perpetual astonishment, he found his store always replenished by an invisible hand. In the day, I believe, he worked sometimes for a neighbouring farmer, because he often went forth and did not return until dinner, yet brought no wood with him. At other times he worked in the garden, but as there was little to do in the frosty season, he read to the old man and Agatha.

"This reading had puzzled me extremely at first, but by degrees I discovered that he uttered many of the same sounds when he read as when he talked. I conjectured, therefore, that he found on the paper signs for speech which he understood, and I ardently longed to comprehend these also; but how was that possible when

I did not even understand the sounds for which they stood as signs? I improved, however, sensibly in this science, but not sufficiently to follow up any kind of conversation, although I applied my whole mind to the endeavour, for I easily perceived that, although I eagerly longed to discover myself to the cottagers, I ought not to make the attempt until I had first become master of their language, which knowledge might enable me to make them overlook the deformity of my figure, for with this also the contrast perpetually presented to my eyes had made me acquainted.

"I had admired the perfect forms of my cottagers — their grace, beauty, and delicate complexions; but how was I terrified when I viewed myself in a transparent pool! At first I started back, unable to believe that it was indeed I who was reflected in the mirror; and when I became fully convinced that I was in reality the monster that I am, I was filled with the bitterest sensations of despondence and mortification. Alas! I did not yet entirely know the fatal effects of this miserable deformity.

"As the sun became warmer and the light of day longer, the snow vanished, and I beheld the bare trees and the black earth. From this time Felix was more employed, and the heart-moving indications of impending famine disappeared. Their food, as I afterwards found, was coarse, but it was wholesome; and they procured a sufficiency of it. Several new kinds of plants sprang up in the garden, which they dressed; and these signs of comfort increased daily as the season advanced.

"The old man, leaning on his son, walked each day at noon, when it did not rain, as I found it was called when the heavens poured forth its waters. This frequently took place, but a high wind quickly dried the earth, and the season became far more pleasant than it had been.

"My mode of life in my hovel was uniform. During the morning I attended the motions of the cottagers, and when they were dispersed in various occupations, I slept; the remainder of the day was spent in observing my friends. When they had retired to rest, if there was any moon or the night was star-light, I went into the woods and collected my own food and fuel for the cottage. When I returned, as often as it was necessary, I cleared their path from the snow and performed those offices that I had seen done by Felix. I afterwards found that these labours, performed by an invisible hand, greatly astonished them; and once or twice I heard them, on these occasions, utter the words 'good spirit,' 'wonderful'; but I did not then understand the signification of these terms.

"My thoughts now became more active, and I longed to discover the motives and feelings of these lovely creatures; I was inquisitive to know why Felix appeared so miserable and Agatha so sad. I thought (foolish wretch!) that it might be in my power to restore happiness to these deserving people. When I slept or was absent, the forms of the venerable blind father, the gentle Agatha, and the excellent Felix flitted before me. I looked upon them as superior beings who would be the arbiters of my future destiny. I formed in my imagination a thousand pictures of presenting myself to them, and their reception of me. I imagined that they would be disgusted, until, by my gentle demeanour and conciliating words, I should first win their favour and afterwards their love.

"These thoughts exhilarated me and led me to apply with fresh ardour to the acquiring the art of language. My organs were indeed harsh, but supple; and although my voice was very unlike the soft music of their tones, yet I pronounced such words as I understood with tolerable ease. It was as the ass and the lap-dog; yet surely the gentle ass whose intentions were affectionate, although his manners were rude, deserved better treatment than blows and execration.

"The pleasant showers and genial warmth of spring greatly altered the aspect of the earth. Men who before this change seemed to have been hid in caves dispersed themselves and were employed in various arts of cultivation. The birds sang in more cheerful notes, and the leaves began to bud forth on the trees. Happy, happy earth! Fit habitation for gods, which, so short a time before, was bleak, damp, and unwholesome. My spirits were elevated by the enchanting appearance of nature; the past was blotted from my memory, the present was tranquil, and the future gilded by bright rays of hope and anticipations of joy." ◀

CHAPTER 13

I NOW HASTEN to the more moving part of my story. I shall relate events that impressed me with feelings which, from what I had been, have made me what I am.

"Spring advanced rapidly; the weather became fine and the skies cloudless. It surprised me that what before was desert and gloomy should now bloom with the most beautiful flowers and verdure. My senses were gratified and refreshed by a thousand scents of delight and a thousand sights of beauty.

"It was on one of these days, when my cottagers periodically rested from labour—the old man played on his guitar, and the children listened to him—that I observed the countenance of Felix was melancholy beyond expression; he sighed frequently, and once his father paused in his music, and I conjectured by his manner that he inquired the cause of his son's sorrow. Felix replied in a cheerful accent, and the old man was recommencing his music when someone tapped at the door.[1]

"It was a lady on horseback, accompanied by a country-man as a guide. The lady was dressed in a dark suit and covered with a thick black veil. Agatha asked a question, to which the stranger only replied by pronouncing, in a sweet accent, the name of Felix. Her voice was musical but unlike that of either of my friends. On hearing this word, Felix came up hastily to the lady, who, when she saw him, threw up her veil, and I beheld a countenance of angelic beauty and expression. Her hair of a shining raven black, and curiously braided; her eyes were dark, but gentle, although animated; her features of a regular proportion, and her complexion wondrously fair, each cheek tinged with a lovely pink.

"Felix seemed ravished with delight when he saw her, every trait of sorrow vanished from his face, and it instantly expressed a degree of ecstatic joy, of which I could hardly have believed it capable; his eyes sparkled, as his cheek flushed with pleasure; and at that moment I thought him as beautiful as the stranger. She appeared affected by different feelings; wiping a few tears from her lovely eyes, she held out her hand to Felix, who kissed it rapturously and called her, as well as I could distinguish, his sweet Arabian. She did not appear to understand him, but smiled. He assisted her to dismount, and dismissing her guide, conducted her into the cottage. Some conversation took place between him and his father, and the young stranger knelt at the old man's feet and would have kissed his hand, but he raised her and embraced her affectionately.

"I soon perceived that although the stranger uttered articulate sounds and appeared to have a language of her own, she was neither understood by nor herself understood the cottagers. They made many signs which I did not comprehend, but I saw that her presence diffused gladness through the cottage, dispelling their sorrow as the sun dissipates the morning mists. Felix seemed peculiarly happy and with smiles of delight welcomed his Arabian. Agatha, the ever-gentle Agatha, kissed the hands of the lovely stranger, and pointing to her brother, made signs which appeared to me to mean that he had been sorrowful until she came. Some hours passed thus, while they, by their countenances, expressed joy, the cause of which I did not comprehend. Presently I found, by the frequent recurrence of some sound which the stranger repeated after them, that she was endeavouring to learn their language; and the idea instantly occurred to me that I should make use of the same instructions to the same end. The stranger learned about twenty words at the first lesson; most of them, indeed, were those which I had before understood, but I profited by the others.

"As night came on, Agatha and the Arabian retired early. When they separated Felix kissed the hand of the stranger and said, 'Good night sweet Safie.' He sat up much longer, conversing with his father, and by the frequent repetition of her name I conjectured that their lovely guest was the subject of their conversation. I ardently desired to understand them, and bent every faculty towards that purpose, but found it utterly impossible.

"The next morning Felix went out to his work, and after the usual occupations of Agatha were finished, the Arabian sat at the feet of the old man, and taking his guitar, played some airs so entrancingly beautiful that they at once drew tears of sorrow and delight from my eyes. She sang, and her voice flowed in a rich cadence, swelling or dying away like a nightingale of the woods.

"When she had finished, she gave the guitar to Agatha, who at first declined it. She played a simple air, and her voice accompanied it in sweet accents, but unlike the wondrous strain of the stranger. The old man appeared enraptured and said some words which Agatha endeavoured to explain to Safie, and by which he appeared to wish to express that she bestowed on him the greatest delight by her music.

"The days now passed as peaceably as before, with the sole alteration that joy had taken place of sadness in the countenances of my friends. Safie was always gay and happy; she and I improved rapidly in the knowledge of language, so that in two months I began to comprehend most of the words uttered by my protectors.

"In the meanwhile also the black ground was covered with herbage, and the green banks interspersed with innumerable flowers, sweet to the scent and the eyes, stars of pale radiance among the moonlight woods; the sun became warmer, the nights clear and balmy; and my nocturnal rambles were an extreme pleasure to me, although they were considerably shortened by the late setting and early rising of the sun, for I never ventured abroad during daylight, fearful of meeting with the same treatment I had formerly endured in the first village which I entered.

"My days were spent in close attention, that I might more speedily master the language; and I may boast that I improved more rapidly than the Arabian, who understood very little and conversed in broken accents, whilst I comprehended and could imitate almost every word that was spoken.

"While I improved in speech, I also learned the science of letters as it was taught to the stranger, and this opened before me a wide field for wonder and delight.

"The book from which Felix instructed Safie was Volney's *Ruins of Empires*. I should not have understood the purport of this book had not Felix, in reading it, given very minute explanations. He had chosen this work, he said, because the declamatory style was framed in imitation of the Eastern authors. Through this work I obtained a cursory knowledge of history and a view of the several empires at present existing in the world; it gave me an insight into the manners, governments, and religions of the different nations of the earth. I heard of the slothful Asiatics, of the stupendous genius and mental activity of the Grecians, of the wars and wonderful virtue of the early Romans—of their subsequent degenerating—of the decline of that mighty empire, of chivalry, Christianity, and kings. I heard of the discovery of the American hemisphere and wept with Safie over the hapless fate of its original inhabitants.

"These wonderful narrations inspired me with strange feelings. Was man, indeed, at once so powerful, so virtuous and magnificent, yet so vicious and base? He appeared at one time a mere scion of the evil principle and at another as all that can be conceived of noble and godlike. To be a great and virtuous man appeared the highest honour that can befall a sensitive being; to be base and vicious, as many on record have been, appeared the lowest degradation, a condition more abject than that of the blind mole or harmless worm. For a long time I could not conceive how one man could go forth to murder his fellow, or even why there were laws and governments; but when I heard details of vice and bloodshed, my wonder ceased and I turned away with disgust and loathing.

"Every conversation of the cottagers now opened new wonders to me. While I listened to the instructions which Felix bestowed upon the Arabian, the strange system of human society was explained to me. I heard of the division of property, of immense wealth and squalid poverty, of rank, descent, and noble blood.

"The words induced me to turn towards myself. I learned that the possessions most esteemed by your fellow creatures were high and unsullied descent united with riches. A man might be respected with only one of these advantages, but without either he was considered, except in very rare instances, as a vagabond and a slave, doomed to waste his powers for the profits of the chosen few! And what was I? Of my creation and creator I was absolutely ignorant, but I knew that I possessed no money, no friends, no kind of property. I was, besides, endued with a figure hideously deformed and loathsome; I was not even of the same nature as man. I was more agile than they and could subsist upon coarser diet; I bore the extremes of heat and cold with less injury to my frame; my stature far exceeded theirs. When I looked around I saw and heard of none like me. Was I, then, a monster, a blot upon the earth, from which all men fled and whom all men disowned?

"I cannot describe to you the agony that these reflections inflicted upon me; I tried to dispel them, but sorrow only increased with knowledge. Oh, that I had forever remained in my native wood, nor known nor felt beyond the sensations of hunger, thirst, and heat!

"Of what a strange nature is knowledge! It clings to the mind when it has once seized on it like a lichen on the rock. I wished sometimes to shake off all thought and feeling, but I learned that there was but one means to overcome the sensation of pain, and that was death—a state which I feared yet did not understand. I admired virtue and good feelings and loved the gentle manners and amiable qualities of my cottagers, but I was shut out from intercourse with them, except through means which I obtained by stealth, when I was unseen and unknown, and which rather increased than satisfied the desire I had of becoming one among my fellows. The gentle words of Agatha and the animated smiles of the charming Arabian were not for me. The mild exhortations of the old man and the lively conversation of the loved Felix were not for me. Miserable, unhappy wretch!

"Other lessons were impressed upon me even more deeply. I heard of the difference of sexes, and the birth and growth of children, how the father doted on the smiles of the infant, and the lively sallies of the older child, how all the life and cares of the mother were wrapped up in the precious charge, how the mind of youth expanded and gained knowledge, of brother, sister, and all the various relationships which bind one human being to another in mutual bonds.

"But where were my friends and relations? No father had watched my infant days, no mother had blessed me with smiles and caresses; or if they had, all my past life was now a blot, a blind vacancy in which I distinguished nothing. From my earliest remembrance I had been as I then was in height and proportion. I had never yet seen a being resembling me or who claimed any intercourse with me. What was I? The question again recurred, to be answered only with groans.

"I will soon explain to what these feelings tended, but allow me now to return to the cottagers, whose story excited in me such various feelings of indignation, delight, and wonder, but which all terminated in additional love and reverence for my protectors (for so I loved, in an innocent, half-painful self-deceit, to call them)." ◄

CHAPTER 13
Annotations

1. The monster admires the De Lacey family and Safie for their beauty, their grace, their kindness to each other, and relates to Victor the complex and cruel political situations that rendered the lovely family impoverished and exiled. Along the way, through the figure of Safie, the monster refers to the situation of Christians in the Middle East. Eastern Orthodox Christians — including Syrian, Lebanese, Coptic, Ethiopian, and Greek — were the earliest practitioners of Christianity. Shelley's novel expresses a prejudiced belief that Christianity is a benevolent religion and Islam a dangerous one, an unfortunate bias very much in keeping with Shelley's time and culture. In particular, George Gordon Lord Byron, the poet and Shelley's close friend, volunteered to fight in the Greek War for Independence (1821-1833), as Greece fought to free itself from the Ottoman Empire. Byron died in 1824 for his pains. The idyllic picture that the monster draws of the cottagers, however, is only a partial image. For the cottagers will ultimately betray and despise him just as all other human beings do because of the way he looks. Thus, Mary Shelley proceeds to systematically destroy any vestige or stronghold of human goodness in her novel. The De Lacey family and Safie appear good because they are beautiful and kind to each other. But they will ultimately prove to have no more generosity toward the monster than do cruder people. Safie alone does not make a categorical decision to reject the monster: she simply faints with horror on seeing him. Safie, of course, is set parallel to the monster in that she represents the non-Western Other in the text. Unlike the monster, however, Safie is brought into the circle of the human by dint of her beauty and her mother's Christianity. The monster has no mother, and no religion. ◄

CHAPTER 14

S OME TIME ELAPSED before I learned the history of my friends. It was one which could not fail to impress itself deeply on my mind, unfolding as it did a number of circumstances, each interesting and wonderful to one so utterly inexperienced as I was.

"The name of the old man was De Lacey. He was descended from a good family in France, where he had lived for many years in affluence, respected by his superiors and beloved by his equals. His son was bred in the service of his country, and Agatha had ranked with ladies of the highest distinction. A few months before my arrival they had lived in a large and luxurious city called Paris, surrounded by friends and possessed of every enjoyment which virtue, refinement of intellect, or taste, accompanied by a moderate fortune, could afford.

"The father of Safie had been the cause of their ruin. He was a Turkish merchant and had inhabited Paris for many years, when, for some reason which I could not learn, he became obnoxious to the government. He was seized and cast into prison the very day that Safie arrived from Constantinople to join him. He was tried and condemned to death. The injustice of his sentence was very flagrant; all Paris was indignant; and it was judged that his religion and wealth rather than the crime alleged against him had been the cause of his condemnation.

"Felix had accidentally been present at the trial; his horror and indignation were uncontrollable when he heard the decision of the court. He made, at that moment, a solemn vow to deliver him and then looked around for the means. After many fruitless attempts to gain admittance to the prison, he found a strongly grated window in an unguarded part of the building, which lighted the dungeon of the unfortunate Muhammadan, who, loaded with chains, waited in despair the execution of the barbarous sentence. Felix visited the grate at night and made known to the prisoner his intentions in his favour. The Turk, amazed and delighted, endeavoured to kindle the zeal of his deliverer by promises of reward and wealth. Felix rejected his offers with contempt, yet when he saw the lovely Safie, who was allowed to visit her father and who by her gestures expressed her lively gratitude, the youth could not help owning to his own mind that the captive possessed a treasure which would fully reward his toil and hazard.

"The Turk quickly perceived the impression that his daughter had made on the heart of Felix and endeavoured to secure him more entirely in his interests by the promise of her hand in marriage so soon as he should be conveyed to a place of safety. Felix was too delicate to accept this offer, yet he looked forward to the probability of the event as to the consummation of his happiness.

"During the ensuing days, while the preparations were going forward for the escape of the merchant, the zeal of Felix was warmed by several letters that he received from this lovely girl, who found means to express her thoughts in the language of her lover by the aid of an old man, a servant of her father who understood French. She thanked him in the most ardent terms for his intended services towards her parent, and at the same time she gently deplored her own fate.

"I have copies of these letters, for I found means, during my residence in the hovel, to procure the implements of writing; and the letters were often in the hands of Felix or Agatha. Before I depart I will give them to you; they will prove the truth of my tale; but at present, as the sun is already far declined, I shall only have time to repeat the substance of them to you.

"Safie related that her mother was a Christian Arab, seized and made a slave by the Turks; recommended by her beauty, she had won the heart of the father of Safie, who married her. The young girl spoke in high and enthusiastic terms of her mother, who, born in freedom, spurned the bondage to which she was now reduced. She instructed her daughter in the tenets of her religion and taught her to aspire to higher powers of intellect and an independence of spirit forbidden to the female followers of Muhammad. This lady died, but her lessons were indelibly impressed on the mind of Safie, who sickened at the prospect of again returning to Asia and being immured within the walls of a harem, allowed only to occupy herself with infantile amusements, ill-suited to the temper of her soul, now accustomed to grand ideas and a noble emulation for virtue. The prospect of marrying a Christian and remaining in a country where women were allowed to take a rank in society was enchanting to her.

"The day for the execution of the Turk was fixed, but on the night previous to it he quitted his prison and before morning was distant many leagues from Paris. Felix had procured passports in the name of his father, sister, and himself. He had previously communicated his plan to the former, who aided the deceit by quitting his house, under the pretence of a journey and concealed himself, with his daughter, in an obscure part of Paris.

"Felix conducted the fugitives through France to Lyons and across Mont Cenis to Leghorn, where the merchant had decided to wait a favourable opportunity of passing into some part of the Turkish dominions.

"Safie resolved to remain with her father until the moment of his departure, before which time the Turk renewed his promise that she should be united to his deliverer; and Felix remained with them in expectation of that event; and in the meantime he enjoyed the society of the Arabian, who exhibited towards him the simplest and tenderest affection. They conversed with one another through the means of an interpreter, and sometimes with the interpretation of looks; and Safie sang to him the divine airs of her native country.

"The Turk allowed this intimacy to take place and encouraged the hopes of the youthful lovers, while in his heart he had formed far other plans. He loathed the idea that his daughter should be united to a Christian, but he feared the resentment of Felix if he should appear lukewarm, for he knew that he was still in the power of his deliverer if he should choose to betray him to the Italian state which they inhabited. He revolved a thousand plans by which he should be enabled to prolong the deceit until it might be no longer necessary, and secretly to take his daughter with him when he departed. His plans were facilitated by the news which arrived from Paris.

"The government of France were greatly enraged at the escape of their victim and spared no pains to detect and punish his deliverer. The plot of Felix was quickly discovered, and De Lacey and Agatha were thrown into prison. The news reached Felix and roused him from his dream of pleasure. His blind and aged father and his gentle sister lay in a noisome dungeon while he enjoyed the free air and the society of her whom he loved. This idea was torture to him. He quickly arranged with the Turk that if the latter should find a favourable opportunity for escape before Felix could return to Italy, Safie should remain as a boarder at a convent at Leghorn; and then, quitting the lovely Arabian, he hastened to Paris and delivered himself up to the vengeance of the law, hoping to free De Lacey and Agatha by this proceeding.

"He did not succeed. They remained confined for five months before the trial took place, the result of which deprived them of their fortune and condemned them to a perpetual exile from their native country.

"They found a miserable asylum in the cottage in Germany, where I discovered them. Felix soon learned that the treacherous Turk, for whom he and his family endured such unheard-of oppression, on discovering that his deliverer was thus reduced to poverty and ruin, became a traitor to good feeling and honour and had quitted Italy with his daughter, insultingly sending Felix a pittance of money to aid him, as he said, in some plan of future maintenance.

"Such were the events that preyed on the heart of Felix and rendered him, when I first saw him, the most miserable of his family. He could have endured poverty, and while this distress had been the meed of his virtue, he gloried in it; but the ingratitude of the Turk and the loss of his beloved Safie were misfortunes more bitter and irreparable. The arrival of the Arabian now infused new life into his soul.

"When the news reached Leghorn that Felix was deprived of his wealth and rank, the merchant commanded his daughter to think no more of her lover, but to prepare to return to her native country. The generous nature of Safie was outraged by this command; she attempted to expostulate with her father, but he left her angrily, reiterating his tyrannical mandate.

"A few days after, the Turk entered his daughter's apartment and told her hastily that he had reason to believe that his residence at Leghorn had been divulged and that he should speedily be delivered up to the French government; he had consequently hired a vessel to convey him to Constantinople, for which city he should sail in a few hours. He intended to leave his daughter under the care of a confidential servant, to follow at her leisure with the greater part of his property, which had not yet arrived at Leghorn.

"When alone, Safie resolved in her own mind the plan of conduct that it would become her to pursue in this emergency. A residence in Turkey was abhorrent to her; her religion and her feelings were alike averse to it. By some papers of her father which fell into her hands she heard of the exile of her lover and learnt the name of the spot where he then resided. She hesitated some time, but at length she formed her determination. Taking with her some jewels that belonged to her and a sum of money, she quitted Italy with an attendant, a native of Leghorn, but who understood the common language of Turkey, and departed for Germany.

"She arrived in safety at a town about twenty leagues from the cottage of De Lacey, when her attendant fell dangerously ill. Safie nursed her with the most devoted affection, but the poor girl died, and the Arabian was left alone, unacquainted with the language of the country and utterly ignorant of the customs of the world. She fell, however, into good hands. The Italian had mentioned the name of the spot for which they were bound, and after her death the woman of the house in which they had lived took care that Safie should arrive in safety at the cottage of her lover." ◀

CHAPTER 15

S UCH WAS THE HISTORY of my beloved cottagers. It impressed me deeply. I learned, from the views of social life which it developed, to admire their virtues and to deprecate the vices of mankind.

"As yet I looked upon crime as a distant evil, benevolence and generosity were ever present before me, inciting within me a desire to become an actor in the busy scene where so many admirable qualities were called forth and displayed. But in giving an account of the progress of my intellect, I must not omit a circumstance which occurred in the beginning of the month of August of the same year.

"One night during my accustomed visit to the neighbouring wood where I collected my own food and brought home firing for my protectors, I found on the ground a leathern portmanteau containing several articles of dress and some books. I eagerly seized the prize and returned with it to my hovel. Fortunately the books were written in the language, the elements of which I had acquired at the cottage; they consisted of Paradise Lost, a volume of *Plutarch's Lives,* and *The Sorrows of Werter.* The possession of these treasures gave me extreme delight; I now continually studied and exercised my mind upon these histories, whilst my friends were employed in their ordinary occupations.

"I can hardly describe to you the effect of these books. They produced in me an infinity of new images and feelings, that sometimes raised me to ecstasy, but more frequently sunk me into the lowest dejection. In *The Sorrows of Werter,* besides the interest of its simple and affecting story, so many opinions are canvassed and so many lights thrown upon what had hitherto been to me obscure subjects that I found in it a never-ending source of speculation and astonishment. The gentle and domestic manners it described, combined with lofty sentiments and feelings, which had for their object something out of self, accorded well with my experience among my protectors and with the wants which were forever alive in my own bosom. But I thought Werter himself a more divine being than I had ever beheld or imagined; his character contained no pretension, but it sank deep. The disquisitions upon death and suicide were calculated to fill me with wonder. I did not pretend to enter into the merits of the case, yet I inclined towards the opinions of the hero, whose extinction I wept, without precisely understanding it.

"As I read, however, I applied much personally to my own feelings and condition. I found myself similar yet at the same time strangely unlike to the beings concerning whom I read and to whose conversation I was a listener. I sympathized with and partly understood them, but I was unformed in mind; I was dependent on none and related to none. 'The path of my departure was free,' and there was none to lament my annihilation. My person was hideous and my stature gigantic. What did this mean? Who was I? What was I? Whence did I come? What was my destination? These questions continually recurred, but I was unable to solve them.

"The volume of Plutarch's *Lives* which I possessed contained the histories of the first founders of the ancient republics. This book had a far different effect upon me from *The Sorrows of Werter*. I learned from Werter's imaginations despondency and gloom, but Plutarch taught me high thoughts; he elevated me above the wretched sphere of my own reflections, to admire and love the heroes of past ages. Many things I read surpassed my understanding and experience. I had a very confused knowledge of kingdoms, wide extents of country, mighty rivers, and boundless seas. But I was perfectly unacquainted with towns and large assemblages of men. The cottage of my protectors had been the only school in which I had studied human nature, but this book developed new and mightier scenes of action. I read of men concerned in public affairs, governing or massacring their species. I felt the greatest ardour for virtue rise within me, and abhorrence for vice, as far as I understood the signification of those terms, relative as they were, as I applied them, to pleasure and pain alone. Induced by these feelings, I was of course led to admire peaceable lawgivers, Numa, Solon, and Lycurgus, in preference to Romulus and Theseus. The patriarchal lives of my protectors caused these impressions to take a firm hold on my mind; perhaps, if my first introduction to humanity had been made by a young soldier, burning for glory and slaughter, I should have been imbued with different sensations.

"But *Paradise Lost* excited different and far deeper emotions. I read it, as I had read the other volumes which had fallen into my hands, as a true history. It moved every feeling of wonder and awe that the picture of an omnipotent God warring with his creatures was capable of exciting. I often referred the several situations, as their similarity struck me, to my own. Like Adam, I was apparently united by no link to any other being in existence; but his state was far different from mine in every other respect. He had come forth from the hands of God a perfect creature, happy and prosperous, guarded by the especial care of his Creator; he was allowed to converse with and acquire knowledge from beings of a superior nature, but I was wretched, helpless, and alone. Many times I considered Satan as the fitter emblem of my condition, for often, like him, when I viewed the bliss of my protectors, the bitter gall of envy rose within me.

"Another circumstance strengthened and confirmed these feelings. Soon after my arrival in the hovel I discovered some papers in the pocket of the dress which I had taken from your laboratory. At first I had neglected them, but now that I was able to decipher the characters in which they were written, I began to study them with diligence. It was your journal of the four months that preceded my creation. You minutely described in these papers every step you took in the progress of your work; this history was mingled with accounts of domestic occurrences. You doubtless recollect these papers. Here they are. Everything is related in them which bears reference to my accursed origin; the whole detail of that series of disgusting circumstances which produced it is set in view; the minutest description of my odious and loathsome person is given, in language which painted your own horrors and rendered mine indelible. I sickened as I read. 'Hateful day when I received life!' I exclaimed in agony. 'Accursed creator! Why did you form a monster so hideous that even YOU turned from me in disgust? God, in pity, made man beautiful and alluring, after his own image; but my form is a filthy type of yours, more horrid even from the very resemblance. Satan had his companions, fellow devils, to admire and encourage him, but I am solitary and abhorred.'

"These were the reflections of my hours of despondency and solitude; but when I contemplated the virtues of the cottagers, their amiable and benevolent dispositions, I persuaded myself that when they should become acquainted with my admiration of their virtues they would compassionate me and overlook my personal deformity. Could they turn from their door one, however monstrous, who solicited their compassion and friendship? I resolved, at least, not to despair, but in every way to fit myself for an interview with them which would decide my fate. I postponed this attempt for some months longer, for the importance attached to its success inspired me with a dread lest I should fail. Besides, I found that my understanding improved so much with every day's experience that I was unwilling to commence this undertaking until a few more months should have added to my sagacity.

"Several changes, in the meantime, took place in the cottage. The presence of Safie diffused happiness among its inhabitants, and I also found that a greater degree of plenty reigned there. Felix and Agatha spent more time in amusement and conversation, and were assisted in their labours by servants. They did not appear rich, but they were contented and happy; their feelings were serene and peaceful, while mine became every day more tumultuous. Increase of knowledge only discovered to me more clearly what a wretched outcast I was. I cherished hope, it is true, but it vanished when I beheld my person reflected in water or my shadow in the moonshine, even as that frail image and that inconstant shade.

"I endeavoured to crush these fears and to fortify myself for the trial which in a few months I resolved to undergo; and sometimes I allowed my thoughts, unchecked by reason, to ramble in the fields of Paradise, and dared to fancy amiable and lovely creatures sympathizing with my feelings and cheering my gloom; their angelic countenances breathed smiles of consolation. But it was all a dream; no Eve soothed my sorrows nor shared my thoughts; I was alone. I remembered Adam's supplication to his Creator. But where was mine? He had abandoned me, and in the bitterness of my heart I cursed him.[2]

"Autumn passed thus. I saw, with surprise and grief, the leaves decay and fall, and nature again assume the barren and bleak appearance it had worn when I first beheld the woods and the lovely moon. Yet I did not heed the bleakness of the weather; I was better fitted by my conformation for the endurance of cold than heat. But my chief delights were the sight of the flowers, the birds, and all the gay apparel of summer; when those deserted me, I turned with more attention towards the cottagers. Their happiness was not decreased by the absence of summer. They loved and sympathized with one another; and their joys, depending on each other, were not interrupted by the casualties that took place around them. The more I saw of them, the greater became my desire to claim their protection and kindness; my heart yearned to be known and loved by these amiable creatures; to see their sweet looks directed towards me with affection was the utmost limit of my ambition. I dared not think that they would turn them from me with disdain and horror. The poor that stopped at their door were never driven away. I asked, it is true, for greater treasures than a little food or rest: I required kindness and sympathy; but I did not believe myself utterly unworthy of it.

"The winter advanced, and an entire revolution of the seasons had taken place since I awoke into life. My attention at this time was solely directed towards my plan of introducing myself into the cottage of my protectors. I revolved many projects, but that on which I finally fixed was to enter the dwelling when the blind old man should be alone. I had sagacity enough to discover that the unnatural hideousness of my person was the chief object of horror with those who had formerly beheld me. My voice, although harsh, had nothing terrible in it; I thought, therefore, that if in the absence of his children I could gain the good will and mediation of the old De Lacey, I might by his means be tolerated by my younger protectors.

"One day, when the sun shone on the red leaves that strewed the ground and diffused cheerfulness, although it denied warmth, Safie, Agatha, and Felix departed on a long country walk, and the old man, at his own desire, was left alone in the cottage. When his children had departed, he took up his guitar and played several mournful but sweet airs, more sweet and mournful than I had ever heard him play before. At first his countenance was illuminated with pleasure, but as he continued, thoughtfulness and sadness succeeded; at length, laying aside the instrument, he sat absorbed in reflection.

"My heart beat quick; this was the hour and moment of trial, which would decide my hopes or realize my fears. The servants were gone to a neighbouring fair. All was silent in and around the cottage; it was an excellent opportunity; yet, when I proceeded to execute my plan, my limbs failed me and I sank to the ground. Again I rose, and exerting all the firmness of which I was master, removed the planks which I had placed before my hovel to conceal my retreat. The fresh air revived me, and with renewed determination I approached the door of their cottage.

"I knocked. 'Who is there?' said the old man. 'Come in.'

"I entered. 'Pardon this intrusion,' said I; 'I am a traveller in want of a little rest; you would greatly oblige me if you would allow me to remain a few minutes before the fire.'

"'Enter,' said De Lacey, 'and I will try in what manner I can to relieve your wants; but, unfortunately, my children are from home, and as I am blind, I am afraid I shall find it difficult to procure food for you.'

"'Do not trouble yourself, my kind host; I have food; it is warmth and rest only that I need.'

"I sat down, and a silence ensued. I knew that every minute was precious to me, yet I remained irresolute in what manner to commence the interview, when the old man addressed me. 'By your language, stranger, I suppose you are my countryman; are you French?'

"'No; but I was educated by a French family and understand that language only. I am now going to claim the protection of some friends, whom I sincerely love, and of whose favour I have some hopes.'

"'Are they Germans?'

"'No, they are French. But let us change the subject. I am an unfortunate and deserted creature, I look around and I have no relation or friend upon earth. These amiable people to whom I go have never seen me and know little of me. I am full of fears, for if I fail there, I am an outcast in the world forever.'

"'Do not despair. To be friendless is indeed to be unfortunate, but the hearts of men, when unprejudiced by any obvious self-interest, are full of brotherly love and charity. Rely, therefore, on your hopes; and if these friends are good and amiable, do not despair.'

"'They are kind—they are the most excellent creatures in the world; but, unfortunately, they are prejudiced against me. I have good dispositions; my life has been hitherto harmless and in some degree beneficial; but a fatal prejudice clouds their eyes, and where they ought to see a feeling and kind friend, they behold only a detestable monster.'

"'That is indeed unfortunate; but if you are really blameless, cannot you undeceive them?'

"'I am about to undertake that task; and it is on that account that I feel so many overwhelming terrors. I tenderly love these friends; I have, unknown to them, been for many months in the habits of daily kindness towards them; but they believe that I wish to injure them, and it is that prejudice which I wish to overcome.'

"'Where do these friends reside?'

"'Near this spot.'

"The old man paused and then continued, 'If you will unreservedly confide to me the particulars of your tale, I perhaps may be of use in undeceiving them. I am blind and cannot judge of your countenance, but there is something in your words which persuades me that you are sincere. I am poor and an exile, but it will afford me true pleasure to be in any way serviceable to a human creature.'

"'Excellent man! I thank you and accept your generous offer. You raise me from the dust by this kindness; and I trust that, by your aid, I shall not be driven from the society and sympathy of your fellow creatures.'

"'Heaven forbid! Even if you were really criminal, for that can only drive you to desperation, and not instigate you to virtue. I also am unfortunate; I and my family have been condemned, although innocent; judge, therefore, if I do not feel for your misfortunes.'

"'How can I thank you, my best and only benefactor? From your lips first have I heard the voice of kindness directed towards me; I shall be forever grateful; and your present humanity assures me of success with those friends whom I am on the point of meeting.'

"'May I know the names and residence of those friends?'

"I paused. This, I thought, was the moment of decision, which was to rob me of or bestow happiness on me forever. I struggled vainly for firmness sufficient to answer him, but the effort destroyed all my remaining strength; I sank on the chair and sobbed aloud. At that moment I heard the steps of my younger protectors. I had not a moment to lose, but seizing the hand of the old man, I cried, 'Now is the time! Save and protect me! You and your family are the friends whom I seek. Do not you desert me in the hour of trial!'

"'Great God!' exclaimed the old man. 'Who are you?'

"At that instant the cottage door was opened, and Felix, Safie, and Agatha entered. Who can describe their horror and consternation on beholding me? Agatha fainted, and Safie, unable to attend to her friend, rushed out of the cottage. Felix darted forward, and with supernatural force tore me from his father, to whose knees I clung, in a transport of fury, he dashed me to the ground and struck me violently with a stick. I could have torn him limb from limb, as the lion rends the antelope. But my heart sank within me as with bitter sickness, and I refrained. I saw him on the point of repeating his blow, when, overcome by pain and anguish, I quitted the cottage, and in the general tumult escaped unperceived to my hovel." ◄

CHAPTER 15
Annotations

1. The monster's discovery of three books, Plutarch's *Lives, The Sorrows of Young Werther*, and *Paradise Lost,* is of central important to Shelley's novel. Two of these works are clear precursor texts to *Frankenstein; or, the Modern Prometheus.* Goethe and Milton, in their works *Sorrows of Young Werther* and *Paradise Lost* are literary references for Shelley's Frankenstein. I have discussed Goethe's influence in other notes, as well as briefly mentioning Milton. Here, it is worth noting that the scene where the monster sees his own reflection and is horrified by it is a re-working of Milton's scene in *Paradise Lost* of Eve seeing her reflection, for the first time, and being entranced with her own beauty. So clear is the parallel that some have argued the monster is Shelley's monstrous "Eve." I think, though, that the parallel Shelley draws is much subtler. She is not saying that female embodiment is monstrous, nor that she experiences her own female embodiment as monstrous. Instead, she is pointing out—by setting the monster and Milton's Eve in parallel scenes of self-gazing—that women are often perceived by men as monstrously different, and that this misprision causes monstrous suffering for women. Recall that in Shelley's time the rule of law was coverture; that is, a married woman became a null person, legally she was subsumed by her husband. Likewise, medical belief, at the time, held that women who engaged in intellectual activity perverted their gender and could damage their reproductive organs simply through becoming well-educated. The monstrousness is not femaleness itself but male perception of it.

    Beyond this, the monster's tale reveals something essential and darkly true about education. The monster has superhuman strength; he also has superhuman intelligence. The monster learns the English language just by observing the De Lacey family from a distance. Moreover, he learns language so quickly that in a short period of time he knows English well enough to read Milton. His intelligence is extraordinary: he teaches himself from these literary works. And yet despite this extraordinary intelligence, the monster is reviled by human beings simply because of the way he looks. Shelley builds the case for the monster's sympathetic reception by describing his intelligence and sensitivity as a reader.

Likewise, the books she chooses shape a shorthand cartography of the path of Western culture: from the early Republics, through Christianity, to the rise of Romanticism. The thwarted *bildungsroman* that is *Frankenstein* the novel here is articulated through the monster's striving to understand his identity in the context of Plutarch, Milton, Goethe. What I mean is that the seed of the monster's identity rather than unfolding into meaning is snuffed and becomes null, ultimately, *through his encounter with Western thought*. In particular, the unpublished papers of Frankenstein that the monster carries—proof of the greatest scientific breakthrough of all time, the "cure" for death—describe to the monster in bitter detail how hated he is by his creator. In other words, just as the monster begins to discover himself as a person through literature—and the novel gestures repeatedly toward the *bildungsroman*, or, "coming of age story,"—Shelley decimates this positive potentiality by bringing in the scientist's notes on his creation, notes that consign his creation to monstrous Otherness. Shelley here takes on Enlightenment ideas of how to educate the young and twists them out of frame by hypothesizing a young person—remember that the monster is newly born—who shares no visual attributes that excite the sympathy of other human beings. Her monster becomes the test case by which she gives the lie to idealized theories of human perfectibility precisely because he is so extraordinarily intelligent and sensitive.

2. The monster, in the previous passages, is changed forever by the cruelty of the De Lacey family, who see him as a monster because of his appearance and do not make any attempt whatsoever to understand him. The narrative building up to this crushing revelation of human shallowness is critical to understanding Shelley's novel. The monster describes himself in terms that align with Jean-Jacques Rousseau's key Enlightenment argument, in *Émile*, that nature is the best teacher, that feeling for nature and the influence of nature produce the purest exemplar of humanity. The monster's reactions to nature show that he is just such a noble person—he loves the natural world, and is moved to tender melancholy by autumn, even though his superhuman constitution allows him to tolerate cold without difficulty. So deeply sensitive to nature, even so the monster is not perceived by human beings as noble, nor of delicate sensibility. Instead, human beings respond only to his appearance: larger and differently formed from themselves.

Shelley suggests, here, that Rousseau's idealization of isolation belies our fundamental need for community, to be connected with others through benevolent reciprocity—something the monster never receives. When the monster saves a young child from drowning, human beings responding to his appearance—not his actions—shoot him with a gun, wounding him, and changing him. The De Lacey family likewise respond with violent repulsion to the monster because they find him ugly, even though he has gently and generously loved and cared for them. ◄

CHAPTER 16

CURSED, CURSED CREATOR! Why did I live? Why, in that instant, did I not extinguish the spark of existence which you had so wantonly bestowed? I know not; despair had not yet taken possession of me; my feelings were those of rage and revenge. I could with pleasure have destroyed the cottage and its inhabitants and have glutted myself with their shrieks and misery.

"When night came I quitted my retreat and wandered in the wood; and now, no longer restrained by the fear of discovery, I gave vent to my anguish in fearful howlings. I was like a wild beast that had broken the toils, destroying the objects that obstructed me and ranging through the wood with a stag-like swiftness. Oh! What a miserable night I passed! The cold stars shone in mockery, and the bare trees waved their branches above me; now and then the sweet voice of a bird burst forth amidst the universal stillness. All, save I, were at rest or in enjoyment; I, like the arch-fiend, bore a hell within me, and finding myself unsympathized with, wished to tear up the trees, spread havoc and destruction around me, and then to have sat down and enjoyed the ruin.

"But this was a luxury of sensation that could not endure; I became fatigued with excess of bodily exertion and sank on the damp grass in the sick impotence of despair. There was none among the myriads of men that existed who would pity or assist me; and should I feel kindness towards my enemies? No; from that moment I declared everlasting war against the species, and more than all, against him who had formed me and sent me forth to this insupportable misery.

"The sun rose; I heard the voices of men and knew that it was impossible to return to my retreat during that day. Accordingly I hid myself in some thick underwood, determining to devote the ensuing hours to reflection on my situation.

"The pleasant sunshine and the pure air of day restored me to some degree of tranquillity; and when I considered what had passed at the cottage, I could not help believing that I had been too hasty in my conclusions. I had certainly acted imprudently. It was apparent that my conversation had interested the father in my behalf, and I was a fool in having exposed my person to the horror of his children. I ought to have familiarized the old De Lacey to me, and by degrees to have discovered myself to the rest of his family, when they should have been prepared for my approach. But I did not believe my errors to be irretrievable, and after much consideration I resolved to return to the cottage, seek the old man, and by my representations win him to my party.

"These thoughts calmed me, and in the afternoon I sank into a profound sleep; but the fever of my blood did not allow me to be visited by peaceful dreams. The horrible scene of the preceding day was forever acting before my eyes; the females were flying and the enraged Felix tearing me from his father's feet. I awoke exhausted, and finding that it was already night, I crept forth from my hiding-place, and went in search of food.

"When my hunger was appeased, I directed my steps towards the well-known path that conducted to the cottage. All there was at peace. I crept into my hovel and remained in silent expectation of the accustomed hour when the family arose. That hour passed, the sun mounted high in the heavens, but the cottagers did not appear. I trembled violently, apprehending some dreadful misfortune. The inside of the cottage was dark, and I heard no motion; I cannot describe the agony of this suspense.

"Presently two countrymen passed by, but pausing near the cottage, they entered into conversation, using violent gesticulations; but I did not understand what they said, as they spoke the language of the country, which differed from that of my protectors. Soon after, however, Felix approached with another man; I was surprised, as I knew that he had not quitted the cottage that morning, and waited anxiously to discover from his discourse the meaning of these unusual appearances.

"'Do you consider,' said his companion to him, 'that you will be obliged to pay three months' rent and to lose the produce of your garden? I do not wish to take any unfair advantage, and I beg therefore that you will take some days to consider of your determination.'

"'It is utterly useless,' replied Felix; 'we can never again inhabit your cottage. The life of my father is in the greatest danger, owing to the dreadful circumstance that I have related. My wife and my sister will never recover from their horror. I entreat you not to reason with me any more. Take possession of your tenement and let me fly from this place.'

"Felix trembled violently as he said this. He and his companion entered the cottage, in which they remained for a few minutes, and then departed. I never saw any of the family of De Lacey more.

"I continued for the remainder of the day in my hovel in a state of utter and stupid despair. My protectors had departed and had broken the only link that held me to the world. For the first time the feelings of revenge and hatred filled my bosom, and I did not strive to control them, but allowing myself to be borne away by the stream, I bent my mind towards injury and death. When I thought of my friends, of the mild voice of De Lacey, the gentle eyes of Agatha, and the exquisite beauty of the Arabian, these thoughts vanished and a gush of tears somewhat soothed me. But again when I reflected that they had spurned and deserted me, anger returned, a rage of anger, and unable to injure anything human, I turned my fury towards inanimate objects. As night advanced I placed a variety of combustibles around the cottage, and after having destroyed every vestige of cultivation in the garden, I waited with forced impatience until the moon had sunk to commence my operations.

"As the night advanced, a fierce wind arose from the woods and quickly dispersed the clouds that had loitered in the heavens; the blast tore along like a mighty avalanche and produced a kind of insanity in my spirits that burst all bounds of reason and reflection. I lighted the dry branch of a tree and danced with fury around the devoted cottage, my eyes still fixed on the western horizon, the edge of which the moon nearly touched. A part of its orb was at length hid, and I waved my brand; it sank, and with a loud scream I fired the straw, and heath, and bushes, which I had collected. The wind fanned the fire, and the cottage was quickly enveloped by the flames, which clung to it and licked it with their forked and destroying tongues.

"As soon as I was convinced that no assistance could save any part of the habitation, I quitted the scene and sought for refuge in the woods.

"And now, with the world before me, whither should I bend my steps? I resolved to fly far from the scene of my misfortunes; but to me, hated and despised, every country must be equally horrible. At length the thought of you crossed my mind. I learned from your papers that you were my father, my creator; and to whom could I apply with more fitness than to him who had given me life? Among the lessons that Felix had bestowed upon Safie, geography had not been omitted; I had learned from these the relative situations of the different countries of the earth. You had mentioned Geneva as the name of your native town, and towards this place I resolved to proceed.

"But how was I to direct myself? I knew that I must travel in a southwesterly direction to reach my destination, but the sun was my only guide. I did not know the names of the towns that I was to pass through, nor could I ask information from a single human being; but I did not despair. From you only could I hope for succour, although towards you I felt no sentiment but that of hatred. Unfeeling, heartless creator! You had endowed me with perceptions and passions and then cast me abroad an object for the scorn and horror of mankind. But on you only had I any claim for pity and redress, and from you I determined to seek that justice which I vainly attempted to gain from any other being that wore the human form.

"My travels were long and the sufferings I endured intense. It was late in autumn when I quitted the district where I had so long resided. I travelled only at night, fearful of encountering the visage of a human being. Nature decayed around me, and the sun became heatless; rain and snow poured around me; mighty rivers were frozen; the surface of the earth was hard and chill, and bare, and I found no shelter. Oh, earth! How often did I imprecate curses on the cause of my being! The mildness of my nature had fled, and all within me was turned to gall and bitterness. The nearer I approached to your habitation, the more deeply did I feel the spirit of revenge enkindled in my heart. Snow fell, and the waters were hardened, but I rested not. A few incidents now and then directed me, and I possessed a map of the country; but I often wandered wide from my path. The agony of my feelings allowed me no respite; no incident occurred from which my rage and misery could not extract its food; but a circumstance that happened when I arrived on the confines of Switzerland, when the sun had recovered its warmth and the earth again began to look green, confirmed in an especial manner the bitterness and horror of my feelings.

"I generally rested during the day and travelled only when I was secured by night from the view of man. One morning, however, finding that my path lay through a deep wood, I ventured to continue my journey after the sun had risen; the day, which was one of the first of spring, cheered even me by the loveliness of its sunshine and the balminess of the air. I felt emotions of gentleness and pleasure, that had long appeared dead, revive within me. Half surprised by the novelty of these sensations, I allowed myself to be borne away by them, and forgetting my solitude and deformity, dared to be happy. Soft tears again bedewed my cheeks, and I even raised my humid eyes with thankfulness towards the blessed sun, which bestowed such joy upon me.

"I continued to wind among the paths of the wood, until I came to its boundary, which was skirted by a deep and rapid river, into which many of the trees bent their branches, now budding with the fresh spring. Here I paused, not exactly knowing what path to pursue, when I heard the sound of voices, that induced me to conceal myself under the shade of a cypress. I was scarcely hid when a young girl came running towards the spot where I was concealed, laughing, as if she ran from someone in sport. She continued her course along the precipitous sides of the river, when suddenly her foot slipped, and she fell into the rapid stream. I rushed from my hiding-place and with extreme labour, from the force of the current, saved her and dragged her to shore. She was senseless, and I endeavoured by every means in my power to restore animation, when I was suddenly interrupted by the approach of a rustic, who was probably the person from whom she had playfully fled. On seeing me, he darted towards me, and tearing the girl from my arms, hastened towards the deeper parts of the wood. I followed speedily, I hardly knew why; but when the man saw me draw near, he aimed a gun, which he carried, at my body and fired. I sank to the ground, and my injurer, with increased swiftness, escaped into the wood.

"This was then the reward of my benevolence! I had saved a human being from destruction, and as a recompense I now writhed under the miserable pain of a wound which shattered the flesh and bone. The feelings of kindness and gentleness which I had entertained but a few moments before gave place to hellish rage and gnashing of teeth. Inflamed by pain, I vowed eternal hatred and vengeance to all mankind. But the agony of my wound overcame me; my pulses paused, and I fainted.

"For some weeks I led a miserable life in the woods, endeavouring to cure the wound which I had received. The ball had entered my shoulder, and I knew not whether it had remained there or passed through; at any rate I had no means of extracting it. My sufferings were augmented also by the oppressive sense of the injustice and ingratitude of their infliction. My daily vows rose for revenge—a deep and deadly revenge, such as would alone compensate for the outrages and anguish I had endured.

"After some weeks my wound healed, and I continued my journey. The labours I endured were no longer to be alleviated by the bright sun or gentle breezes of spring; all joy was but a mockery which insulted my desolate state and made me feel more painfully that I was not made for the enjoyment of pleasure.

"But my toils now drew near a close, and in two months from this time I reached the environs of Geneva.

"It was evening when I arrived, and I retired to a hiding-place among the fields that surround it to meditate in what manner I should apply to you. I was oppressed by fatigue and hunger and far too unhappy to enjoy the gentle breezes of evening or the prospect of the sun setting behind the stupendous mountains of Jura.

"At this time a slight sleep relieved me from the pain of reflection, which was disturbed by the approach of a beautiful child, who came running into the recess I had chosen, with all the sportiveness of infancy. Suddenly, as I gazed on him, an idea seized me that this little creature was unprejudiced and had lived too short a time to have imbibed a horror of deformity. If, therefore, I could seize him and educate him as my companion and friend, I should not be so desolate in this peopled earth.

"Urged by this impulse, I seized on the boy as he passed and drew him towards me. As soon as he beheld my form, he placed his hands before his eyes and uttered a shrill scream; I drew his hand forcibly from his face and said, 'Child, what is the meaning of this? I do not intend to hurt you; listen to me.'

"He struggled violently. 'Let me go,' he cried; 'monster! Ugly wretch! You wish to eat me and tear me to pieces. You are an ogre. Let me go, or I will tell my papa.'

"'Boy, you will never see your father again; you must come with me.'

"'Hideous monster! Let me go. My papa is a syndic—he is M. Franken-stein—he will punish you. You dare not keep me.'

"'Frankenstein! you belong then to my enemy—to him towards whom I have sworn eternal revenge; you shall be my first victim.'

"The child still struggled and loaded me with epithets which carried despair to my heart; I grasped his throat to silence him, and in a moment he lay dead at my feet.

"I gazed on my victim, and my heart swelled with exultation and hellish triumph; clapping my hands, I exclaimed, 'I too can create desolation; my enemy is not invulnerable; this death will carry despair to him, and a thousand other miseries shall torment and destroy him.'

"As I fixed my eyes on the child, I saw something glittering on his breast. I took it; it was a portrait of a most lovely woman. In spite of my malignity, it softened and attracted me. For a few moments I gazed with delight on her dark eyes, fringed by deep lashes, and her lovely lips; but presently my rage returned; I remembered that I was forever deprived of the delights that such beautiful creatures could bestow and that she whose resemblance I contemplated would, in regarding me, have changed that air of divine benignity to one expressive of disgust and affright.

"Can you wonder that such thoughts transported me with rage? I only wonder that at that moment, instead of venting my sensations in exclamations and agony, I did not rush among mankind and perish in the attempt to destroy them.

"While I was overcome by these feelings, I left the spot where I had com-mitted the murder, and seeking a more secluded hiding-place, I entered a barn which had appeared to me to be empty. A woman was sleeping on some straw; she was young, not indeed so beautiful as her whose portrait I held, but of an agreeable aspect and blooming in the loveliness of youth and health. Here, I thought, is one of those whose joy-imparting smiles are bestowed on all but me. And then I bent over her and whispered, 'Awake, fairest, thy lover is near — he who would give his life but to obtain one look of affection from thine eyes; my beloved, awake!'

"The sleeper stirred; a thrill of terror ran through me. Should she indeed awake, and see me, and curse me, and denounce the murderer? Thus would she assuredly act if her darkened eyes opened and she beheld me. The thought was madness; it stirred the fiend within me — not I, but she, shall suffer; the murder I have committed because I am forever robbed of all that she could give me, she shall atone. The crime had its source in her; be hers the punishment! Thanks to the lessons of Felix and the sanguinary laws of man, I had learned now to work mischief. I bent over her and placed the portrait securely in one of the folds of her dress. She moved again, and I fled.

"For some days I haunted the spot where these scenes had taken place, sometimes wishing to see you, sometimes resolved to quit the world and its miseries forever. At length I wandered towards these mountains, and have ranged through their immense recesses, consumed by a burning passion which you alone can gratify. We may not part until you have promised to comply with my requisition. I am alone and miserable; man will not associate with me; but one as deformed and horrible as myself would not deny herself to me. My companion must be of the same species and have the same defects. This being you must create." ◄

CHAPTER 17

T HE BEING FINISHED SPEAKING and fixed his looks upon me in the expectation of a reply. But I was bewildered, perplexed, and unable to arrange my ideas sufficiently to understand the full extent of his proposition. He continued,

"You must create a female for me with whom I can live in the interchange of those sympathies necessary for my being. This you alone can do, and I demand it of you as a right which you must not refuse to concede."

The latter part of his tale had kindled anew in me the anger that had died away while he narrated his peaceful life among the cottagers, and as he said this I could no longer suppress the rage that burned within me.

"I do refuse it," I replied; "and no torture shall ever extort a consent from me. You may render me the most miserable of men, but you shall never make me base in my own eyes. Shall I create another like yourself, whose joint wickedness might desolate the world. Begone! I have answered you; you may torture me, but I will never consent."

"You are in the wrong," replied the fiend; "and instead of threatening, I am content to reason with you. I am malicious because I am miserable. Am I not shunned and hated by all mankind? You, my creator, would tear me to pieces and triumph; remember that, and tell me why I should pity man more than he pities me? You would not call it murder if you could precipitate me into one of those ice-rifts and destroy my frame, the work of your own hands. Shall I respect man when he condemns me? Let him live with me in the interchange of kindness, and instead of injury I would bestow every benefit upon him with tears of gratitude at his acceptance. But that cannot be; the human senses are insurmountable barriers to our union. Yet mine shall not be the submission of abject slavery. I will revenge my injuries; if I cannot inspire love, I will cause fear, and chiefly towards you my arch-enemy, because my creator, do I swear inextinguishable hatred. Have a care; I will work at your destruction, nor finish until I desolate your heart, so that you shall curse the hour of your birth."

A fiendish rage animated him as he said this; his face was wrinkled into contortions too horrible for human eyes to behold; but presently he calmed himself and proceeded—

"I intended to reason. This passion is detrimental to me, for you do not reflect that YOU are the cause of its excess. If any being felt emotions of benevolence towards me, I should return them a hundred and a hundredfold; for that one creature's sake I would make peace with the whole kind! But I now indulge in dreams of bliss that cannot be realized. What I ask of you is reasonable and moderate; I demand a creature of another sex, but as hideous as myself; the gratification is small, but it is all that I can receive, and it shall content me. It is true, we shall be monsters, cut off from all the world; but on that account we shall be more attached to one another. Our lives will not be happy, but they will be harmless and free from the misery I now feel. Oh! My creator, make me happy; let me feel gratitude towards you for one benefit! Let me see that I excite the sympathy of some existing thing; do not deny me my request!"

I was moved. I shuddered when I thought of the possible consequences of my consent, but I felt that there was some justice in his argument. His tale and the feelings he now expressed proved him to be a creature of fine sensations, and did I not as his maker owe him all the portion of happiness that it was in my power to bestow? He saw my change of feeling and continued,

"If you consent, neither you nor any other human being shall ever see us again; I will go to the vast wilds of South America. My food is not that of man; I do not destroy the lamb and the kid to glut my appetite; acorns and berries afford me sufficient nourishment. My companion will be of the same nature as myself and will be content with the same fare. We shall make our bed of dried leaves; the sun will shine on us as on man and will ripen our food. The picture I present to you is peaceful and human, and you must feel that you could deny it only in the wantonness of power and cruelty. Pitiless as you have been towards me, I now see compassion in your eyes; let me seize the favourable moment and persuade you to promise what I so ardently desire."

"You propose," replied I, "to fly from the habitations of man, to dwell in those wilds where the beasts of the field will be your only companions. How can you, who long for the love and sympathy of man, persevere in this exile? You will return and again seek their kindness, and you will meet with their detestation; your evil passions will be renewed, and you will then have a companion to aid you in the task of destruction. This may not be; cease to argue the point, for I cannot consent."

"How inconstant are your feelings! But a moment ago you were moved by my representations, and why do you again harden yourself to my complaints? I swear to you, by the earth which I inhabit, and by you that made me, that with the companion you bestow I will quit the neighbourhood of man and dwell, as it may chance, in the most savage of places. My evil passions will have fled, for I shall meet with sympathy! My life will flow quietly away, and in my dying moments I shall not curse my maker."

His words had a strange effect upon me. I compassionated him and sometimes felt a wish to console him, but when I looked upon him, when I saw the filthy mass that moved and talked, my heart sickened and my feelings were altered to those of horror and hatred. I tried to stifle these sensations; I thought that as I could not sympathize with him, I had no right to withhold from him the small portion of happiness which was yet in my power to bestow.

"You swear," I said, "to be harmless; but have you not already shown a degree of malice that should reasonably make me distrust you? May not even this be a feint that will increase your triumph by affording a wider scope for your revenge?"

"How is this? I must not be trifled with, and I demand an answer. If I have no ties and no affections, hatred and vice must be my portion; the love of another will destroy the cause of my crimes, and I shall become a thing of whose existence everyone will be ignorant. My vices are the children of a forced solitude that I abhor, and my virtues will necessarily arise when I live in communion with an equal. I shall feel the affections of a sensitive being and become linked to the chain of existence and events from which I am now excluded."[1]

I paused some time to reflect on all he had related and the various arguments which he had employed. I thought of the promise of virtues which he had displayed on the opening of his existence and the subsequent blight of all kindly feeling by the loathing and scorn which his protectors had manifested towards him. His power and threats were not omitted in my calculations; a creature who could exist in the ice caves of the glaciers and hide himself from pursuit among the ridges of inaccessible precipices was a being possessing faculties it would be vain to cope with. After a long pause of reflection I concluded that the justice due both to him and my fellow creatures demanded of me that I should comply with his request. Turning to him, therefore, I said,

"I consent to your demand, on your solemn oath to quit Europe forever, and every other place in the neighbourhood of man, as soon as I shall deliver into your hands a female who will accompany you in your exile."

"I swear," he cried, "by the sun, and by the blue sky of heaven, and by the fire of love that burns my heart, that if you grant my prayer, while they exist you shall never behold me again. Depart to your home and commence your labours; I shall watch their progress with unutterable anxiety; and fear not but that when you are ready I shall appear."

Saying this, he suddenly quitted me, fearful, perhaps, of any change in my sentiments. I saw him descend the mountain with greater speed than the flight of an eagle, and quickly lost among the undulations of the sea of ice.

His tale had occupied the whole day, and the sun was upon the verge of the horizon when he departed. I knew that I ought to hasten my descent towards the valley, as I should soon be encompassed in darkness; but my heart was heavy, and my steps slow. The labour of winding among the little paths of the mountain and fixing my feet firmly as I advanced perplexed me, occupied as I was by the emotions which the occurrences of the day had produced. Night was far advanced when I came to the halfway resting-place and seated myself beside the fountain. The stars shone at intervals as the clouds passed from over them; the dark pines rose before me, and every here and there a broken tree lay on the ground; it was a scene of wonderful solemnity and stirred strange thoughts within me. I wept bitterly, and clasping my hands in agony, I exclaimed, "Oh! Stars and clouds and winds, ye are all about to mock me; if ye really pity me, crush sensation and memory; let me become as nought; but if not, depart, depart, and leave me in darkness."

These were wild and miserable thoughts, but I cannot describe to you how the eternal twinkling of the stars weighed upon me and how I listened to every blast of wind as if it were a dull ugly siroc on its way to consume me.

Morning dawned before I arrived at the village of Chamounix; I took no rest, but returned immediately to Geneva. Even in my own heart I could give no expression to my sensations — they weighed on me with a mountain's weight and their excess destroyed my agony beneath them. Thus I returned home, and entering the house, presented myself to the family. My haggard and wild appearance awoke intense alarm, but I answered no question, scarcely did I speak. I felt as if I were placed under a ban — as if I had no right to claim their sympathies — as if never more might I enjoy companionship with them. Yet even thus I loved them to adoration; and to save them, I resolved to dedicate myself to my most abhorred task. The prospect of such an occupation made every other circumstance of existence pass before me like a dream, and that thought only had to me the reality of life. ◄

CHAPTER 17
Annotations

1. The monster, after describing to Victor his murder of Victor's infant brother, states that he has become murderous because no one on earth loves him, no one returns his affection. It is interesting to note that psychologist Donald Winnicott (1896-1971) in the twentieth century theorized that infants develop the capacity for empathy, and kindness, and morality, by seeing in the faces of their parents (Winnicott was particularly concerned with the mother's role) expressions of pleasure and warmth directed toward the child. Winnicott called this parental gentleness a "holding" environment. Shelley predicts Winnicott's theory by a century and more when the monster explains to Frankenstein that precisely the fact that he has never been seen by any other creature as worthy of love causes him to behave murderously. The monster asks Frankenstein to create a female monster for him to love, whom he assumes will also love him. Here, Shelley at once empathizes with the monster's plight but also, simultaneously, points to the denigrated subject position of woman: she who is created to serve at another's pleasure, to mirror pleasure for the male subject. ◄

CHAPTER 18

D AY AFTER DAY, WEEK AFTER WEEK, passed away on my return to Geneva; and I could not collect the courage to recommence my work. I feared the vengeance of the disappointed fiend, yet I was unable to overcome my repugnance to the task which was enjoined me. I found that I could not compose a female without again devoting several months to profound study and laborious disquisition. I had heard of some discoveries having been made by an English philosopher, the knowledge of which was material to my success, and I sometimes thought of obtaining my father's consent to visit England for this purpose; but I clung to every pretence of delay and shrank from taking the first step in an undertaking whose immediate necessity began to appear less absolute to me. A change indeed had taken place in me; my health, which had hitherto declined, was now much restored; and my spirits, when unchecked by the memory of my unhappy promise, rose proportionably. My father saw this change with pleasure, and he turned his thoughts towards the best method of eradicating the remains of my melancholy, which every now and then would return by fits, and with a devouring blackness overcast the approaching sunshine. At these moments I took refuge in the most perfect solitude. I passed whole days on the lake alone in a little boat, watching the clouds and listening to the rippling of the waves, silent and listless. But the fresh air and bright sun seldom failed to restore me to some degree of composure, and on my return I met the salutations of my friends with a readier smile and a more cheerful heart.

It was after my return from one of these rambles that my father, calling me aside, thus addressed me,

"I am happy to remark, my dear son, that you have resumed your former pleasures and seem to be returning to yourself. And yet you are still unhappy and still avoid our society. For some time I was lost in conjecture as to the cause of this, but yesterday an idea struck me, and if it is well founded, I conjure you to avow it. Reserve on such a point would be not only useless, but draw down treble misery on us all."

I trembled violently at his exordium, and my father continued — "I confess, my son, that I have always looked forward to your marriage with our dear Elizabeth as the tie of our domestic comfort and the stay of my declining years. You were attached to each other from your earliest infancy; you studied together, and appeared, in dispositions and tastes, entirely suited to one another. But so blind is the experience of man that what I conceived to be the best assistants to my plan may have entirely destroyed it. You, perhaps, regard her as your sister, without any wish that she might become your wife. Nay, you may have met with another whom you may love; and considering yourself as bound in honour to Elizabeth, this struggle may occasion the poignant misery which you appear to feel."

"My dear father, reassure yourself. I love my cousin tenderly and sincerely. I never saw any woman who excited, as Elizabeth does, my warmest admiration and affection. My future hopes and prospects are entirely bound up in the expectation of our union."

"The expression of your sentiments of this subject, my dear Victor, gives me more pleasure than I have for some time experienced. If you feel thus, we shall assuredly be happy, however present events may cast a gloom over us. But it is this gloom which appears to have taken so strong a hold of your mind that I wish to dissipate. Tell me, therefore, whether you object to an immediate solemnization of the marriage. We have been unfortunate, and recent events have drawn us from that everyday tranquillity befitting my years and infirmities. You are younger; yet I do not suppose, possessed as you are of a competent fortune, that an early marriage would at all interfere with any future plans of honour and utility that you may have formed. Do not suppose, however, that I wish to dictate happiness to you or that a delay on your part would cause me any serious uneasiness. Interpret my words with candour and answer me, I conjure you, with confidence and sincerity."

I listened to my father in silence and remained for some time incapable of offering any reply. I revolved rapidly in my mind a multitude of thoughts and endeavoured to arrive at some conclusion. Alas! To me the idea of an immediate union with my Elizabeth was one of horror and dismay. I was bound by a solemn promise which I had not yet fulfilled and dared not break, or if I did, what manifold miseries might not impend over me and my devoted family! Could I enter into a festival with this deadly weight yet hanging round my neck and bowing me to the ground? I must perform my engagement and let the monster depart with his mate before I allowed myself to enjoy the delight of a union from which I expected peace.

I remembered also the necessity imposed upon me of either journeying to England or entering into a long correspondence with those philosophers of that country whose knowledge and discoveries were of indispensable use to me in my present undertaking. The latter method of obtaining the desired intelligence was dilatory and unsatisfactory; besides, I had an insurmountable aversion to the idea of engaging myself in my loathsome task in my father's house while in habits of familiar intercourse with those I loved. I knew that a thousand fearful accidents might occur, the slightest of which would disclose a tale to thrill all connected with me with horror. I was aware also that I should often lose all self-command, all capacity of hiding the harrowing sensations that would possess me during the progress of my unearthly occupation. I must absent myself from all I loved while thus employed. Once commenced, it would quickly be achieved, and I might be restored to my family in peace and happiness. My promise fulfilled, the monster would depart forever. Or (so my fond fancy imaged) some accident might meanwhile occur to destroy him and put an end to my slavery forever.

These feelings dictated my answer to my father. I expressed a wish to visit England, but concealing the true reasons of this request, I clothed my desires under a guise which excited no suspicion, while I urged my desire with an earnestness that easily induced my father to comply. After so long a period of an absorbing melancholy that resembled madness in its intensity and effects, he was glad to find that I was capable of taking pleasure in the idea of such a journey, and he hoped that change of scene and varied amusement would, before my return, have restored me entirely to myself.

The duration of my absence was left to my own choice; a few months, or at most a year, was the period contemplated. One paternal kind precaution he had taken to ensure my having a companion. Without previously communicating with me, he had, in concert with Elizabeth, arranged that Clerval should join me at Strasbourg. This interfered with the solitude I coveted for the prosecution of my task; yet at the commencement of my journey the presence of my friend could in no way be an impediment, and truly I rejoiced that thus I should be saved many hours of lonely, maddening reflection. Nay, Henry might stand between me and the intrusion of my foe. If I were alone, would he not at times force his abhorred presence on me to remind me of my task or to contemplate its progress?

To England, therefore, I was bound, and it was understood that my union with Elizabeth should take place immediately on my return. My father's age rendered him extremely averse to delay. For myself, there was one reward I promised myself from my detested toils—one consolation for my unparalleled sufferings; it was the prospect of that day when, enfranchised from my miserable slavery, I might claim Elizabeth and forget the past in my union with her.

I now made arrangements for my journey, but one feeling haunted me which filled me with fear and agitation. During my absence I should leave my friends unconscious of the existence of their enemy and unprotected from his attacks, exasperated as he might be by my departure. But he had promised to follow me wherever I might go, and would he not accompany me to England? This imagination was dreadful in itself, but soothing inasmuch as it supposed the safety of my friends. I was agonized with the idea of the possibility that the reverse of this might happen. But through the whole period during which I was the slave of my creature I allowed myself to be governed by the impulses of the moment; and my present sensations strongly intimated that the fiend would follow me and exempt my family from the danger of his machinations.

It was in the latter end of September that I again quitted my native country. My journey had been my own suggestion, and Elizabeth therefore acquiesced, but she was filled with disquiet at the idea of my suffering, away from her, the inroads of misery and grief. It had been her care which provided me a companion in Clerval—and yet a man is blind to a thousand minute circumstances which call forth a woman's sedulous attention. She longed to bid me hasten my return; a thousand conflicting emotions rendered her mute as she bade me a tearful, silent farewell.

I threw myself into the carriage that was to convey me away, hardly knowing whither I was going, and careless of what was passing around. I remembered only, and it was with a bitter anguish that I reflected on it, to order that my chemical instruments should be packed to go with me. Filled with dreary imaginations, I passed through many beautiful and majestic scenes, but my eyes were fixed and unobserving. I could only think of the bourne of my travels and the work which was to occupy me whilst they endured.

After some days spent in listless indolence, during which I traversed many leagues, I arrived at Strasbourg, where I waited two days for Clerval. He came. Alas, how great was the contrast between us! He was alive to every new scene, joyful when he saw the beauties of the setting sun, and more happy when he beheld it rise and recommence a new day. He pointed out to me the shifting colours of the landscape and the appearances of the sky. "This is what it is to live," he cried; "how I enjoy existence! But you, my dear Frankenstein, wherefore are you desponding and sorrowful!" In truth, I was occupied by gloomy thoughts and neither saw the descent of the evening star nor the golden sunrise reflected in the Rhine. And you, my friend, would be far more amused with the journal of Clerval, who observed the scenery with an eye of feeling and delight, than in listening to my reflections. I, a miserable wretch, haunted by a curse that shut up every avenue to enjoyment.

We had agreed to descend the Rhine in a boat from Strasbourg to Rotterdam, whence we might take shipping for London. During this voyage we passed many willowy islands and saw several beautiful towns. We stayed a day at Mannheim, and on the fifth from our departure from Strasbourg, arrived at Mainz. The course of the Rhine below Mainz becomes much more picturesque. The river descends rapidly and winds between hills, not high, but steep, and of beautiful forms. We saw many ruined castles standing on the edges of precipices, surrounded by black woods, high and inaccessible. This part of the Rhine, indeed, presents a singularly variegated landscape. In one spot you view rugged hills, ruined castles overlooking tremendous precipices, with the dark Rhine rushing beneath; and on the sudden turn of a promontory, flourishing vineyards with green sloping banks and a meandering river and populous towns occupy the scene.

We travelled at the time of the vintage and heard the song of the labourers as we glided down the stream. Even I, depressed in mind, and my spirits continually agitated by gloomy feelings, even I was pleased. I lay at the bottom of the boat, and as I gazed on the cloudless blue sky, I seemed to drink in a tranquillity to which I had long been a stranger. And if these were my sensations, who can describe those of Henry? He felt as if he had been transported to fairy-land and enjoyed a happiness seldom tasted by man. "I have seen," he said, "the most beautiful scenes of my own country; I have visited the lakes of Lucerne and Uri, where the snowy mountains descend almost perpendicularly to the water, casting black and impenetrable shades, which would cause a gloomy and mournful appearance were it not for the most verdant islands that believe the eye by their gay appearance; I have seen this lake agitated by a tempest, when the wind tore up whirlwinds of water and gave you an idea of what the water-spout must be on the great ocean; and the waves dash with fury the base of the mountain, where the priest and his mistress were overwhelmed by an avalanche and where their dying voices are still said to be heard amid the pauses of the nightly wind; I have seen the mountains of La Valais, and the Pays de Vaud; but this country, Victor, pleases me more than all those wonders. The mountains of Switzerland are more majestic and strange, but there is a charm in the banks of this divine river that I never before saw equalled. Look at that castle which overhangs yon precipice; and that also on the island, almost concealed amongst the foliage of those lovely trees; and now that group of labourers coming from among their vines; and that village half hid in the recess of the mountain. Oh, surely the spirit that inhabits and guards this place has a soul more in harmony with man than those who pile the glacier or retire to the inaccessible peaks of the mountains of our own country." Clerval! Beloved friend! Even now it delights me to record your words and to dwell on the praise of which you are so eminently deserving. He was a being formed in the "very poetry of nature." His wild and enthusiastic imagination was chastened by the sensibility of his heart. His soul overflowed with ardent affections, and his friendship was of that devoted and wondrous nature that the world-minded teach us to look for only in the imagination. But even human sympathies were not sufficient to satisfy his eager mind. The scenery of external nature, which others regard only with admiration, he loved with ardour: —

— The sounding cataract
Haunted him like a passion: the tall rock,
The mountain, and the deep and gloomy wood,
Their colours and their forms, were then to him
An appetite; a feeling, and a love,
That had no need of a remoter charm,
By thought supplied, or any interest
Unborrow'd from the eye.
Wordsworth's "Tintern Abbey".

And where does he now exist? Is this gentle and lovely being lost forever? Has this mind, so replete with ideas, imaginations fanciful and magnificent, which formed a world, whose existence depended on the life of its creator; — has this mind perished? Does it now only exist in my memory? No, it is not thus; your form so divinely wrought, and beaming with beauty, has decayed, but your spirit still visits and consoles your unhappy friend.

Pardon this gush of sorrow; these ineffectual words are but a slight tribute to the unexampled worth of Henry, but they soothe my heart, overflowing with the anguish which his remembrance creates. I will proceed with my tale.

Beyond Cologne we descended to the plains of Holland; and we resolved to post the remainder of our way, for the wind was contrary and the stream of the river was too gentle to aid us. Our journey here lost the interest arising from beautiful scenery, but we arrived in a few days at Rotterdam, whence we proceeded by sea to England. It was on a clear morning, in the latter days of December, that I first saw the white cliffs of Britain. The banks of the Thames presented a new scene; they were flat but fertile, and almost every town was marked by the remembrance of some story. We saw Tilbury Fort and remembered the Spanish

Armada, Gravesend, Woolwich, and Greenwich — places which I had heard of even in my country.

At length we saw the numerous steeples of London, St. Paul's towering above all, and the Tower famed in English history. ◄

CHAPTER 19

L ONDON WAS OUR PRESENT POINT of rest; we determined to remain several months in this wonderful and celebrated city. Clerval desired the intercourse of the men of genius and talent who flourished at this time, but this was with me a secondary object; I was principally occupied with the means of obtaining the information necessary for the completion of my promise and quickly availed myself of the letters of introduction that I had brought with me, addressed to the most distinguished natural philosophers.

If this journey had taken place during my days of study and happiness, it would have afforded me inexpressible pleasure. But a blight had come over my existence, and I only visited these people for the sake of the information they might give me on the subject in which my interest was so terribly profound. Company was irksome to me; when alone, I could fill my mind with the sights of heaven and earth; the voice of Henry soothed me, and I could thus cheat myself into a transitory peace. But busy, uninteresting, joyous faces brought back despair to my heart. I saw an insurmountable barrier placed between me and my fellow men; this barrier was sealed with the blood of William and Justine, and to reflect on the events connected with those names filled my soul with anguish.

But in Clerval I saw the image of my former self; he was inquisitive and anxious to gain experience and instruction. The difference of manners which he observed was to him an inexhaustible source of instruction and amusement. He was also pursuing an object he had long had in view. His design was to visit India, in the belief that he had in his knowledge of its various languages, and in the views he had taken of its society, the means of materially assisting the progress of European colonization and trade. In Britain only could he further the execution of his plan. He was forever busy, and the only check to his enjoyments was my sorrowful and dejected mind. I tried to conceal this as much as possible, that I might not debar him from the pleasures natural to one who was entering on a new scene of life, undisturbed by any care or bitter recollection. I often refused to accompany him, alleging another engagement, that I might remain alone. I now also began to collect the materials necessary for my new creation, and this was to me like the torture of single drops of water continually falling on the head. Every thought that was devoted to it was an extreme anguish, and every word that I spoke in allusion to it caused my lips to quiver, and my heart to palpitate.

After passing some months in London, we received a letter from a person in Scotland who had formerly been our visitor at Geneva. He mentioned the beauties of his native country and asked us if those were not sufficient allurements to induce us to prolong our journey as far north as Perth, where he resided. Clerval eagerly desired to accept this invitation, and I, although I abhorred society, wished to view again mountains and streams and all the wondrous works with which Nature adorns her chosen dwelling-places. We had arrived in England at the beginning of October, and it was now February. We accordingly determined to commence our journey towards the north at the expiration of another month. In this expedition we did not intend to follow the great road to Edinburgh, but to visit Windsor, Oxford, Matlock, and the Cumberland lakes, resolving to arrive at the completion of this tour about the end of July. I packed up my chemical instruments and the materials I had collected, resolving to finish my labours in some obscure nook in the northern highlands of Scotland.

We quitted London on the 27th of March and remained a few days at Windsor, rambling in its beautiful forest. This was a new scene to us mountaineers; the majestic oaks, the quantity of game, and the herds of stately deer were all novelties to us.

From thence we proceeded to Oxford. As we entered this city our minds were filled with the remembrance of the events that had been transacted there more than a century and a half before. It was here that Charles I. had collected his forces. This city had remained faithful to him, after the whole nation had forsaken his cause to join the standard of Parliament and liberty. The memory of that unfortunate king and his companions, the amiable Falkland, the insolent Goring, his queen, and son, gave a peculiar interest to every part of the city which they might be supposed to have inhabited. The spirit of elder days found a dwelling here, and we delighted to trace its footsteps. If these feelings had not found an imaginary gratification, the appearance of the city had yet in itself sufficient beauty to obtain our admiration. The colleges are ancient and picturesque; the streets are almost magnificent; and the lovely Isis, which flows beside it through meadows of exquisite verdure, is spread forth into a placid expanse of waters, which reflects its majestic assemblage of towers, and spires, and domes, embosomed among aged trees.

I enjoyed this scene, and yet my enjoyment was embittered both by the memory of the past and the anticipation of the future. I was formed for peaceful happiness. During my youthful days discontent never visited my mind, and if I was ever overcome by ennui, the sight of what is beautiful in nature or the study of what is excellent and sublime in the productions of man could always interest my heart and communicate elasticity to my spirits. But I am a blasted tree; the bolt has entered my soul; and I felt then that I should survive to exhibit what I shall soon cease to be—a miserable spectacle of wrecked humanity, pitiable to others and intolerable to myself.

We passed a considerable period at Oxford, rambling among its environs and endeavouring to identify every spot which might relate to the most animating epoch of English history. Our little voyages of discovery were often prolonged by the successive objects that presented themselves. We visited the tomb of the illustrious Hampden and the field on which that patriot fell. For a moment my soul was elevated from its debasing and miserable fears to contemplate the divine ideas of liberty and self sacrifice of which these sights were the monuments and the remembrancers. For an instant I dared to shake off my chains and look around me with a free and lofty spirit, but the iron had eaten into my flesh, and I sank again, trembling and hopeless, into my miserable self.

We left Oxford with regret and proceeded to Matlock, which was our next place of rest. The country in the neighbourhood of this village resembled, to a greater degree, the scenery of Switzerland; but everything is on a lower scale, and the green hills want the crown of distant white Alps which always attend on the piny mountains of my native country. We visited the wondrous cave and the little cabinets of natural history, where the curiosities are disposed in the same manner as in the collections at Servox and Chamounix. The latter name made me tremble when pronounced by Henry, and I hastened to quit Matlock, with which that terrible scene was thus associated.

From Derby, still journeying northwards, we passed two months in Cumberland and Westmorland. I could now almost fancy myself among the Swiss mountains. The little patches of snow which yet lingered on the northern sides of the mountains, the lakes, and the dashing of the rocky streams were all familiar and dear sights to me. Here also we made some acquaintances, who almost contrived to cheat me into happiness. The delight of Clerval was proportionably greater than mine; his mind expanded in the company of men of talent, and he found in his own nature greater capacities and resources than he could have imagined himself to have possessed while he associated with his inferiors. "I could pass my life here," said he to me; "and among these mountains I should scarcely regret Switzerland and the Rhine."

But he found that a traveller's life is one that includes much pain amidst its enjoyments. His feelings are forever on the stretch; and when he begins to sink into repose, he finds himself obliged to quit that on which he rests in pleasure for something new, which again engages his attention, and which also he forsakes for other novelties.

We had scarcely visited the various lakes of Cumberland and Westmorland and conceived an affection for some of the inhabitants when the period of our appointment with our Scotch friend approached, and we left them to travel on. For my own part I was not sorry. I had now neglected my promise for some time, and I feared the effects of the daemon's disappointment. He might remain in Switzerland and wreak his vengeance on my relatives. This idea pursued me and tormented me at every moment from which I might otherwise have snatched repose and peace. I waited for my letters with feverish impatience; if they were delayed I was miserable and overcome by a thousand fears; and when they arrived and I saw the superscription of Elizabeth or my father, I hardly dared to read and ascertain my fate. Sometimes I thought that the fiend followed me and might expedite my remissness by murdering my companion. When these thoughts possessed me, I would not quit Henry for a moment, but followed him as his shadow, to protect him from the fancied rage of his destroyer. I felt as if I had committed some great crime, the consciousness of which haunted me. I was guiltless, but I had indeed drawn down a horrible curse upon my head, as mortal as that of crime.

I visited Edinburgh with languid eyes and mind; and yet that city might have interested the most unfortunate being. Clerval did not like it so well as Oxford, for the antiquity of the latter city was more pleasing to him. But the beauty and regularity of the new town of Edinburgh, its romantic castle and its environs, the most delightful in the world, Arthur's Seat, St. Bernard's Well, and the Pentland Hills compensated him for the change and filled him with cheerfulness and admiration. But I was impatient to arrive at the termination of my journey.

We left Edinburgh in a week, passing through Coupar, St. Andrew's, and along the banks of the Tay, to Perth, where our friend expected us. But I was in no mood to laugh and talk with strangers or enter into their feelings or plans with the good humour expected from a guest; and accordingly I told Clerval that I wished to make the tour of Scotland alone. "Do you," said I, "enjoy yourself, and let this be our rendezvous. I may be absent a month or two; but do not interfere with my motions, I entreat you; leave me to peace and solitude for a short time; and when I return, I hope it will be with a lighter heart, more congenial to your own temper."

Henry wished to dissuade me, but seeing me bent on this plan, ceased to remonstrate. He entreated me to write often. "I had rather be with you," he said, "in your solitary rambles, than with these Scotch people, whom I do not know; hasten, then, my dear friend, to return, that I may again feel myself somewhat at home, which I cannot do in your absence."

Having parted from my friend, I determined to visit some remote spot of Scotland and finish my work in solitude. I did not doubt but that the monster followed me and would discover himself to me when I should have finished, that he might receive his companion. With this resolution I traversed the northern highlands and fixed on one of the remotest of the Orkneys as the scene of my labours. It was a place fitted for such a work, being hardly more than a rock whose high sides were continually beaten upon by the waves. The soil was barren, scarcely affording pasture for a few miserable cows, and oatmeal for its inhabitants, which consisted of five persons, whose gaunt and scraggy limbs gave tokens of their miserable fare. Vegetables and bread, when they indulged in such luxuries, and even fresh water, was to be procured from the mainland, which was about five miles distant.

On the whole island there were but three miserable huts, and one of these was vacant when I arrived. This I hired. It contained but two rooms, and these exhibited all the squalidness of the most miserable penury. The thatch had fallen in, the walls were unplastered, and the door was off its hinges. I ordered it to be repaired, bought some furniture, and took possession, an incident which would doubtless have occasioned some surprise had not all the senses of the cottagers been benumbed by want and squalid poverty. As it was, I lived ungazed at and unmolested, hardly thanked for the pittance of food and clothes which I gave, so much does suffering blunt even the coarsest sensations of men.

In this retreat I devoted the morning to labour; but in the evening, when the weather permitted, I walked on the stony beach of the sea to listen to the waves as they roared and dashed at my feet. It was a monotonous yet ever-changing scene. I thought of Switzerland; it was far different from this desolate and appalling landscape. Its hills are covered with vines, and its cottages are scattered thickly in the plains. Its fair lakes reflect a blue and gentle sky, and when troubled by the winds, their tumult is but as the play of a lively infant when compared to the roarings of the giant ocean.

In this manner I distributed my occupations when I first arrived, but as I proceeded in my labour, it became every day more horrible and irksome to me.

Sometimes I could not prevail on myself to enter my laboratory for several days, and at other times I toiled day and night in order to complete my work. It was, indeed, a filthy process in which I was engaged. During my first experiment, a kind of enthusiastic frenzy had blinded me to the horror of my employment; my mind was intently fixed on the consummation of my labour, and my eyes were shut to the horror of my proceedings. But now I went to it in cold blood, and my heart often sickened at the work of my hands.

Thus situated, employed in the most detestable occupation, immersed in a solitude where nothing could for an instant call my attention from the actual scene in which I was engaged, my spirits became unequal; I grew restless and nervous. Every moment I feared to meet my persecutor. Sometimes I sat with my eyes fixed on the ground, fearing to raise them lest they should encounter the object which I so much dreaded to behold. I feared to wander from the sight of my fellow creatures lest when alone he should come to claim his companion.

In the mean time I worked on, and my labour was already considerably advanced. I looked towards its completion with a tremulous and eager hope, which I dared not trust myself to question but which was intermixed with obscure forebodings of evil that made my heart sicken in my bosom. ◄

CHAPTER 20

I SAT ONE EVENING IN MY LABORATORY; the sun had set, and the moon was just rising from the sea; I had not sufficient light for my employment, and I remained idle, in a pause of consideration of whether I should leave my labour for the night or hasten its conclusion by an unremitting attention to it. As I sat, a train of reflection occurred to me which led me to consider the effects of what I was now doing. Three years before, I was engaged in the same manner and had created a fiend whose unparalleled barbarity had desolated my heart and filled it forever with the bitterest remorse. I was now about to form another being of whose dispositions I was alike ignorant; she might become ten thousand times more malignant than her mate and delight, for its own sake, in murder and wretchedness. He had sworn to quit the neighbourhood of man and hide himself in deserts, but she had not; and she, who in all probability was to become a thinking and reasoning animal, might refuse to comply with a compact made before her creation. They might even hate each other; the creature who already lived loathed his own deformity, and might he not conceive a greater abhorrence for it when it came before his eyes in the female form? She also might turn with disgust from him to the superior beauty of man; she might quit him, and he be again alone, exasperated by the fresh provocation of being deserted by one of his own species. Even if they were to leave Europe and inhabit the deserts of the new world, yet one of the first results of those sympathies for which the daemon thirsted would be children, and a race of devils would be propagated upon the earth who might make the very existence of the species of man a condition precarious and full of terror. Had I right, for my own benefit, to inflict this curse upon everlasting generations? I had before been moved by the sophisms of the being I had created; I had been struck senseless by his fiendish threats; but now, for the first time, the wickedness of my promise burst upon me; I shuddered to think that future ages might curse me as their pest, whose selfishness had not hesitated to buy its own peace at the price, perhaps, of the existence of the whole human race.

I trembled and my heart failed within me, when, on looking up, I saw by the light of the moon the daemon at the casement. A ghastly grin wrinkled his lips as he gazed on me, where I sat fulfilling the task which he had allotted to me. Yes, he had followed me in my travels; he had loitered in forests, hid himself in caves, or taken refuge in wide and desert heaths; and he now came to mark my progress and claim the fulfilment of my promise.

As I looked on him, his countenance expressed the utmost extent of malice and treachery. I thought with a sensation of madness on my promise of creating another like to him, and trembling with passion, tore to pieces the thing on which I was engaged. The wretch saw me destroy the creature on whose future existence he depended for happiness, and with a howl of devilish despair and revenge, withdrew.

I left the room, and locking the door, made a solemn vow in my own heart never to resume my labours; and then, with trembling steps, I sought my own apartment. I was alone; none were near me to dissipate the gloom and relieve me from the sickening oppression of the most terrible reveries.

Several hours passed, and I remained near my window gazing on the sea; it was almost motionless, for the winds were hushed, and all nature reposed under the eye of the quiet moon. A few fishing vessels alone specked the water, and now and then the gentle breeze wafted the sound of voices as the fishermen called to one another. I felt the silence, although I was hardly conscious of its extreme profundity, until my ear was suddenly arrested by the paddling of oars near the shore, and a person landed close to my house.

In a few minutes after, I heard the creaking of my door, as if some one endeavoured to open it softly. I trembled from head to foot; I felt a presentiment of who it was and wished to rouse one of the peasants who dwelt in a cottage not far from mine; but I was overcome by the sensation of helplessness, so often felt in frightful dreams, when you in vain endeavour to fly from an impending danger, and was rooted to the spot. Presently I heard the sound of footsteps along the passage; the door opened, and the wretch whom I dreaded appeared.

Shutting the door, he approached me and said in a smothered voice, "You have destroyed the work which you began; what is it that you intend? Do you dare to break your promise? I have endured toil and misery; I left Switzerland with you; I crept along the shores of the Rhine, among its willow islands and over the summits of its hills. I have dwelt many months in the heaths of England and among the deserts of Scotland. I have endured incalculable fatigue, and cold, and hunger; do you dare destroy my hopes?"

"Begone! I do break my promise; never will I create another like yourself, equal in deformity and wickedness."

"Slave, I before reasoned with you, but you have proved yourself unworthy of my condescension. Remember that I have power; you believe yourself miserable, but I can make you so wretched that the light of day will be hateful to you. You are my creator, but I am your master; obey!"

"The hour of my irresolution is past, and the period of your power is arrived. Your threats cannot move me to do an act of wickedness; but they confirm me in a determination of not creating you a companion in vice. Shall I, in cool blood, set loose upon the earth a daemon whose delight is in death and wretchedness? Begone! I am firm, and your words will only exasperate my rage."

The monster saw my determination in my face and gnashed his teeth in the impotence of anger. "Shall each man," cried he, "find a wife for his bosom, and each beast have his mate, and I be alone? I had feelings of affection, and they were requited by detestation and scorn. Man! You may hate, but beware! Your hours will pass in dread and misery, and soon the bolt will fall which must ravish from you your happiness forever. Are you to be happy while I grovel in the intensity of my wretchedness? You can blast my other passions, but revenge remains — revenge, henceforth dearer than light or food! I may die, but first you, my tyrant and tormentor, shall curse the sun that gazes on your misery. Beware, for I am fearless and therefore powerful. I will watch with the wiliness of a snake, that I may sting with its venom. Man, you shall repent of the injuries you inflict."

"Devil, cease; and do not poison the air with these sounds of malice. I have declared my resolution to you, and I am no coward to bend beneath words. Leave me; I am inexorable."

"It is well. I go; but remember, I shall be with you on your wedding-night."

I started forward and exclaimed, "Villain! Before you sign my death-warrant, be sure that you are yourself safe."

I would have seized him, but he eluded me and quitted the house with precipitation. In a few moments I saw him in his boat, which shot across the waters with an arrowy swiftness and was soon lost amidst the waves.

All was again silent, but his words rang in my ears. I burned with rage to pursue the murderer of my peace and precipitate him into the ocean. I walked up and down my room hastily and perturbed, while my imagination conjured up a thousand images to torment and sting me. Why had I not followed him and closed with him in mortal strife? But I had suffered him to depart, and he had directed his course towards the mainland. I shuddered to think who might be the next victim sacrificed to his insatiate revenge. And then I thought again of his words—"I WILL BE WITH YOU ON YOUR WEDDING-NIGHT." That, then, was the period fixed for the fulfilment of my destiny. In that hour I should die and at once satisfy and extinguish his malice. The prospect did not move me to fear; yet when I thought of my beloved Elizabeth, of her tears and endless sorrow, when she should find her lover so barbarously snatched from her, tears, the first I had shed for many months, streamed from my eyes, and I resolved not to fall before my enemy without a bitter struggle.

The night passed away, and the sun rose from the ocean; my feelings became calmer, if it may be called calmness when the violence of rage sinks into the depths of despair. I left the house, the horrid scene of the last night's contention, and walked on the beach of the sea, which I almost regarded as an insuperable barrier between me and my fellow creatures; nay, a wish that such should prove the fact stole across me.

I desired that I might pass my life on that barren rock, wearily, it is true, but uninterrupted by any sudden shock of misery. If I returned, it was to be sacrificed or to see those whom I most loved die under the grasp of a daemon whom I had myself created.[1]

I walked about the isle like a restless spectre, separated from all it loved and miserable in the separation. When it became noon, and the sun rose higher, I lay down on the grass and was overpowered by a deep sleep. I had been awake the whole of the preceding night, my nerves were agitated, and my eyes inflamed by watching and misery. The sleep into which I now sank refreshed me; and when I awoke, I again felt as if I belonged to a race of human beings like myself, and I began to reflect upon what had passed with greater composure; yet still the words of the fiend rang in my ears like a death-knell; they appeared like a dream, yet distinct and oppressive as a reality.

The sun had far descended, and I still sat on the shore, satisfying my appetite, which had become ravenous, with an oaten cake, when I saw a fishing-boat land close to me, and one of the men brought me a packet; it contained letters from Geneva, and one from Clerval entreating me to join him. He said that he was wearing away his time fruitlessly where he was, that letters from the friends he had formed in London desired his return to complete the negotiation they had entered into for his Indian enterprise. He could not any longer delay his departure; but as his journey to London might be followed, even sooner than he now conjectured, by his longer voyage, he entreated me to bestow as much of my society on him as I could spare. He besought me, therefore, to leave my solitary isle and to meet him at Perth, that we might proceed southwards together. This letter in a degree recalled me to life, and I determined to quit my island at the expiration of two days. Yet, before I departed, there was a task to perform, on which I shuddered to reflect; I must pack up my chemical instruments, and for that purpose I must enter the room which had been the scene of my odious work, and I must handle those utensils the sight of which was sickening to me. The next morning, at daybreak, I summoned sufficient courage and unlocked the door of my laboratory. The remains of the half-finished creature, whom I had destroyed, lay scattered on the floor, and I almost felt as if I had mangled the living flesh of a human being. I paused to collect myself and then entered the chamber. With trembling hand I conveyed the instruments out of the room, but I reflected that I ought not to leave the relics of my work to excite the horror and suspicion of the peasants; and I accordingly put them into a basket, with a great quantity of stones, and laying them up, determined to throw them into the sea that very night; and in the meantime I sat upon the beach, employed in cleaning and arranging my chemical apparatus.

Nothing could be more complete than the alteration that had taken place in my feelings since the night of the appearance of the daemon. I had before regarded my promise with a gloomy despair as a thing that, with whatever consequences, must be fulfilled; but I now felt as if a film had been taken from before my eyes and that I for the first time saw clearly. The idea of renewing my labours did not for one instant occur to me; the threat I had heard weighed on my thoughts, but I did not reflect that a voluntary act of mine could avert it. I had resolved in my own mind that to create another like the fiend I had first made would be an act of the basest and most atrocious selfishness, and I banished from my mind every thought that could lead to a different conclusion.

Between two and three in the morning the moon rose; and I then, putting my basket aboard a little skiff, sailed out about four miles from the shore. The scene was perfectly solitary; a few boats were returning towards land, but I sailed away from them. I felt as if I was about the commission of a dreadful crime and avoided with shuddering anxiety any encounter with my fellow creatures. At one time the moon, which had before been clear, was suddenly overspread by a thick cloud, and I took advantage of the moment of darkness and cast my basket into the sea; I listened to the gurgling sound as it sank and then sailed away from the spot. The sky became clouded, but the air was pure, although chilled by the northeast breeze that was then rising. But it refreshed me and filled me with such agreeable sensations that I resolved to prolong my stay on the water, and fixing the rudder in a direct position, stretched myself at the bottom of the boat. Clouds hid the moon, everything was obscure, and I heard only the sound of the boat as its keel cut through the waves; the murmur lulled me, and in a short time I slept soundly. I do not know how long I remained in this situation, but when I awoke I found that the sun had already mounted considerably. The wind was high, and the waves continually threatened the safety of my little skiff. I found that the wind was northeast and must have driven me far from the coast from which I had embarked. I endeavoured to change my course but quickly found that if I again made the attempt the boat would be instantly filled with water. Thus situated, my only resource was to drive before the wind. I confess that I felt a few sensations of terror. I had no compass with me and was so slenderly acquainted with the geography of this part of the world that the sun was of little benefit to me. I might be driven into the wide Atlantic and feel all the tortures of starvation or be swallowed up in the immeasurable waters that roared and buffeted around me. I had already been out many hours and felt the torment of a burning thirst, a prelude to my other sufferings. I looked on the heavens, which were covered by clouds that flew before the wind, only to be replaced by others; I looked upon the sea; it was to be my grave. "Fiend," I exclaimed, "your task is already fulfilled!" I thought of Elizabeth, of my father, and of Clerval—all left behind, on whom the monster might satisfy his sanguinary and merciless passions. This idea plunged me into a reverie so despairing and frightful that even now, when the scene is on the point of closing before me forever, I shudder to reflect on it.

Some hours passed thus; but by degrees, as the sun declined towards the horizon, the wind died away into a gentle breeze and the sea became free from breakers. But these gave place to a heavy swell; I felt sick and hardly able to hold the rudder, when suddenly I saw a line of high land towards the south.

Almost spent, as I was, by fatigue and the dreadful suspense I endured for several hours, this sudden certainty of life rushed like a flood of warm joy to my heart, and tears gushed from my eyes.

How mutable are our feelings, and how strange is that clinging love we have of life even in the excess of misery! I constructed another sail with a part of my dress and eagerly steered my course towards the land. It had a wild and rocky appearance, but as I approached nearer I easily perceived the traces of cultivation. I saw vessels near the shore and found myself suddenly transported back to the neighbourhood of civilized man. I carefully traced the windings of the land and hailed a steeple which I at length saw issuing from behind a small promontory. As I was in a state of extreme debility, I resolved to sail directly towards the town, as a place where I could most easily procure nourishment. Fortunately I had money with me.

As I turned the promontory I perceived a small neat town and a good harbour, which I entered, my heart bounding with joy at my unexpected escape.

As I was occupied in fixing the boat and arranging the sails, several people crowded towards the spot. They seemed much surprised at my appearance, but instead of offering me any assistance, whispered together with gestures that at any other time might have produced in me a slight sensation of alarm. As it was, I merely remarked that they spoke English, and I therefore addressed them in that language. "My good friends," said I, "will you be so kind as to tell me the name of this town and inform me where I am?"

"You will know that soon enough," replied a man with a hoarse voice. "Maybe you are come to a place that will not prove much to your taste, but you will not be consulted as to your quarters, I promise you."

I was exceedingly surprised on receiving so rude an answer from a stranger, and I was also disconcerted on perceiving the frowning and angry countenances of his companions. "Why do you answer me so roughly?" I replied. "Surely it is not the custom of Englishmen to receive strangers so inhospitably."

"I do not know," said the man, "what the custom of the English may be, but it is the custom of the Irish to hate villains." While this strange dialogue continued, I perceived the crowd rapidly increase. Their faces expressed a mixture of curiosity and anger, which annoyed and in some degree alarmed me.

I inquired the way to the inn, but no one replied. I then moved forward, and a murmuring sound arose from the crowd as they followed and surrounded me, when an ill-looking man approaching tapped me on the shoulder and said, "Come, sir, you must follow me to Mr. Kirwin's to give an account of yourself."

"Who is Mr. Kirwin? Why am I to give an account of myself? Is not this a free country?"

"Ay, sir, free enough for honest folks. Mr. Kirwin is a magistrate, and you are to give an account of the death of a gentleman who was found murdered here last night."

This answer startled me, but I presently recovered myself. I was innocent; that could easily be proved; accordingly I followed my conductor in silence and was led to one of the best houses in the town. I was ready to sink from fatigue and hunger, but being surrounded by a crowd, I thought it politic to rouse all my strength, that no physical debility might be construed into apprehension or conscious guilt. Little did I then expect the calamity that was in a few moments to overwhelm me and extinguish in horror and despair all fear of ignominy or death. I must pause here, for it requires all my fortitude to recall the memory of the frightful events which I am about to relate, in proper detail, to my recollection. ◄

CHAPTER 20
Annotations

1. Intensifying the nightmare quality of this Gothic story rife with double meanings and narrative doublings, Victor is urged to marry Elizabeth, whom he claims to love but for whose safety he fears should she become affianced to him, just after he agrees to build a female monster to become the mate of his male monster. Here we see the Biblical allusion of Shelley's novel moving outside Milton's take on the same terrain. As Shelley writes it, the monster takes the place of Adam, now, and Eve will be secondary to him. Notably, the creation story in the Old Testament in fact divides into two stories, one in which Adam and Eve are created at the same time and with apparently equal footing and the other wherein Eve is secondary, created from Adam's bone. Shelley appears to be following the second narrative and yet she interrupts this narrative by having Victor destroy the new Eve, before giving the female creature life. An ever-tightening bond is drawn between Victor and the monster as the novel connects their "wives"—the new female monster and Elizabeth. This connection is initially made by the narrative's placing the decision for Victor to marry Elizabeth right after the monster's request that Victor build him a mate. Subsequently, after Victor destroys this fully-fashioned but not yet brought to life female monster, the living male monster seals the connection between Victor, the male monster, the female monster, and Elizabeth, by vowing to "be with [Victor] on [his] wedding night."

   There is a queer subtext here, one brought forward in James Whales' classic movie *Bride of Frankenstein* (1935), that suggests a gay eroticism in the novel. The bond between Victor Frankenstein and his monster is stronger than that of any other two characters. In this reading, Elizabeth and the female monster have to be destroyed so that Victor and his male monster can remain always together. However, their bond is painful, destructive, rather than regenerative and renewing. For Whale as for Shelley, both of whom lived during times that deemed homosexuality immoral, the representation of gay love as violent, destructive, and deathly was not a reflection of what gay male love actually is—a love that can be as regenerative and beautiful as any other kind of love—but rather of views of queer life at the time of Shelley's writing (1818), and at the time of Whale's movie (1935). Whale ultimately took his own life, and one can see a kind of depressive merging—Whale's depression merging with Mary Shelley's — in his influential representations of her works. If Shelley's monster and Victor are entwined like fatal lovers, her novel presents this male-on-male sexuality as toxic.

What's interesting, though, is that Shelley also represents the love between Henry Clerval and Victor Frankenstein as beautiful, soulful, rarified, lively, and far more pure than Frankenstein's dully incestuous love for Elizabeth, who though adopted was raised as his sister. Moreover, the narrative engine of the whole novel is Walton's profound, selfless, and one may say Romantic (if not also romantic) love for Victor Frankenstein. Remember that the novel is presented to us as letters written by Walton to his sister, recounting Victor Frankenstein's words. Hence, male-on-male love, and admiration, is a key trope for textual creation and transmission in *Frankenstein*. ◄

CHAPTER 21

I WAS SOON INTRODUCED into the presence of the magistrate, an old benevolent man with calm and mild manners. He looked upon me, however, with some degree of severity, and then, turning towards my conductors, he asked who appeared as witnesses on this occasion.

About half a dozen men came forward; and, one being selected by the magistrate, he deposed that he had been out fishing the night before with his son and brother-in-law, Daniel Nugent, when, about ten o'clock, they observed a strong northerly blast rising, and they accordingly put in for port. It was a very dark night, as the moon had not yet risen; they did not land at the harbour, but, as they had been accustomed, at a creek about two miles below. He walked on first, carrying a part of the fishing tackle, and his companions followed him at some distance.

As he was proceeding along the sands, he struck his foot against something and fell at his length on the ground. His companions came up to assist him, and by the light of their lantern they found that he had fallen on the body of a man, who was to all appearance dead. Their first supposition was that it was the corpse of some person who had been drowned and was thrown on shore by the waves, but on examination they found that the clothes were not wet and even that the body was not then cold. They instantly carried it to the cottage of an old woman near the spot and endeavoured, but in vain, to restore it to life. It appeared to be a handsome young man, about five and twenty years of age. He had apparently been strangled, for there was no sign of any violence except the black mark of fingers on his neck.

The first part of this deposition did not in the least interest me, but when the mark of the fingers was mentioned I remembered the murder of my brother and felt myself extremely agitated; my limbs trembled, and a mist came over my eyes, which obliged me to lean on a chair for support. The magistrate observed me with a keen eye and of course drew an unfavourable augury from my manner.

The son confirmed his father's account, but when Daniel Nugent was called he swore positively that just before the fall of his companion, he saw a boat, with a single man in it, at a short distance from the shore; and as far as he could judge by the light of a few stars, it was the same boat in which I had just landed. A woman deposed that she lived near the beach and was standing at the door of her cottage, waiting for the return of the fishermen, about an hour before she heard of the discovery of the body, when she saw a boat with only one man in it push off from that part of the shore where the corpse was afterwards found.

Another woman confirmed the account of the fishermen having brought the body into her house; it was not cold. They put it into a bed and rubbed it, and Daniel went to the town for an apothecary, but life was quite gone.

Several other men were examined concerning my landing, and they agreed that, with the strong north wind that had arisen during the night, it was very probable that I had beaten about for many hours and had been obliged to return nearly to the same spot from which I had departed. Besides, they observed that it appeared that I had brought the body from another place, and it was likely that as I did not appear to know the shore, I might have put into the harbour ignorant of the distance of the town of —— from the place where I had deposited the corpse.

Mr. Kirwin, on hearing this evidence, desired that I should be taken into the room where the body lay for interment, that it might be observed what effect the sight of it would produce upon me. This idea was probably suggested by the extreme agitation I had exhibited when the mode of the murder had been described. I was accordingly conducted, by the magistrate and several other persons, to the inn. I could not help being struck by the strange coincidences that had taken place during this eventful night; but, knowing that I had been conversing with several persons in the island I had inhabited about the time that the body had been found, I was perfectly tranquil as to the consequences of the affair. I entered the room where the corpse lay and was led up to the coffin. How can I describe my sensations on beholding it? I feel yet parched with horror, nor can I reflect on that terrible moment without shuddering and agony. The examination, the presence of the magistrate and witnesses, passed like a dream from my memory when I saw the lifeless form of Henry Clerval stretched before me. I gasped for breath, and throwing myself on the body, I exclaimed, "Have my murderous machinations deprived you also, my dearest Henry, of life? Two I have already destroyed; other victims await their destiny; but you, Clerval, my friend, my benefactor—"

The human frame could no longer support the agonies that I endured, and I was carried out of the room in strong convulsions. A fever succeeded to this. I lay for two months on the point of death; my ravings, as I afterwards heard, were frightful; I called myself the murderer of William, of Justine, and of Clerval. Sometimes I entreated my attendants to assist me in the destruction of the fiend by whom I was tormented; and at others I felt the fingers of the monster already grasping my neck, and screamed aloud with agony and terror. Fortunately, as I spoke my native language, Mr. Kirwin alone understood me; but my gestures and bitter cries were sufficient to affright the other witnesses. Why did I not die? More miserable than man ever was before, why did I not sink into forgetfulness and rest? Death snatches away many blooming children, the only hopes of their doting parents; how many brides and youthful lovers have been one day in the bloom of health and hope, and the next a prey for worms and the decay of the tomb! Of what materials was I made that I could thus resist so many shocks, which, like the turning of the wheel, continually renewed the torture?

But I was doomed to live and in two months found myself as awaking from a dream, in a prison, stretched on a wretched bed, surrounded by jailers, turnkeys, bolts, and all the miserable apparatus of a dungeon. It was morning, I remember, when I thus awoke to understanding; I had forgotten the particulars of what had happened and only felt as if some great misfortune had suddenly overwhelmed me; but when I looked around and saw the barred windows and the squalidness of the room in which I was, all flashed across my memory and I groaned bitterly.[1]

This sound disturbed an old woman who was sleeping in a chair beside me. She was a hired nurse, the wife of one of the turnkeys, and her countenance expressed all those bad qualities which often characterize that class. The lines of her face were hard and rude, like that of persons accustomed to see without sympathizing in sights of misery. Her tone expressed her entire indifference; she addressed me in English, and the voice struck me as one that I had heard during my sufferings. "Are you better now, sir?" said she.

I replied in the same language, with a feeble voice, "I believe I am; but if it be all true, if indeed I did not dream, I am sorry that I am still alive to feel this misery and horror."

"For that matter," replied the old woman, "if you mean about the gentle-man you murdered, I believe that it were better for you if you were dead, for I fancy it will go hard with you! However, that's none of my business; I am sent to nurse you and get you well; I do my duty with a safe conscience; it were well if everybody did the same."

I turned with loathing from the woman who could utter so unfeeling a speech to a person just saved, on the very edge of death; but I felt languid and unable to reflect on all that had passed. The whole series of my life appeared to me as a dream; I sometimes doubted if indeed it were all true, for it never presented itself to my mind with the force of reality.

As the images that floated before me became more distinct, I grew feverish; a darkness pressed around me; no one was near me who soothed me with the gentle voice of love; no dear hand supported me. The physician came and prescribed medicines, and the old woman prepared them for me; but utter carelessness was visible in the first, and the expression of brutality was strongly marked in the visage of the second. Who could be interested in the fate of a murderer but the hangman who would gain his fee?

These were my first reflections, but I soon learned that Mr. Kirwin had shown me extreme kindness. He had caused the best room in the prison to be prepared for me (wretched indeed was the best); and it was he who had provided a physician and a nurse. It is true, he seldom came to see me, for although he ardently desired to relieve the sufferings of every human creature, he did not wish to be present at the agonies and miserable ravings of a murderer. He came, therefore, sometimes to see that I was not neglected, but his visits were short and with long intervals. One day, while I was gradually recovering, I was seated in a chair, my eyes half open and my cheeks livid like those in death. I was overcome by gloom and misery and often reflected I had better seek death than desire to remain in a world which to me was replete with wretchedness. At one time I considered whether I should not declare myself guilty and suffer the penalty of the law, less innocent than poor Justine had been. Such were my thoughts when the door of my apartment was opened and Mr. Kirwin entered. His countenance expressed sympathy and compassion; he drew a chair close to mine and addressed me in French, "I fear that this place is very shocking to you; can I do anything to make you more comfortable?"

"I thank you, but all that you mention is nothing to me; on the whole earth there is no comfort which I am capable of receiving."

"I know that the sympathy of a stranger can be but of little relief to one borne down as you are by so strange a misfortune. But you will, I hope, soon quit this melancholy abode, for doubtless evidence can easily be brought to free you from the criminal charge."

"That is my least concern; I am, by a course of strange events, become the most miserable of mortals. Persecuted and tortured as I am and have been, can death be any evil to me?"

"Nothing indeed could be more unfortunate and agonizing than the strange chances that have lately occurred. You were thrown, by some surprising accident, on this shore, renowned for its hospitality, seized immediately, and charged with murder. The first sight that was presented to your eyes was the body of your friend, murdered in so unaccountable a manner and placed, as it were, by some fiend across your path."

As Mr. Kirwin said this, notwithstanding the agitation I endured on this retrospect of my sufferings, I also felt considerable surprise at the knowledge he seemed to possess concerning me. I suppose some astonishment was exhibited in my countenance, for Mr. Kirwin hastened to say, "Immediately upon your being taken ill, all the papers that were on your person were brought me, and I examined them that I might discover some trace by which I could send to your relations an account of your misfortune and illness. I found several letters, and, among others, one which I discovered from its commencement to be from your father. I instantly wrote to Geneva; nearly two months have elapsed since the departure of my letter. But you are ill; even now you tremble; you are unfit for agitation of any kind."

"This suspense is a thousand times worse than the most horrible event; tell me what new scene of death has been acted, and whose murder I am now to lament?"

"Your family is perfectly well," said Mr. Kirwin with gentleness; "and someone, a friend, is come to visit you."

I know not by what chain of thought the idea presented itself, but it instantly darted into my mind that the murderer had come to mock at my misery and taunt me with the death of Clerval, as a new incitement for me to comply with his hellish desires. I put my hand before my eyes, and cried out in agony, "Oh! Take him away! I cannot see him; for God's sake, do not let him enter!"

Mr. Kirwin regarded me with a troubled countenance. He could not help regarding my exclamation as a presumption of my guilt and said in rather a severe tone, "I should have thought, young man, that the presence of your father would have been welcome instead of inspiring such violent repugnance."

"My father!" cried I, while every feature and every muscle was relaxed from anguish to pleasure. "Is my father indeed come? How kind, how very kind! But where is he, why does he not hasten to me?"

My change of manner surprised and pleased the magistrate; perhaps he thought that my former exclamation was a momentary return of delirium, and now he instantly resumed his former benevolence. He rose and quitted the room with my nurse, and in a moment my father entered it.

Nothing, at this moment, could have given me greater pleasure than the arrival of my father. I stretched out my hand to him and cried, "Are you, then, safe—and Elizabeth—and Ernest?" My father calmed me with assurances of their welfare and endeavoured, by dwelling on these subjects so interesting to my heart, to raise my desponding spirits; but he soon felt that a prison cannot be the abode of cheerfulness.

"What a place is this that you inhabit, my son!" said he, looking mournfully at the barred windows and wretched appearance of the room. "You travelled to seek happiness, but a fatality seems to pursue you. And poor Clerval—"

The name of my unfortunate and murdered friend was an agitation too great to be endured in my weak state; I shed tears. "Alas! Yes, my father," replied I; "some destiny of the most horrible kind hangs over me, and I must live to fulfil it, or surely I should have died on the coffin of Henry."

We were not allowed to converse for any length of time, for the precarious state of my health rendered every precaution necessary that could ensure tranquillity. Mr. Kirwin came in and insisted that my strength should not be exhausted by too much exertion. But the appearance of my father was to me like that of my good angel, and I gradually recovered my health.

As my sickness quitted me, I was absorbed by a gloomy and black melancholy that nothing could dissipate. The image of Clerval was forever before me, ghastly and murdered. More than once the agitation into which these reflections threw me made my friends dread a dangerous relapse. Alas! Why did they preserve so miserable and detested a life? It was surely that I might fulfil my destiny, which is now drawing to a close. Soon, oh, very soon, will death extinguish these throbbings and relieve me from the mighty weight of anguish that bears me to the dust; and, in executing the award of justice, I shall also sink to rest. Then the appearance of death was distant, although the wish was ever present to my thoughts; and I often sat for hours motionless and speechless, wishing for some mighty revolution that might bury me and my destroyer in its ruins.

The season of the assizes approached. I had already been three months in prison, and although I was still weak and in continual danger of a relapse, I was obliged to travel nearly a hundred miles to the country town where the court was held. Mr. Kirwin charged himself with every care of collecting witnesses and arranging my defence. I was spared the disgrace of appearing publicly as a criminal, as the case was not brought before the court that decides on life and death. The grand jury rejected the bill, on its being proved that I was on the Orkney Islands at the hour the body of my friend was found; and a fortnight after my removal I was liberated from prison.

My father was enraptured on finding me freed from the vexations of a criminal charge, that I was again allowed to breathe the fresh atmosphere and permitted to return to my native country. I did not participate in these feelings, for to me the walls of a dungeon or a palace were alike hateful. The cup of life was poisoned forever, and although the sun shone upon me, as upon the happy and gay of heart, I saw around me nothing but a dense and frightful darkness, penetrated by no light but the glimmer of two eyes that glared upon me. Sometimes they were the expressive eyes of Henry, languishing in death, the dark orbs nearly covered by the lids and the long black lashes that fringed them; sometimes it was the watery, clouded eyes of the monster, as I first saw them in my chamber at Ingolstadt.

My father tried to awaken in me the feelings of affection. He talked of Geneva, which I should soon visit, of Elizabeth and Ernest; but these words only drew deep groans from me. Sometimes, indeed, I felt a wish for happiness and thought with melancholy delight of my beloved cousin or longed, with a devouring maladie du pays, to see once more the blue lake and rapid Rhone, that had been so dear to me in early childhood; but my general state of feeling was a torpor in which a prison was as welcome a residence as the divinest scene in nature; and these fits were seldom interrupted but by paroxysms of anguish and despair. At these moments I often endeavoured to put an end to the existence I loathed, and it required unceasing attendance and vigilance to restrain me from committing some dreadful act of violence.

Yet one duty remained to me, the recollection of which finally triumphed over my selfish despair. It was necessary that I should return without delay to Geneva, there to watch over the lives of those I so fondly loved and to lie in wait for the murderer, that if any chance led me to the place of his concealment, or if he dared again to blast me by his presence, I might, with unfailing aim, put an end to the existence of the monstrous image which I had endued with the mockery of a soul still more monstrous. My father still desired to delay our departure, fearful that I could not sustain the fatigues of a journey, for I was a shattered wreck—the shadow of a human being. My strength was gone. I was a mere skeleton, and fever night and day preyed upon my wasted frame. Still, as I urged our leaving Ireland with such inquietude and impatience, my father thought it best to yield. We took our passage on board a vessel bound for Havre-de-Grace and sailed with a fair wind from the Irish shores. It was midnight. I lay on the deck looking at the stars and listening to the dashing of the waves. I hailed the darkness that shut Ireland from my sight, and my pulse beat with a feverish joy when I reflected that I should soon see Geneva. The past appeared to me in the light of a frightful dream; yet the vessel in which I was, the wind that blew me from the detested shore of Ireland, and the sea which surrounded me told me too forcibly that I was deceived by no vision and that Clerval, my friend and dearest companion, had fallen a victim to me and the monster of my creation. I repassed, in my memory, my whole life—my quiet happiness while residing with my family in Geneva, the death of my mother, and my departure for Ingolstadt. I remembered, shuddering, the mad enthusiasm that hurried me on to the creation of my hideous enemy, and I called to mind the night in which he first lived. I was unable to pursue the train of thought; a thousand feelings pressed upon me, and I wept bitterly. Ever since my recovery from the fever I had been in the custom of taking every night a small quantity of laudanum, for it was by means of this drug only that I was enabled to gain the rest necessary for the preservation of life. Oppressed by the recollection of my various misfortunes, I now swallowed double my usual quantity and soon slept profoundly. But sleep did not afford me respite from thought and misery; my dreams presented a thousand objects that scared me. Towards morning I was possessed by a kind of nightmare; I felt the fiend's grasp in my neck and could not free myself from it; groans and cries rang in my ears. My father, who was watching over me, perceiving my restlessness, awoke me; the dashing waves were around, the cloudy sky above, the fiend was not here: a sense of security, a feeling that a truce was established between the present hour and the irresistible, disastrous future imparted to me a kind of calm forgetfulness, of which the human mind is by its structure peculiarly susceptible. ◄

CHAPTER 21
Annotations

1. Clerval's death, by the erotically charged method of strangulation, seals Victor Frankenstein's belief that he has no way out of his predicament. Once Frankenstein destroys the female monster, going back on his promise to the male monster, that monster becomes bent on destroying everyone Victor loves. It is notable that Victor Frankenstein made a solemn vow to the monster *which he then broke*, putting him in the wrong in the precise sense that he has broken a vow. Now he approaches making another vow, marrying Elizabeth, and Victor (rightly) fears it will end badly. In Shelley's uncanny novel, Victor Frankenstein fears his secret is so fantastical no one will believe it. This feeling of assurance of disbelief, coupled with Victor's two major bouts of brain fever (a catch-all term for illness brought on by stress and exhaustion) suggest that Victor may at some point be seen by others as a person whose sanity is in doubt.

    Here, the connection between *Frankenstein* the novel and *Mathilda* the novella is strikingly clear: both works turn on the narrative engine of a secret that cannot be told and cannot be solved. Mathilda, as I will discuss, cannot tell Woodville that she is a victim of paternal incest because that knowledge is too horrifying for people to believe (even though, in fact, it happens). Similarly, Victor feels he cannot tell the story of the monster's creation because no one will credence his reality. One may, then, interpret *Frankenstein* and *Mathilda* as stories that at their heart are concerned with the impossibility of telling the truth of one's deepest reality, a trauma that cannot be remedied even through language. ◄

CHAPTER 22

T HE VOYAGE CAME TO AN END. We landed, and proceeded to Paris. I soon found that I had overtaxed my strength and that I must repose before I could continue my journey. My father's care and attentions were indefatigable, but he did not know the origin of my sufferings and sought erroneous methods to remedy the incurable ill. He wished me to seek amusement in society. I abhorred the face of man. Oh, not abhorred! They were my brethren, my fellow beings, and I felt attracted even to the most repulsive among them, as to creatures of an angelic nature and celestial mechanism. But I felt that I had no right to share their intercourse. I had unchained an enemy among them whose joy it was to shed their blood and to revel in their groans. How they would, each and all, abhor me and hunt me from the world did they know my unhallowed acts and the crimes which had their source in me!

My father yielded at length to my desire to avoid society and strove by various arguments to banish my despair. Sometimes he thought that I felt deeply the degradation of being obliged to answer a charge of murder, and he endeavoured to prove to me the futility of pride.

"Alas! My father," said I, "how little do you know me. Human beings, their feelings and passions, would indeed be degraded if such a wretch as I felt pride. Justine, poor unhappy Justine, was as innocent as I, and she suffered the same charge; she died for it; and I am the cause of this—I murdered her. William, Justine, and Henry—they all died by my hands."

My father had often, during my imprisonment, heard me make the same assertion; when I thus accused myself, he sometimes seemed to desire an explanation, and at others he appeared to consider it as the offspring of delirium, and that, during my illness, some idea of this kind had presented itself to my imagination, the remembrance of which I preserved in my convalescence.

I avoided explanation and maintained a continual silence concerning the wretch I had created. I had a persuasion that I should be supposed mad, and this in itself would forever have chained my tongue. But, besides, I could not bring myself to disclose a secret which would fill my hearer with consternation and make fear and unnatural horror the inmates of his breast. I checked, therefore, my impatient thirst for sympathy and was silent when I would have given the world to have confided the fatal secret. Yet, still, words like those I have recorded would burst uncontrollably from me. I could offer no explanation of them, but their truth in part relieved the burden of my mysterious woe. Upon this occasion my father said, with an expression of unbounded wonder, "My dearest Victor, what infatuation is this? My dear son, I entreat you never to make such an assertion again."

"I am not mad," I cried energetically; "the sun and the heavens, who have viewed my operations, can bear witness of my truth. I am the assassin of those most innocent victims; they died by my machinations. A thousand times would I have shed my own blood, drop by drop, to have saved their lives; but I could not, my father, indeed I could not sacrifice the whole human race."

The conclusion of this speech convinced my father that my ideas were deranged, and he instantly changed the subject of our conversation and endeavoured to alter the course of my thoughts. He wished as much as possible to obliterate the memory of the scenes that had taken place in Ireland and never alluded to them or suffered me to speak of my misfortunes.

As time passed away I became more calm; misery had her dwelling in my heart, but I no longer talked in the same incoherent manner of my own crimes; sufficient for me was the consciousness of them. By the utmost self-violence I curbed the imperious voice of wretchedness, which sometimes desired to declare itself to the whole world, and my manners were calmer and more composed than they had ever been since my journey to the sea of ice. A few days before we left Paris on our way to Switzerland, I received the following letter from Elizabeth:

"My dear Friend,

"It gave me the greatest pleasure to receive a letter from my uncle dated at Paris; you are no longer at a formidable distance, and I may hope to see you in less than a fortnight. My poor cousin, how much you must have suffered! I expect to see you looking even more ill than when you quitted Geneva. This winter has been passed most miserably, tortured as I have been by anxious suspense; yet I hope to see peace in your countenance and to find that your heart is not totally void of comfort and tranquillity.

"Yet I fear that the same feelings now exist that made you so miserable a year ago, even perhaps augmented by time. I would not disturb you at this period, when so many misfortunes weigh upon you, but a conversation that I had with my uncle previous to his departure renders some explanation necessary before we meet. Explanation! You may possibly say, What can Elizabeth have to explain? If you really say this, my questions are answered and all my doubts satisfied. But you are distant from me, and it is possible that you may dread and yet be pleased with this explanation; and in a probability of this being the case, I dare not any longer postpone writing what, during your absence, I have often wished to express to you but have never had the courage to begin.

"You well know, Victor, that our union had been the favourite plan of your parents ever since our infancy. We were told this when young, and taught to look forward to it as an event that would certainly take place. We were affectionate playfellows during childhood, and, I believe, dear and valued friends to one another as we grew older. But as brother and sister often entertain a lively affection towards each other without desiring a more intimate union, may not such also be our case? Tell me, dearest Victor. Answer me, I conjure you by our mutual happiness, with simple truth—Do you not love another?

"You have travelled; you have spent several years of your life at Ingolstadt; and I confess to you, my friend, that when I saw you last autumn so unhappy, flying to solitude from the society of every creature, I could not help supposing that you might regret our connection and believe yourself bound in honour to fulfil the wishes of your parents, although they opposed themselves to your inclinations. But this is false reasoning. I confess to you, my friend, that I love you and that in my airy dreams of futurity you have been my constant friend and companion. But it is your happiness I desire as well as my own when I declare to you that our marriage would render me eternally miserable unless it were the dictate of your own free choice. Even now I weep to think that, borne down as you are by the cruellest misfortunes, you may stifle, by the word 'honour,' all hope of that love and happiness which would alone restore you to yourself. I, who have so disinterested an affection for you, may increase your miseries tenfold by being an obstacle to your wishes. Ah! Victor, be assured that your cousin and playmate has too sincere a love for you not to be made miserable by this supposition. Be happy, my friend; and if you obey me in this one request, remain satisfied that nothing on earth will have the power to interrupt my tranquillity.

"Do not let this letter disturb you; do not answer tomorrow, or the next day, or even until you come, if it will give you pain. My uncle will send me news of your health, and if I see but one smile on your lips when we meet, occasioned by this or any other exertion of mine, I shall need no other happiness.

"Elizabeth Lavenza
"Geneva, May 18th, 17— "

THIS LETTER REVIVED IN MY MEMORY what I had before forgotten, the threat of the fiend—"I WILL BE WITH YOU ON YOUR WEDDING-NIGHT!" Such was my sentence, and on that night would the daemon employ every art to destroy me and tear me from the glimpse of happiness which promised partly to console my sufferings. On that night he had determined to consummate his crimes by my death. Well, be it so; a deadly struggle would then assuredly take place, in which if he were victorious I should be at peace and his power over me be at an end. If he were vanquished, I should be a free man. Alas! What freedom? Such as the peasant enjoys when his family have been massacred before his eyes, his cottage burnt, his lands laid waste, and he is turned adrift, homeless, penniless, and alone, but free. Such would be my liberty except that in my Elizabeth I possessed a treasure, alas, balanced by those horrors of remorse and guilt which would pursue me until death.

Sweet and beloved Elizabeth! I read and reread her letter, and some softened feelings stole into my heart and dared to whisper paradisiacal dreams of love and joy; but the apple was already eaten, and the angel's arm bared to drive me from all hope. Yet I would die to make her happy. If the monster executed his threat, death was inevitable; yet, again, I considered whether my marriage would hasten my fate. My destruction might indeed arrive a few months sooner, but if my torturer should suspect that I postponed it, influenced by his menaces, he would surely find other and perhaps more dreadful means of revenge.

He had vowed TO BE WITH ME ON MY WEDDING-NIGHT, yet he did not consider that threat as binding him to peace in the meantime, for as if to show me that he was not yet satiated with blood, he had murdered Clerval immediately after the enunciation of his threats. I resolved, therefore, that if my immediate union with my cousin would conduce either to hers or my father's happiness, my adversary's designs against my life should not retard it a single hour.

In this state of mind I wrote to Elizabeth. My letter was calm and affectionate. "I fear, my beloved girl," I said, "little happiness remains for us on earth; yet all that I may one day enjoy is centred in you. Chase away your idle fears; to you alone do I consecrate my life and my endeavours for contentment. I have one secret, Elizabeth, a dreadful one; when revealed to you, it will chill your frame with horror, and then, far from being surprised at my misery, you will only wonder that I survive what I have endured. I will confide this tale of misery and terror to you the day after our marriage shall take place, for, my sweet cousin, there must be perfect confidence between us. But until then, I conjure you, do not mention or allude to it. This I most earnestly entreat, and I know you will comply."

In about a week after the arrival of Elizabeth's letter we returned to Geneva. The sweet girl welcomed me with warm affection, yet tears were in her eyes as she beheld my emaciated frame and feverish cheeks. I saw a change in her also. She was thinner and had lost much of that heavenly vivacity that had before charmed me; but her gentleness and soft looks of compassion made her a more fit companion for one blasted and miserable as I was. The tranquillity which I now enjoyed did not endure. Memory brought madness with it, and when I thought of what had passed, a real insanity possessed me; sometimes I was furious and burnt with rage, sometimes low and despondent. I neither spoke nor looked at anyone, but sat motionless, bewildered by the multitude of miseries that overcame me.

Elizabeth alone had the power to draw me from these fits; her gentle voice would soothe me when transported by passion and inspire me with human feelings when sunk in torpor. She wept with me and for me. When reason returned, she would remonstrate and endeavour to inspire me with resignation. Ah! It is well for the unfortunate to be resigned, but for the guilty there is no peace. The agonies of remorse poison the luxury there is otherwise sometimes found in indulging the excess of grief. Soon after my arrival my father spoke of my immediate marriage with Elizabeth. I remained silent.

"Have you, then, some other attachment?"

"None on earth. I love Elizabeth and look forward to our union with delight. Let the day therefore be fixed; and on it I will consecrate myself, in life or death, to the happiness of my cousin."

"My dear Victor, do not speak thus. Heavy misfortunes have befallen us, but let us only cling closer to what remains and transfer our love for those whom we have lost to those who yet live. Our circle will be small but bound close by the ties of affection and mutual misfortune. And when time shall have softened your despair, new and dear objects of care will be born to replace those of whom we have been so cruelly deprived."

Such were the lessons of my father. But to me the remembrance of the threat returned; nor can you wonder that, omnipotent as the fiend had yet been in his deeds of blood, I should almost regard him as invincible, and that when he had pronounced the words "I SHALL BE WITH YOU ON YOUR WED-DING-NIGHT," I should regard the threatened fate as unavoidable. But death was no evil to me if the loss of Elizabeth were balanced with it, and I therefore, with a contented and even cheerful countenance, agreed with my father that if my cousin would consent, the ceremony should take place in ten days, and thus put, as I imagined, the seal to my fate.

Great God! If for one instant I had thought what might be the hellish intention of my fiendish adversary, I would rather have banished myself forever from my native country and wandered a friendless outcast over the earth than have consented to this miserable marriage. But, as if possessed of magic powers, the monster had blinded me to his real intentions; and when I thought that I had prepared only my own death, I hastened that of a far dearer victim.

As the period fixed for our marriage drew nearer, whether from cowardice or a prophetic feeling, I felt my heart sink within me. But I concealed my feelings by an appearance of hilarity that brought smiles and joy to the countenance of my father, but hardly deceived the ever-watchful and nicer eye of Elizabeth. She looked forward to our union with placid contentment, not unmingled with a little fear, which past misfortunes had impressed, that what now appeared certain and tangible happiness might soon dissipate into an airy dream and leave no trace but deep and everlasting regret. Preparations were made for the event, congratulatory visits were received, and all wore a smiling appearance. I shut up, as well as I could, in my own heart the anxiety that preyed there and entered with seeming earnestness into the plans of my father, although they might only serve as the decorations of my tragedy. Through my father's exertions a part of the inheritance of Elizabeth had been restored to her by the Austrian government. A small possession on the shores of Como belonged to her. It was agreed that, immediately after our union, we should proceed to Villa Lavenza and spend our first days of happiness beside the beautiful lake near which it stood.

In the meantime I took every precaution to defend my person in case the fiend should openly attack me. I carried pistols and a dagger constantly about me and was ever on the watch to prevent artifice, and by these means gained a greater degree of tranquillity. Indeed, as the period approached, the threat appeared more as a delusion, not to be regarded as worthy to disturb my peace, while the happiness I hoped for in my marriage wore a greater appearance of certainty as the day fixed for its solemnization drew nearer and I heard it continually spoken of as an occurrence which no accident could possibly prevent.

Elizabeth seemed happy; my tranquil demeanour contributed greatly to calm her mind. But on the day that was to fulfil my wishes and my destiny, she was melancholy, and a presentiment of evil pervaded her; and perhaps also she thought of the dreadful secret which I had promised to reveal to her on the following day. My father was in the meantime overjoyed and in the bustle of preparation only recognized in the melancholy of his niece the diffidence of a bride.

After the ceremony was performed a large party assembled at my father's, but it was agreed that Elizabeth and I should commence our journey by water, sleeping that night at Evian and continuing our voyage on the following day. The day was fair, the wind favourable; all smiled on our nuptial embarkation.

Those were the last moments of my life during which I enjoyed the feeling of happiness. We passed rapidly along; the sun was hot, but we were sheltered from its rays by a kind of canopy while we enjoyed the beauty of the scene, sometimes on one side of the lake, where we saw Mont Saleve, the pleasant banks of Montalegre, and at a distance, surmounting all, the beautiful Mont Blanc and the assemblage of snowy mountains that in vain endeavour to emulate her; sometimes coasting the opposite banks, we saw the mighty Jura opposing its dark side to the ambition that would quit its native country, and an almost insurmountable barrier to the invader who should wish to enslave it.

I took the hand of Elizabeth. "You are sorrowful, my love. Ah! If you knew what I have suffered and what I may yet endure, you would endeavour to let me taste the quiet and freedom from despair that this one day at least permits me to enjoy."

"Be happy, my dear Victor," replied Elizabeth; "there is, I hope, nothing to distress you; and be assured that if a lively joy is not painted in my face, my heart is contented. Something whispers to me not to depend too much on the prospect that is opened before us, but I will not listen to such a sinister voice. Observe how fast we move along and how the clouds, which sometimes obscure and sometimes rise above the dome of Mont Blanc, render this scene of beauty still more interesting. Look also at the innumerable fish that are swimming in the clear waters, where we can distinguish every pebble that lies at the bottom. What a divine day! How happy and serene all nature appears!"

Thus Elizabeth endeavoured to divert her thoughts and mine from all reflection upon melancholy subjects. But her temper was fluctuating; joy for a few instants shone in her eyes, but it continually gave place to distraction and reverie.

The sun sank lower in the heavens; we passed the river Drance and observed its path through the chasms of the higher and the glens of the lower hills. The Alps here come closer to the lake, and we approached the amphitheatre of mountains which forms its eastern boundary. The spire of Evian shone under the woods that surrounded it and the range of mountain above mountain by which it was overhung.

The wind, which had hitherto carried us along with amazing rapidity, sank at sunset to a light breeze; the soft air just ruffled the water and caused a pleasant motion among the trees as we approached the shore, from which it wafted the most delightful scent of flowers and hay. The sun sank beneath the horizon as we landed, and as I touched the shore I felt those cares and fears revive which soon were to clasp me and cling to me forever. ◄

CHAPTER 23

I T WAS EIGHT O'CLOCK when we landed; we walked for a short time on the shore, enjoying the transitory light, and then retired to the inn and contemplated the lovely scene of waters, woods, and mountains, obscured in darkness, yet still displaying their black outlines.

The wind, which had fallen in the south, now rose with great violence in the west. The moon had reached her summit in the heavens and was beginning to descend; the clouds swept across it swifter than the flight of the vulture and dimmed her rays, while the lake reflected the scene of the busy heavens, rendered still busier by the restless waves that were beginning to rise. Suddenly a heavy storm of rain descended.

I had been calm during the day, but so soon as night obscured the shapes of objects, a thousand fears arose in my mind. I was anxious and watchful, while my right hand grasped a pistol which was hidden in my bosom; every sound terrified me, but I resolved that I would sell my life dearly and not shrink from the conflict until my own life or that of my adversary was extinguished. Elizabeth observed my agitation for some time in timid and fearful silence, but there was something in my glance which communicated terror to her, and trembling, she asked, "What is it that agitates you, my dear Victor? What is it you fear?"

"Oh! Peace, peace, my love," replied I; "this night, and all will be safe; but this night is dreadful, very dreadful."

I passed an hour in this state of mind, when suddenly I reflected how fearful the combat which I momentarily expected would be to my wife, and I earnestly entreated her to retire, resolving not to join her until I had obtained some knowledge as to the situation of my enemy.

She left me, and I continued some time walking up and down the passages of the house and inspecting every corner that might afford a retreat to my adversary. But I discovered no trace of him and was beginning to conjecture that some fortunate chance had intervened to prevent the execution of his menaces when suddenly I heard a shrill and dreadful scream. It came from the room into which Elizabeth had retired. As I heard it, the whole truth rushed into my mind, my arms dropped, the motion of every muscle and fibre was suspended; I could feel the blood trickling in my veins and tingling in the extremities of my limbs. This state lasted but for an instant; the scream was repeated, and I rushed into the room. Great God! Why did I not then expire! Why am I here to relate the destruction of the best hope and the purest creature on earth? She was there, lifeless and inanimate, thrown across the bed, her head hanging down and her pale and distorted features half covered by her hair. Everywhere I turn I see the same figure—her bloodless arms and relaxed form flung by the murderer on its bridal bier. Could I behold this and live? Alas! Life is obstinate and clings closest where it is most hated. For a moment only did I lose recollection; I fell senseless on the ground.

When I recovered I found myself surrounded by the people of the inn; their countenances expressed a breathless terror, but the horror of others appeared only as a mockery, a shadow of the feelings that oppressed me. I escaped from them to the room where lay the body of Elizabeth, my love, my wife, so lately living, so dear, so worthy. She had been moved from the posture in which I had first beheld her, and now, as she lay, her head upon her arm and a handkerchief thrown across her face and neck, I might have supposed her asleep. I rushed towards her and embraced her with ardour, but the deadly languor and coldness of the limbs told me that what I now held in my arms had ceased to be the Elizabeth whom I had loved and cherished. The murderous mark of the fiend's grasp was on her neck, and the breath had ceased to issue from her lips. While I still hung over her in the agony of despair, I happened to look up. The windows of the room had before been darkened, and I felt a kind of panic on seeing the pale yellow light of the moon illuminate the chamber. The shutters had been thrown back, and with a sensation of horror not to be described, I saw at the open window a figure the most hideous and abhorred. A grin was on the face of the monster; he seemed to jeer, as with his fiendish finger he pointed towards the corpse of my wife. I rushed towards the window, and drawing a pistol from my bosom, fired; but he eluded me, leaped from his station, and running with the swiftness of lightning, plunged into the lake.

The report of the pistol brought a crowd into the room. I pointed to the spot where he had disappeared, and we followed the track with boats; nets were cast, but in vain. After passing several hours, we returned hopeless, most of my companions believing it to have been a form conjured up by my fancy. After having landed, they proceeded to search the country, parties going in different directions among the woods and vines.

I attempted to accompany them and proceeded a short distance from the house, but my head whirled round, my steps were like those of a drunken man, I fell at last in a state of utter exhaustion; a film covered my eyes, and my skin was parched with the heat of fever. In this state I was carried back and placed on a bed, hardly conscious of what had happened; my eyes wandered round the room as if to seek something that I had lost.

After an interval I arose, and as if by instinct, crawled into the room where the corpse of my beloved lay. There were women weeping around; I hung over it and joined my sad tears to theirs; all this time no distinct idea presented itself to my mind, but my thoughts rambled to various subjects, reflecting confusedly on my misfortunes and their cause. I was bewildered, in a cloud of wonder and horror. The death of William, the execution of Justine, the murder of Clerval, and lastly of my wife; even at that moment I knew not that my only remaining friends were safe from the malignity of the fiend; my father even now might be writhing under his grasp, and Ernest might be dead at his feet. This idea made me shudder and recalled me to action. I started up and resolved to return to Geneva with all possible speed.[1]

There were no horses to be procured, and I must return by the lake; but the wind was unfavourable, and the rain fell in torrents. However, it was hardly morning, and I might reasonably hope to arrive by night. I hired men to row and took an oar myself, for I had always experienced relief from mental torment in bodily exercise. But the overflowing misery I now felt, and the excess of agitation that I endured rendered me incapable of any exertion. I threw down the oar, and leaning my head upon my hands, gave way to every gloomy idea that arose. If I looked up, I saw scenes which were familiar to me in my happier time and which I had contemplated but the day before in the company of her who was now but a shadow and a recollection. Tears streamed from my eyes. The rain had ceased for a moment, and I saw the fish play in the waters as they had done a few hours before; they had then been observed by Elizabeth. Nothing is so painful to the human mind as a great and sudden change. The sun might shine or the clouds might lower, but nothing could appear to me as it had done the day before. A fiend had snatched from me every hope of future happiness; no creature had ever been so miserable as I was; so frightful an event is single in the history of man. But why should I dwell upon the incidents that followed this last overwhelming event? Mine has been a tale of horrors; I have reached their acme, and what I must now relate can but be tedious to you. Know that, one by one, my friends were snatched away; I was left desolate. My own strength is exhausted, and I must tell, in a few words, what remains of my hideous narration. I arrived at Geneva. My father and Ernest yet lived, but the former sunk under the tidings that I bore. I see him now, excellent and venerable old man! His eyes wandered in vacancy, for they had lost their charm and their delight—his Elizabeth, his more than daughter, whom he doted on with all that affection which a man feels, who in the decline of life, having few affections, clings more earnestly to those that remain. Cursed, cursed be the fiend that brought misery on his grey hairs and doomed him to waste in wretchedness! He could not live under the horrors that were accumulated around him; the springs of existence suddenly gave way; he was unable to rise from his bed, and in a few days he died in my arms.

What then became of me? I know not; I lost sensation, and chains and darkness were the only objects that pressed upon me. Sometimes, indeed, I dreamt that I wandered in flowery meadows and pleasant vales with the friends of my youth, but I awoke and found myself in a dungeon. Melancholy followed, but by degrees I gained a clear conception of my miseries and situation and was then released from my prison. For they had called me mad, and during many months, as I understood, a solitary cell had been my habitation.

Liberty, however, had been a useless gift to me, had I not, as I awakened to reason, at the same time awakened to revenge. As the memory of past misfortunes pressed upon me, I began to reflect on their cause—the monster whom I had created, the miserable daemon whom I had sent abroad into the world for my destruction. I was possessed by a maddening rage when I thought of him, and desired and ardently prayed that I might have him within my grasp to wreak a great and signal revenge on his cursed head.

Nor did my hate long confine itself to useless wishes; I began to reflect on the best means of securing him; and for this purpose, about a month after my release, I repaired to a criminal judge in the town and told him that I had an accusation to make, that I knew the destroyer of my family, and that I required him to exert his whole authority for the apprehension of the murderer. The magistrate listened to me with attention and kindness.

"Be assured, sir," said he, "no pains or exertions on my part shall be spared to discover the villain."

"I thank you," replied I; "listen, therefore, to the deposition that I have to make. It is indeed a tale so strange that I should fear you would not credit it were there not something in truth which, however wonderful, forces conviction. The story is too connected to be mistaken for a dream, and I have no motive for falsehood." My manner as I thus addressed him was impressive but calm; I had formed in my own heart a resolution to pursue my destroyer to death, and this purpose quieted my agony and for an interval reconciled me to life. I now related my history briefly but with firmness and precision, marking the dates with accuracy and never deviating into invective or exclamation.

The magistrate appeared at first perfectly incredulous, but as I continued he became more attentive and interested; I saw him sometimes shudder with horror; at others a lively surprise, unmingled with disbelief, was painted on his countenance. When I had concluded my narration I said, "This is the being whom I accuse and for whose seizure and punishment I call upon you to exert your whole power. It is your duty as a magistrate, and I believe and hope that your feelings as a man will not revolt from the execution of those functions on this occasion." This address caused a considerable change in the physiognomy of my own auditor. He had heard my story with that half kind of belief that is given to a tale of spirits and supernatural events; but when he was called upon to act officially in consequence, the whole tide of his incredulity returned. He, however, answered mildly, "I would willingly afford you every aid in your pursuit, but the creature of whom you speak appears to have powers which would put all my exertions to defiance. Who can follow an animal which can traverse the sea of ice and inhabit caves and dens where no man would venture to intrude? Besides, some months have elapsed since the commission of his crimes, and no one can conjecture to what place he has wandered or what region he may now inhabit."

"I do not doubt that he hovers near the spot which I inhabit, and if he has indeed taken refuge in the Alps, he may be hunted like the chamois and destroyed as a beast of prey. But I perceive your thoughts; you do not credit my narrative and do not intend to pursue my enemy with the punishment which is his desert." As I spoke, rage sparkled in my eyes; the magistrate was intimidated. "You are mistaken," said he. "I will exert myself, and if it is in my power to seize the monster, be assured that he shall suffer punishment proportionate to his crimes. But I fear, from what you have yourself described to be his properties, that this will prove impracticable; and thus, while every proper measure is pursued, you should make up your mind to disappointment."

"That cannot be; but all that I can say will be of little avail. My revenge is of no moment to you; yet, while I allow it to be a vice, I confess that it is the devouring and only passion of my soul. My rage is unspeakable when I reflect that the murderer, whom I have turned loose upon society, still exists. You refuse my just demand; I have but one resource, and I devote myself, either in my life or death, to his destruction."

I trembled with excess of agitation as I said this; there was a frenzy in my manner, and something, I doubt not, of that haughty fierceness which the martyrs of old are said to have possessed. But to a Genevan magistrate, whose mind was occupied by far other ideas than those of devotion and heroism, this elevation of mind had much the appearance of madness. He endeavoured to soothe me as a nurse does a child and reverted to my tale as the effects of delirium.

"Man," I cried, "how ignorant art thou in thy pride of wisdom! Cease; you know not what it is you say."

I broke from the house angry and disturbed and retired to meditate on some other mode of action. ◄

CHAPTER 23
Annotations

1. The monster carries through with his threat to kill Elizabeth, killing her on her wedding night. This crossing by which the fate of the destroyed female monster becomes also Elizabeth's fate clears the way for Victor to have a relationship solely with his male monster. From now on, Victor's whole world will consist of chasing the monster until he meets Walton, tells his story, and expires. But this double death of the female monster and Elizabeth is notable for its suggestion that heterosexual sex itself is violent. Rather than losing her virginity on her wedding night, Elizabeth is murdered in her wedding bed. Likewise, Victor's assault on the female monster can be read as a kind of rape on the eve of the new creature's 'marriage' to the male monster. Shelley, with these twin scenes of death instead of sexual communion, flesh torn apart instead of marriages consummated, undoes any chance for her novel to have a happy outcome.

    It is precisely the destruction of women that seals the novel's status as insolvable horror. One can read this narrative fact many ways: maybe Mary Shelley felt that her life with Percy, despite being excessively procreative, was not one in which Percy Shelley was able to act as an actual father by looking after the safety and well-being of his progeny. Maybe she was excavating tropes of the male Gothic to make a claim for a feminist re-working of the genre. And also maybe Mary Shelley realized that in some ways heterosexual procreative sex is violent, an enemy of female empowerment, and she sought—narratively— to tear it apart but then could not go forward and imagine this rending as a utopic beginning and instead turned it to tragedy. Regardless, the death of Elizabeth on her bridal bed is the imagistic and symbolic high-water mark of the monster's violence, a scene evocative of Henry Fuseli's 1781 painting, *The Nightmare*, depicting a woman ravished by malevolent night spirits. This dramatic bridal-bed death punctuates the novel as a Gothic work. ◀

CHAPTER 24

MY PRESENT SITUATION was one in which all voluntary thought was swallowed up and lost. I was hurried away by fury; revenge alone endowed me with strength and composure; it moulded my feelings and allowed me to be calculating and calm at periods when otherwise delirium or death would have been my portion.

My first resolution was to quit Geneva forever; my country, which, when I was happy and beloved, was dear to me, now, in my adversity, became hateful. I provided myself with a sum of money, together with a few jewels which had belonged to my mother, and departed. And now my wanderings began which are to cease but with life. I have traversed a vast portion of the earth and have endured all the hardships which travellers in deserts and barbarous countries are wont to meet. How I have lived I hardly know; many times have I stretched my failing limbs upon the sandy plain and prayed for death. But revenge kept me alive; I dared not die and leave my adversary in being.

When I quitted Geneva my first labour was to gain some clue by which I might trace the steps of my fiendish enemy. But my plan was unsettled, and I wandered many hours round the confines of the town, uncertain what path I should pursue. As night approached I found myself at the entrance of the cemetery where William, Elizabeth, and my father reposed. I entered it and approached the tomb which marked their graves. Everything was silent except the leaves of the trees, which were gently agitated by the wind; the night was nearly dark, and the scene would have been solemn and affecting even to an uninterested observer. The spirits of the departed seemed to flit around and to cast a shadow, which was felt but not seen, around the head of the mourner.

The deep grief which this scene had at first excited quickly gave way to rage and despair. They were dead, and I lived; their murderer also lived, and to destroy him I must drag out my weary existence. I knelt on the grass and kissed the earth and with quivering lips exclaimed, "By the sacred earth on which I kneel, by the shades that wander near me, by the deep and eternal grief that I feel, I swear; and by thee, O Night, and the spirits that preside over thee, to pursue the daemon who caused this misery, until he or I shall perish in mortal conflict. For this purpose I will preserve my life; to execute this dear revenge will I again behold the sun and tread the green herbage of earth, which otherwise should vanish from my eyes forever. And I call on you, spirits of the dead, and on you, wandering ministers of vengeance, to aid and conduct me in my work. Let the cursed and hellish monster drink deep of agony; let him feel the despair that now torments me." I had begun my adjuration with solemnity and an awe which almost assured me that the shades of my murdered friends heard and approved my devotion, but the furies possessed me as I concluded, and rage choked my utterance.

I was answered through the stillness of night by a loud and fiendish laugh. It rang on my ears long and heavily; the mountains re-echoed it, and I felt as if all hell surrounded me with mockery and laughter. Surely in that moment I should have been possessed by frenzy and have destroyed my miserable existence but that my vow was heard and that I was reserved for vengeance. The laughter died away, when a well-known and abhorred voice, apparently close to my ear, addressed me in an audible whisper, "I am satisfied, miserable wretch! You have determined to live, and I am satisfied."

I darted towards the spot from which the sound proceeded, but the devil eluded my grasp. Suddenly the broad disk of the moon arose and shone full upon his ghastly and distorted shape as he fled with more than mortal speed.

I pursued him, and for many months this has been my task. Guided by a slight clue, I followed the windings of the Rhone, but vainly. The blue Mediterranean appeared, and by a strange chance, I saw the fiend enter by night and hide himself in a vessel bound for the Black Sea. I took my passage in the same ship, but he escaped, I know not how.

Amidst the wilds of Tartary and Russia, although he still evaded me, I have ever followed in his track. Sometimes the peasants, scared by this horrid apparition, informed me of his path; sometimes he himself, who feared that if I lost all trace of him I should despair and die, left some mark to guide me. The snows descended on my head, and I saw the print of his huge step on the white plain. To you first entering on life, to whom care is new and agony unknown, how can you understand what I have felt and still feel? Cold, want, and fatigue were the least pains which I was destined to endure; I was cursed by some devil and carried about with me my eternal hell; yet still a spirit of good followed and directed my steps and when I most murmured would suddenly extricate me from seemingly insurmountable difficulties. Sometimes, when nature, overcome by hunger, sank under the exhaustion, a repast was prepared for me in the desert that restored and inspirited me. The fare was, indeed, coarse, such as the peasants of the country ate, but I will not doubt that it was set there by the spirits that I had invoked to aid me. Often, when all was dry, the heavens cloudless, and I was parched by thirst, a slight cloud would bedim the sky, shed the few drops that revived me, and vanish.[1]

I followed, when I could, the courses of the rivers; but the daemon generally avoided these, as it was here that the population of the country chiefly collected. In other places human beings were seldom seen, and I generally subsisted on the wild animals that crossed my path. I had money with me and gained the friendship of the villagers by distributing it; or I brought with me some food that I had killed, which, after taking a small part, I always presented to those who had provided me with fire and utensils for cooking.

My life, as it passed thus, was indeed hateful to me, and it was during sleep alone that I could taste joy. O blessed sleep! Often, when most miserable, I sank to repose, and my dreams lulled me even to rapture. The spirits that guarded me had provided these moments, or rather hours, of happiness that I might retain strength to fulfil my pilgrimage. Deprived of this respite, I should have sunk under my hardships. During the day I was sustained and inspirited by the hope of night, for in sleep I saw my friends, my wife, and my beloved country; again I saw the benevolent countenance of my father, heard the silver tones of my Elizabeth's voice, and beheld Clerval enjoying health and youth. Often, when wearied by a toilsome march, I persuaded myself that I was dreaming until night should come and that I should then enjoy reality in the arms of my dearest friends. What agonizing fondness did I feel for them! How did I cling to their dear forms, as sometimes they haunted even my waking hours, and persuade myself that they still lived! At such moments vengeance, that burned within me, died in my heart, and I pursued my path towards the destruction of the daemon more as a task enjoined by heaven, as the mechanical impulse of some power of which I was unconscious, than as the ardent desire of my soul. What his feelings were whom I pursued I cannot know. Sometimes, indeed, he left marks in writing on the barks of the trees or cut in stone that guided me and instigated my fury. "My reign is not yet over" — these words were legible in one of these inscriptions — "you live, and my power is complete. Follow me; I seek the everlasting ices of the north, where you will feel the misery of cold and frost, to which I am impassive. You will find near this place, if you follow not too tardily, a dead hare; eat and be refreshed. Come on, my enemy; we have yet to wrestle for our lives, but many hard and miserable hours must you endure until that period shall arrive."

Scoffing devil! Again do I vow vengeance; again do I devote thee, miserable fiend, to torture and death. Never will I give up my search until he or I perish; and then with what ecstasy shall I join my Elizabeth and my departed friends, who even now prepare for me the reward of my tedious toil and horrible pilgrimage!

As I still pursued my journey to the northward, the snows thickened and the cold increased in a degree almost too severe to support. The peasants were shut up in their hovels, and only a few of the most hardy ventured forth to seize the animals whom starvation had forced from their hiding-places to seek for prey. The rivers were covered with ice, and no fish could be procured; and thus I was cut off from my chief article of maintenance. The triumph of my enemy increased with the difficulty of my labours. One inscription that he left was in these words: "Prepare! Your toils only begin; wrap yourself in furs and provide food, for we shall soon enter upon a journey where your sufferings will satisfy my everlasting hatred."

My courage and perseverance were invigorated by these scoffing words; I resolved not to fail in my purpose, and calling on heaven to support me, I continued with unabated fervour to traverse immense deserts, until the ocean appeared at a distance and formed the utmost boundary of the horizon. Oh! How unlike it was to the blue seasons of the south! Covered with ice, it was only to be distinguished from land by its superior wildness and ruggedness. The Greeks wept for joy when they beheld the Mediterranean from the hills of Asia, and hailed with rapture the boundary of their toils. I did not weep, but I knelt down and with a full heart thanked my guiding spirit for conducting me in safety to the place where I hoped, notwithstanding my adversary's gibe, to meet and grapple with him.

Some weeks before this period I had procured a sledge and dogs and thus traversed the snows with inconceivable speed. I know not whether the fiend possessed the same advantages, but I found that, as before I had daily lost ground in the pursuit, I now gained on him, so much so that when I first saw the ocean he was but one day's journey in advance, and I hoped to intercept him before he should reach the beach. With new courage, therefore, I pressed on, and in two days arrived at a wretched hamlet on the seashore. I inquired of the inhabitants concerning the fiend and gained accurate information. A gigantic monster, they said, had arrived the night before, armed with a gun and many pistols, putting to flight the inhabitants of a solitary cottage through fear of his terrific appearance. He had carried off their store of winter food, and placing it in a sledge, to draw which he had seized on a numerous drove of trained dogs, he had harnessed them, and the same night, to the joy of the horror-struck villagers, had pursued his journey across the sea in a direction that led to no land; and they conjectured that he must speedily be destroyed by the breaking of the ice or frozen by the eternal frosts.

On hearing this information I suffered a temporary access of despair. He had escaped me, and I must commence a destructive and almost endless journey across the mountainous ices of the ocean, amidst cold that few of the inhabitants could long endure and which I, the native of a genial and sunny climate, could not hope to survive. Yet at the idea that the fiend should live and be triumphant, my rage and vengeance returned, and like a mighty tide, overwhelmed every other feeling. After a slight repose, during which the spirits of the dead hovered round and instigated me to toil and revenge, I prepared for my journey. I exchanged my land-sledge for one fashioned for the inequalities of the frozen ocean, and purchasing a plentiful stock of provisions, I departed from land.

I cannot guess how many days have passed since then, but I have endured misery which nothing but the eternal sentiment of a just retribution burning within my heart could have enabled me to support. Immense and rugged mountains of ice often barred up my passage, and I often heard the thunder of the ground sea, which threatened my destruction. But again the frost came and made the paths of the sea secure.

By the quantity of provision which I had consumed, I should guess that I had passed three weeks in this journey; and the continual protraction of hope, returning back upon the heart, often wrung bitter drops of despondency and grief from my eyes. Despair had indeed almost secured her prey, and I should soon have sunk beneath this misery. Once, after the poor animals that conveyed me had with incredible toil gained the summit of a sloping ice mountain, and one, sinking under his fatigue, died, I viewed the expanse before me with anguish, when suddenly my eye caught a dark speck upon the dusky plain. I strained my sight to discover what it could be and uttered a wild cry of ecstasy when I distinguished a sledge and the distorted proportions of a well-known form within. Oh! With what a burning gush did hope revisit my heart! Warm tears filled my eyes, which I hastily wiped away, that they might not intercept the view I had of the daemon; but still my sight was dimmed by the burning drops, until, giving way to the emotions that oppressed me, I wept aloud.

But this was not the time for delay; I disencumbered the dogs of their dead companion, gave them a plentiful portion of food, and after an hour's rest, which was absolutely necessary, and yet which was bitterly irksome to me, I continued my route. The sledge was still visible, nor did I again lose sight of it except at the moments when for a short time some ice-rock concealed it with its intervening crags. I indeed perceptibly gained on it, and when, after nearly two days' journey, I beheld my enemy at no more than a mile distant, my heart bounded within me.

But now, when I appeared almost within grasp of my foe, my hopes were suddenly extinguished, and I lost all trace of him more utterly than I had ever done before. A ground sea was heard; the thunder of its progress, as the waters rolled and swelled beneath me, became every moment more ominous and terrific. I pressed on, but in vain. The wind arose; the sea roared; and, as with the mighty shock of an earthquake, it split and cracked with a tremendous and overwhelming sound. The work was soon finished; in a few minutes a tumultuous sea rolled between me and my enemy, and I was left drifting on a scattered piece of ice that was continually lessening and thus preparing for me a hideous death. In this manner many appalling hours passed; several of my dogs died, and I myself was about to sink under the accumulation of distress when I saw your vessel riding at anchor and holding forth to me hopes of succour and life. I had no conception that vessels ever came so far north and was astounded at the sight. I quickly destroyed part of my sledge to construct oars, and by these means was enabled, with infinite fatigue, to move my ice raft in the direction of your ship. I had determined, if you were going southwards, still to trust myself to the mercy of the seas rather than abandon my purpose. I hoped to induce you to grant me a boat with which I could pursue my enemy. But your direction was northwards. You took me on board when my vigour was exhausted, and I should soon have sunk under my multiplied hardships into a death which I still dread, for my task is unfulfilled.

Oh! When will my guiding spirit, in conducting me to the daemon, allow me the rest I so much desire; or must I die, and he yet live? If I do, swear to me, Walton, that he shall not escape, that you will seek him and satisfy my vengeance in his death. And do I dare to ask of you to undertake my pilgrimage, to endure the hardships that I have undergone? No; I am not so selfish. Yet, when I am dead, if he should appear, if the ministers of vengeance should conduct him to you, swear that he shall not live—swear that he shall not triumph over my accumulated woes and survive to add to the list of his dark crimes. He is eloquent and persuasive, and once his words had even power over my heart; but trust him not. His soul is as hellish as his form, full of treachery and fiend-like malice. Hear him not; call on the names of William, Justine, Clerval, Elizabeth, my father, and of the wretched Victor, and thrust your sword into his heart. I will hover near and direct the steel aright.

Walton, in continuation
August 26th, 17 —

YOU HAVE READ THIS STRANGE and terrific story, Margaret; and do you not feel your blood congeal with horror, like that which even now curdles mine? Sometimes, seized with sudden agony, he could not continue his tale; at others, his voice broken, yet piercing, uttered with difficulty the words so replete with anguish. His fine and lovely eyes were now lighted up with indignation, now subdued to downcast sorrow and quenched in infinite wretchedness. Sometimes he commanded his countenance and tones and related the most horrible incidents with a tranquil voice, suppressing every mark of agitation; then, like a volcano bursting forth, his face would suddenly change to an expression of the wildest rage as he shrieked out imprecations on his persecutor.

His tale is connected and told with an appearance of the simplest truth, yet I own to you that the letters of Felix and Safie, which he showed me, and the apparition of the monster seen from our ship, brought to me a greater conviction of the truth of his narrative than his asseverations, however earnest and connected. Such a monster has, then, really existence! I cannot doubt it, yet I am lost in surprise and admiration. Sometimes I endeavoured to gain from Frankenstein the particulars of his creature's formation, but on this point he was impenetrable. "Are you mad, my friend?" said he. "Or whither does your senseless curiosity lead you? Would you also create for yourself and the world a demoniacal enemy? Peace, peace! Learn my miseries and do not seek to increase your own." Frankenstein discovered that I made notes concerning his history; he asked to see them and then himself corrected and augmented them in many places, but principally in giving the life and spirit to the conversations he held with his enemy. "Since you have preserved my narration," said he, "I would not that a mutilated one should go down to posterity."

Thus has a week passed away, while I have listened to the strangest tale that ever imagination formed. My thoughts and every feeling of my soul have been drunk up by the interest for my guest which this tale and his own elevated and gentle manners have created. I wish to soothe him, yet can I counsel one so infinitely miserable, so destitute of every hope of consolation, to live? Oh, no! The only joy that he can now know will be when he composes his shattered spirit to peace and death. Yet he enjoys one comfort, the offspring of solitude and delirium; he believes that when in dreams he holds converse with his friends and derives from that communion consolation for his miseries or excitements to his vengeance, that they are not the creations of his fancy, but the beings themselves who visit him from the regions of a remote world. This faith gives a solemnity to his reveries that render them to me almost as imposing and interesting as truth.

Our conversations are not always confined to his own history and misfortunes. On every point of general literature he displays unbounded knowledge and a quick and piercing apprehension. His eloquence is forcible and touching; nor can I hear him, when he relates a pathetic incident or endeavours to move the passions of pity or love, without tears. What a glorious creature must he have been in the days of his prosperity, when he is thus noble and godlike in ruin! He seems to feel his own worth and the greatness of his fall.

"When younger," said he, "I believed myself destined for some great enterprise. My feelings are profound, but I possessed a coolness of judgment that fitted me for illustrious achievements. This sentiment of the worth of my nature supported me when others would have been oppressed, for I deemed it criminal to throw away in useless grief those talents that might be useful to my fellow creatures. When I reflected on the work I had completed, no less a one than the creation of a sensitive and rational animal, I could not rank myself with the herd of common projectors. But this thought, which supported me in the commencement of my career, now serves only to plunge me lower in the dust. All my speculations and hopes are as nothing, and like the archangel who aspired to omnipotence, I am chained in an eternal hell. My imagination was vivid, yet my powers of analysis and application were intense; by the union of these qualities I conceived the idea and executed the creation of a man. Even now I cannot recollect without passion my reveries while the work was incomplete. I trod heaven in my thoughts, now exulting in my powers, now burning with the idea of their effects. From my infancy I was imbued with high hopes and a lofty ambition; but how am I sunk! Oh! My friend, if you had known me as I once was, you would not recognize me in this state of degradation. Despondency rarely visited my heart; a high destiny seemed to bear me on, until I fell, never, never again to rise." Must I then lose this admirable being? I have longed for a friend; I have sought one who would sympathize with and love me. Behold, on these desert seas I have found such a one, but I fear I have gained him only to know his value and lose him. I would reconcile him to life, but he repulses the idea.

"I thank you, Walton," he said, "for your kind intentions towards so miserable a wretch; but when you speak of new ties and fresh affections, think you that any can replace those who are gone? Can any man be to me as Clerval was, or any woman another Elizabeth? Even where the affections are not strongly moved by any superior excellence, the companions of our childhood always possess a certain power over our minds which hardly any later friend can obtain. They know our infantine dispositions, which, however they may be afterwards modified, are never eradicated; and they can judge of our actions with more certain conclusions as to the integrity of our motives. A sister or a brother can never, unless indeed such symptoms have been shown early, suspect the other of fraud or false dealing, when another friend, however strongly he may be attached, may, in spite of himself, be contemplated with suspicion. But I enjoyed friends, dear not only through habit and association, but from their own merits; and wherever I am, the soothing voice of my Elizabeth and the conversation of Clerval will be ever whispered in my ear. They are dead, and but one feeling in such a solitude can persuade me to preserve my life. If I were engaged in any high undertaking or design, fraught with extensive utility to my fellow creatures, then could I live to fulfil it. But such is not my destiny; I must pursue and destroy the being to whom I gave existence; then my lot on earth will be fulfilled and I may die."

September 2nd
My beloved Sister,

I WRITE TO YOU, ENCOMPASSED by peril and ignorant whether I am ever doomed to see again dear England and the dearer friends that inhabit it. I am surrounded by mountains of ice which admit of no escape and threaten every moment to crush my vessel. The brave fellows whom I have persuaded to be my companions look towards me for aid, but I have none to bestow. There is something terribly appalling in our situation, yet my courage and hopes do not desert me. Yet it is terrible to reflect that the lives of all these men are endangered through me. If we are lost, my mad schemes are the cause.

And what, Margaret, will be the state of your mind? You will not hear of my destruction, and you will anxiously await my return. Years will pass, and you will have visitings of despair and yet be tortured by hope. Oh! My beloved sister, the sickening failing of your heart-felt expectations is, in prospect, more terrible to me than my own death.

But you have a husband and lovely children; you may be happy. Heaven bless you and make you so!

My unfortunate guest regards me with the tenderest compassion. He endeavours to fill me with hope and talks as if life were a possession which he valued. He reminds me how often the same accidents have happened to other navigators who have attempted this sea, and in spite of myself, he fills me with cheerful auguries. Even the sailors feel the power of his eloquence; when he speaks, they no longer despair; he rouses their energies, and while they hear his voice they believe these vast mountains of ice are mole-hills which will vanish before the resolutions of man. These feelings are transitory; each day of expectation delayed fills them with fear, and I almost dread a mutiny caused by this despair.

September 5th

A SCENE HAS JUST PASSED of such uncommon interest that, although it is highly probable that these papers may never reach you, yet I cannot forbear recording it.

We are still surrounded by mountains of ice, still in imminent danger of being crushed in their conflict. The cold is excessive, and many of my unfortunate comrades have already found a grave amidst this scene of desolation. Frankenstein has daily declined in health; a feverish fire still glimmers in his eyes, but he is exhausted, and when suddenly roused to any exertion, he speedily sinks again into apparent lifelessness.

I mentioned in my last letter the fears I entertained of a mutiny. This morning, as I sat watching the wan countenance of my friend—his eyes half closed and his limbs hanging listlessly—I was roused by half a dozen of the sailors, who demanded admission into the cabin. They entered, and their leader addressed me. He told me that he and his companions had been chosen by the other sailors to come in deputation to me to make me a requisition which, in justice, I could not refuse. We were immured in ice and should probably never escape, but they feared that if, as was possible, the ice should dissipate and a free passage be opened, I should be rash enough to continue my voyage and lead them into fresh dangers, after they might happily have surmounted this. They insisted, therefore, that I should engage with a solemn promise that if the vessel should be freed I would instantly direct my course southwards.

This speech troubled me. I had not despaired, nor had I yet conceived the idea of returning if set free. Yet could I, in justice, or even in possibility, refuse this demand? I hesitated before I answered, when Frankenstein, who had at first been silent, and indeed appeared hardly to have force enough to attend, now roused himself; his eyes sparkled, and his cheeks flushed with momentary vigour. Turning towards the men, he said, "What do you mean? What do you demand of your captain? Are you, then, so easily turned from your design? Did you not call this a glorious expedition?

"And wherefore was it glorious? Not because the way was smooth and placid as a southern sea, but because it was full of dangers and terror, because at every new incident your fortitude was to be called forth and your courage exhibited, because danger and death surrounded it, and these you were to brave and over-come. For this was it a glorious, for this was it an honourable undertaking. You were hereafter to be hailed as the benefactors of your species, your names adored as belonging to brave men who encountered death for honour and the benefit of mankind. And now, behold, with the first imagination of danger, or, if you will, the first mighty and terrific trial of your courage, you shrink away and are content to be handed down as men who had not strength enough to endure cold and peril; and so, poor souls, they were chilly and returned to their warm firesides. Why, that requires not this preparation; ye need not have come thus far and dragged your captain to the shame of a defeat merely to prove yourselves cowards. Oh! Be men, or be more than men. Be steady to your purposes and firm as a rock. This ice is not made of such stuff as your hearts may be; it is mutable and cannot withstand you if you say that it shall not. Do not return to your families with the stigma of disgrace marked on your brows. Return as heroes who have fought and conquered and who know not what it is to turn their backs on the foe." He spoke this with a voice so modulated to the different feelings expressed in his speech, with an eye so full of lofty design and heroism, that can you wonder that these men were moved? They looked at one another and were unable to reply. I spoke; I told them to retire and consider of what had been said, that I would not lead them farther north if they strenuously desired the contrary, but that I hoped that, with reflection, their courage would return. They retired and I turned towards my friend, but he was sunk in languor and almost deprived of life.

How all this will terminate, I know not, but I had rather die than return shamefully, my purpose unfulfilled. Yet I fear such will be my fate; the men, unsupported by ideas of glory and honour, can never willingly continue to endure their present hardships.

September 7th

THE DIE IS CAST; I have consented to return if we are not destroyed. Thus are my hopes blasted by cowardice and indecision; I come back ignorant and disappointed. It requires more philosophy than I possess to bear this injustice with patience.

September 12th

IT IS PAST; I AM RETURNING to England. I have lost my hopes of utility and glory; I have lost my friend. But I will endeavour to detail these bitter circumstances to you, my dear sister; and while I am wafted towards England and towards you, I will not despond.

September 9th, the ice began to move, and roarings like thunder were heard at a distance as the islands split and cracked in every direction. We were in the most imminent peril, but as we could only remain passive, my chief attention was occupied by my unfortunate guest whose illness increased in such a degree that he was entirely confined to his bed. The ice cracked behind us and was driven with force towards the north; a breeze sprang from the west, and on the 11th the passage towards the south became perfectly free. When the sailors saw this and that their return to their native country was apparently assured, a shout of tumultuous joy broke from them, loud and long-continued. Frankenstein, who was dozing, awoke and asked the cause of the tumult. "They shout," I said, "because they will soon return to England."

"Do you, then, really return?"

"Alas! Yes; I cannot withstand their demands. I cannot lead them unwillingly to danger, and I must return."

"Do so, if you will; but I will not. You may give up your purpose, but mine is assigned to me by heaven, and I dare not. I am weak, but surely the spirits who assist my vengeance will endow me with sufficient strength." Saying this, he endeavoured to spring from the bed, but the exertion was too great for him; he fell back and fainted.

It was long before he was restored, and I often thought that life was entirely extinct. At length he opened his eyes; he breathed with difficulty and was unable to speak. The surgeon gave him a composing draught and ordered us to leave him undisturbed. In the meantime he told me that my friend had certainly not many hours to live.

His sentence was pronounced, and I could only grieve and be patient. I sat by his bed, watching him; his eyes were closed, and I thought he slept; but presently he called to me in a feeble voice, and bidding me come near, said, "Alas! The strength I relied on is gone; I feel that I shall soon die, and he, my enemy and persecutor, may still be in being. Think not, Walton, that in the last moments of my existence I feel that burning hatred and ardent desire of revenge I once expressed; but I feel myself justified in desiring the death of my adversary. During these last days I have been occupied in examining my past conduct; nor do I find it blamable. In a fit of enthusiastic madness I created a rational creature and was bound towards him to assure, as far as was in my power, his happiness and well-being.

"This was my duty, but there was another still paramount to that. My duties towards the beings of my own species had greater claims to my attention because they included a greater proportion of happiness or misery. Urged by this view, I refused, and I did right in refusing, to create a companion for the first creature. He showed unparalleled malignity and selfishness in evil; he destroyed my friends; he devoted to destruction beings who possessed exquisite sensations, happiness, and wisdom; nor do I know where this thirst for vengeance may end. Miserable himself that he may render no other wretched, he ought to die. The task of his destruction was mine, but I have failed. When actuated by selfish and vicious motives, I asked you to undertake my unfinished work, and I renew this request now, when I am only induced by reason and virtue.

"Yet I cannot ask you to renounce your country and friends to fulfil this task; and now that you are returning to England, you will have little chance of meeting with him. But the consideration of these points, and the well balancing of what you may esteem your duties, I leave to you; my judgment and ideas are already disturbed by the near approach of death. I dare not ask you to do what I think right, for I may still be misled by passion.

"That he should live to be an instrument of mischief disturbs me; in other respects, this hour, when I momentarily expect my release, is the only happy one which I have enjoyed for several years. The forms of the beloved dead flit before me, and I hasten to their arms. Farewell, Walton! Seek happiness in tranquillity and avoid ambition, even if it be only the apparently innocent one of distinguishing yourself in science and discoveries. Yet why do I say this? I have myself been blasted in these hopes, yet another may succeed."

His voice became fainter as he spoke, and at length, exhausted by his effort, he sank into silence. About half an hour afterwards he attempted again to speak but was unable; he pressed my hand feebly, and his eyes closed forever, while the irradiation of a gentle smile passed away from his lips.

Margaret, what comment can I make on the untimely extinction of this glorious spirit? What can I say that will enable you to understand the depth of my sorrow? All that I should express would be inadequate and feeble. My tears flow; my mind is overshadowed by a cloud of disappointment. But I journey towards England, and I may there find consolation.

I am interrupted. What do these sounds portend? It is midnight; the breeze blows fairly, and the watch on deck scarcely stir. Again there is a sound as of a human voice, but hoarser; it comes from the cabin where the remains of Frankenstein still lie. I must arise and examine. Good night, my sister.

Great God! what a scene has just taken place! I am yet dizzy with the remembrance of it. I hardly know whether I shall have the power to detail it; yet the tale which I have recorded would be incomplete without this final and wonderful catastrophe. I entered the cabin where lay the remains of my ill-fated and admirable friend. Over him hung a form which I cannot find words to describe—gigantic in stature, yet uncouth and distorted in its proportions. As he hung over the coffin, his face was concealed by long locks of ragged hair; but one vast hand was extended, in colour and apparent texture like that of a mummy. When he heard the sound of my approach, he ceased to utter exclamations of grief and horror and sprung towards the window. Never did I behold a vision so horrible as his face, of such loathsome yet appalling hideousness. I shut my eyes involuntarily and endeavoured to recollect what were my duties with regard to this destroyer. I called on him to stay.

He paused, looking on me with wonder, and again turning towards the lifeless form of his creator, he seemed to forget my presence, and every feature and gesture seemed instigated by the wildest rage of some uncontrollable passion.

"That is also my victim!" he exclaimed. "In his murder my crimes are consummated; the miserable series of my being is wound to its close! Oh, Frankenstein! Generous and self-devoted being! What does it avail that I now ask thee to pardon me? I, who irretrievably destroyed thee by destroying all thou lovedst. Alas! He is cold, he cannot answer me." His voice seemed suffocated, and my first impulses, which had suggested to me the duty of obeying the dying request of my friend in destroying his enemy, were now suspended by a mixture of curiosity and compassion. I approached this tremendous being; I dared not again raise my eyes to his face, there was something so scaring and unearthly in his ugliness. I attempted to speak, but the words died away on my lips. The monster continued to utter wild and incoherent self-reproaches. At length I gathered resolution to address him in a pause of the tempest of his passion.

"Your repentance," I said, "is now superfluous. If you had listened to the voice of conscience and heeded the stings of remorse before you had urged your diabolical vengeance to this extremity, Frankenstein would yet have lived."

"And do you dream?" said the daemon. "Do you think that I was then dead to agony and remorse? He," he continued, pointing to the corpse, "he suffered not in the consummation of the deed. Oh! Not the ten-thousandth portion of the anguish that was mine during the lingering detail of its execution. A frightful selfishness hurried me on, while my heart was poisoned with remorse. Think you that the groans of Clerval were music to my ears? My heart was fashioned to be susceptible of love and sympathy, and when wrenched by misery to vice and hatred, it did not endure the violence of the change without torture such as you cannot even imagine.

"After the murder of Clerval I returned to Switzerland, heart-broken and overcome. I pitied Frankenstein; my pity amounted to horror; I abhorred myself. But when I discovered that he, the author at once of my existence and of its unspeakable torments, dared to hope for happiness, that while he accumulated wretchedness and despair upon me he sought his own enjoyment in feelings and passions from the indulgence of which I was forever barred, then impotent envy and bitter indignation filled me with an insatiable thirst for vengeance. I recollected my threat and resolved that it should be accomplished. I knew that I was preparing for myself a deadly torture, but I was the slave, not the master, of an impulse which I detested yet could not disobey. Yet when she died! Nay, then I was not miserable. I had cast off all feeling, subdued all anguish, to riot in the excess of my despair. Evil thenceforth became my good. Urged thus far,

I had no choice but to adapt my nature to an element which I had willingly chosen. The completion of my demoniacal design became an insatiable passion. And now it is ended; there is my last victim!"

I was at first touched by the expressions of his misery; yet, when I called to mind what Frankenstein had said of his powers of eloquence and persuasion, and when I again cast my eyes on the lifeless form of my friend, indignation was rekindled within me. "Wretch!" I said. "It is well that you come here to whine over the desolation that you have made. You throw a torch into a pile of buildings, and when they are consumed, you sit among the ruins and lament the fall. Hypocritical fiend! If he whom you mourn still lived, still would he be the object, again would he become the prey, of your accursed vengeance. It is not pity that you feel; you lament only because the victim of your malignity is withdrawn from your power."

"Oh, it is not thus—not thus," interrupted the being. "Yet such must be the impression conveyed to you by what appears to be the purport of my actions. Yet I seek not a fellow feeling in my misery. No sympathy may I ever find. When I first sought it, it was the love of virtue, the feelings of happiness and affection with which my whole being overflowed, that I wished to be participated. But now that virtue has become to me a shadow, and that happiness and affection are turned into bitter and loathing despair, in what should I seek for sympathy? I am content to suffer alone while my sufferings shall endure; when I die, I am well satisfied that abhorrence and opprobrium should load my memory. Once my fancy was soothed with dreams of virtue, of fame, and of enjoyment. Once I falsely hoped to meet with beings who, pardoning my outward form, would love me for the excellent qualities which I was capable of unfolding. I was nourished with high thoughts of honour and devotion. But now crime has degraded me beneath the meanest animal. No guilt, no mischief, no malignity, no misery, can be found comparable to mine. When I run over the frightful catalogue of my sins, I cannot believe that I am the same creature whose thoughts were once filled with sublime and transcendent visions of the beauty and the majesty of goodness. But it is even so; the fallen angel becomes a malignant devil. Yet even that enemy of God and man had friends and associates in his desolation; I am alone.

"You, who call Frankenstein your friend, seem to have a knowledge of my crimes and his misfortunes. But in the detail which he gave you of them he could not sum up the hours and months of misery which I endured wasting in impotent passions. For while I destroyed his hopes, I did not satisfy my own desires. They were forever ardent and craving; still I desired love and fellowship, and I was still spurned. Was there no injustice in this? Am I to be thought the only criminal, when all humankind sinned against me? Why do you not hate Felix, who drove his friend from his door with contumely? Why do you not execrate the rustic who sought to destroy the saviour of his child? Nay, these are virtuous and immaculate beings! I, the miserable and the abandoned, am an abortion, to be spurned at, and kicked, and trampled on. Even now my blood boils at the recollection of this injustice.

"But it is true that I am a wretch. I have murdered the lovely and the helpless; I have strangled the innocent as they slept and grasped to death his throat who never injured me or any other living thing. I have devoted my creator, the select specimen of all that is worthy of love and admiration among men, to misery; I have pursued him even to that irremediable ruin.

"There he lies, white and cold in death. You hate me, but your abhorrence cannot equal that with which I regard myself. I look on the hands which executed the deed; I think on the heart in which the imagination of it was conceived and long for the moment when these hands will meet my eyes, when that imagination will haunt my thoughts no more.

"Fear not that I shall be the instrument of future mischief. My work is nearly complete. Neither yours nor any man's death is needed to consummate the series of my being and accomplish that which must be done, but it requires my own. Do not think that I shall be slow to perform this sacrifice. I shall quit your vessel on the ice raft which brought me thither and shall seek the most northern extremity of the globe; I shall collect my funeral pile and consume to ashes this miserable frame, that its remains may afford no light to any curious and unhallowed wretch who would create such another as I have been. I shall die. I shall no longer feel the agonies which now consume me or be the prey of feelings unsatisfied, yet unquenched. He is dead who called me into being; and when I shall be no more, the very remembrance of us both will speedily vanish. I shall no longer see the sun or stars or feel the winds play on my cheeks.

"Light, feeling, and sense will pass away; and in this condition must I find my happiness. Some years ago, when the images which this world affords first opened upon me, when I felt the cheering warmth of summer and heard the rustling of the leaves and the warbling of the birds, and these were all to me, I should have wept to die; now it is my only consolation. Polluted by crimes and torn by the bitterest remorse, where can I find rest but in death?

"Farewell! I leave you, and in you the last of humankind whom these eyes will ever behold. Farewell, Frankenstein! If thou wert yet alive and yet cherished a desire of revenge against me, it would be better satiated in my life than in my destruction. But it was not so; thou didst seek my extinction, that I might not cause greater wretchedness; and if yet, in some mode unknown to me, thou hadst not ceased to think and feel, thou wouldst not desire against me a vengeance greater than that which I feel. Blasted as thou wert, my agony was still superior to thine, for the bitter sting of remorse will not cease to rankle in my wounds until death shall close them forever.

"But soon," he cried with sad and solemn enthusiasm, "I shall die, and what I now feel be no longer felt. Soon these burning miseries will be extinct. I shall ascend my funeral pile triumphantly and exult in the agony of the torturing flames. The light of that conflagration will fade away; my ashes will be swept into the sea by the winds. My spirit will sleep in peace, or if it thinks, it will not surely think thus. Farewell."

He sprang from the cabin window as he said this, upon the ice raft which lay close to the vessel.[2] He was soon borne away by the waves and lost in darkness and distance.[3] ◄

CHAPTER 24
Annotations

1. The monster lures Frankenstein, pulling him into a senseless chase around the world. After killing William, Justine (by proxy), Clerval, and Elizabeth, the monster does not attempt to kill Victor's father or adult brother. He seems, for some mysterious reason, to leave intact the Frankenstein patriarchal line. Instead, having killed those who were vulnerable to and beloved by Victor, the monster then taunts his creator with the idea that he will "wrestle" with him. This image of Jacob wrestling with the angel is potent, but the homoerotic press of the monster's invitation to Victor is even more potent. The two are bound together by a visceral bond of chase, and the eroticization of the chase is inescapable (though also unfulfilled). Strikingly, the monster lures Victor to the farthest north, apparently the Arctic Circle. The idea that this terrain is uninhabitable reveals Shelley's immersion in the colonizing thrust of her culture and time. As I've noted, indigenous peoples from the Saami, to the Nenet, to the Yupik, and others, have inhabited the realm for many centuries. The novel states that the monster is able to withstand the extreme conditions of the far north, whereas Victor cannot, further associating the monster with indigenous peoples. They, of course do not have differential physical attributes that permit them to survive in the Arctic Circle but rather have developed cultures that make life sustainable in this realm). The far north, in *Frankenstein*, stands as a symbol for the limit of the human, much as does the monster; it also stands as a symbol for the sublime, the end of the domestic, a realm of conquest, as the British were fascinated with planting their flag. Though the explorations of Sir James Clark Ross occurred a couple decades after Shelley wrote her first novel, she predicts them. The north as the limit of the human is the fitting place for Shelley to bring her novel of nihilism for its conclusion.

2. After Frankenstein dies, the monster appears and expresses — perhaps unsurprisingly — his love for his creator. Before Walton, he repents his crimes and vows to do no further "mischief." And yet, there is no narrative explanation for this change of heart. The monster's words do explain why he does not murder Walton who, as Frankenstein's dear friend, should be a target for the monster. But the monster's closing soliloquy does not explain his changed attitude. Walton suggests, in his letter to his sister that contains the monster's last speech, that the monster's eloquence can disarm the listener, suggesting

the monster may well be lying about his intention to commit no further violence. Here, Shelley clearly sets the monster as a parallel figure to John Milton's Lucifer, in *Paradise Lost,* the fallen angel. But Shelley's monster is ambiguous and ambivalent as a signifier of violence. He is rather more a signifier of loss, grief, and the outcast condition of the motherless child. It is notable that Shelley's novel ends with ambiguity: the monster disappears into "darkness and distance," into the north. He is not going to return to England, with Walton's failed expedition. He is staying in the place of the sublime. And though he claims he will commit no more violence, Walton's caution — in the letter to his sister — suggests that the novel's open-ended conclusion could mean the monster survives, and moreover, does not cease to commit violence. If Shelley wanted her reader to be certain that the monster's life, and capacity to commit violence, were over, she would have closed the novel with his death. But instead, she presses her narrative into a space of sublime ambiguity: the monster disappears into the far north. That is all we know.

The monster's appearance before Walton has the dramatic effect, also, of proving Victor's story. Up until the moment that Walton sees the monster, we can think that maybe the monster is a metaphor for Victor's own murderousness. That is, that maybe Victor is lying the whole time and coming up with this figure of a monster to cover the fact that he himself murdered William, Clerval, and Elizabeth. But once the monster appears that tack of reading is closed. The monster is not a figment of Victor's imagination but real.

3. Here, I turn to a brief discussion of the tropes, or ways of telling, that Mary Shelley deploys in *Frankenstein*, for they have significant bearing on her approach to writing *Mathilda*. We are never given direct access to Victor Frankenstein's voice nor to the monster's voice. Instead, the entire story is told through Walton's transcription. Beyond this, even Walton's voice is arguably not the ultimate agent of the telling of the story but rather his sister (the letters' recipient) is the storyteller. While, as many have pointed out, Walton's sister bears the same initials as Mary Wollstonecraft Shelley herself, what is perhaps more significant is that Frankenstein's story is presented as a story so wildly painful, and so hard to believe, that it must be transferred through several narrative bands to the reader. It is a molten story, about a secret that cannot be believed, and that causes immense destruction because it cannot be told. Finally, it is told, but only after the secret has worked its destructive force.

In this narrative trait, *Frankenstein* is like *Mathilda*. Both the novel and the novella are structured around the problem of a secret so dire, so violent, so outside everyday experience, as to be unacceptable to be conveyed. And yet, also, for both works the story's not being told destroys all those connected to it. In this sense, Shelley makes clear the extreme force and power of stories, especially secret stories.

Structurally, both *Frankenstein* and *Mathilda* handle a molten and secret story by diffusing the narrative through witnesses who then intercede to carry the story to the reader. The narrative of Frankenstein is not told to us by the monster, not told to us by Victor, Clerval, Elizabeth; it is not conveyed to the reader by anyone directly connected to the events described. Instead, it is a story within a story within a story: conveyed through multiple turns of narrative so that we are, in a sense, protected from the intensity of the story. It is given to us through multiple narrators, each with less and less at stake in the horror presented. Recall that Shelley describes the monster as terrifying merely to look upon. In this sense, the monster is himself a figure for the unbearable secret, an emblem of that which we cannot bear to know but which is also entirely, searingly, real and true. The monster is that monstrous secret which we need to be able to see.

Similarly, *Mathilda* is a novella centered around an intolerable secret. Mathilda's story of paternal incestuous desire is rendered "safe" for readers by two narrative gestures. Mathilda is dying when she tells the story. The "poison" of the incest secret, then, is dying with her. Moreover, the entire story is transmitted for Woodville, Mathilda's poet friend. Hence, we can assume that we are reading not directly Mathilda's manuscript but rather Woodville's transcription of it. Here again, we the readers are protected from the horror of the secret by a narrative structure that at once permits the secret to be told but also diffuses the intensity of its conveyance by placing narrative structures between the core secret/story and the reader. Shelley later came superstitiously to believe that *Mathilda* in particular was a novella that had the capacity to actually cause harm to her and those she loved. After her husband's death, by drowning, she drew a parallel between the scene of the father's death, in *Mathilda*, and her actual, lived, approach to the scene of Percy Bysshe Shelley's death by drowning. This superstitious belief that what she wrote could then affect her real life — not because it was published and people reacted to it, but because it had a magical power to shape her fate — indicates Shelley's feeling that secrets, stories, and the ways they are told, have immense power, dangerous power, over real life. This belief is evinced in the intricate narrative structures in which she encases her molten stories of sexuality, paternal vice, and the aching wound of the abused child. ◄

Mathilda

CHAPTER 1

Florence. Nov. 9th 1819

IT IS ONLY FOUR O'CLOCK; but it is winter and the sun has already set: there are no clouds in the clear, frosty sky to reflect its slant beams, but the air itself is tinged with a slight roseate colour which is again reflected on the snow that covers the ground. I live in a lone cottage on a solitary, wide heath: no voice of life reaches me. I see the desolate plain covered with white, save a few black patches that the noonday sun has made at the top of those sharp pointed hillocks from which the snow, sliding as it fell, lay thinner than on the plain ground: a few birds are pecking at the hard ice that covers the pools—for the frost has been of long continuance.[1]

I am in a strange state of mind. I am alone—quite alone—in the world—the blight of misfortune has passed over me and withered me; I know that I am about to die and I feel happy—joyous.—I feel my pulse; it beats fast: I place my thin hand on my cheek; it burns: there is a slight, quick spirit within me which is now emitting its last sparks. I shall never see the snows of another winter—I do believe that I shall never again feel the vivifying warmth of another summer sun; and it is in this persuasion that I begin to write my tragic history. Perhaps a history such as mine had better die with me, but a feeling that I cannot define leads me on and I am too weak both in body and mind to resist the slightest impulse. While life was strong within me I thought indeed that there was a sacred horror in my tale that rendered it unfit for utterance, and now about to die I pollute its mystic terrors. It is as the wood of the Eumenides none but the dying may enter; and Oedipus is about to die.

What am I writing? — I must collect my thoughts. I do not know that any will peruse these pages except you, my friend, who will receive them at my death. I do not address them to you alone because it will give me pleasure to dwell upon our friendship in a way that would be needless if you alone read what I shall write. I shall relate my tale therefore as if I wrote for strangers. You have often asked me the cause of my solitary life; my tears; and above all of my impenetrable and unkind silence. In life I dared not; in death I unveil the mystery. Others will toss these pages lightly over: to you, Woodville, kind, affectionate friend, they will be dear — the precious memorials of a heart-broken girl who, dying, is still warmed by gratitude towards you: your tears will fall on the words that record my misfortunes; I know they will — and while I have life I thank you for your sympathy.

But enough of this. I will begin my tale: it is my last task, and I hope I have strength sufficient to fulfill it. I record no crimes; my faults may easily be pardoned; for they proceeded not from evil motive but from want of judgement; and I believe few would say that they could, by a different conduct and superior wisdom, have avoided the misfortunes to which I am the victim. My fate has been governed by necessity, a hideous necessity. It required hands stronger than mine; stronger I do believe than any human force to break the thick, adamantine chain that has bound me, once breathing nothing but joy, ever possessed by a warm love & delight in goodness, — to misery only to be ended, and now about to be ended, in death. But I forget myself, my tale is yet untold. I will pause a few moments, wipe my dim eyes, and endeavour to lose the present obscure but heavy feeling of unhappiness in the more acute emotions of the past.

I was born in England. My father was a man of rank: he had lost his father early, and was educated by a weak mother with all the indulgence she thought due to a nobleman of wealth. He was sent to Eton and afterwards to college; & allowed from childhood the free use of large sums of money; thus enjoying from his earliest youth the independance which a boy with these advantages, always acquires at a public school.

Under the influence of these circumstances his passions found a deep soil wherein they might strike their roots and flourish either as flowers or weeds as was their nature. By being always allowed to act for himself his character became strongly and early marked and exhibited a various surface on which a quick sighted observer might see the seeds of virtues and of misfortunes. His careless extravagance, which made him squander immense sums of money to satisfy passing whims, which from their apparent energy he dignified with the name of passions, often displayed itself in unbounded generosity. Yet while he earnestly occupied himself about the wants of others his own desires were gratified to their fullest extent. He gave his money, but none of his own wishes were sacrifised to his gifts; he gave his time, which he did not value, and his affections which he was happy in any manner to have called into action.

I do not say that if his own desires had been put in competition with those of others that he would have displayed undue selfishness, but this trial was never made. He was nurtured in prosperity and attended by all its advantages; every one loved him and wished to gratify him. He was ever employed in promoting the pleasures of his companions—but their pleasures were his; and if he bestowed more attention upon the feelings of others than is usual with schoolboys it was because his social temper could never enjoy itself if every brow was not as free from care as his own.

While at school, emulation and his own natural abilities made him hold a conspicuous rank in the forms among his equals; at college he discarded books; he believed that he had other lessons to learn than those which they could teach him. He was now to enter into life and he was still young enough to consider study as a school-boy shackle, employed merely to keep the unruly out of mischief but as having no real connexion with life—whose wisdom of riding—gaming &c. he considered with far deeper interest—So he quickly entered into all college follies although his heart was too well moulded to be contaminated by them—it might be light but it was never cold. He was a sincere and sympathizing friend—but he had met with none who superior or equal to himself could aid him in unfolding his mind, or make him seek for fresh stores of thought by exhausting the old ones. He felt himself superior in quickness of judgement to those around him: his talents, his rank and wealth made him the chief of his party, and in that station he rested not only contented but glorying, conceiving it to be the only ambition worthy for him to aim at in the world.

By a strange narrowness of ideas he viewed all the world in connexion only as it was or was not related to his little society. He considered queer and out of fashion all opinions that were exploded by his circle of intimates, and he became at the same time dogmatic and yet fearful of not coinciding with the only sentiments he could consider orthodox. To the generality of spectators he appeared careless of censure, and with high disdain to throw aside all dependance on public prejudices; but at the same time that he strode with a triumphant stride over the rest of the world, he cowered, with self disguised lowliness, to his own party, and although its chief never dared express an opinion or a feeling until he was assured that it would meet with the approbation of his companions.

Yet he had one secret hidden from these dear friends; a secret he had nurtured from his earliest years, and although he loved his fellow collegiates he would not trust it to the delicacy or sympathy of any one among them. He loved. He feared that the intensity of his passion might become the subject of their ridicule; and he could not bear that they should blaspheme it by considering that trivial and transitory which he felt was the life of his life.

There was a gentleman of small fortune who lived near his family mansion who had three lovely daughters. The eldest was far the most beautiful, but her beauty was only an addition to her other qualities—her understanding was clear & strong and her disposition angelically gentle. She and my father had been playmates from infancy: Diana, even in her childhood had been a favourite with his mother; this partiality encreased with the years of this beautiful and lively girl and thus during his school & college vacations they were perpetually together. Novels and all the various methods by which youth in civilized life are led to a knowledge of the existence of passions before they really feel them, had produced a strong effect on him who was so peculiarly susceptible of every impression. At eleven years of age Diana was his favourite playmate but he already talked the language of love. Although she was elder than he by nearly two years the nature of her education made her more childish at least in the knowledge and expression of feeling; she received his warm protestations with innocence, and returned them unknowing of what they meant. She had read no novels and associated only with her younger sisters, what could she know of the difference between love and friendship? And when the development of her understanding disclosed the true nature of this intercourse to her, her affections were already engaged to her friend, and all she feared was lest other attractions and fickleness might make him break his infant vows.

But they became every day more ardent and tender. It was a passion that had grown with his growth; it had become entwined with every faculty and every sentiment and only to be lost with life. None knew of their love except their own two hearts; yet although in all things else, and even in this he dreaded the censure of his companions, for thus truly loving one inferior to him in fortune, nothing was ever able for a moment to shake his purpose of uniting himself to her as soon as he could muster courage sufficient to meet those difficulties he was determined to surmount.

Diana was fully worthy of his deepest affection. There were few who could boast of so pure a heart, and so much real humbleness of soul joined to a firm reliance on her own integrity and a belief in that of others. She had from her birth lived a retired life. She had lost her mother when very young, but her father had devoted himself to the care of her education—He had many peculiar ideas which influenced the system he had adopted with regard to her—She was well acquainted with the heroes of Greece and Rome or with those of England who had lived some hundred years ago, while she was nearly ignorant of the passing events of the day: she had read few authors who had written during at least the last fifty years but her reading with this exception was very extensive. Thus although she appeared to be less initiated in the mysteries of life and society than he her knowledge was of a deeper kind and laid on firmer foundations; and if even her beauty and sweetness had not fascinated him her understanding would ever have held his in thrall. He looked up to her as his guide, and such was his adoration that he delighted to augment to his own mind the sense of inferiority with which she sometimes impressed him.

When he was nineteen his mother died. He left college on this event and shaking off for a while his old friends he retired to the neighbourhood of his Diana and received all his consolation from her sweet voice and dearer caresses. This short seperation from his companions gave him courage to assert his independance. He had a feeling that however they might express ridicule of his intended marriage they would not dare display it when it had taken place; therefore seeking the consent of his guardian which with some difficulty he obtained, and of the father of his mistress which was more easily given, without acquainting any one else of his intention, by the time he had attained his twentieth birthday he had become the husband of Diana.

He loved her with passion and her tenderness had a charm for him that would not permit him to think of aught but her. He invited some of his college friends to see him but their frivolity disgusted him. Diana had torn the veil which had before kept him in his boyhood: he was become a man and he was surprised how he could ever have joined in the cant words and ideas of his fellow collegiates or how for a moment he had feared the censure of such as these. He discarded his old friendships not from fickleness but because they were indeed unworthy of him. Diana filled up all his heart: he felt as if by his union with her he had received a new and better soul. She was his monitress as he learned what were the true ends of life. It was through her beloved lessons that he cast off his old pursuits and gradually formed himself to become one among his fellow men; a distinguished member of society, a Patriot; and an enlightened lover of truth and virtue. — He loved her for her beauty and for her amiable disposition but he seemed to love her more for what he considered her superior wisdom. They studied, they rode together; they were never seperate and seldom admitted a third to their society.

Thus my father, born in affluence, and always prosperous, clombe without the difficulty and various disappointments that all human beings seem destined to encounter, to the very topmost pinacle of happiness: Around him was sunshine, and clouds whose shapes of beauty made the prospect divine concealed from him the barren reality which lay hidden below them. From this dizzy point he was dashed at once as he unawares congratulated himself on his felicity. Fifteen months after their marriage I was born, and my mother died a few days after my birth.

A sister of my father was with him at this period. She was nearly fifteen years older than he, and was the offspring of a former marriage of his father. When the latter died this sister was taken by her maternal relations: they had seldom seen one another, and were quite unlike in disposition. This aunt, to whose care I was afterwards consigned, has often related to me the effect that this catastrophe had on my father's strong and susceptible character. From the moment of my mother's death untill his departure she never heard him utter a single word: buried in the deepest melancholy he took no notice of any one; often for hours his eyes streamed tears or a more fearful gloom overpowered him. All outward things seemed to have lost their existence relatively to him and only one circumstance could in any degree recall him from his motionless and mute despair: he would never see me. He seemed insensible to the presence of any one else, but if, as a trial to awaken his sensibility, my aunt brought me into the room he would instantly rush out with every symptom of fury and distraction. At the end of a month he suddenly quitted his house and, unatteneded [sic] by any servant, departed from that part of the country without by word or writing informing any one of his intentions. My aunt was only relieved of her anxiety concerning his fate by a letter from him dated Hamburgh.

How often have I wept over that letter which untill I was sixteen was the only relick I had to remind me of my parents. "Pardon me," it said, "for the uneasiness I have unavoidably given you: but while in that unhappy island, where every thing breathes _her_ spirit whom I have lost for ever, a spell held me. It is broken: I have quitted England for many years, perhaps for ever. But to convince you that selfish feeling does not entirely engross me I shall remain in this town untill you have made by letter every arrangement that you judge necessary. When I leave this place do not expect to hear from me: I must break all ties that at present exist. I shall become a wanderer, a miserable outcast—alone! alone!"—In another part of the letter he mentioned me—"As for that unhappy little being whom I could not see, and hardly dare mention, I leave her under your protection. Take care of her and cherish her: one day I may claim her at your hands; but futurity is dark, make the present happy to her."

My father remained three months at Hamburgh; when he quitted it he changed his name, my aunt could never discover that which he adopted and only by faint hints, could conjecture that he had taken the road of Germany and Hungary to Turkey.

Thus this towering spirit who had excited interest and high expectation in all who knew and could value him became at once, as it were, extinct. He existed from this moment for himself only. His friends remembered him as a brilliant vision which would never again return to them. The memory of what he had been faded away as years passed; and he who before had been as a part of themselves and of their hopes was now no longer counted among the living. ◀

CHAPTER 1
Annotations

1. *Mathilda* is a more intimate narrative than *Frankenstein*. As we begin reading, we feel we are being directly addressed by a person who is all alone and thus speaking only to us. As we'll see, the narrative is actually addressed to someone else—Woodville—placing the reader as a kind of interloper, who sees a text that began as an intimate secret between the speaker and Woodville. Even so, as we begin Shelley's novella, we have the feeling of being brought deeply and quickly into someone else's secret, private world. This speaker tells us that she is alone and lives in a "lone" cottage, that is, she is isolated, and she is dying. We feel we are being summoned to the death bed confession of someone who will tell us everything: that is the way the narrative establishes itself, with intensity, intimacy, and urgency. We are told that if we continue to read we will learn a "sacred horror," a secret that is both set apart and in some sense holy and also too horrific to have been made public while the speaker was still concerned with having a public identity. In this sense, we know we are going to learn a secret that annihilates the speaker's public identity and also, paradoxically, creates her true identity. As the speaker turns to address the friend, Woodville, for whom the story is told, she challenges us, her readers, to care as much as he about her suffering. Since Shelley is writing fiction, here, the speaker is not Mary Shelley but the novella's eponymous heroine Mathilda, and Woodville of course is also a fictional character. What is not fictional is us—the readers—and we are challenged to take the narrative seriously, to not turn "lightly" through it. ◀

CHAPTER 2

NOW COME TO MY OWN STORY. During the early part of my life there is little to relate, and I will be brief; but I must be allowed to dwell a little on the years of my childhood that it may be apparent how when one hope failed all life was to be a blank; and how when the only affection I was permitted to cherish was blasted my existence was extinguished with it.

I have said that my aunt was very unlike my father. I believe that without the slightest tinge of a bad heart she had the coldest that ever filled a human breast: it was totally incapable of any affection. She took me under her protection because she considered it her duty; but she had too long lived alone and undisturbed by the noise and prattle of children to allow that I should disturb her quiet. She had never been married; and for the last five years had lived perfectly alone on an estate, that had descended to her through her mother, on the shores of Loch Lomond in Scotland. My father had expressed a wish in his letters that she should reside with me at his family mansion which was situated in a beautiful country near Richmond in Yorkshire. She would not consent to this proposition, but as soon as she had arranged the affairs which her brother's departure had caused to fall to her care, she quitted England and took me with her to her scotch estate.

The care of me while a baby, and afterwards untill I had reached my eighth year devolved on a servant of my mother's, who had accompanied us in our retirement for that purpose. I was placed in a remote part of the house, and only saw my aunt at stated hours. These occurred twice a day; once about noon she came to my nursery, and once after her dinner I was taken to her. She never caressed me, and seemed all the time I staid in the room to fear that I should annoy her by some childish freak. My good nurse always schooled me with the greatest care before she ventured into the parlour—and the awe my aunt's cold looks and few constrained words inspired was so great that I seldom disgraced her lessons or was betrayed from the exemplary stillness which I was taught to observe during these short visits.

Under my good nurse's care I ran wild about our park and the neighbouring fields. The offspring of the deepest love I displayed from my earliest years the greatest sensibility of disposition. I cannot say with what passion I loved every thing even the inanimate objects that surrounded me. I believe that I bore an individual attachment to every tree in our park; every animal that inhabited it knew me and I loved them. Their occasional deaths filled my infant heart with anguish. I cannot number the birds that I have saved during the long and severe winters of that climate; or the hares and rabbits that I have defended from the attacks of our dogs, or have nursed when accidentally wounded.[1]

When I was seven years of age my nurse left me. I now forget the cause of her departure if indeed I ever knew it. She returned to England, and the bitter tears she shed at parting were the last I saw flow for love of me for many years. My grief was terrible: I had no friend but her in the whole world. By degrees I became reconciled to solitude but no one supplied her place in my affections. I lived in a desolate country where

— — — there were none to praise   And very few to love.[2]

It is true that I now saw a little more of my aunt, but she was in every way an unsocial being; and to a timid child she was as a plant beneath a thick covering of ice; I should cut my hands in endeavouring to get at it. So I was entirely thrown upon my own resourses. The neighbouring minister was engaged to give me lessons in reading, writing and french, but he was without family and his manners even to me were always perfectly characteristic of the profession in the exercise of whose functions he chiefly shone, that of a schoolmaster. I sometimes strove to form friendships with the most attractive of the girls who inhabited the neighbouring village; but I believe I should never have succeeded [even] had not my aunt interposed her authority to prevent all intercourse between me and the peasantry; for she was fearful lest I should acquire the Scotch accent and dialect; a little of it I had, although great pains was taken that my tongue should not disgrace my English origin.

As I grew older my liberty increased with my desires, and my wanderings extended from our park to the neighbouring country. Our house was situated on the shores of the lake and the lawn came down to the water's edge. I rambled amidst the wild scenery of this lovely country and became a complete mountaineer: I passed hours on the steep brow of a mountain that overhung a waterfall or rowed myself in a little skiff to some one of the islands. I wandered for ever about these lovely solitudes, gathering flower after flower *Ond' era pinta tutta la mia via* singing as I might the wild melodies of the country, or occupied by pleasant day dreams. My greatest pleasure was the enjoyment of a serene sky amidst these verdant woods: yet I loved all the changes of Nature; and rain, and storm, and the beautiful clouds of heaven brought their delights with them. When rocked by the waves of the lake my spirits rose in triumph as a horseman feels with pride the motions of his high fed steed.

But my pleasures arose from the contemplation of nature alone, I had no companion: my warm affections finding no return from any other human heart were forced to run waste on inanimate objects. Sometimes indeed I wept when my aunt received my caresses with repulsive coldness, and when I looked round and found none to love; but I quickly dried my tears. As I grew older books in some degree supplied the place of human intercourse: the library of my aunt was very small; Shakespear, Milton, Pope and Cowper were the strangley [sic] assorted poets of her collection; and among the prose authors a translation of Livy and Rollin's ancient history were my chief favourites although as I emerged from childhood I found others highly interesting which I had before neglected as dull.

When I was twelve years old it occurred to my aunt that I ought to learn music; she herself played upon the harp. It was with great hesitation that she persuaded herself to undertake my instruction; yet believing this accomplishment a necessary part of my education, and balancing the evils of this measure or of having some one in the house to instruct me she submitted to the inconvenience. A harp was sent for that my playing might not interfere with hers, and I began: she found me a docile and when I had conquered the first rudiments a very apt scholar. I had acquired in my harp a companion in rainy days; a sweet soother of my feelings when any untoward accident ruffled them: I often addressed it as my only friend; I could pour forth to it my hopes and loves, and I fancied that its sweet accents answered me. I have now mentioned all my studies.

I was a solitary being, and from my infant years, ever since my dear nurse left me, I had been a dreamer. I brought Rosalind and Miranda and the lady of Comus to life to be my companions, or on my isle acted over their parts imagining myself to be in their situations. Then I wandered from the fancies of others and formed affections and intimacies with the aerial creations of my own brain — but still clinging to reality I gave a name to these conceptions and nursed them in the hope of realization. I clung to the memory of my parents; my mother I should never see, she was dead: but the idea of [my] unhappy, wandering father was the idol of my imagination. I bestowed on him all my affections; there was a miniature of him that I gazed on continually; I copied his last letter and read it again and again. Sometimes it made me weep; and at other [times] I repeated with transport those words, — "One day I may claim her at your hands." I was to be his consoler, his companion in after years. My favourite vision was that when I grew up I would leave my aunt, whose coldness lulled my conscience, and disguised like a boy I would seek my father through the world. My imagination hung upon the scene of recognition; his miniature, which I should continually wear exposed on my breast, would be the means and I imaged the moment to my mind a thousand and a thousand times, perpetually varying the circumstances. Sometimes it would be in a desart; in a populous city; at a ball; we should perhaps meet in a vessel; and his first words constantly were, "My daughter, I love thee"! What extactic moments have I passed in these dreams! How many tears I have shed; how often have I laughed aloud.

This was my life for sixteen years. At fourteen and fifteen I often thought that the time was come when I should commence my pilgrimage, which I had cheated my own mind into believing was my imperious duty: but a reluctance to quit my Aunt; a remorse for the grief which, I could not conceal from myself, I should occasion her for ever withheld me. Sometimes when I had planned the next morning for my escape a word of more than usual affection from her lips made me postpone my resolution. I reproached myself bitterly for what I called a culpable weakness; but this weakness returned upon me whenever the critical moment approached, and I never found courage to depart. ◄

CHAPTER 2
Annotations

1. Shelley's description of the father is extraordinarily revealing. He is a person who has never been told *no*. He has been wealthy and coddled and this has allowed his "passions" to grow unabated. Shelley indicates that he is a man who has never had to think about other people, never had to see the world from another's perspective, never constrained himself out of respect for someone else's needs or wants. In this description, then, she conveys that he has the capacity to incestuously abuse his child because he lacks empathy. The problematic but still useful term *sociopath* seems to describe Mathilda's father, this "man of rank." He cannot feel empathy for others, Shelley suggests, because he has never been asked to do so and at a certain point lost the capacity to develop that empathy. His love for Diana, his wife, seems to be a kind of narcissistic mirroring in which the two cut themselves off from the world. When she dies in childbirth, he feels no empathy for their child, a newborn baby; instead, he is "insensible to the presence of anyone else." Thus, the incest secret that Mathilda will divulge begins with the father's inability to feel empathy for his child. This insight on Shelley's part is extraordinary, indicating her intuitive understanding that child sexual abuse does not arise from passion or love but from a critical lack of empathy on the part of the parent. Already, then, Shelley's approach to telling the incest tale is radically different from that of other Romantic authors. Incest was a popular theme for Romantic writers. But Shelley's handling of the theme is not fanciful. Rather she is deeply and psychologically realistic in her representation of this family tragedy.

2. Shelley quotes one of Romantic poet William Wordsworth's "Lucy" poems

    > She dwelt among the untrodden ways
    > Beside the springs of Dove,
    > A Maid whom there were none to praise
    > And very few to love:
    > A violet by a mossy stone
    > Half hidden from the eye!
    > —Fair as a star, when only one
    > Is shining in the sky.
    > She lived unknown, and few could know

When Lucy ceased to be;
But she is in her grave, and, oh,
The difference to me!

Wordsworth, the major Romantic poet of the generation just preceding Shelley's, in this poem idealizes and, well, *romanticizes* the idea of the isolated, virginal maiden. Shelley quotes the poem to suggest that Mathilda is a sympathetic figure, and more importantly a "pure" figure. She is not a temptress who lures her father but an isolated child. Similarly, on the following page Shelley quotes Dante's *Purgatorio* in describing Mathilda's childhood wanderings in nature. By quoting Dante, here, Shelley places her novella in purgatory: Mathilda's story is itself the means by which she absolves herself of the taint of incest. It is important to see that Mary Shelley's strategy in both her works *Frankenstein* and *Mathilda* is deeply intertextual. That is, she conceives of these works as being in conversation with other, earlier literary texts. *Mathilda*, indeed, begins as a reworking of the unfinished draft of her mother's, Mary Wollstonecraft's, *Cave of Fancy*. The frequency with which Shelley alludes to and/or quotes other authors—Milton, Wordsworth, Dante, Goethe—indicates her seriousness as a very young writer (remember she is a teenager writing *Frankenstein*, and barely out of her teens writing *Mathilda*), as she seeks to establish her voice in conversation with the literatures that precede her. At the same time, there is a sense of futility conveyed in the way she uses these allusions and quotes, as if she were somehow pointing out that for all their eloquence and brilliance, these earlier writers have not solved the horrific and dystopic problems faced by her characters. ◄

CHAPTER 3

I T WAS ON MY SIXTEENTH BIRTHDAY that my aunt received a letter from my father. I cannot describe the tumult of emotions that arose within me as I read it. It was dated from London; he had returned! I could only relieve my transports by tears, tears of unmingled joy. He had returned, and he wrote to know whether my aunt would come to London or whether he should visit her in Scotland. How delicious to me were the words of his letter that concerned me: "I cannot tell you," it said, "how ardently I desire to see my Mathilda. I look on her as the creature who will form the happiness of my future life: she is all that exists on earth that interests me. I can hardly prevent myself from hastening immediately to you but I am necessarily detained a week and I write because if you come here I may see you somewhat sooner." I read these words with devouring eyes; I kissed them, wept over them and exclaimed, "He will love me!" —

My aunt would not undertake so long a journey, and in a fortnight we had another letter from my father, it was dated Edinburgh: he wrote that he should be with us in three days. "As he approached his desire of seeing me," he said, "became more and more ardent, and he felt that the moment when he should first clasp me in his arms would be the happiest of his life."[1]

How irksome were these three days to me! All sleep and appetite fled from me; I could only read and re-read his letter, and in the solitude of the woods imagine the moment of our meeting. On the eve of the third day I retired early to my room; I could not sleep but paced all night about my chamber and, as you may in Scotland at midsummer, watched the crimson track of the sun as it almost skirted the northern horizon. At day break I hastened to the woods; the hours past on while I indulged in wild dreams that gave wings to the slothful steps of time, and beguiled my eager impatience. My father was expected at noon but when I wished to return to meet him I found that I had lost my way: it seemed that in every attempt to find it I only became more involved in the intracacies of the woods, and the trees hid all trace by which I might be guided. I grew impatient, I wept; [sic] and wrung my hands but still I could not discover my path.

It was past two o'clock when by a sudden turn I found myself close to the lake near a cove where a little skiff was moored — It was not far from our house and I saw my father and aunt walking on the lawn. I jumped into the boat, and well accustomed to such feats, I pushed it from shore, and exerted all my strength to row swiftly across. As I came, dressed in white, covered only by my tartan rachan, my hair streaming on my shoulders, and shooting across with greater speed that it could be supposed I could give to my boat, my father has often told me that I looked more like a spirit than a human maid. I approached the shore, my father held the boat, I leapt lightly out, and in a moment was in his arms.

And now I began to live. All around me was changed from a dull uniformity to the brightest scene of joy and delight. The happiness I enjoyed in the company of my father far exceeded my sanguine expectations. We were for ever together; and the subjects of our conversations were inexhaustible. He had passed the sixteen years of absence among nations nearly unknown to Europe; he had wandered through Persia, Arabia and the north of India and had penetrated among the habitations of the natives with a freedom permitted to few Europeans. His relations of their manners, his anecdotes and descriptions of scenery whiled away delicious hours, when we were tired of talking of our own plans of future life.

The voice of affection was so new to me that I hung with delight upon his words when he told me what he had felt concerning me during these long years of apparent forgetfulness. "At first" — said he, "I could not bear to think of my poor little girl; but afterwards as grief wore off and hope again revisited me I could only turn to her, and amidst cities and desarts her little fairy form, such as I imagined it, for ever flitted before me. The northern breeze as it refreshed me was sweeter and more balmy for it seemed to carry some of your spirit along with it. I often thought that I would instantly return and take you along with me to some fertile island where we should live at peace for ever. As I returned my fervent hopes were dashed by so many fears; my impatience became in the highest degree painful. I dared not think that the sun should shine and the moon rise not on your living form but on your grave. But, no, it is not so; I have my Mathilda, my consolation, and my hope." —

My father was very little changed from what he described himself to be before his misfortunes. It is intercourse with civilized society; it is the disappointment of cherished hopes, the falsehood of friends, or the perpetual clash of mean passions that changes the heart and damps the ardour of youthful feelings; lonely wanderings in a wild country among people of simple or savage manners may inure the body but will not tame the soul, or extinguish the ardour and freshness of feeling incident to youth. The burning sun of India, and the freedom from all restraint had rather encreased the energy of his character: before he bowed under, now he was impatient of any censure except that of his own mind. He had seen so many customs and witnessed so great a variety of moral creeds that he had been obliged to form an independant one for himself which had no relation to the peculiar notions of any one country: his early prejudices of course influenced his judgement in the formation of his principles, and some raw colledge ideas were strangely mingled with the deepest deductions of his penetrating mind.

The vacuity his heart endured of any deep interest in life during his long absence from his native country had had a singular effect upon his ideas. There was a curious feeling of unreality attached by him to his foreign life in comparison with the years of his youth. All the time he had passed out of England was as a dream, and all the interest of his soul, all his affections belonged to events which had happened and persons who had existed sixteen years before. It was strange when you heard him talk to see how he passed over this lapse of time as a night of visions; while the remembrances of his youth standing seperate as they did from his after life had lost none of their vigour. He talked of my Mother as if she had lived but a few weeks before; not that he expressed poignant grief, but his discription of her person, and his relation of all anecdotes connected with her was thus fervent and vivid.[2]

In all this there was a strangeness that attracted and enchanted me. He was, as it were, now awakened from his long, visionary sleep, and he felt some what like one of the seven sleepers, or like Nourjahad, in that sweet imitation of an eastern tale: Diana was gone; his friends were changed or dead, and now on his awakening I was all that he had to love on earth.

How dear to me were the waters, and mountains, and woods of Loch Lomond now that I had so beloved a companion for my rambles. I visited with my father every delightful spot, either on the islands, or by the side of the tree-sheltered waterfalls; every shady path, or dingle entangled with underwood and fern. My ideas were enlarged by his conversation. I felt as if I were recreated and had about me all the freshness and life of a new being: I was, as it were, transported since his arrival from a narrow spot of earth into a universe boundless to the imagination and the understanding. My life had been before as a pleasing country rill, never destined to leave its native fields, but when its task was fulfilled quietly to be absorbed, and leave no trace. Now it seemed to me to be as a various river flowing through a fertile and lovely lanscape, ever changing and ever beautiful. Alas! I knew not the desart it was about to reach; the rocks that would tear its waters, and the hideous scene that would be reflected in a more distorted manner in its waves. Life was then brilliant; I began to learn to hope and what brings a more bitter despair to the heart than hope destroyed?

Is it not strange that grief should quickly follow so divine a happiness? I drank of an enchanted cup but gall was at the bottom of its long drawn sweetness. My heart was full of deep affection, but it was calm from its very depth and fulness. I had no idea that misery could arise from love, and this lesson that all at last must learn was taught me in a manner few are obliged to receive it. I lament now, I must ever lament, those few short months of Paradisaical bliss; I disobeyed no command, I ate no apple, and yet I was ruthlessly driven from it. Alas! my companion did, and I was precipitated in his fall. But I wander from my relation — let woe come at its appointed time; I may at this stage of my story still talk of happiness.

Three months passed away in this delightful intercourse, when my aunt fell ill. I passed a whole month in her chamber nursing her, but her disease was mortal and she died, leaving me for some time inconsolable, Death is so dreadful to the living; the chains of habit are so strong even when affection does not link them that the heart must be agonized when they break. But my father was beside me to console me and to drive away bitter memories by bright hopes: methought that it was sweet to grieve that he might dry my tears.

Then again he distracted my thoughts from my sorrow by comparing it with his despair when he lost my mother. Even at that time I shuddered at the picture he drew of his passions: he had the imagination of a poet, and when he described the whirlwind that then tore his feelings he gave his words the impress of life so vividly that I believed while I trembled. I wondered how he could ever again have entered into the offices of life after his wild thoughts seemed to have given him affinity with the unearthly; while he spoke so tremendous were the ideas which he conveyed that it appeared as if the human heart were far too bounded for their conception. His feelings seemed better fitted for a spirit whose habitation is the earthquake and the volcano than for one confined to a mortal body and human lineaments. But these were merely memories; he was changed since then. He was now all love, all softness; and when I raised my eyes in wonder at him as he spoke the smile on his lips told me that his heart was possessed by the gentlest passions.

Two months after my aunt's death we removed to London where I was led by my father to attend to deeper studies than had before occupied me. My improvement was his delight; he was with me during all my studies and assisted or joined with me in every lesson. We saw a great deal of society, and no day passed that my father did not endeavour to embellish by some new enjoyment. The tender attachment that he bore me, and the love and veneration with which I returned it cast a charm over every moment. The hours were slow for each minute was employed; we lived more in one week than many do in the course of several months and the variety and novelty of our pleasures gave zest to each.

We perpetually made excursions together. And whether it were to visit beautiful scenery, or to see fine pictures, or sometimes for no object but to seek amusement as it might chance to arise, I was always happy when near my father. It was a subject of regret to me whenever we were joined by a third person, yet if I turned with a disturbed look towards my father, his eyes fixed on me and beaming with tenderness instantly restored joy to my heart. O, hours of intense delight! Short as ye were ye are made as long to me as a whole life when looked back upon through the mist of grief that rose immediately after as if to shut ye from my view. Alas! ye were the last of happiness that I ever enjoyed; a few, a very few weeks and all was destroyed. Like Psyche I lived for awhile in an enchanted palace, amidst odours, and music, and every luxurious delight; when suddenly I was left on a barren rock; a wide ocean of despair rolled around me: above all was black, and my eyes closed while I still inhabited a universal death. Still I would not hurry on; I would pause for ever on the recollections of these happy weeks; I would repeat every word, and how many do I remember, record every enchantment of the faery habitation. But, no, my tale must not pause; it must be as rapid as was my fate,—I can only describe in short although strong expressions my precipitate and irremediable change from happiness to despair.[3] ◄

CHAPTER 3
Annotations

1. *Mathilda* and *Frankenstein* are narratives of troubled, in fact catastrophic, "coming of age" stories. The crisis point for Victor Frankenstein, Mathilda's father, and for Mathilda herself is the end of childhood (with these characters being in their late teens and early twenties when the troubles commence). Rather than entering the world, struggling, and triumphing, Victor Frankenstein, Mathilda's father, and Mathilda, instead "come of age" into entirely unresolvable and unhealable horrors. Frankenstein leaves his family of origin to study but as a scholar what he does is create a monster. Mathilda's father becomes a man, in his own eyes, only through marrying her mother but this marriage ends after little more than a year with his wife's death, at which point Mathilda's father literally erases himself, taking up an assumed name and traveling where he is unknown. Mathilda, also, as we will learn, tells the tale of a brutally thwarted "coming of age" story. This sense of coming of age not into struggle and then triumph but rather into circumstances that either make it impossible for the protagonist to succeed or, if you prefer, that reveal that deep and fatal flaws of the protagonist, is a commonality between the works. They are stories of foreclosed possibility. Notably, while Mathilda's father and Victor Frankenstein appear to experience fates that are the working out of their own flawed characters, Mathilda appears to suffer a fate that has nothing to do with her personality but instead is impressed upon her because of her father's character. Shelley suggests that 'coming of age' is dangerous in a different way for women than for men; men face — in her novels — their own character flaws whereas women face men's character flaws.

2. The words of Mathilda's father, in the letter announcing his return to her — after sixteen years of travel — suggest to the careful reader that far from having changed during his travels the man has only become more himself, more solipsistic, more narcissistic. He writes, of his daughter Mathilda, "I look on her as the creature who will form the happiness of my future life: she is all that exists on earth that interests me." And while these words initially bring Mathilda joy, because in her extreme social isolation she craves to be the object of affection and love, we can see in his words warning signs. He does not express a desire to take care of his teenage daughter, to help her become a happy adult; he does not express a wish to "make it up to her" for all the years he abandoned her. No. He expresses the opposite: that she

will bring *him* happiness. That she will be his sole interest. In other words, he will reconfigure the narcissistic relationship that he had with her mother with the daughter now in the place of his ego-double. Ominously, Mathilda, a child, will have no defense against his selfish desire to use her—or use her up—to provide his sole happiness on earth. Likewise, the repeated use of the word "ardent" to describe his desire for Mathilda, his young daughter, is disturbing. Ardent is a term used to describe the passion between lovers, not a parent and child. Ardent etymologically means "burning," hence, a passion that consumes. The idea of different kinds of love goes back to classical times, with the term *agape* signifying love for a family member, in contrast to *eros*, sexual love. Mathilda's father uses the language of ardency, signifying that even before he meets his daughter he is already in his mind crossing the boundary between *agape*—love for a family member—and *eros,* sexual love.

3.   The father, we learn, spent the sixteen years after his wife died in childbirth traveling in countries described by the narrative as "savage." There are several interlocking strands to ravel here. Firstly, non-European countries are used in this narrative as symbols for places where there is no civilization and hence no restraint on human desire. This is a complete misunderstanding of what it means to be not European. All cultures are civilized; that is what it means to be a human culture, and there are no human beings who are not part of some culture of some kind. From there, then, the idea that there are human cultures that have no restraint and act entirely according to impulse is also a Euro-centric racist belief, and an entirely wrong one. Mathilda's father uses his history as a traveler outside of Europe to excuse his incestuous passion for his teenage daughter, even though there is no known culture in the world that actually finds father-daughter incest acceptable. But Mathilda, our narrator, accepts his excuse, falling into the Euro-patriarchal frame of thought that excuses her father's violence. She tells us, "The burning sun of India, and the freedom from all restraint had rather increased the energy of his character: before he bowed under, now he was impatient of any censure except that of his own mind." The reality is, the father has used his privilege and wealth to live in other places without respecting their cultures and morals. ◀

CHAPTER 4

A MONG OUR MOST ASSIDUOUS VISITORS was a young man of rank, well informed, and agreable in his person. After we had spent a few weeks in London his attentions towards me became marked and his visits more frequent. I was too much taken up by my own occupations and feelings to attend much to this, and then indeed I hardly noticed more than the bare surface of events as they passed around me; but I now remember that my father was restless and uneasy whenever this person visited us, and when we talked together watched us with the greatest apparent anxiety although he himself maintained a profound silence. At length these obnoxious visits suddenly ceased altogether, but from that moment I must date the change of my father: a change that to remember makes me shudder and then filled me with the deepest grief. There were no degrees which could break my fall from happiness to misery; it was as the stroke of lightning—sudden and entire. Alas! I now met frowns where before I had been welcomed only with smiles: he, my beloved father, shunned me, and either treated me with harshness or a more heart-breaking coldness. We took no more sweet counsel together; and when I tried to win him again to me, his anger, and the terrible emotions that he exhibited drove me to silence and tears.

And this was sudden. The day before we had passed alone together in the country; I remember we had talked of future travels that we should undertake together—. There was an eager delight in our tones and gestures that could only spring from deep & mutual love joined to the most unrestrained confidence[;]

and now the next day, the next hour, I saw his brows contracted, his eyes fixed in sullen fierceness on the ground, and his voice so gentle and so dear made me shiver when he addressed me. Often, when my wandering fancy brought by its various images now consolation and now aggravation of grief to my heart, I have compared myself to Proserpine who was gaily and heedlessly gathering flowers on the sweet plain of Enna, when the King of Hell snatched her away to the abodes of death and misery. Alas! I who so lately knew of nought but the joy of life; who had slept only to dream sweet dreams and awoke to incomparable happiness, I now passed my days and nights in tears. I who sought and had found joy in the love-breathing countenance of my father now when I dared fix on him a supplicating look it was ever answered by an angry frown. I dared not speak to him; and when sometimes I had worked up courage to meet him and to ask an explanation one glance at his face where a chaos of mighty passion seemed for ever struggling made me tremble and shrink to silence. I was dashed down from heaven to earth as a silly sparrow when pounced on by a hawk; my eyes swam and my head was bewildered by the sudden apparition of grief. Day after day passed marked only by my complaints and my tears; often I lifted my soul in vain prayer for a softer descent from joy to woe, or if that were denied me that I might be allowed to die, and fade for ever under the cruel blast that swept over me,

— — — for what should I do here, Like a decaying flower, still withering Under his bitter words, whose kindly heat Should give my poor heart life?

Sometimes I said to myself, this is an enchantment, and I must strive against it. My father is blinded by some malignant vision which I must remove. And then, like David, I would try music to win the evil spirit from him; and once while singing I lifted my eyes towards him and saw his fixed on me and filled with tears; all his muscles seemed relaxed to softness. I sprung towards him with a cry of joy and would have thrown myself into his arms, but he pushed me roughly from him and left me. And even from this slight incident he contracted fresh gloom and an additional severity of manner.

There are many incidents that I might relate which shewed the diseased yet incomprehensible state of his mind; but I will mention one that occurred while we were in company with several other persons. On this occasion I chanced to say that I thought Myrrha the best of Alfieri's tragedies; as I said this I chanced to cast my eyes on my father and met his: for the first time the expression of those beloved eyes displeased me, and I saw with affright that his whole frame shook with some concealed emotion that in spite of his efforts half conquered him: as this tempest faded from his soul he became melancholy and silent. Every day some new scene occured and displayed in him a mind working as [it] were with an unknown horror that now he could master but which at times threatened to overturn his reason, and to throw the bright seat of his intelligence into a perpetual chaos.

I will not dwell longer than I need on these disastrous circumstances. I might waste days in describing how anxiously I watched every change of fleeting circumstance that promised better days, and with what despair I found that each effort of mine aggravated his seeming madness. To tell all my grief I might as well attempt to count the tears that have fallen from these eyes, or every sign that has torn my heart. I will be brief for there is in all this a horror that will not bear many words, and I sink almost a second time to death while I recall these sad scenes to my memory. Oh, my beloved father! Indeed you made me miserable beyond all words, but how truly did I even then forgive you, and how entirely did you possess my whole heart while I endeavoured, as a rainbow gleams upon a cataract, to soften thy tremendous sorrows.

Thus did this change come about. I seem perhaps to have dashed too suddenly into the description, but thus suddenly did it happen. In one sentence I have passed from the idea of unspeakable happiness to that of unspeakable grief but they were thus closely linked together. We had remained five months in London three of joy and two of sorrow. My father and I were now seldom alone or if we were he generally kept silence with his eyes fixed on the ground—the dark full orbs in which before I delighted to read all sweet and gentle feeling shadowed from my sight by their lids and the long lashes that fringed them. When we were in company he affected gaiety but I wept to hear his hollow laugh—begun by an empty smile and often ending in a bitter sneer such as never before this fatal period had wrinkled his lips. When others were there he often spoke to me and his eyes perpetually followed my slightest motion. His accents whenever he addressed me were cold and constrained although his voice would tremble when he perceived that my full heart choked the answer to words proffered with a mien yet new to me.[1]

But days of peaceful melancholy were of rare occurence[:] they were often broken in upon by gusts of passion that drove me as a weak boat on a stormy sea to seek a cove for shelter; but the winds blew from my native harbour and I was cast far, far out untill shattered I perished when the tempest had passed and the sea was apparently calm. I do not know that I can describe his emotions: sometimes he only betrayed them by a word or gesture, and then retired to his chamber and I crept as near it as I dared and listened with fear to every sound, yet still more dreading a sudden silence—dreading I knew not what, but ever full of fear.

It was after one tremendous day when his eyes had glared on me like lightning—and his voice sharp and broken seemed unable to express the extent of his emotion that in the evening when I was alone he joined me with a calm countenance, and not noticing my tears which I quickly dried when he approached, told me that in three days that [sic] he intended to remove with me to his estate in Yorkshire, and bidding me prepare left me hastily as if afraid of being questioned.

This determination on his part indeed surprised me. This estate was that which he had inhabited in childhood and near which my mother resided while a girl; this was the scene of their youthful loves and where they had lived after their marriage; in happier days my father had often told me that however he might appear weaned from his widow sorrow, and free from bitter recollections elsewhere, yet he would never dare visit the spot where he had enjoyed her society or trust himself to see the rooms that so many years ago they had inhabited together; her favourite walks and the gardens the flowers of which she had delighted to cultivate. And now while he suffered intense misery he determined to plunge into still more intense, and strove for greater emotion than that which already tore him. I was perplexed, and most anxious to know what this portended; ah, what could it po[r]tend but ruin!

I saw little of my father during this interval, but he appeared calmer although not less unhappy than before. On the morning of the third day he informed me that he had determined to go to Yorkshire first alone, and that I should follow him in a fortnight unless I heard any thing from him in the mean time that should contradict this command. He departed the same day, and four days afterwards I received a letter from his steward telling me in his name to join him with as little delay as possible. After travelling day and night I arrived with an anxious, yet a hoping heart, for why should he send for me if it were only to avoid me and to treat me with the apparent aversion that he had in London. I met him at the distance of thirty miles from our mansion. His demeanour was sad; for a moment he appeared glad to see me and then he checked himself as if unwilling to betray his feelings. He was silent during our ride, yet his manner was kinder than before and I thought I beheld a softness in his eyes that gave me hope.

When we arrived, after a little rest, he led me over the house and pointed out to me the rooms which my mother had inhabited. Although more than sixteen years had passed since her death nothing had been changed; her work box, her writing desk were still there and in her room a book lay open on the table as she had left it. My father pointed out these circumstances with a serious and unaltered mien, only now and then fixing his deep and liquid eyes upon me; there was something strange and awful in his look that overcame me, and in spite of myself I wept, nor did he attempt to console me, but I saw his lips quiver and the muscles of his countenance seemed convulsed.

We walked together in the gardens and in the evening when I would have retired he asked me to stay and read to him; and first said, "When I was last here your mother read Dante to me; you shall go on where she left off." And then in a moment he said, "No, that must not be; you must not read Dante. Do you choose a book." I took up Spencer and read the descent of Sir Guyon to the halls of Avarice; while he listened his eyes fixed on me in sad profound silence.

I heard the next morning from the steward that upon his arrival he had been in a most terrible state of mind: he had passed the first night in the garden lying on the damp grass; he did not sleep but groaned perpetually. "Alas!" said the old man, who gave me this account with tears in his eyes, "it wrings my heart to see my lord in this state: when I heard that he was coming down here with you, my young lady, I thought we should have the happy days over again that we enjoyed during the short life of my lady your mother — But that would be too much happiness for us poor creatures born to tears — and that was why she was taken from us so soon; [s]he was too beautiful and good for us. It was a happy day as we all thought it when my lord married her: I knew her when she was a child and many a good turn has she done for me in my old lady's time — You are like her although there is more of my lord in you — But has he been thus ever since his return? All my joy turned to sorrow when I first beheld him with that melancholy countenance enter these doors as it were the day after my lady's funeral — He seemed to recover himself a little after he had bidden me write to you — but still it is a woful [sic] thing to see him so unhappy." These were the feelings of an old, faithful servant: what must be those of an affectionate daughter. Alas! Even then my heart was almost broken.

We spent two months together in this house. My father spent the greater part of his time with me; he accompanied me in my walks, listened to my music, and leant over me as I read or painted. When he conversed with me his manner was cold and constrained; his eyes only seemed to speak, and as he turned their black, full lustre towards me they expressed a living sadness. There was somthing in those dark deep orbs so liquid, and intense that even in happiness I could never meet their full gaze that mine did not overflow. Yet it was with sweet tears; now there was a depth of affliction in their gentle appeal that rent my heart with sympathy; they seemed to desire peace for me; for himself a heart patient to suffer; a craving for sympathy, yet a perpetual self denial. It was only when he was absent from me that his passion subdued him, — that he clinched his hands — knit his brows — and with haggard looks called for death to his despair, raving wildly, untill exhausted he sank down nor was revived untill I joined him.

While we were in London there was a harshness and sullenness in his sorrow which had now entirely disappeared. There I shrunk and fled from him, now I only wished to be with him that I might soothe him to peace. When he was silent I tried to divert him, and when sometimes I stole to him during the energy of his passion I wept but did not desire to leave him. Yet he suffered fearful agony; during the day he was more calm, but at night when I could not be with him he seemed to give the reins to his grief: he often passed his nights either on the floor in my mother's room, or in the garden; and when in the morning he saw me view with poignant grief his exhausted frame, and his person languid almost to death with watching he wept; but during all this time he spoke no word by which I might guess the cause of his unhappiness. If I ventured to enquire he would either leave me or press his finger on his lips, and with a deprecating look that I could not resist, turn away. If I wept he would gaze on me in silence but he was no longer harsh and although he repulsed every caress yet it was with gentleness.[2]

He seemed to cherish a mild grief and softer emotions although sad as a relief from despair—He contrived in many ways to nurse his melancholy as an antidote to wilder passion. He perpetually frequented the walks that had been favourites with him when he and my mother wandered together talking of love and happiness; he collected every relick that remained of her and always sat opposite her picture which hung in the room fixing on it a look of sad despair—and all this was done in a mystic and awful silence. If his passion subdued him he locked himself in his room; and at night when he wandered restlessly about the house, it was when every other creature slept.

It may easily be imagined that I wearied myself with conjecture to guess the cause of his sorrow. The solution that seemed to me the most probable was that during his residence in London he had fallen in love with some unworthy person, and that his passion mastered him although he would not gratify it: he loved me too well to sacrifise me to this inclination, and that he had now visited this house that by reviving the memory of my mother whom he so passionately adored he might weaken the present impression. This was possible; but it was a mere conjecture unfounded on any fact. Could there be guilt in it? He was too upright and noble to do aught that his conscience would not approve; I did not yet know of the crime there may be in involuntary feeling and therefore ascribed his tumultuous starts and gloomy looks wholly to the struggles of his mind and not any as they were partly due to the worst fiend of all—Remorse.

But still do I flatter myself that this would have passed away. His paroxisms of passion were terrific but his soul bore him through them triumphant, though almost destroyed by victory; but the day would finally have been won had not I, foolish and presumtuous wretch! hurried him on untill there was no recall, no hope. My rashness gave the victory in this dreadful fight to the enemy who triumphed over him as he lay fallen and vanquished. I! I alone was the cause of his defeat and justly did I pay the fearful penalty. I said to myself, let him receive sympathy and these struggles will cease. Let him confide his misery to another heart and half the weight of it will be lightened. I will win him to me; he shall not deny his grief to me and when I know his secret then will I pour a balm into his soul and again I shall enjoy the ravishing delight of beholding his smile, and of again seeing his eyes beam if not with pleasure at least with gentle love and thankfulness. This will I do, I said. Half I accomplished; I gained his secret and we were both lost for ever. ◄

CHAPTER 4
Annotations

1.   These passages are most intimately entwined with Wollstonecraft's *Cave of Fancy*, which turns on the idea of love arising through tutorship. Likewise, by embedding two references to Myrrha, who is described in Ovid as a daughter in love with her father, Shelley sets up a precedent for her tale. In her sylvan purgatory, Shelley's Mathilda is presented as being like Myrrha in the eighth circle of hell in Dante's *Purgatorio*. Likewise, Mathilda directly mentions to her father Alfieri's play, *Mirra*, with both Dante and Alfieri referencing Ovid. And yet, Ovid's, Dante's, and Alfieri's Myrrha differ radically from Mary Shelley's character, Mathilda. Mary Shelley's Mathilda is not incestuously in love with her father. On the contrary, he is incestuously in love with her, and she refuses him. Shelley's build-up to the incest crisis, in great contrast to other Romantic writers, is psychologically astute and realistic. In Shelley's insightful novella, the father is described as becoming jealous when a young man is attracted to his teenage daughter. Shelley has carefully laid the groundwork, so to speak, so that the attentive reader realizes the father is a person who is concerned only with his own pleasure. When the daughter becomes the object of another man's attention, the father cannot bear it. He becomes despondent and hateful, behaving toward his daughter very much like a spurned suitor rather than like a father whose interest should be in his daughter's welfare and future. Remember, Shelley described his love for his daughter as "ardent," that is burning and consuming. He wants to consume his teenage daughter, not support her in becoming an adult.

   Here, I cannot emphasize enough the extraordinary degree to which Mary Shelley intuits the psychology of the incestuously abusive father. A reader familiar with Judith Lewis Herman's groundbreaking study *Father-Daughter Incest,* however, will immediately be struck by how entirely psychologically accurate Shelley is in her depiction of the incestuous father. It is this psychologically realistic accuracy that radically sets apart the novella *Mathilda* from other literary depictions of incest preceding her work.

2.   Driven by jealousy for his daughter's suitor, the father takes Mathilda away from London — and the young man who is interested in Mathilda — to the mansion where he was living with her mother before the mother's death, in effect re-staging his earlier relationship with Diana. He tells Mathilda, once

they are ensconced at the estate, "'When I was last here your mother read Dante to me; you shall go on where she left off.' And then in a moment he said, 'No, that must not be; you must not read Dante.'" The father asks his daughter to "go on where she [the mother] left off" and then fights against himself, telling Mathilda not to read what her mother was reading just before her death. This staging of the scene wherein the daughter takes the place of the mother is the nightmare toward which *Mathilda*, the novella, converges, and it is striking that reading Dante — or not reading Dante — is the mechanism moving the narrative. The theme of purgatory, and the presentation of Mathilda as a soul in purgatory, is the constant substructure of the narrative, conveyed and also moved forward by repeated allusions to Dante's *Purgatorio*. We are pulled into the nightmare of the novella because we are indeed "reading Dante" as we read Shelley. ◄

CHAPTER 5

NEARLY A YEAR HAD PAST since my father's return, and the seasons had almost finished their round—It was now the end of May; the woods were clothed in their freshest verdure, and the sweet smell of the new mown grass was in the fields. I thought that the balmy air and the lovely face of Nature might aid me in inspiring him with mild sensations, and give him gentle feelings of peace and love preparatory to the confidence I determined to win from him.

I chose therefore the evening of one of these days for my attempt. I invited him to walk with me, and led him to a neighbouring wood of beech trees whose light shade shielded us from the slant and dazzling beams of the descending sun—After walking for some time in silence I seated my self with him on a mossy hillock—It is strange but even now I seem to see the spot—the slim and smooth trunks were many of them wound round by ivy whose shining leaves of the darkest green contrasted with the white bark and the light leaves of the young sprouts of beech that grew from their parent trunks—the short grass was mingled with moss and was partly covered by the dead leaves of the last autumn that driven by the winds had here and there collected in little hillocks—there were a few moss grown stumps about—The leaves were gently moved by the breeze and through their green canopy you could see the bright blue sky—As evening came on the distant trunks were reddened by the sun and the wind died entirely away while a few birds flew past us to their evening rest.

Well it was here we sat together, and when you hear all that past—all that of terrible tore our souls even in this placid spot, which but for strange passions might have been a paradise to us, you will not wonder that I remember it as I looked on it that its calm might give me calm, and inspire me not only with courage but with persuasive words. I saw all these things and in a vacant manner noted them in my mind while I endeavoured to arrange my thoughts in fitting order for my attempt. My heart beat fast as I worked myself up to speak to him, for I was determined not to be repulsed but I trembled to imagine what effect my words might have on him; at length, with much hesitation I began:

"Your kindness to me, my dearest father, and the affection—the excessive affection—that you had for me when you first returned will I hope excuse me in your eyes that I dare speak to you, although with the tender affection of a daughter, yet also with the freedom of a friend and equal. But pardon me, I entreat you and listen to me: do not turn away from me; do not be impatient; you may easily intimidate me into silence, but my heart is bursting, nor can I willingly consent to endure for one moment longer the agony of uncertitude which for the last four months has been my portion.

"Listen to me, dearest friend, and permit me to gain your confidence. Are the happy days of mutual love which have passed to be to me as a dream never to return? Alas! You have a secret grief that destroys us both: but you must permit me to win this secret from you. Tell me, can I do nothing? You well know that on the whole earth there is no sacrifise that I would not make, no labour that I would not undergo with the mere hope that I might bring you ease. But if no endeavour on my part can contribute to your happiness, let me at least know your sorrow, and surely my earnest love and deep sympathy must soothe your despair.

"I fear that I speak in a constrained manner: my heart is overflowing with the ardent desire I have of bringing calm once more to your thoughts and looks; but I fear to aggravate your grief, or to raise that in you which is death to me, anger and distaste. Do not then continue to fix your eyes on the earth; raise them on me for I can read your soul in them: speak to me to me [sic], and pardon my presumption. Alas! I am a most unhappy creature!"

I was breathless with emotion, and I paused fixing my earnest eyes on my father, after I had dashed away the intrusive tears that dimmed them. He did not raise his, but after a short silence he replied to me in a low voice: "You are indeed presumptuous, Mathilda, presumptuous and very rash. In the heart of one like me there are secret thoughts working, and secret tortures which you ought not to seek to discover. I cannot tell you how it adds to my grief to know that I am the cause of uneasiness to you; but this will pass away, and I hope that soon we shall be as we were a few months ago. Restrain your impatience or you may mar what you attempt to alleviate. Do not again speak to me in this strain; but wait in submissive patience the event of what is passing around you."

"Oh, yes!" I passionately replied, "I will be very patient; I will not be rash or presumptuous: I will see the agonies, and tears, and despair of my father, my only friend, my hope, my shelter, I will see it all with folded arms and downcast eyes. You do not treat me with candour; it is not true what you say; this will not soon pass away, it will last forever if you deign not to speak to me; to admit my consolations.

"Dearest, dearest father, pity me and pardon me: I entreat you do not drive me to despair; indeed I must not be repulsed; there is one thing that which [sic] although it may torture me to know, yet that you must tell me. I demand, and most solemnly I demand if in any way I am the cause of your unhappiness. Do you not see my tears which I in vain strive against—You hear unmoved my voice broken by sobs—Feel how my hand trembles: my whole heart is in the words I speak and you must not endeavour to silence me by mere words barren of meaning: the agony of my doubt hurries me on, and you must reply. I beseech you; by your former love for me now lost, I adjure you to answer that one question. Am I the cause of your grief?"

He raised his eyes from the ground, but still turning them away from me, said: "Besought by that plea I will answer your rash question. Yes, you are the sole, the agonizing cause of all I suffer, of all I must suffer untill I die. Now, beware! Be silent! Do not urge me to your destruction. I am struck by the storm, rooted up, laid waste: but you can stand against it; you are young and your passions are at peace. One word I might speak and then you would be implicated in my destruction; yet that word is hovering on my lips. Oh! There is a fearful chasm; but I adjure you to beware!"

"Ah, dearest friend!" I cried, "do not fear! Speak that word; it will bring peace, not death. If there is a chasm our mutual love will give us wings to pass it, and we shall find flowers, and verdure, and delight on the other side." I threw myself at his feet, and took his hand, "Yes, speak, and we shall be happy; there will no longer be doubt, no dreadful uncertainty; trust me, my affection will soothe your sorrow; speak that word and all danger will be past, and we shall love each other as before, and for ever."

He snatched his hand from me, and rose in violent disorder: "What do you mean? You know not what you mean. Why do you bring me out, and torture me, and tempt me, and kill me—Much happier would [it] be for you and for me if in your frantic curiosity you tore my heart from my breast and tried to read its secrets in it as its life's blood was dropping from it. Thus you may console me by reducing me to nothing—but your words I cannot bear; soon they will make me mad, quite mad, and then I shall utter strange words, and you will believe them, and we shall be both lost for ever. I tell you I am on the very verge of insanity; why, cruel girl, do you drive me on: you will repent and I shall die."

When I repeat his words I wonder at my pertinacious folly; I hardly know what feelings resis[t]lessly impelled me. I believe it was that coming out with a determination not to be repulsed I went right forward to my object without well weighing his replies: I was led by passion and drew him with frantic heedlessness into the abyss that he so fearfully avoided—I replied to his terrific words: "You fill me with affright it is true, dearest father, but you only confirm my resolution to put an end to this state of doubt. I will not be put off thus: do you think that I can live thus fearfully from day to day—the sword in my bosom yet kept from its mortal wound by a hair—a word!—I demand that dreadful word; though it be as a flash of lightning to destroy me, speak it.

"Alas! Alas! What am I become? But a few months have elapsed since I believed that I was all the world to you; and that there was no happiness or grief for you on earth unshared by your Mathilda—your child: that happy time is no longer, and what I most dreaded in this world is come upon me. In the despair of my heart I see what you cannot conceal: you no longer love me. I adjure you, my father, has not an unnatural passion seized upon your heart? Am I not the most miserable worm that crawls? Do I not embrace your knees, and you most cruelly repulse me? I know it—I see it—you hate me!"

I was transported by violent emotion, and rising from his feet, at which I had thrown myself, I leant against a tree, wildly raising my eyes to heaven. He began to answer with violence: "Yes, yes, I hate you! You are my bane, my poison, my disgust! Oh! No[!]" And then his manner changed, and fixing his eyes on me with an expression that convulsed every nerve and member of my frame—"you are none of all these; you are my light, my only one, my life.—My daughter, I love you!" The last words died away in a hoarse whisper, but I heard them and sunk on the ground, covering my face and almost dead with excess of sickness and fear: a cold perspiration covered my forehead and I shivered in every limb—But he continued, clasping his hands with a frantic gesture:

"Now I have dashed from the top of the rock to the bottom! Now I have precipitated myself down the fearful chasm! The danger is over; she is alive! Oh, Mathilda, lift up those dear eyes in the light of which I live. Let me hear the sweet tones of your beloved voice in peace and calm. Monster as I am, you are still, as you ever were, lovely, beautiful beyond expression. What I have become since this last moment I know not; perhaps I am changed in mien as the fallen archangel. I do believe I am for I have surely a new soul within me, and my blood riots through my veins: I am burnt up with fever. But these are precious moments; devil as I am become, yet that is my Mathilda before me whom I love as one was never before loved: and she knows it now; she listens to these words which I thought, fool as I was, would blast her to death. Come, come, the worst is past: no more grief, tears or despair; were not those the words you uttered? — We have leapt the chasm I told you of, and now, mark me, Mathilda, we are to find flowers, and verdure and delight, or is it hell, and fire, and tortures? Oh! Beloved One, I am borne away; I can no longer sustain myself; surely this is death that is coming. Let me lay my head near your heart; let me die in your arms!" — He sunk to the earth fainting, while I, nearly as lifeless, gazed on him in despair.

Yes it was despair I felt; for the first time that phantom seized me; the first and only time for it has never since left me — After the first moments of speechless agony I felt her fangs on my heart: I tore my hair; I raved aloud; at one moment in pity for his sufferings I would have clasped my father in my arms; and then starting back with horror I spurned him with my foot; I felt as if stung by a serpent, as if scourged by a whip of scorpions which drove me — Ah! Whither — Whither?[1]

Well, this could not last. One idea rushed on my mind; never, never may I speak to him again. As this terrible conviction came upon it melted my soul to tenderness and love — I gazed on him as to take my last farewell — he lay insensible — his eyes closed and his cheeks deathly pale. Above, the leaves of the beech wood cast a flickering shadow on his face, and waved in mournful melody over him — I saw all these things and said, "Aye, this is his grave!" And then I wept aloud, and raised my eyes to heaven to entreat for a respite to my despair and an alleviation for his unnatural suffering — the tears that gushed in a warm & healing stream from my eyes relieved the burthen that oppressed my heart almost to madness. I wept for a long time untill I saw him about to revive, when horror and misery again recurred, and the tide of my sensations rolled back to their former channel: with a terror I could not restrain — I sprung up and fled, with winged speed, along the paths of the wood and across the fields untill nearly dead I reached our house and just ordering the servants to seek my father at the spot I indicated, I shut myself up in my own room. ◄

CHAPTER 5
Annotations

1. Mary Shelley is writing in the early nineteenth-century, before Sigmund Freud (1856-1939) developed a process of psychoanalysis and theory to support his process based on a belief that telling secrets, learning secrets, was healing. Philosopher Michel Foucault (1926-1984) has argued that for a century or more preceding Freud, European culture was moving toward the paradigm of full confession as healing. Foucault charts changes in the religious practice of confession, from general recognition of sin to an impetus to state specific detailed histories of one's sins and sinful thoughts. For Foucault, this move toward detailed confession is the shift into modernity, wherein man becomes "a confessing animal." Shelley, in *Mathilda,* predicts the flaws in the Freudian paradigm of confessing secrets as a mode of healing, somewhat in the way that she predicts, in *Frankenstein,* pitfalls of the pietism of science. For Mathilda clearly believes—and the narrative also believes—that if she had not pressed her father to tell her what was troubling him, he may have found a way to control himself, or remove himself, and life would have moved forward without the explicit expression of the father's incestuous desire.

    Here, Shelley's paradoxical and dystopic vision of secrets and stories comes to the fore. In both the novel *Frankenstein* and the novella *Mathilda,* an impossible secret carries fatal force. By *impossible* I mean a secret that cannot be told without causing ruin and destruction and also a secret that by not being told causes ruin and destruction. In *Mathilda,* it's not clear that had the father not told Mathilda of his incestuous desire for her everything would have been alright. That conjecture may be Mathilda's way of assuming guilt for a situation that she did not cause: she considers herself guilty for having 'forced' her father to divulge the secret of his incestuous desire for her, but beyond her explicit claim of guilt, the narrative of the novella, *Mathilda,* does not support her own view. On the contrary, like *Frankenstein*, *Mathilda* is motivated by the conundrum of a secret that cannot be told and must be told: that will bring ruin if told and if not told.

    To understand this painful narrative structure, we can consider the history of the novel and ask where Mary Shelley, writing in the early nineteenth century, fits in this history. While *Mathilda* is somewhat between genres—a novella—*Frankenstein* stays within the genre of the novel. Thomas Pavel, in *The Lives of the Novel: A History,* argues that in the late eighteenth- and early nineteenth- centuries the novel begins to change in Europe and Great Britain, reframing the productive tension between perfect and villainous characters, becoming more realistic. We can think of Mary Shelley's *Frankenstein* and also *Mathilda* as fitting into this epochal shift while brilliantly commenting on it. Both Shelley's early works take on the trope of the perfect protagonist and then veer radically away from that perfection, creating two characters — Victor Frankenstein and Mathilda's father — who are described in idealized terms and who then commit unforgivable acts. What is most notable about Shelley's work is her bringing in a feminine point of view that tells the story of male dominance and its excesses — which become villainous — in psychologically realistic ways. *Mathilda* is much subtler as a psychological portrait of an abusive father, whereas *Frankenstein* is more ruggedly symbolic.

Even so, both works draw their narrative energy from the secret acts of these idolized, ruined men. What is original to Mary Shelley, in the novel's development as a genre, is the immense and I think superstitiously fervent, emphasis on the force of secrets. Certainly, she draws from the Gothic, from Walpole's *The Castle of Otranto* (1764) as prototype for the novel as the repository of familial secret sins. But for Shelley the Gothic force of the novel is twinned with psychological realism: in *Mathilda* in particular we are brought into the psychological anguish of the incest survivor. Shelley takes Gothic turns and gives them the force of nightmares that people actually have — her own nightmare in the case of *Frankenstein*, and one simply cannot say from whence *Mathilda* derives its force. Observation of another's suffering? Of her own? While scholars argue that *Mathilda* picks up the incest theme from its popularity among Romantic poets, which is certainly correct, Shelley goes beyond this trope into a novella of painfully realistic psychological despair. As I've discussed at length in *The Posthumous Voice in Women's Writing from Mary Shelley to Sylvia Plath,* Percy Bysshe Shelley was writing *The Cenci* — the story of incest victim and parricide Beatrice Cenci — around the same time that Mary Shelley was writing *Mathilda:* comparing these texts is profoundly enlightening as to how sharply Mary Shelley differs and diverges from the Romantic script of handling incest. ◀

CHAPTER 6

MY CHAMBER WAS IN A RETIRED PART of the house, and looked upon the garden so that no sound of the other inhabitants could reach it; and here in perfect solitude I wept for several hours. When a servant came to ask me if I would take food I learnt from him that my father had returned, and was apparently well and this relieved me from a load of anxiety, yet I did not cease to weep bitterly. At first, as the memory of former happiness contrasted to my present despair came across me, I gave relief to the oppression of heart that I felt by words, and groans, and heart rending sighs: but nature became wearied, and this more violent grief gave place to a passionate but mute flood of tears: my whole soul seemed to dissolve [in] them. I did not wring my hands, or tear my hair, or utter wild exclamations, but as Boccacio describes the intense and quiet grief [of] Sigismunda over the heart of Guiscardo, I sat with my hands folded, silently letting fall a perpetual stream from my eyes. Such was the depth of my emotion that I had no feeling of what caused my distress, my thoughts even wandered to many indifferent objects; but still neither moving limb or feature my tears fell untill, as if the fountains were exhausted, they gradually subsided, and I awoke to life as from a dream.

When I had ceased to weep reason and memory returned upon me, and I began to reflect with greater calmness on what had happened, and how it became me to act—A few hours only had passed but a mighty revolution had taken place with regard to me—the natural work of years had been transacted since the morning: my father was as dead to me, and I felt for a moment as if he with white hairs were laid in his coffin and I—youth vanished in approaching age, were weeping at his timely dissolution. But it was not so, I was yet young, Oh! far too young, nor was he dead to others; but I, most miserable, must never see or speak to him again. I must fly from him with more earnestness than from my greatest enemy: in solitude or in cities I must never more behold him. That consideration made me breathless with anguish, and impressing itself on my imagination I was unable for a time to follow up any train of ideas. Ever after this, I thought, I would live in the most dreary seclusion. I would retire to the Continent and become a nun; not for religion's sake, for I was not a Catholic, but that I might be for ever shut out from the world. I should there find solitude where I might weep, and the voices of life might never reach me.

But my father; my beloved and most wretched father? Would he die? Would he never overcome the fierce passion that now held pityless dominion over him? Might he not many, many years hence, when age had quenched the burning sensations that he now experienced, might he not then be again a father to me? This reflection unwrinkled my brow, and I could feel (and I wept to feel it) a half melancholy smile draw from my lips their expression of suffering: I dared indulge better hopes for my future life; years must pass but they would speed lightly away winged by hope, or if they passed heavily, still they would pass and I had not lost my father for ever. Let him spend another sixteen years of desolate wandering: let him once more utter his wild complaints to the vast woods and the tremendous cataracts of another clime: let him again undergo fearful danger and soul-quelling hardships: let the hot sun of the south again burn his passion worn cheeks and the cold night rains fall on him and chill his blood.[1]

To this life, miserable father, I devote thee!—Go!—Be thy days passed with savages, and thy nights under the cope of heaven! Be thy limbs worn and thy heart chilled, and all youth be dead within thee! Let thy hairs be as snow; thy walk trembling and thy voice have lost its mellow tones! Let the liquid lustre of thine eyes be quenched; and then return to me, return to thy Mathilda, thy child, who may then be clasped in thy loved arms, while thy heart beats with sinless emotion. Go, Devoted One, and return thus!—This is my curse, a daughter's curse: go, and return pure to thy child, who will never love aught but thee.

These were my thoughts; and with trembling hands I prepared to begin a letter to my unhappy parent. I had now spent many hours in tears and mournful meditation; it was past twelve o'clock; all was at peace in the house, and the gentle air that stole in at my window did not rustle the leaves of the twining plants that shadowed it. I felt the entire tranquillity of the hour when my own breath and involuntary sobs were all the sounds that struck upon the air. On a sudden I heard a gentle step ascending the stairs; I paused breathless, and as it approached glided into an obscure corner of the room; the steps paused at my door, but after a few moments they again receded, descended the stairs and I heard no more.

This slight incident gave rise in me to the most painful reflections; nor do I now dare express the emotions I felt. That he should be restless I understood; that he should wander as an unlaid ghost and find no quiet from the burning hell that consumed his heart. But why approach my chamber? Was not that sacred? I felt almost ready to faint while he had stood there, but I had not betrayed my wakefulness by the slightest motion, although I had heard my own heart beat with violent fear. He had withdrawn. Oh, never, never, may I see him again! Tomorrow night the same roof may not cover us; he or I must depart. The mutual link of our destinies is broken; we must be divided by seas — by land. The stars and the sun must not rise at the same period to us: he must not say, looking at the setting crescent of the moon, "Mathilda now watches its fall." — No, all must be changed. Be it light with him when it is darkness with me! Let him feel the sun of summer while I am chilled by the snows of winter! Let there be the distance of the antipodes between us!

At length the east began to brighten, and the comfortable light of morning streamed into my room. I was weary with watching and for some time I had combated with the heavy sleep that weighed down my eyelids: but now, no longer fearful, I threw myself on my bed. I sought for repose although I did not hope for forgetfulness; I knew I should be pursued by dreams, but did not dread the frightful one that I really had. I thought that I had risen and went to seek my father to inform him of my determination to seperate myself from him. I sought him in the house, in the park, and then in the fields and the woods, but I could not find him. At length I saw him at some distance, seated under a tree, and when he perceived me he waved his hand several times, beckoning me to approach; there was something unearthly in his mien that awed and chilled me, but I drew near. When at a short distance from him I saw that he was deadlily [sic] pale, and clothed in flowing garments of white. Suddenly he started up and fled from me; I pursued him: we sped over the fields, and by the skirts of woods, and on the banks of rivers; he flew fast and I followed. We came at last, methought, to the brow of a huge cliff that over hung the sea which, troubled by the winds, dashed against its base at a distance. I heard the roar of the waters: he held his course right on towards the brink and I became breathless with fear lest he should plunge down the dreadful precipice; I tried to augment my speed, but my knees failed beneath me, yet I had just reached him; just caught a part of his flowing robe, when he leapt down and I awoke with a violent scream. I was trembling and my pillow was wet with my tears; for a few moments my heart beat hard, but the bright beams of the sun and the chirping of the birds quickly restored me to myself, and I rose with a languid spirit, yet wondering what events the day would bring forth. Some time passed before I summoned courage to ring the bell for my servant, and when she came I still dared not utter my father's name. I ordered her to bring my breakfast to my room, and was again left alone — yet still I could make no resolve, but only thought that I might write a note to my father to beg his permission to pay a visit to a relation who lived about thirty miles off, and who had before invited me to her house, but I had refused for then I could not quit my suffering father. When the servant came back she gave me a letter.

"From whom is this letter[?]" I asked trembling.

"Your father left it, madam, with his servant, to be given to you when you should rise."

"My father left it! Where is he? Is he not here?"

"No; he quitted the house before four this morning."

"Good God! He is gone! But tell how this was; speak quick!"

Her relation was short. He had gone in the carriage to the nearest town where he took a post chaise and horses with orders for the London road. He dismissed his servants there, only telling them that he had a sudden call of business and that they were to obey me as their mistress untill his return. ◄

CHAPTER 6
Annotations

1. For the contemporary reader, the divulging of the incest secret — that is, Mathilda's father's sexual and romantic passion for his young daughter — will seem almost a non-occurrence in these passages. The father claims that he hates his daughter, that she is his poison. Of course, it is this feeling of being hated that tortures Mathilda, who has lived a life of such extreme isolation and craves paternal, familial affection. The father then reveals that he hates Mathilda because he loves her. What he means is that he *loves* loves her: not as a father but as a lover. On making this confession, he hopes Mathilda will agree to be in this incestuous love bond with him, and states unequivocally that he loves her more than he ever loved her mother.

    This passage's overlap with *Frankenstein* is striking. Like *Frankenstein, Mathilda* is centered by the moment when a parent and child find insolvable monstrosity in their bond. Whereas Victor Frankenstein finds his carefully created 'child' monstrous once it comes to life, Mathilda's father finds his daughter poisonous because he is sexually attracted to her. And yet, Mathilda's father claims that he is the "monster" rather than Mathilda. In this sense, the two narratives intersect and cross-over each other. Whereas Frankenstein's monster is described as physically hideous progeny, Mathilda is described as incomparably beautiful. Whereas the progeny is called the "monster" in *Frankenstein*, in *Mathilda* the parent is described as a "monster." Both scenes generate narrative structures motivated by the need of the parent and child to avoid each other, and equally motivated by their inability to live without each other. ◄

CHAPTER 7

WITH A BEATING HEART AND FEARFUL, I knew not why, I dismissed the servant and locking my door, sat down to read my father's letter. These are the words that it contained.

"My dear Child

"I HAVE BETRAYED YOUR CONFIDENCE; I have endeavoured to pollute your mind, and have made your innocent heart acquainted with the looks and language of unlawful and monstrous passion. I must expiate these crimes, and must endeavour in some degree to proportionate my punishment to my guilt. You are I doubt not prepared for what I am about to announce; we must seperate and be divided for ever.

"I deprive you of your parent and only friend. You are cast out shelterless on the world: your hopes are blasted; the peace and security of your pure mind destroyed; memory will bring to you frightful images of guilt, and the anguish of innocent love betrayed. Yet I who draw down all this misery upon you; I who cast you forth and remorselessly have set the seal of distrust and agony on the heart and brow of my own child, who with devilish levity have endeavoured to steal away her loveliness to place in its stead the foul deformity of sin; I, in the overflowing anguish of my heart, supplicate you to forgive me.

"I do not ask your pity; you must and do abhor me: but pardon me, Mathilda, and let not your thoughts follow me in my banishment with unrelenting anger. I must never more behold you; never more hear your voice; but the soft whisperings of your forgiveness will reach me and cool the burning of my disordered brain and heart; I am sure I should feel it even in my grave. And I dare enforce this request by relating how miserably I was betrayed into this net of fiery anguish and all my struggles to release myself: indeed if your soul were less pure and bright I would not attempt to exculpate myself to you; I should fear that if I led you to regard me with less abhorrence you might hate vice less: but in addressing you I feel as if I appealed to an angelic judge. I cannot depart without your forgiveness and I must endeavour to gain it, or I must despair. I conjure you therefore to listen to my words, and if with the good guilt may be in any degree extenuated by sharp agony, and remorse that rends the brain as madness perhaps you may think, though I dare not, that I have some claim to your compassion.

"I entreat you to call to your remembrance our first happy life on the shores of Loch Lomond. I had arrived from a weary wandering of sixteen years, during which, although I had gone through many dangers and misfortunes, my affections had been an entire blank. If I grieved it was for your mother, if I loved it was your image; these sole emotions filled my heart in quietness. The human creatures around me excited in me no sympathy and I thought that the mighty change that the death of your mother had wrought within me had rendered me callous to any future impression. I saw the lovely and I did not love, I imagined therefore that all warmth was extinguished in my heart except that which led me ever to dwell on your then infantine image.

"It is a strange link in my fate that without having seen you I should passionately love you. During my wanderings I never slept without first calling down gentle dreams on your head. If I saw a lovely woman, I thought, does my Mathilda resemble her? All delightful things, sublime scenery, soft breezes, exquisite music seemed to me associated with you and only through you to be pleasant to me. At length I saw you. You appeared as the deity of a lovely region, the ministering Angel of a Paradise to which of all human kind you admitted only me. I dared hardly consider you as my daughter; your beauty, artlessness and untaught wisdom seemed to belong to a higher order of beings; your voice breathed forth only words of love: if there was aught of earthly in you it was only what you derived from the beauty of the world; you seemed to have gained a grace from the mountain breezes — the waterfalls and the lake; and this was all of earthly except your affections that you had; there was no dross, no bad feeling in the composition. You yet even have not seen enough of the world to know the stupendous difference that exists between the women we meet in dayly life and a nymph of the woods such as you were, in whose eyes alone mankind may study for centuries & grow wiser & purer. Those divine lights which shone on me as did those of Beatrice upon Dante, and well might I say with him yet with what different feelings

E quasi mi perdei gli occhi chini.

Can you wonder, Mathilda, that I dwelt on your looks, your words, your motions, & drank in unmixed delight?

"But I am afraid that I wander from my purpose. I must be more brief for night draws on apace and all my hours in this house are counted. Well, we removed to London, and still I felt only the peace of sinless passion. You were ever with me, and I desired no more than to gaze on your countenance, and to know that I was all the world to you; I was lapped in a fool's paradise of enjoyment and security. Was my love blamable? If it was I was ignorant of it; I desired only that which I possessed, and if I enjoyed from your looks, and words, and most innocent caresses a rapture usually excluded from the feelings of a parent towards his child, yet no uneasiness, no wish, no casual idea awoke me to a sense of guilt. I loved you as a human father might be supposed to love a daughter borne to him by a heavenly mother; as Anchises might have regarded the child of Venus if the sex had been changed; love mingled with respect and adoration. Perhaps also my passion was lulled to content by the deep and exclusive affection you felt for me.

"But when I saw you become the object of another's love; when I imagined that you might be loved otherwise than as a sacred type and image of loveliness and excellence; or that you might love another with a more ardent affection than that which you bore to me, then the fiend awoke within me; I dismissed your lover; and from that moment I have known no peace. I have sought in vain for sleep and rest; my lids refused to close, and my blood was for ever in a tumult. I awoke to a new life as one who dies in hope might wake in Hell. I will not sully your imagination by recounting my combats, my self-anger and my despair. Let a veil be drawn over the unimaginable sensations of a guilty father; the secrets of so agonized a heart may not be made vulgar. All was uproar, crime, remorse and hate, yet still the tenderest love; and what first awoke me to the firm resolve of conquering my passion and of restoring her father to my child was the sight of your bitter and sympathizing sorrows. It was this that led me here: I thought that if I could again awaken in my heart the grief I had felt at the loss of your mother, and the many associations with her memory which had been laid to sleep for seventeen years, that all love for her child would become extinct. In a fit of heroism I determined to go alone; to quit you, the life of my life, and not to see you again untill I might guiltlessly. But it would not do: I rated my fortitude too high, or my love too low. I should certainly have died if you had not hastened to me. Would that I had been indeed extinguished!

"And now, Mathilda I must make you my last confession. I have been miserably mistaken in imagining that I could conquer my love for you; I never can. The sight of this house, these fields and woods which my first love inhabited seems to have encreased it: in my madness I dared say to myself—Diana died to give her birth; her mother's spirit was transferred into her frame, and she ought to be as Diana to me. With every effort to cast it off, this love clings closer, this guilty love more unnatural than hate, that withers your hopes and destroys me for ever.

Better have loved despair, & safer kissed her.

No time or space can tear from my soul that which makes a part of it. Since my arrival here I have not for a moment ceased to feel the hell of passion which has been implanted in me to burn untill all be cold, and stiff, and dead. Yet I will not die; alas! how dare I go where I may meet Diana, when I have disobeyed her last request; her last words said in a faint voice when all feeling but love, which survives all things else was already dead, she then bade me make her child happy: that thought alone gives a double sting to death. I will wander away from you, away from all life—in the solitude I shall seek I alone shall breathe of human kind. I must endure life; and as it is my duty so I shall untill the grave dreaded yet desired, receive me free from pain: for while I feel it will be pain that must make up the whole sum of my sensations. Is not this a fearful curse that I labour under? Do I not look forward to a miserable future? My child, if after this life I am permitted to see you again, if pain can purify the heart, mine will be pure: if remorse may expiate guilt, I shall be guiltless.

"I have been at the door of your chamber: every thing is silent. You sleep. Do you indeed sleep, Mathilda? Spirits of Good, behold the tears of my earnest prayer! Bless my child! Protect her from the selfish among her fellow creatures: protect her from the agonies of passion, and the despair of disappointment! Peace, Hope and Love be thy guardians, oh, thou soul of my soul: thou in whom I breathe!

"I dare not read my letter over for I have no time to write another, and yet I fear that some expressions in it might displease me. Since I last saw you I have been constantly employed in writing letters, and have several more to write; for I do not intend that any one shall hear of me after I depart. I need not conjure you to look upon me as one of whom all links that once existed between us are broken. Your own delicacy will not allow you, I am convinced, to attempt to trace me. It is far better for your peace that you should be ignorant of my destination. You will not follow me, for when I bannish myself would you nourish guilt by obtruding yourself upon me? You will not do this, I know you will not. You must forget me and all the evil that I have taught you. Cast off the only gift that I have bestowed upon you, your grief, and rise from under my blighting influence as no flower so sweet ever did rise from beneath so much evil.

"You will never hear from me again: receive these then as the last words of mine that will ever reach you; and although I have forfeited your filial love, yet regard them I conjure you as a father's command. Resolutely shake of[f] the wretchedness that this first misfortune in early life must occasion you. Bear boldly up against the storm: continue wise and mild, but believe it, and indeed it is, your duty to be happy. You are very young; let not this check for more than a moment retard your glorious course; hold on, beloved one. The sun of youth is not set for you; it will restore vigour and life to you; do not resist with obstinate grief its beneficent influence, oh, my child! bless me with the hope that I have not utterly destroyed you.

"Farewell, Mathilda. I go with the belief that I have your pardon. Your gentle nature would not permit you to hate your greatest enemy and though I be he, although I have rent happiness from your grasp; though I have passed over your young love and hopes as the angel of destruction, finding beauty and joy, and leaving blight and despair, yet you will forgive me, and with eyes overflowing with tears I thank you; my beloved one, I accept your pardon with a gratitude that will never die, and that will, indeed it will, outlive guilt and remorse.

"Farewell for ever!"

The moment I finished this letter I ordered the carriage and prepared to follow my father. The words of his letter by which he had dissuaded me from this step were those that determined me. Why did he write them? He must know that if I believed that his intention was merely to absent himself from me that instead of opposing him it would be that which I should myself require—or if he thought that any lurking feeling, yet he could not think that, should lead me to him would he endeavour to overthrow the only hope he could have of ever seeing me again; a lover, there was madness in the thought, yet he was my lover, would not act thus. No, he had determined to die, and he wished to spare me the misery of knowing it. The few ineffectual words he had said concerning his duty were to me a further proof—and the more I studied the letter the more did I perceive a thousand slight expressions that could only indicate a knowledge that life was now over for him. He was about to die! My blood froze at the thought: a sickening feeling of horror came over me that allowed not of tears. As I waited for the carriage I walked up and down with a quick pace; then kneeling and passionately clasping my hands I tried to pray but my voice was choked by convulsive sobs—Oh the sun shone, the air was balmy—he must yet live for if he were dead all would surely be black as night to me!

The motion of the carriage knowing that it carried me towards him and that I might perhaps find him alive somewhat revived my courage: yet I had a dreadful ride. Hope only supported me, the hope that I should not be too late. I did not weep, but I wiped the perspiration from my brow, and tried to still my brain and heart beating almost to madness. Oh! I must not be mad when I see him; or perhaps it were as well that I should be, my distraction might calm his, and recall him to the endurance of life. Yet untill I find him I must force reason to keep her seat, and I pressed my forehead hard with my hands—Oh do not leave me; or I shall forget what I am about—instead of driving on as we ought with the speed of lightning they will attend to me, and we shall be too late. Oh! God help me! Let him be alive! It is all dark; in my abject misery I demand no more: no hope, no good: only passion, and guilt, and horror; but alive! Alive! My sensations choked me—No tears fell yet I sobbed, and breathed short and hard; one only thought possessed me, and I could only utter one word, that half screaming was perpetually on my lips; Alive! Alive!—

I had taken the steward with me for he, much better than I, could make the requisite enquiries—the poor old man could not restrain his tears as he saw my deep distress and knew the cause—he sometimes uttered a few broken words of consolation: in moments like these the mistress and servant become in a manner equals and when I saw his old dim eyes wet with sympathizing tears; his gray hair thinly scattered on an age-wrinkled brow I thought oh if my father were as he is—decrepid & hoary—then I should be spared this pain—

When I had arrived at the nearest town I took post horses and followed the road my father had taken. At every inn where we changed horses we heard of him, and I was possessed by alternate hope and fear. A length I found that he had altered his route; at first he had followed the London road; but now he changed it, and upon enquiry I found that the one which he now pursued led towards the sea. My dream recurred to my thoughts; I was not usually superstitious but in wretchedness every one is so. The sea was fifty miles off, yet it was towards it that he fled. The idea was terrible to my half crazed imagination, and almost over-turned the little self possession that still remained to me. I journied all day; every moment my misery encreased and the fever of my blood became intolerable. The summer sun shone in an unclouded sky; the air was close but all was cool to me except my own scorching skin. Towards evening dark thunder clouds arose above the horrizon and I heard its distant roll—after sunset they darkened the whole sky and it began to rain, the lightning lighted up the whole country and the thunder drowned the noise of our carriage. At the next inn my father had not taken horses; he had left a box there saying he would return, and had walked over the fields to the town of — — a seacost town eight miles off.

For a moment I was almost paralyzed by fear; but my energy returned and I demanded a guide to accompany me in following his steps. The night was tempestuous but my bribe was high and I easily procured a countryman. We passed through many lanes and over fields and wild downs; the rain poured down in torrents; and the loud thunder broke in terrible crashes over our heads. Oh! What a night it was! And I passed on with quick steps among the high, dank grass amid the rain and tempest. My dream was for ever in my thoughts, and with a kind of half insanity that often possesses the mind in despair, I said aloud; "Courage! We are not near the sea; we are yet several miles from the ocean" — Yet it was towards the sea that our direction lay and that heightened the confusion of my ideas. Once, overcome by fatigue, I sunk on the wet earth; about two hundred yards distant, alone in a large meadow stood a magnificent oak; the lightnings shewed its myriad boughs torn by the storm. A strange idea seized me; a person must have felt all the agonies of doubt concerning the life and death of one who is the whole world to them before they can enter into my feelings — for in that state, the mind working unrestrained by the will makes strange and fanciful combinations with outward circumstances and weaves the chances and changes of nature into an immediate connexion with the event they dread. It was with this feeling that I turned to the old Steward who stood pale and trembling beside me; "Mark, Gaspar, if the next flash of lightning rend not that oak my father will be alive."

I had scarcely uttered these words than a flash instantly followed by a tremendous peal of thunder descended on it; and when my eyes recovered their sight after the dazzling light, the oak no longer stood in the meadow — The old man uttered a wild exclamation of horror when he saw so sudden an interpretation given to my prophesy. I started up, my strength returned; [sic] with my terror; I cried, "Oh, God! Is this thy decree? Yet perhaps I shall not be too late."

Although still several miles distant we continued to approach the sea. We came at last to the road that led to the town of— —and at an inn there we heard that my father had passed by somewhat before sunset; he had observed the approaching storm and had hired a horse for the next town which was situated a mile from the sea that he might arrive there before it should commence: this town was five miles off. We hired a chaise here, and with four horses drove with speed through the storm. My garments were wet and clung around me, and my hair hung in straight locks on my neck when not blown aside by the wind. I shivered, yet my pulse was high with fever. Great God! What agony I endured. I shed no tears but my eyes wild and inflamed were starting from my head; I could hardly support the weight that pressed upon my brain. We arrived at the town of — — in a little more than half an hour. When my father had arrived the storm had already begun, but he had refused to stop and leaving his horse there he walked on — towards the sea. Alas! it was double cruelty in him to have chosen the sea for his fatal resolve; it was adding madness to my despair.

The poor old servant who was with me endeavoured to persuade me to remain here and to let him go alone — I shook my head silently and sadly; sick almost to death I leant upon his arm, and as there was no road for a chaise dragged my weary steps across the desolate downs to meet my fate, now too certain for the agony of doubt. Almost fainting I slowly approached the fatal waters; when we had quitted the town we heard their roaring. I whispered to myself in a muttering voice — "The sound is the same as that which I heard in my dream. It is the knell of my father which I hear."

The rain had ceased; there was no more thunder and lightning; the wind had paused. My heart no longer beat wildly; I did not feel any fever: but I was chilled; my knees sunk under me — I almost slept as I walked with excess of weariness; every limb trembled. I was silent: all was silent except the roaring of the sea which became louder and more dreadful. Yet we advanced slowly: sometimes I thought that we should never arrive; that the sound of waves would still allure us, and that we should walk on for ever and ever: field succeeding field, never would our weary journey cease, nor night nor day; but still we should hear the dashing of the sea, and to all this there would be no end. Wild beyond the imagination of the happy are the thoughts bred by misery and despair.

At length we reached the overhanging beach; a cottage stood beside the path; we knocked at the door and it was opened: the bed within instantly caught my eye; something stiff and straight lay on it, covered by a sheet; the cottagers looked aghast. The first words that they uttered confirmed what I before knew. I did not feel shocked or overcome: I believe that I asked one or two questions and listened to the answers. I har[d]ly know, but in a few moments I sank lifeless to the ground; and so would that then all had been at an end! ◄

CHAPTER 8

WAS CARRIED TO THE NEXT TOWN: fever succeeded to convulsions and faint-ings, & for some weeks my unhappy spirit hovered on the very verge of death. But life was yet strong within me; I recovered: nor did it a little aid my returning health that my recollections were at first vague, and that I was too weak to feel any violent emotion. I often said to myself, my father is dead. He loved me with a guilty passion, and stung by remorse and despair he killed himself. Why is it that I feel no horror? Are these circumstances not dreadful? Is it not enough that I shall never more meet the eyes of my beloved father; never more hear his voice; no caress, no look? All cold, and stiff, and dead! Alas! I am quite callous: the night I was out in was fearful and the cold rain that fell about my heart has acted like the waters of the cavern of Antiparos and has changed it to stone. I do not weep or sigh; but I must reason with myself, and force myself to feel sorrow and despair. This is not resignation that I feel, for I am dead to all regret.[1]

I communed in this manner with myself, but I was silent to all around me. I hardly replied to the slightest question, and was uneasy when I saw a human creature near me. I was surrounded by my female relations, but they were all of them nearly strangers to me: I did not listen to their consolations; and so little did they work their designed effect that they seemed to me to be spoken in an unknown tongue. I found if sorrow was dead within me, so was love and desire of sympathy. Yet sorrow only slept to revive more fierce, but love never woke again — its ghost, ever hovering over my father's grave, alone survived — since his death all the world was to me a blank except where woe had stampt its burning words telling me to smile no more—the living were not fit companions for me, and I was ever meditating by what means I might shake them all off, and never be heard of again.

My convalescence rapidly advanced, yet this was the thought that haunted me, and I was for ever forming plans how I might hereafter contrive to escape the tortures that were prepared for me when I should mix in society, and to find that solitude which alone could suit one whom an untold grief seperated from her fellow creatures. Who can be more solitary even in a crowd than one whose history and the never ending feelings and remembrances arising from it is [sic] known to no living soul. There was too deep a horror in my tale for confidence; I was on earth the sole depository of my own secret. I might tell it to the winds and to the desart heaths but I must never among my fellow creatures, either by word or look give allowance to the smallest conjecture of the dread reality: I must shrink before the eye of man lest he should read my father's guilt in my glazed eyes: I must be silent lest my faltering voice should betray unimagined horrors. Over the deep grave of my secret I must heap an impenetrable heap of false smiles and words: cunning frauds, treacherous laughter and a mixture of all light deceits would form a mist to blind others and be as the poisonous simoon to me. I, the offspring of love, the child of the woods, the nursling of Nature's bright self was to submit to this? I dared not.

How must I escape? I was rich and young, and had a guardian appointed for me; and all about me would act as if I were one of their great society, while I must keep the secret that I really was cut off from them for ever. If I fled I should be pursued; in life there was no escape for me: why then I must die. I shuddered; I dared not die even though the cold grave held all I loved; although I might say with Job

Where is now my hope? For my hope who shall see it?

They shall go down together to the bars of the pit, when our   rest together is in the dust—

Yes my hope was corruption and dust and all to which death brings us. — Or after life—No, no, I will not persuade myself to die, I may not, dare not. And then I wept; yes, warm tears once more struggled into my eyes soothing yet bitter; and after I had wept much and called with unavailing anguish, with outstretched arms, for my cruel father; after my weak frame was exhausted by all variety of plaint I sank once more into reverie, and once more reflected on how I might find that which I most desired; dear to me if aught were dear, a death-like solitude.

I dared not die, but I might feign death, and thus escape from my comforters: they will believe me united to my father, and so indeed I shall be. For alone, when no voice can disturb my dream, and no cold eye meet mine to check its fire, then

I may commune with his spirit; on a lone heath, at noon or at midnight, still I should be near him. His last injunction to me was that I should be happy; perhaps he did not mean the shadowy happiness that I promised myself, yet it was that alone which I could taste. He did not conceive that ever again I could make one of the smiling hunters that go coursing after bubles that break to nothing when caught, and then after a new one with brighter colours; my hope also had proved a buble, but it had been so lovely, so adorned that I saw none that could attract me after it; besides I was wearied with the pursuit, nearly dead with weariness.

I would feign to die; my contented heirs would seize upon my wealth, and I should purchase freedom. But then my plan must be laid with art; I would not be left destitute, I must secure some money. Alas! to what loathsome shifts must I be driven? Yet a whole life of falsehood was otherwise my portion: and when remorse at being the contriver of any cheat made me shrink from my design I was irresistably led back and confirmed in it by the visit of some aunt or cousin, who would tell me that death was the end of all men. And then say that my father had surely lost his wits ever since my mother's death; that he was mad and that I was fortunate, for in one of his fits he might have killed me instead of destroying his own crazed being. And all this, to be sure, was delicately put; not in broad words for my feelings might be hurt but

Whispered so and so   In dark hint soft and low with downcast eyes, and sympathizing smiles or whimpers; and I listened with quiet countenance while every nerve trembled; I that dared not utter aye or no to all this blasphemy. Oh, this was a delicious life quite void of guile! I with my dove's look and fox's heart: for indeed I felt only the degradation of falsehood, and not any sacred sentiment of conscious innocence that might redeem it. I who had before clothed myself in the bright garb of sincerity must now borrow one of divers colours: it might sit awkwardly at first, but use would enable me to place it in elegant folds, to lie with grace. Aye, I might die my soul with falsehood untill I had quite hid its native colour. Oh, beloved father! Accept the pure heart of your unhappy daughter; permit me to join you unspotted as I was or you will not recognize my altered semblance. As grief might change Constance so would deceit change me untill in heaven you would say, "This is not my child" — My father, to be happy both now and when again we meet I must fly from all this life which is mockery to one like me. In solitude only shall I be myself; in solitude I shall be thine.

Alas! I even now look back with disgust at my artifices and contrivances by which, after many painful struggles, I effected my retreat. I might enter into a long detail of the means I used, first to secure myself a slight maintenance for the remainder of my life, and afterwards to ensure the conviction of my death: I might, but I will not. I even now blush at the falsehoods I uttered; my heart sickens: I will leave this complication of what I hope I may in a manner call innocent deceit to be imagined by the reader. The remembrance haunts me like a crime—I know that if I were to endeavour to relate it my tale would at length remain unfinished. I was led to London, and had to endure for some weeks cold looks, cold words and colder consolations: but I escaped; they tried to bind me with fetters that they thought silken, yet which weighed on me like iron, although I broke them more easily than a girth formed of a single straw and fled to freedom.

The few weeks that I spent in London were the most miserable of my life: a great city is a frightful habitation to one sorrowing. The sunset and the gentle moon, the blessed motion of the leaves and the murmuring of waters are all sweet physicians to a distempered mind. The soul is expanded and drinks in quiet, a lulling medecine [sic]—to me it was as the sight of the lovely water snakes to the bewitched mariner—in loving and blessing Nature I unawares, called down a blessing on my own soul. But in a city all is closed shut like a prison, a wiry prison from which you can peep at the sky only. I can not describe to you what were [sic] the frantic nature of my sensations while I resided there; I was often on the verge of madness. Nay, when I look back on many of my wild thoughts, thoughts with which actions sometimes endeavoured to keep pace; when I tossed my hands high calling down the cope of heaven to fall on me and bury me; when I tore my hair and throwing it to the winds cried, "Ye are free, go seek my father!" And then, like the unfortunate Constance, catching at them again and tying them up, that nought might find him if I might not. How, on my knees I have fancied myself close to my father's grave and struck the ground in anger that it should cover him from me. Oft when I have listened with gasping attention for the sound of the ocean mingled with my father's groans; and then wept untill my strength was gone and I was calm and faint, when I have recollected all this I have asked myself if this were not madness. While in London these and many other dreadful thoughts too harrowing for words were my portion: I lost all this suffering when I was free; when I saw the wild heath around me, and the evening star in the west, then I could weep, gently weep, and be at peace.

Do not mistake me; I never was really mad. I was always conscious of my state when my wild thoughts seemed to drive me to insanity, and never betrayed them to aught but silence and solitude. The people around me saw nothing of all this. They only saw a poor girl broken in spirit, who spoke in a low and gentle voice, and from underneath whose downcast lids tears would sometimes steal which she strove to hide. One who loved to be alone, and shrunk from observation; who never smiled; oh, no! I never smiled—and that was all.

Well, I escaped. I left my guardian's house and I was never heard of again; it was believed from the letters that I left and other circumstances that I planned that I had destroyed myself. I was sought after therefore with less care than would otherwise have been the case; and soon all trace and memory of me was lost. I left London in a small vessel bound for a port in the north of England. And now having succeeded in my attempt, and being quite alone peace returned to me. The sea was calm and the vessel moved gently onwards, I sat upon deck under the open canopy of heaven and methought I was an altered creature. Not the wild, raving & most miserable Mathilda but a youthful Hermitess dedicated to seclusion and whose bosom she must strive to keep free from all tumult and unholy despair—The fanciful nunlike dress that I had adopted; the knowledge that my very existence was a secret known only to myself; the solitude to which I was for ever hereafter destined nursed gentle thoughts in my wounded heart. The breeze that played in my hair revived me, and I watched with quiet eyes the sunbeams that glittered on the waves, and the birds that coursed each other over the waters just brushing them with their plumes. I slept too undisturbed by dreams; and awoke refreshed to again enjoy my tranquil freedom.

In four days we arrived at the harbour to which we were bound. I would not remain on the sea coast, but proceeded immediately inland. I had already planned the situation where I would live. It should be a solitary house on a wide plain near no other habitation: where I could behold the whole horizon, and wander far without molestation from the sight of my fellow creatures. I was not mysanthropic, but I felt that the gentle current of my feelings depended upon my being alone. I fixed myself on a wide solitude. On a dreary heath bestrewen with stones, among which short grass grew; and here and there a few rushes beside a little pool. Not far from my cottage was a small cluster of pines the only trees to be seen for many miles: I had a path cut through the furze from my door to this little wood, from whose topmost branches the birds saluted the rising sun and awoke me to my daily meditation. My view was bounded only by the horizon except on one side where a distant wood made a black spot on the heath, that every where else stretched out its faint hues as far as the eye could reach, wide and very desolate. Here I could mark the net work of the clouds as they wove themselves into thick masses: I could watch the slow rise of the heavy thunder clouds and could see the rack as it was driven across the heavens, or under the pine trees I could enjoy the stillness of the azure sky.

My life was very peaceful. I had one female servant who spent the greater part of the day at a village two miles off. My amusements were simple and very innocent; I fed the birds who built on the pines or among the ivy that covered the wall of my little garden, and they soon knew me: the bolder ones pecked the crumbs from my hands and perched on my fingers to sing their thankfulness. When I had lived here some time other animals visited me and a fox came every day for a portion of food appropriated for him & would suffer me to pat his head. I had besides many books and a harp with which when despairing I could soothe my spirits, and raise myself to sympathy and love.

Love! What had I to love? Oh many things: there was the moonshine, and the bright stars; the breezes and the refreshing rains; there was the whole earth and the sky that covers it: all lovely forms that visited my imagination, all memories of heroism and virtue. Yet this was very unlike my early life although as then I was confined to Nature and books. Then I bounded across the fields; my spirit often seemed to ride upon the winds, and to mingle in joyful sympathy with the ambient air. Then if I wandered slowly I cheered myself with a sweet song or sweeter day dreams. I felt a holy rapture spring from all I saw. I drank in joy with life; my steps were light; my eyes, clear from the love that animated them, sought the heavens, and with my long hair loosened to the winds I gave my body and my mind to sympathy and delight. But now my walk was slow—My eyes were seldom raised and often filled with tears; no song; no smiles; no careless motion that might bespeak a mind intent on what surrounded it—I was gathered up into myself—a selfish solitary creature ever pondering on my regrets and faded hopes.

Mine was an idle, useless life; it was so; but say not to the lily laid prostrate by the storm arise, and bloom as before. My heart was bleeding from its death's wound; I could live no otherwise—Often amid apparent calm I was visited by despair and melancholy; gloom that nought could dissipate or overcome; a hatred of life; a carelessness of beauty; all these would by fits hold me nearly annihilated by their powers. Never for one moment when most placid did I cease to pray for death. I could be found in no state of mind which I would not willingly have exchanged for nothingness. And morning and evening my tearful eyes raised to heaven, my hands clasped tight in the energy of prayer, I have repeated with the poet—

Before I see another day   Oh, let this body die away!

Let me not be reproached then with inutility; I believed that by suicide I should violate a divine law of nature, and I thought that I sufficiently fulfilled my part in submitting to the hard task of enduring the crawling hours & minutes—in bearing the load of time that weighed miserably upon me and that in abstaining from what I in my calm moments considered a crime, I deserved the reward of virtue. There were periods, dreadful ones, during which I despaired—& doubted the existence of all duty & the reality of crime—but I shudder, and turn from the rememberance. ◄

CHAPTER 8
Annotations

1. To convey the horror of the incest secret, Shelley returns to the epistolary form she employed for the opening of *Frankenstein*. In his letter, Mathilda's father references Dante's *Purgatorio,* so that we are very clear that Mathilda, the character, is a figure from Dante and more importantly a figure in purgatory—one who has been tainted and marked by sin but who can expiate that sin through confession of the very story we are reading in the novella *Mathilda*. In his letter, the father states his incestuous desire for his daughter, making clear his wish that his daughter should become his wife, should take Diana's (Mathilda's mother's) place. Importantly, the letter conveys the idea that motivates the entire novella: his sin of incestuously desiring his young daughter absolutely changes her and becomes her problem, her burden.

   This section ends with the father's suicide, and Mathilda's frantic journey to the ocean in an attempt to save him. Here is the scene that Mary Shelley later referred to in deeply superstitious terms when she came to believe that the novella *Mathilda*—that she had written but not published—was an ill omen, predicting the death by drowning of her spouse, Percy Bysshe Shelley. What I want to emphasize here, by conveying this anecdote, is Mary Shelley's intense personal belief that stories and secrets have tremendous force in the real world: that her works *Frankenstein* and *Mathilda* were not merely words but acts, acts with consequences. Perhaps it is the intensity of her belief in the force of words—words as acts—that makes Shelley's early works so enduring. And, paradoxically, this may also explain why after *Frankenstein* and *Mathilda* her work begins to lose a sense of tensile force. Certainly, *The Last Man* is conceptually fascinating and has brilliant passages but beyond that Shelley, after suffering by age twenty-four her husband's horrifying death by drowning and the tragic deaths of all but one of her children, began to veer away from writing that confronts with emotional intensity the dangers and terrors of the mortal world. ◄

CHAPTER 9

THUS I PASSED TWO YEARS. Day after day so many hundreds wore on; they brought no outward changes with them, but some few slowly operated on my mind as I glided on towards death. I began to study more; to sympathize more in the thoughts of others as expressed in books; to read history, and to lose my individuallity among the crowd that had existed before me. Thus perhaps as the sensation of immediate suffering wore off, I became more human. Solitude also lost to me some of its charms: I began again to wish for sympathy; not that I was ever tempted to seek the crowd, but I wished for one friend to love me. You will say perhaps that I gradually became fitted to return to society. I do not think so. For the sympathy that I desired must be so pure, so divested of influence from outward circumstances that in the world I could not fail of being balked by the gross materials that perpetually mingle even with its best feelings. Believe me, I was then less fitted for any communion with my fellow creatures than before. When I left them they had tormented me but it was in the same way as pain and sickness may torment; somthing extraneous to the mind that galled it, and that I wished to cast aside. But now I should have desired sympathy; I should wish to knit my soul to some one of theirs, and should have prepared for myself plentiful draughts of disappointment and suffering; for I was tender as the sensitive plant, all nerve. I did not desire sympathy and aid in ambition or wisdom, but sweet and mutual affection; smiles to cheer me and gentle words of comfort. I wished for one heart in which I could pour unrestrained my plaints, and by the heavenly nature of the soil blessed fruit might spring from such bad seed. Yet how could I find this? The love that is the soul of friendship is a soft spirit seldom found except when two amiable creatures are knit from early youth, or when bound by mutual suffering and pursuits; it comes to some of the elect unsought and unaware; it descends as gentle dew on chosen spots which however barren they were before become under its benign influence fertile in all sweet plants; but when desired it flies; it scoffs at the prayers of its votaries; it will bestow, but not be sought.

I knew all this and did not go to seek sympathy; but there on my solitary heath, under my lowly roof where all around was desart, it came to me as a sun beam in winter to adorn while it helps to dissolve the drifted snow. — Alas the sun shone on blighted fruit; I did not revive under its radiance for I was too utterly undone to feel its kindly power. My father had been and his memory was the life of my life. I might feel gratitude to another but I never more could love or hope as I had done; it was all suffering; even my pleasures were endured, not enjoyed. I was as a solitary spot among mountains shut in on all sides by steep black precipices; where no ray of heat could penetrate; and from which there was no outlet to sunnier fields. And thus it was that although the spirit of friendship soothed me for a while it could not restore me. It came as some gentle visitation; it went and I hardly felt the loss. The spirit of existence was dead within me; be not surprised therefore that when it came I welcomed not more gladly, or when it departed I lamented not more bitterly the best gift of heaven — a friend.[1]

The name of my friend was Woodville. I will briefly relate his history that you may judge how cold my heart must have been not to be warmed by his eloquent words and tender sympathy; and how he also being most unhappy we were well fitted to be a mutual consolation to each other, if I had not been hardened to stone by the Medusa head of Misery. The misfortunes of Woodville were not of the hearts core like mine; his was a natural grief, not to destroy but to purify the heart and from which he might, when its shadow had passed from over him, shine forth brighter and happier than before.

Woodville was the son of a poor clergyman and had received a classical education. He was one of those very few whom fortune favours from their birth; on whom she bestows all gifts of intellect and person with a profusion that knew no bounds, and whom under her peculiar protection, no imperfection however slight, or disappointment however transitory has leave to touch. She seemed to have formed his mind of that excellence which no dross can tarnish, and his understanding was such that no error could pervert. His genius was transcendant, and when it rose as a bright star in the east all eyes were turned towards it in admiration. He was a Poet. That name has so often been degraded that it will not convey the idea of all that he was. He was like a poet of old whom the muses had crowned in his cradle, and on whose lips bees had fed. As he walked among other men he seemed encompassed with a heavenly halo that divided him from and lifted him above them. It was his surpassing beauty, the dazzling fire of his eyes, and his words whose rich accents wrapt the listener in mute and extatic wonder, that made him transcend all others so that before him they appeared only formed to minister to his superior excellence.

He was glorious from his youth. Every one loved him; no shadow of envy or hate cast even from the meanest mind ever fell upon him. He was, as one the peculiar delight of the Gods, railed and fenced in by his own divinity, so that nought but love and admiration could approach him. His heart was simple like a child, unstained by arrogance or vanity. He mingled in society unknowing of his superiority over his companions, not because he undervalued himself but because he did not perceive the inferiority of others. He seemed incapable of conceiving of the full extent of the power that selfishness & vice possesses in the world: when I knew him, although he had suffered disappointment in his dearest hopes, he had not experienced any that arose from the meaness and self love of men: his station was too high to allow of his suffering through their hardheart-edness; and too low for him to have experienced ingratitude and encroaching selfishness: it is one of the blessings of a moderate fortune, that by preventing the possessor from confering pecuniary favours it prevents him also from diving into the arcana of human weakness or malice — To bestow on your fellow men is a Godlike attribute — So indeed it is and as such not one fit for mortality; — the giver like Adam and Prometheus, must pay the penalty of rising above his nature by being the martyr to his own excellence. Woodville was free from all these evils; and if slight examples did come across him he did not notice them but passed on in his course as an angel with winged feet might glide along the earth unimpeded by all those little obstacles over which we of earthly origin stumble. He was a believer in the divinity of genius and always opposed a stern disbelief to the objections of those petty cavillers and minor critics who wish to reduce all men to their own miserable level — "I will make a scientific simile" he would say, "[i]n the manner, if you will, of Dr. Darwin — I consider the alledged errors of a man of genius as the aberrations of the fixed stars. It is our distance from them and our imperfect means of communication that makes them appear to move; in truth they always remain stationary, a glorious centre, giving us a fine lesson of modesty if we would thus receive it."[2]

I have said that he was a poet: when he was three and twenty years of age he first published a poem, and it was hailed by the whole nation with enthusiasm and delight. His good star perpetually shone upon him; a reputation had never before been made so rapidly: it was universal. The multitude extolled the same poems that formed the wonder of the sage in his closet: there was not one dissentient voice.

It was at this time, in the height of his glory, that he became acquainted with Elinor. She was a young heiress of exquisite beauty who lived under the care of her guardian: from the moment they were seen together they appeared formed for each other. Elinor had not the genius of Woodville but she was generous and noble, and exalted by her youth and the love that she every where excited above the knowledge of aught but virtue and excellence. She was lovely; her manners were frank and simple; her deep blue eyes swam in a lustre which could only be given by sensibility joined to wisdom.[3]

They were formed for one another and they soon loved. Woodville for the first time felt the delight of love; and Elinor was enraptured in possessing the heart of one so beautiful and glorious among his fellow men. Could any thing but unmixed joy flow from such a union?

Woodville was a Poet — he was sought for by every society and all eyes were turned on him alone when he appeared; but he was the son of a poor clergyman and Elinor was a rich heiress. Her guardian was not displeased with their mutual affection: the merit of Woodville was too eminent to admit of cavil on account of his inferior wealth; but the dying will of her father did not allow her to marry before she was of age and her fortune depended upon her obeying this injunction. She had just entered her twentieth year, and she and her lover were obliged to submit to this delay. But they were ever together and their happiness seemed that of Paradise: they studied together: formed plans of future occupations, and drinking in love and joy from each other's eyes and words they hardly repined at the delay to their entire union. Woodville for ever rose in glory; and Elinor become more lovely and wise under the lessons of her accomplished lover.

In two months Elinor would be twenty one: every thing was prepared for their union. How shall I relate the catastrophe to so much joy; but the earth would not be the earth it is covered with blight and sorrow if one such pair as these angelic creatures had been suffered to exist for one another: search through the world and you will not find the perfect happiness which their marriage would have caused them to enjoy; there must have been a revolution in the order of things as estab-lished among us miserable earth-dwellers to have admitted of such consummate joy. The chain of necessity ever bringing misery must have been broken and the malignant fate that presides over it would not permit this breach of her eternal laws. But why should I repine at this? Misery was my element, and nothing but what was miserable could approach me; if Woodville had been happy I should never have known him. And can I who for many years was fed by tears, and nourished under the dew of grief, can I pause to relate a tale of woe and death?

Woodville was obliged to make a journey into the country and was detained from day to day in irksome absence from his lovely bride. He received a letter from her to say that she was slightly ill, but telling him to hasten to her, that from his eyes she would receive health and that his company would be her surest medecine. He was detained three days longer and then he hastened to her. His heart, he knew not why prognosticated misfortune; he had not heard from her again; he feared she might be worse and this fear made him impatient and restless for the moment of beholding her once more stand before him arrayed in health and beauty; for a sinister voice seemed always to whisper to him, "You will never more behold her as she was."

When he arrived at her habitation all was silent in it: he made his way through several rooms; in one he saw a servant weeping bitterly: he was faint with fear and could hardly ask, "Is she dead?" and just listened to the dreadful answer, "Not yet." These astounding words came on him as of less fearful import than those which he had expected; and to learn that she was still in being, and that he might still hope was an alleviation to him. He remembered the words of her letter and he indulged the wild idea that his kisses breathing warm love and life would infuse new spirit into her, and that with him near her she could not die; that his presence was the talisman of her life.

He hastened to her sick room; she lay, her cheeks burning with fever, yet her eyes were closed and she was seemingly senseless. He wrapt her in his arms; he imprinted breathless kisses on her burning lips; he called to her in a voice of subdued anguish by the tenderest names; "Return Elinor; I am with you; your life, your love. Return; dearest one, you promised me this boon, that I should bring you health. Let your sweet spirit revive; you cannot die near me: What is death? To see you no more? To part with what is a part of myself; without whom I have no memory and no futurity? Elinor die! This is frenzy and the most miserable despair: you cannot die while I am near."

And again he kissed her eyes and lips, and hung over her inanimate form in agony, gazing on her countenance still lovely although changed, watching every slight convulsion, and varying colour which denoted life still lingering although about to depart. Once for a moment she revived and recognized his voice; a smile, a last lovely smile, played upon her lips. He watched beside her for twelve hours and then she died. ◄

CHAPTER 9
Annotations

1. Mathilda decides that because she can tell no one the truth of the circumstances of her father's suicide—that he killed himself either from guilt over desiring his daughter incestuously or possibly also because she refused to be in an incestuous relationship with him—she will fake her own death. By faking her own death, Mathilda aims to remove herself entirely from society. In effect, she commits suicide socially but stays alive physically. She believes that the incestuous feelings of her father are her burden, that insofar as she carries "an untold grief [she is] separated from [her] fellow creatures." Mathilda characterizes this secret as a "deep grave" and so as to avoid spending her life covering up the incest secret, she decides to feign her own death. In these passages, Mathilda, our narrator, describes herself as deceitful and, oddly, some scholars have taken this self-critique to mean she is complicit in the incestuous bond with her father. But that is not at all what Mary Shelley conveys here: rather, Mathilda the narrator describes in great detail that she becomes deceitful—feigning her own death—so as to retreat from society and thereby find a way to live with what for her is the truth, the gory reality of her father's incestuous desire for her. Mathilda does not desire to retreat into a relationship with her father who in any case is already dead. Instead, she wishes not to compound what she sees as her sin—the sin (in her eyes) of inspiring her father's sexual desire for her—with the further sin of lying about her history. Shelley here reveals poignantly how in patriarchal cultures women, and for that matter girls, are considered the root of the 'sin' of male sexual desire. The traditional Judeo-Christian view of women is that we incite male lust and therefore are the cause of the sins of adultery, rape, and also incest. This is of course a false way of seeing women. But Shelley gives her character Mathilda this worldview which is accurate to the time in which the novella is placed, a time in which the general belief would be that a woman who ignited sexual passion was herself the source of the 'sin' of sexual desire. Mathilda lives with the belief that she has been the cause of her father's ruin. Now, in the twenty-first century, I hope we no longer believe that women are to blame when men sexually abuse them. I hope we no longer blame underage daughters for causing their fathers to incestuously desire them. Shelley's tragedy, then, contends not only with tropes of Romanticism but also with gender politics. Is it reasonable that Mathilda blame herself for her father's abuse of her?

As Mathilda describes her feigning of her own death, one may note that Mary Shelley's half-sister, also a daughter of Mary Wollstonecraft, Fanny Imlay (1794-1816), committed suicide when Mary Shelley was a teenager. Harriet Westbrook Shelley (1795-1816), Percy Shelley's first wife, also committed suicide in 1816. Mary Wollstonecraft (1759-1797), Shelley's mother, twice attempted suicide as a younger woman. Mary Shelley's approach to the subject of a young woman's suicide is a fascinating rewriting of the 'plot' of a young woman's suicide. With Mathilda's decision to feign her death rather than to actually kill herself (she does eventually die, but we'll get to that), Shelley sets out the radical idea that suicide is not caused by female madness—she makes clear the Mathilda is not insane—but rather a response to unbearable social circumstances caused by the injustices of patriarchy. Here, then, paternal incest becomes a marker for the excesses of patriarchy, standing for and at the pinnacle of male abuses of women.

2. Mathilda's hard-won peace through solitude suggests that her suffering stems from human beings, not something intrinsic to herself. Importantly, here Shelley suggests that female suffering is not caused by some inherent flaw in the female mind and character but rather by the way that women are treated in society. In her solitude, however, Mathilda continues to feel suicidal because she is haunted by her father's sexual desire for her; she feels irrevocably tainted. It becomes clear that her retreat was not sufficient to heal herself but instead a move into a death-in-life state.

Anchoresses—to which Mathilda explicitly compares herself—are female religious recluses who, before they remove themselves from society, undergo the traditional funeral rite, indicating that they are dead to the world, though still alive in body. Mathilda takes up this position of the socially dead, though physically still alive, figure but she avows no religion to steady, stabilize, and give larger meaning to her retreat. Rather it is presented as a slow suicide. Her retreat, however, brings into her sphere the poet Woodville, he toward whom the entire narrative is positioned.

The narrative's description of Woodville is off-putting, overwhelmingly suffused with excess of Romantic tropes of the Poet who transcends human needs and indeed bodily existence itself. We ask ourselves, what is Mary Shelley trying to create with this character, Woodville? It seems to me that the lugubrious weight of Mathilda's feeling of personal taint following her father's confession of incestuous desire draws from the narrative a counter-balancing figure—Woodville—who is described as without taint. He is universally loved; good and kind; brilliant and beautiful. He becomes the male figure that can redeem Mathilda's fallen state. There is something profoundly depressing about this configuration: that Shelley posits Mathilda as irrevocably tainted and damaged by her experience of incest, and that she posits the redemption of Mathilda as arriving only through the hands of an idealized male partner. And yet, there is also a dose of realism here. Father-daughter incest is the most psychologically devastating form of sexual abuse, leaving the survivor with a sense of profound mistrust in human beings. Mathilda's depression, sadly, is not out of step with the sequaliae often seen in survivors of father-daughter incest. Likewise, in a patriarchal society, a woman's capacity to save herself is often deeply limited: Woodville as Mathilda's savior, then, while depressing because of the way it undercuts Mathilda's agency is yet another gesture of realistic reflection of the world of and in which Mary Shelley writes. Woodville of course does not actually save Mathilda. Rather, he salvages her story. Remember, Shelley sets up the novella so that we readers encounter the story only on the assumption that Woodville has passed it on to us, since Mathilda makes clear that she gives the story only to Woodville. In this way, even though Woodville plays the dramatic role of the male savior of the story, it is actually Mary Shelley's story. He is merely a trope for conveyance.

Here, it is important to emphasize Mary Shelley's multifaceted approach to structuring her narratives. She structures *Frankenstein* by opening the text with letters written from an outsider to whom the story is given. Hence, the story of Frankenstein's monster is translated through several narrative 'tellers' to reach us the readers. When we hear the monster's voice, in the heart and center of the novel, we are actually being told what Frankenstein heard the monster say and then conveyed to Walton who then conveyed it to his sister, who then conveys the story to us. Thus, we are never given direct access to the monster's interior thoughts, but rather through a prism-like structure receive glints and deep suggestions of his psyche. Likewise, *Mathilda* is structured through letters—recall that some of Mathilda's father's most important utterances are conveyed to the readers as letters—and the whole narrative is an epistle written to Woodville. Just as the novel *Frankenstein* is presented to the reader as Victor Frankenstein's deathbed confession to Walton, so also the novella *Mathilda* is presented to the reader as Mathilda's deathbed confession to Woodville.

A key difference, though, between the two stories is the relationships between Frankenstein and Walton versus that of Mathilda and Woodville. We notice that throughout the novella *Mathilda* we rarely hear Woodville's voice. This creates the uncanny feeling that we ourselves are Woodville, since the text is clearly directed to him and we are given no explanation as to how it came into our hands. Whereas *Frankenstein* is given to us through Walton's letters to his sisters (albeit we do not hear her voice and do not know how she conveyed his letters to the public), *Mathilda* is given to us through Mathilda's epistle to Woodville. In other words, the first novel is a male confession conveyed through a female intercessor whereas the second work, a novella, is a female confession conveyed through a male intercessor. That gender difference is important because of the way *Mathilda,* the narrator of Mathilda, describes and positions Woodville.

Woodville, as I've noted, is described in exalted terms: he is the perfect human being and his perfection is tied, in the narrative, to the fact that he is male. He is explicitly given, in Mathilda's narrative, as the way that her story can be told. He is the safe-keeper of her story and the gentle and good person who can "purify" her of sin by taking on and disseminating her story. I argued in my book, *The Posthumous Voice in Women's Writing from Mary Shelley to Sylvia Plath,* that Woodville's role is to take the story of female trauma that is not considered acceptable in the social world of its day and, by covering Mathilda's trauma with his voice and his name, making it acceptable, palatable, to audiences. It's important to note that *Mathilda* in fact was not palatable to audiences in Mary Shelley's day; it was not published until 1959. However, the way *Mathilda* found its way into the public realm was not through a male poet, but through the carefully brilliant work of the scholar Elizabeth Nitchie. That said, it seems worth thinking about whether Mary Shelley saw Percy Bysshe Shelley, in some sense, as her Woodville, specifically in the sense of being her way of finding a public voice. While an earlier generation of scholars argued that Percy actually wrote, or significantly rewrote, Mary's work, that is no longer considered correct. But what does remain perhaps correct is the role male authors, Percy Shelley and William Godwin, played in helping Mary Shelley reach audience, the gendered dynamics of authorship being such that a woman who writes radically threatening works, such as Mary Shelley, would have trouble finding audience unless through prestigious and influential male intercessors. This reality of publishing reflects the gendered power dynamics of Mary Shelley's day. After the deaths of her husband and father, Shelley's work was often rejected by publishers.

3. Woodville comes to the barren moor where Mathilda is keeping her secret life because he is in mourning for his beloved, Elinor. If we read back into *Frankenstein*, we will notice that Elinor and Elizabeth are described in strikingly similar terms. Likewise, their untimely deaths, at the eve or on the night of marriage, are tied to the bridal state. Being a bride is an exceedingly dangerous position for women in Mary Shelley's early works. Elinor and Elizabeth function as sacrificial victims, their deaths moving the narratives forward. As Mathilda notes, if Woodville had not been suffering, mourning, grieving, he would've had nothing in common with her. Hence, Elinor's death is essential to our being able to receive Mathilda's deathbed confession, which is transmitted through Woodville and, as Mathilda makes clear, could only have been transmitted through him. He is presented as the only human being who could both understand and convey her story, her story that is a secret that cannot be survived. Woodville believes in human perfectibility, and yet Mathilda has knowledge—the incest secret—that makes her unable to believe Woodville's positive view of human nature. But it is his optimism that allows her to assume he can carry her story. ◄

CHAPTER 10

I T WAS SIX MONTHS after this miserable conclusion to his long nursed hopes that I first saw him. He had retired to a part of the country where he was not known that he might peacefully indulge his grief. All the world, by the death of his beloved Elinor, was changed to him, and he could no longer remain in any spot where he had seen her or where her image mingled with the most rapturous hopes had brightened all around with a light of joy which would now be transformed to a darkness blacker than midnight since she, the sun of his life, was set for ever.

He lived for some time never looking on the light of heaven but shrouding his eyes in a perpetual darkness far from all that could remind him of what he had been; but as time softened his grief like a true child of Nature he sought in the enjoyment of her beauties for a consolation in his unhappiness. He came to a part of the country where he was entirely unknown and where in the deepest solitude he could converse only with his own heart. He found a relief to his impatient grief in the breezes of heaven and in the sound of waters and woods. He became fond of riding; this exercise distracted his mind and elevated his spirits; on a swift horse he could for a moment gain respite from the image that else for ever followed him; Elinor on her death bed, her sweet features changed, and the soft spirit that animated her gradually waning into extinction. For many months Woodville had in vain endeavoured to cast off this terrible remembrance; it still hung on him untill memory was too great a burthen for his loaded soul, but when on horseback the spell that seemingly held him to this idea was snapt; then if he thought of his lost bride he pictured her radiant in beauty; he could hear her voice, and fancy her "a sylvan Huntress by his side," while his eyes brightened as he thought he gazed on her cherished form. I had several times seen him ride across the heath and felt angry that my solitude should be disturbed. It was so long [since] I had spoken to any but peasants that I felt a disagreable sensation at being gazed on by one of superior rank. I feared also that it might be some one who had seen me before: I might be recognized, my impostures discovered and I dragged back to a life of worse torture than that I had before endured. These were dreadful fears and they even haunted my dreams.

I was one day seated on the verge of the clump of pines when Woodville rode past. As soon as I perceived him I suddenly rose to escape from his observation by entering among the trees. My rising startled his horse; he reared and plunged and the Rider was at length thrown. The horse then galopped swiftly across the heath and the stranger remained on the ground stunned by his fall. He was not materially hurt, a little fresh water soon recovered him. I was struck by his exceeding beauty, and as he spoke to thank me the sweet but melancholy cadence of his voice brought tears into my eyes.

A short conversation passed between us, but the next day he again stopped at my cottage and by degrees an intimacy grew between us. It was strange to him to see a female in extreme youth, I was not yet twenty, evidently belonging to the first classes of society & possessing every accomplishment an excellent education could bestow, living alone on a desolate health [sic] — One on whose forehead the impress of grief was strongly marked, and whose words and motions betrayed that her thoughts did not follow them but were intent on far other ideas; bitter and overwhelming miseries. I was dressed also in a whimsical nunlike habit which denoted that I did not retire to solitude from necessity, but that I might indulge in a luxury of grief, and fanciful seclusion.

He soon took great interest in me, and sometimes forgot his own grief to sit beside me and endeavour to cheer me. He could not fail to interest even one who had shut herself from the whole world, whose hope was death, and who lived only with the departed. His personal beauty; his conversation which glowed with imagination and sensibility; the poetry that seemed to hang upon his lips and to make the very air mute to listen to him were charms that no one could resist. He was younger, less worn, more passionless than my father and in no degree reminded me of him: he suffered under immediate grief yet its gentle influence instead of calling feelings otherwise dormant into action, seemed only to veil that which otherwise would have been too dazzling for me. When we were together I spoke little yet my selfish mind was sometimes borne away by the rapid course of his ideas; I would lift my eyes with momentary brilliancy until memories that never died and seldom slept would recur, and a tear would dim them.

Woodville for ever tried to lead me to the contemplation of what is beautiful and happy in the world. His own mind was constitunially [sic] bent to a former belief in good [rather] than in evil and this feeling which must even exhilirate the hopeless ever shone forth in his words. He would talk of the wonderful powers of man, of their present state and of their hopes: of what they had been and what they were, and when reason could no longer guide him, his imagination as if inspired shed light on the obscurity that veils the past and the future. He loved to dwell on what might have been the state of the earth before man lived on it, and how he first arose and gradually became the strange, complicated, but as he said, the glorious creature he now is. Covering the earth with their creations and forming by the power of their minds another world more lovely than the visible frame of things, even all the world that we find in their writings. A beautiful creation, he would say, which may claim this superiority to its model, that good and evil is more easily seperated: the good rewarded in the way they themselves desire; the evil punished as all things evil ought to be punished, not by pain which is revolting to all philanthropy to consider but by quiet obscurity, which simply deprives them of their harmful qualities; why kill the serpent when you have extracted his fangs?

The poetry of his language and ideas which my words ill convey held me enchained to his discourses. It was a melancholy pleasure to me to listen to his inspired words; to catch for a moment the light of his eyes; to feel a transient sympathy and then to awaken from the delusion, again to know that all this was nothing, — a dream — a shadow for that there was no reallity for me; my father had for ever deserted me, leaving me only memories which set an eternal barrier between me and my fellow creatures. I was indeed fellow to none. He — Woodville, mourned the loss of his bride: others wept the various forms of misery as they visited them: but infamy and guilt was mingled with my portion; unlawful and detestable passion had poured its poison into my ears and changed all my blood, so that it was no longer the kindly stream that supports life but a cold fountain of bitterness corrupted in its very source. It must be the excess of madness that could make me imagine that I could ever be aught but one alone; struck off from humanity; bearing no affinity to man or woman; a wretch on whom Nature had set her ban.

Sometimes Woodville talked to me of himself. He related his history brief in happiness and woe and dwelt with passion on his and Elinor's mutual love. "She was, he said, "the brightest vision that ever came upon the earth: there was something in her frank countenance, in her voice, and in every motion of her graceful form that overpowered me, as if it were a celestial creature that deigned to mingle with me in intercourse more sweet than man had ever before enjoyed.

Sorrow fled before her; and her smile seemed to possess an influence like light to irradiate all mental darkness. It was not like a human loveliness that these gentle smiles went and came; but as a sunbeam on a lake, now light and now obscure, flitting before as you strove to catch them, and fold them for ever to your heart. I saw this smile fade for ever. Alas! I could never have believed that it was indeed Elinor that died if once when I spoke she had not lifted her almost benighted eyes, and for one moment like nought beside on earth, more lovely than a sunbeam, slighter, quicker than the waving plumage of a bird, dazzling as lightning and like it giving day to night, yet mild and faint, that smile came; it went, and then there was an end of all joy to me."[1]

Thus his own sorrows, or the shapes copied from nature that dwelt in his mind with beauty greater than their own, occupied our talk while I railed in my own griefs with cautious secrecy. If for a moment he shewed curiosity, my eyes fell, my voice died away and my evident suffering made him quickly endeavour to banish the ideas he had awakened; yet he for ever mingled consolation in his talk, and tried to soften my despair by demonstrations of deep sympathy and compassion. "We are both unhappy—" he would say to me; "I have told you my melancholy tale and we have wept together the loss of that lovely spirit that has so cruelly deserted me; but you hide your griefs: I do not ask you to disclose them, but tell me if I may not console you. It seems to me a wild adventure to find in this desart one like you quite solitary: you are young and lovely; your manners are refined and attractive; yet there is in your settled melancholy, and something, I know not what, in your expressive eyes that seems to seperate you from your kind: you shudder; pardon me, I entreat you but I cannot help expressing this once at least the lively interest I feel in your destiny.

"You never smile: your voice is low, and you utter your words as if you were afraid of the slight sound they would produce: the expression of awful and intense sorrow never for a moment fades from your countenance. I have lost for ever the loveliest companion that any man could ever have possessed, one who rather appears to have been a superior spirit who by some strange accident wandered among us earthly creatures, than as belonging to our kind. Yet I smile, and sometimes I speak almost forgetful of the change I have endured. But your sad mien never alters; your pulses beat and you breathe, yet you seem already to belong to another world; and sometimes, pray pardon my wild thoughts, when you touch my hand I am surprised to find your hand warm when all the fire of life seems extinct within you.

"When I look upon you, the tears you shed, the soft deprecating look with which you withstand enquiry; the deep sympathy your voice expresses when I speak of my lesser sorrows add to my interest for you. You stand here shelterless.

You have cast yourself from among us and you wither on this wild plain fo[r]lorn and helpless: some dreadful calamity must have befallen you. Do not turn from me; I do not ask you to reveal it: I only entreat you to listen to me and to become familiar with the voice of consolation and kindness. If pity, and admiration, and gentle affection can wean you from despair let me attempt the task. I cannot see your look of deep grief without endeavouring to restore you to happier feelings. Unbend your brow; relax the stern melancholy of your regard; permit a friend, a sincere, affectionate friend, I will be one, to convey some relief, some momentary pause to your sufferings.

"Do not think that I would intrude upon your confidence: I only ask your patience. Do not for ever look sorrow and never speak it; utter one word of bitter complaint and I will reprove it with gentle exhortation and pour on you the balm of compassion. You must not shut me from all communion with you: do not tell me why you grieve but only say the words, "I am unhappy," and you will feel relieved as if for some time excluded from all intercourse by some magic spell you should suddenly enter again the pale of human sympathy. I entreat you to believe in my most sincere professions and to treat me as an old and tried friend: promise me never to forget me, never causelessly to banish me; but try to love me as one who would devote all his energies to make you happy. Give me the name of friend; I will fulfill its duties; and if for a moment complaint and sorrow would shape themselves into words let me be near to speak peace to your vext soul."

I repeat his persuasions in faint terms and cannot give you at the same time the tone and gesture that animated them. Like a refreshing shower on an arid soil they revived me, and although I still kept their cause secret he led me to pour forth my bitter complaints and to clothe my woe in words of gall and fire. With all the energy of desperate grief I told him how I had fallen at once from bliss to misery; how that for me there was no joy, no hope; that death however bitter would be the welcome seal to all my pangs; death the skeleton was to be beautiful as love. I know not why but I found it sweet to utter these words to human ears; and though I derided all consolation yet I was pleased to see it offered me with gentleness and kindness. I listened quietly, and when he paused would again pour out my misery in expressions that shewed how far too deep my wounds were for any cure.

But now also I began to reap the fruits of my perfect solitude. I had become unfit for any intercourse, even with Woodville the most gentle and sympathizing creature that existed. I had become captious and unreasonable: my temper was utterly spoilt. I called him my friend but I viewed all he did with jealous eyes. If he did not visit me at the appointed hour I was angry, very angry, and told him that if indeed he did feel interest in me it was cold, and could not be fitted for me, a poor worn creature, whose deep unhappiness demanded much more than his worldly heart could give. When for a moment I imagined that his manner was cold I would fretfully say to him—"I was at peace before you came; why have you disturbed me? You have given me new wants and now your trifle with me as if my heart were as whole as yours, as if I were not in truth a shorn lamb thrust out on the bleak hill side, tortured by every blast. I wished for no friend, no sympathy. I avoided you, you know I did, but you forced yourself upon me and gave me those wants which you see with triump[h] give you power over me. Oh the brave power of the bitter north wind which freezes the tears it has caused to shed! But I will not bear this; go: the sun will rise and set as before you came, and I shall sit among the pines or wander on the heath weeping and complaining without wishing for you to listen. You are cruel, very cruel, to treat me who bleed at every pore in this rough manner."

And then, when in answer to my peevish words, I saw his countenance bent with living pity on me, when I saw him

Gli occhi drizzo ver me con quel sembiante   Che madre fa sopra figlioul deliro Paradiso.[2]

I wept and said, "Oh, pardon me! You are good and kind but I am not fit for life. Why am I obliged to live? To drag hour after hour, to see the trees wave their branches restlessly, to feel the air, & to suffer in all I feel keenest agony. My frame is strong, but my soul sinks beneath this endurance of living anguish. Death is the goal that I would attain, but, alas! I do not even see the end of the course. Do you, my compassionate friend, tell me how to die peacefully and innocently and I will bless you: all that I, poor wretch, can desire is a painless death."

But Woodville's words had magic in them, when beginning with the sweetest pity, he would raise me by degrees out of myself and my sorrows until I wondered at my own selfishness: but he left me and despair returned; the work of consolation was ever to begin anew. I often desired his entire absence; for I found that I was grown out of the ways of life and that by long seclusion, although I could support my accustomed grief, and drink the bitter daily draught with some degree of patience, yet I had become unfit for the slightest novelty of feeling. Expectation, and hopes, and affection were all too much for me. I knew this, but at other times I was unreasonable and laid the blame upon him, who was most blameless, and pevishly thought that if his gentle soul were more gentle, if his intense sympathy were more intense, he could drive the fiend from my soul and make me more human. I am, I thought, a tragedy; a character that he comes to see act: now and then he gives me my cue that I may make a speech more to his purpose: perhaps he is already planning a poem in which I am to figure. I am a farce and play to him, but to me this is all dreary reality: he takes all the profit and I bear all the burthen. ◀

CHAPTER 10
Annotations

1. Woodville and Mathilda are both described by the phrase "child of nature," a designation that places them in Romantic terms as deeply connected to the natural world's sublimity. While Shelley's works *Frankenstein* and *Mathilda* are aware of social class, they rarely work against stereotypical notions of class: in these works, people who are highborn, even if they fall onto hard times, are frequently described as retaining clear designations of upper-class status despite material poverty. The Romantic ideal of the "child of nature" ignores the realities of class status and economics. People who actually work in the fields to survive, and the forces that press people to become factory workers in the burgeoning industries of the early nineteenth-century, are *not* considered in the designation of children of nature. The term is rather reserved for the privileged.

   Romanticism is a movement of transition — leading from the early modern into capitalist-industrialist modernity — taking place at the cusp of the Industrial Revolution (1760 to about 1840, in Great Britain). For generations before Shelley's birth, and still during the time she is writing her two earliest works, the British aristocracy (from which her husband hailed but not herself) had money through land. The aristocracy was landed, that is, owned ancestral lands that other people worked for them, and that yielded income for the aristocracy rather than for the laborers of the land. The Industrial Revolution, beginning just before Shelley's birth and culminating in her lifetime, created a new class of people, the bourgeois, who had money but no titles (unless they bought titles or married them). E. P. Thompson's classic work of scholarship, *The Making of the English Working Class,* charts this transition. What's important for readers of Mary Shelley's works to realize is that she expresses in these works values and terms of Romanticism as a movement on the cusp of massive social changes brought about by the Industrial Revolution. The ideal "child of nature" that Shelley echoes in both works is a concept, then, seems to be unaware of class structure as a force that oppresses and devalues the laboring classes, including those people who work the land.

   But Romanticism is complicated and conflicted on this terrain. The poets John Clare and John Keats are exemplars of the ways that Romanticism as a movement handled those who work the land (Clare's social milieu) and those of the laboring class (Keats). Readers will note that throughout *Frankenstein* and *Mathilda* people of noble birth are described as inherently superior to those not of the nobility, regardless of immediate financial circumstances. On the one hand, this reflects an older prejudice, of long standing before the Industrial Revolution. But at the same time, it is a response to the Industrial Revolution, a way of attempting to secure meaning and value apart from and in contrast to wealth earned through industry.

The child of nature as the prime figure of Romanticism is fully expressed in Shelley's drawing of Woodville. Strikingly, however, Mathilda considers her own position to be outside of and beyond redemption by nature, even as she calls herself a child of nature. She also describes herself as poisoned by her father's "unlawful and detestable passion." In words strikingly similar to those of Frankenstein's monster, Mathilda describes herself as "struck off from humanity; bearing no affinity to man or woman; a wretch on whom Nature had set her ban." The incest secret cuts off Mathilda from nature no matter what she does or who she is, hollowing out the Romantic visionary trope of the natural sublime and laying it at the feet of Mary Shelley's exceedingly pessimistic view of humanity.

2. Shelley here quotes Dante to indicate that Woodville offers Mathilda a kind of salvation; but this salvation, we learn is of a very specific kind. He carries Mathilda's words to audience. Mathilda describing Woodville's urging her to confess her secret to him stands as a fascinating parallel to Mathilda's earlier pleading with her father to confess to her the secret cause of his suffering. The incest secret is changing hands. It was the father's incestuous desire for her that set in motion Mathilda's tragic coming of age: his confession of that desire becomes *her* secret. As the novella reaches its close, it is Woodville who beseeches Mathilda to confess her secret sorrow. Notably, while Mathilda berates herself for begging her father to confess the secret—which at the time of course she did not imagine would be the confession of his incestuous desire for her—she applauds Woodville for precisely the same behavior, that is, for trying to persuade someone who appears to be suffering with a heavy secret to speak out.

Cynically, Mathilda at the same time imagines that Woodville wants her to tell him the source of her sorrow so that he can write about it, use it as material for his poetry. That reason for Woodville's actions is never entirely disputed in what remains of the novella, given that Mathilda tells her story for Woodville's ears only, and yet we the readers have access to it, presumably through Woodville. The novella, then, is positioned in this narrow space between the speaker's desire to tell the truth, the wish for someone to hear her truth who takes it seriously and does not make use of her story for personal gain, and the recognition that if we readers are reading her story, that can only be because Woodville *did* make it available to the reading public. Shelley leaves it to us, the readers, to discern whether Woodville makes her story public because he is a good friend to her or whether he makes use of her story to increase his own reputation. But Mathilda understands that the person who suffers from abuse or assault is very rarely the one who benefits when that story is made public, a prescient realization. ◄

CHAPTER 11

I T IS A STRANGE CIRCUMSTANCE but it often occurs that blessings by their use turn to curses; and that I who in solitude had desired sympathy as the only relief I could enjoy should now find it an additional torture to me. During my father's life time I had always been of an affectionate and forbearing disposition, but since those days of joy alas! I was much changed. I had become arrogant, peevish, and above all suspicious. Although the real interest of my narration is now ended and I ought quickly to wind up its melancholy catastrophe, yet I will relate one instance of my sad suspicion and despair and how Woodville with the goodness and almost the power of an angel, softened my rugged feelings and led me back to gentleness.

He had promised to spend some hours with me one afternoon but a violent and continual rain prevented him. I was alone the whole evening. I had passed two whole years alone unrepining, but now I was miserable. He could not really care for me, I thought, for if he did the storm would rather have made him come even if I had not expected him, than, as it did, prevent a promised visit. He would well know that this drear sky and gloomy rain would load my spirit almost to madness: if the weather had been fine I should not have regretted his absence as heavily as I necessarily must shut up in this miserable cottage with no companions but my own wretched thoughts. If he were truly my friend he would have calculated all this; and let me now calculate this boasted friendship, and discover its real worth. He got over his grief for Elinor, and the country became dull to him, so he was glad to find even me for amusement; and when he does not know what else to do he passes his lazy hours here, and calls this friendship—It is true that his presence is a consolation to me, and that his words are sweet, and, when he will he can pour forth thoughts that win me from despair. His words are sweet,—and so, truly, is the honey of the bee, but the bee has a sting, and unkindness is a worse smart than that received from an insect's venom. I will put him to the proof. He says all hope is dead to him, and I know that it is dead to me, so we are both equally fitted for death. Let me try if he will die with me; and as I fear to die alone, if he will accompany [me] to cheer me, and thus he can shew himself my friend in the only manner my misery will permit.

It was madness I believe, but I so worked myself up to this idea that I could think of nothing else. If he dies with me it is well, and there will be an end of two miserable beings; and if he will not, then will I scoff at his friendship and drink the poison before him to shame his cowardice. I planned the whole scene with an earnest heart and franticly set my soul on this project. I procured Laudanum and placing it in two glasses on the table, filled my room with flowers and decorated the last scene of my tragedy with the nicest care. As the hour for his coming approached my heart softened and I wept; not that I gave up my plan, but even when resolved the mind must undergo several revolutions of feeling before it can drink its death.

Now all was ready and Woodville came. I received him at the door of my cottage and leading him solemnly into the room, I said: "My friend, I wish to die. I am quite weary of enduring the misery which hourly I do endure, and I will throw it off. What slave will not, if he may, escape from his chains? Look, I weep: for more than two years I have never enjoyed one moment free from anguish. I have often desired to die; but I am a very coward. It is hard for one so young who was once so happy as I was; [sic] voluntarily to divest themselves of all sensation and to go alone to the dreary grave; I dare not. I must die, yet my fear chills me; I pause and shudder and then for months I endure my excess of wretchedness. But now the time is come when I may quit life, I have a friend who will not refuse to accompany me in this dark journey; such is my request: earnestly do I entreat and implore you to die with me. Then we shall find Elinor and what I have lost. Look, I am prepared; there is the death draught, let us drink it together and willingly & joyfully quit this hated round of daily life.

"You turn from me; yet before you deny me reflect, Woodville, how sweet it were to cast off the load of tears and misery under which we now labour: and surely we shall find light after we have passed the dark valley. That drink will plunge us in a sweet slumber, and when we awaken what joy will be ours to find all our sorrows and fears past. A little patience, and all will be over; aye, a very little patience; for, look, there is the key of our prison; we hold it in our own hands, and are we more debased than slaves to cast it away and give ourselves up to voluntary bondage? Even now if we had courage we might be free. Behold, my cheek is flushed with pleasure at the imagination of death; all that we love are dead. Come, give me your hand, one look of joyous sympathy and we will go together and seek them; a lulling journey; where our arrival will bring bliss and our waking be that of angels. Do you delay? Are you a coward, Woodville? Oh fie! Cast off this blank look of human melancholy. Oh! that I had words to express the luxury of death that I might win you. I tell you we are no longer miserable mortals; we are about to become Gods; spirits free and happy as gods. What fool on a bleak shore, seeing a flowery isle on the other side with his lost love beckoning to him from it would pause because the wave is dark and turbid?

"What if some little payne the passage have   That makes frayle flesh to fear the bitter wave?   Is not short payne well borne that brings long ease,   And lays the soul to sleep in quiet grave?[1]

"Do you mark my words; I have learned the language of despair: I have it all by heart, for I am Despair; and a strange being am I, joyous, triumphant Despair. But those words are false, for the wave may be dark but it is not bitter. We lie down, and close our eyes with a gentle good night, and when we wake, we are free. Come then, no more delay, thou tardy one! Behold the pleasant potion! Look, I am a spirit of good, and not a human maid that invites thee, and with winning accents, (oh, that they would win thee!) says, Come and drink."

As I spoke I fixed my eyes upon his countenance, and his exquisite beauty, the heavenly compassion that beamed from his eyes, his gentle yet earnest look of deprecation and wonder even before he spoke wrought a change in my high strained feelings taking from me all the sterness of despair and filling me only with the softest grief. I saw his eyes humid also as he took both my hands in his; and sitting down near me, he said:

"This is a sad deed to which you would lead me, dearest friend, and your woe must indeed be deep that could fill you with these unhappy thoughts. You long for death and yet you fear it and wish me to be your companion. But I have less courage than you and even thus accompanied I dare not die. Listen to me, and then reflect if you ought to win me to your project, even if with the over-bearing eloquence of despair you could make black death so inviting that the fair heaven should appear darkness. Listen I entreat you to the words of one who has himself nurtured desperate thoughts, and longed with impatient desire for death, but who has at length trampled the phantom under foot, and crushed his sting. Come, as you have played Despair with me I will play the part of Una with you and bring you hurtless from his dark cavern. Listen to me, and let yourself be softened by words in which no selfish passion lingers.

"We know not what all this wide world means; its strange mixture of good and evil. But we have been placed here and bid live and hope. I know not what we are to hope; but there is some good beyond us that we must seek; and that is our earthly task. If misfortune come against us we must fight with her; we must cast her aside, and still go on to find out that which it is our nature to desire. Whether this prospect of future good be the preparation for another existence I know not; or whether that it is merely that we, as workmen in God's vineyard, must lend a hand to smooth the way for our posterity. If it indeed be that; if the efforts of the virtuous now, are to make the future inhabitants of this fair world more happy; if the labours of those who cast aside selfishness, and try to know the truth of things, are to free the men of ages, now far distant but which will one day come, from the burthen under which those who now live groan, and like you weep bitterly; if they free them but from one of what are now the necessary evils of life, truly I will not fail but will with my whole soul aid the work. From my youth I have said, I will be virtuous; I will dedicate my life for the good of others; I will do my best to extirpate evil and if the spirit who protects ill should so influence circumstances that I should suffer through my endeavour, yet while there is hope and hope there ever must be, of success, cheerfully do I gird myself to my task.

"I have powers; my countrymen think well of them. Do you think I sow my seed in the barren air, & have no end in what I do? Believe me, I will never desert life untill this last hope is torn from my bosom, that in some way my labours may form a link in the chain of gold with which we ought all to strive to drag Happiness from where she sits enthroned above the clouds, now far beyond our reach, to inhabit the earth with us. Let us suppose that Socrates, or Shakespeare, or Rousseau had been seized with despair and died in youth when they were as young as I am; do you think that we and all the world should not have lost incalculable improvement in our good feelings and our happiness thro' their destruction. I am not like one of these; they influenced millions: but if I can influence but a hundred, but ten, but one solitary individual, so as in any way to lead him from ill to good, that will be a joy to repay me for all my sufferings, though they were a million times multiplied; and that hope will support me to bear them.

"And those who do not work for posterity; or working, as may be my case, will not be known by it; yet they, believe me, have also their duties. You grieve because you are unhappy; it is happiness you seek but you despair of obtaining it. But if you can bestow happiness on another; if you can give one other person only one hour of joy ought you not to live to do it? And every one has it in their power to do that. The inhabitants of this world suffer so much pain. In crowded cities, among cultivated plains, or on the desart mountains, pain is thickly sown, and if we can tear up but one of these noxious weeds, or more, if in its stead we can sow one seed of corn, or plant one fair flower, let that be motive sufficient against suicide. Let us not desert our task while there is the slightest hope that we may in a future day do this.

"Indeed I dare not die. I have a mother whose support and hope I am. I have a friend who loves me as his life, and in whose breast I should infix a mortal sting if I ungratefully left him. So I will not die. Nor shall you, my friend; cheer up; cease to weep, I entreat you. Are you not young, and fair, and good? Why should you despair? Or if you must for yourself, why for others? If you can never be happy, can you never bestow happiness? Oh! believe me, if you beheld on lips pale with grief one smile of joy and gratitude, and knew that you were parent of that smile, and that without you it had never been, you would feel so pure and warm a happiness that you would wish to live for ever again and again to enjoy the same pleasure.[2]

"Come, I see that you have already cast aside the sad thoughts you before franticly indulged. Look in that mirror; when I came your brow was contracted, your eyes deep sunk in your head, your lips quivering; your hands trembled violently when I took them; but now all is tranquil and soft. You are grieved and there is grief in the expression of your countenance but it is gentle and sweet. You allow me to throw away this cursed drink; you smile; oh, Congratulate me, hope is triumphant, and I have done some good."

These words are shadowy as I repeat them but they were indeed words of fire and produced a warm hope in me (I, miserable wretch, to hope!) that tingled like pleasure in my veins. He did not leave me for many hours; not until he had improved the spark that he had kindled, and with an angelic hand fostered the return of somthing that seemed like joy. He left me but I still was calm, and after I had saluted the starry sky and dewy earth with eyes of love and a contented good night, I slept sweetly, visited by dreams, the first of pleasure I had had for many long months.

But this was only a momentary relief and my old habits of feeling returned; for I was doomed while in life to grieve, and to the natural sorrow of my father's death and its most terrific cause, immagination added a tenfold weight of woe. I believed myself to be polluted by the unnatural love I had inspired, and that I was a creature cursed and set apart by nature. I thought that like another Cain, I had a mark set on my forehead to shew mankind that there was a barrier between me and they [sic]. Woodville had told me that there was in my countenance an expression as if I belonged to another world; so he had seen that sign: and there it lay a gloomy mark to tell the world that there was that within my soul that no silence could render sufficiently obscure. Why when fate drove me to become this outcast from human feeling; this monster with whom none might mingle in converse and love; why had she not from that fatal and most accursed moment, shrouded me in thick mists and placed real darkness between me and my fellows so that I might never more be seen?, [sic] and as I passed, like a murky cloud loaded with blight, they might only perceive me by the cold chill I should cast upon them; telling them, how truly, that something unholy was near? Then I should have lived upon this dreary heath unvisited, and blasting none by my unhallowed gaze. Alas! I verily believe that if the near prospect of death did not dull and soften my bitter [fe]elings, if for a few months longer I had continued to live as I then lived, strong in body, but my soul corrupted to its core by a deadly cancer, if day after day I had dwelt on these dreadful sentiments I should have become mad, and should have fancied myself a living pestilence: so horrible to my own solitary thoughts did this form, this voice, and all this wretched self appear; for had it not been the source of guilt that wants a name?

This was superstition. I did not feel thus franticly when first I knew that the holy name of father was become a curse to me: but my lonely life inspired me with wild thoughts; and then when I saw Woodville & day after day he tried to win my confidence and I never dared give words to my dark tale, I was impressed more strongly with the withering fear that I was in truth a marked creature, a pariah, only fit for death.[3] ◄

CHAPTER 11
Annotations

1. Mathilda here quotes Edmund Spenser, after quoting Dante. We recall that when her father took her back to the house where her mother died (and where she was born) he asked her to read Dante from the place where her mother had left off reading at her death, and then he hurriedly changed his mind. Thereupon, Mathilda reads Spenser. In quoting Dante and Spenser to provide dramatic language for Mathilda, Shelley positions her text in relation to these master texts. Dante and Spenser stand as progenitors for Italian and English literatures, fathers of their national literatures.

   Shelley stages, by quoting Dante, Spenser, and Wordsworth, at crucial points in her text, the struggle for female authority and authorship. She struggles to give Mathilda—and herself—a voice that might be if not equal in stature to these men at the very least in their lineage, and yet she does so precisely in the context of telling a story of father-daughter incest. In other words, the idea that the daughter can be an inheritor of the father's literary lineage is profoundly troubled in *Mathilda*, precisely because the entire story is about a father's abuse of power. In this scene, where Mathilda is attempting to persuade Woodville to commit suicide with her, he refuses, thereby preserving his chance at becoming part of the literary legacy of England—Spenser's son as it were. But Mathilda sees death as her only recompense. After being abusively and sexually desired by her own father, Mathilda can no longer imagine the possibilities of female voice. Mary Shelley, though, hedges her bets. In describing Mathilda's suicidality, she stages her own despair and survives it, living on to write not only this novella but many other later works.

2. Having longed for death, Mathilda at length becomes ill apparently with tuberculosis, called "consumption" in the novella. Tuberculosis was a common cause of death for young adults in the nineteenth-century. However, Mary Shelley writing in 1819 did not know—as at that time no one knew—that tuberculosis is contagious. Hence, Mathilda could not have contracted consumption from having spent the night out of doors and getting drenched. However, it is possible she contracted the disease earlier, and that stressing her immune system by not sleeping and by exposing herself to extreme weather brought the disease from a latent to an active stage. Regardless, choosing to have Mathilda die of tuberculosis, or consumption as it was called in the

nineteenth-century, means that Mary Shelley places her heroine in good literary company. John Keats, and later Emily Brontë and Anne Brontë, died young of the disease, one of the most feared in nineteenth-century England. The disease was also, however, called *the blessed death* because the victim typically retained mental clarity up until the point of death. This, then, is the disease that takes Mathilda's life in a way that allows her, while dying, to lucidly write down her story. During the final pages of her novella, Shelley quotes Dante and Wordsworth, placing Mathilda in the literature of Dante's *Purgatorio* and *Paradiso,* and also placing her among Wordsworth's poetry mourning the anonymous maid "Lucy" in his Lucy poems. Mathilda dies into male literature, ceding her voice and allowing Dante, Spenser, and Wordsworth to carry her text.

As she closes her life, the narrative of the novella circles back to its beginning. Recall that as the novella opens we are told we are reading the deathbed confession of a person who is granting us the intimate privilege of her last words. Now as the novel reaches its conclusion we are returned to precisely that scene. In other words, the entire time of the novella we have been enthralled by this one voice of this one speaker who addresses us from a place between life and death, at the boundary of life and death. This boundary position matches the deeper history of Shelley's drafting of *Mathilda,* in which she originally envisioned her character telling her story actually from purgatory — that is, *after* death — and later revised so that the more realistic story is yet suffused throughout with references to Dante's *Purgatorio,* thereby signifying to the reader that, yes, we are in purgatory when we are with Mathilda and her incest story.

What is purgatory? It is the place where souls of the dead who have sinned but who can be forgiven go to expiate their sins before rising to heaven. Those who have committed mortal sin cannot go to heaven through purgatory, in traditional Catholic theology. Mathilda's placement in purgatory indicates that she has not committed a mortal sin. Accepting her father's incestuous advances and living in incest with him would have been a mortal sin, so we must read the novella as Shelley's statement of her novel's eponymous narrator's ultimate *innocence.* Shelley was not a Catholic, but she clearly structures *Mathilda* in relation to Dante's *Purgatorio* and *Paradiso,* both conceptually and allusively and, in this sense, uses the Catholic concept of the terrain of purgatory as a key mechanism of her text. Mathilda dies without committing suicide, and is thereby released of any grave that is, mortal, sin (although, in a play on words, Shelley refers to the secret of the father's incestuous desire for Mathilda as a "grave"). Mathilda's placement in purgatory means she is purifying herself of her father's taint, and doing so specifically by confessing it. Confession, here, is crucial because it carries theological implications. To die with an unconfessed sin makes reaching purgatory and, through its purgation, heaven, impossible in traditional theology. For Woodville to carry Mathilda's story, then, is for him to release her from damnation. For us to read her story is to release her from damnation.

Insofar as Mary Shelley was not Catholic, one is mistaken to read *Mathilda* through dogmatic religious interpretation. Rather instead I think she explores in *Mathilda* the idea that silence is a form of damnation, and purgatory a space through which language purifies the speaker. I think that for her damnation and purgatory have specific gendered and non-religious parameters: damnation is the silenced position of the feminine, and purgatory the working through of this silence toward voice. *Mathilda* is, oddly, a novel of survival. Of course, the narrator dies very young, and the whole story is told on her deathbed. And yet, she survives what her father did to her and survives specifically in language and through language. She survives to tell the tale, and that is what matters.

3. The increasing frequency with which Mary Shelley quotes from male authors as she reaches the close of *Mathilda* suggests a loss of voice. Edmund Spenser's *Faerie Queen,* and Dante's *Purgatorio,* give ballast and frame to the young Shelley's work, but they also begin to intrude, taking voice from her. And this question of voice is the entire drama of *Mathilda*: how do we lose voice, how do we regain it? This question structures the narrative dramatically. Just as *Frankenstein* ends with the death of Victor Frankenstein, and the disappearance of the monster, with Walton and his sister left to carry the story to readers, so also *Mathilda* ends with the death of the narrator, who is the novella's protagonist, with Woodville presumably left to carry the story to audience. Both works, then, share this dramatic structure of being stories told to us by a speaker who is dying *because of* the story they are telling us. The pessimism of this structure is clear: the main protagonist in both works is someone who does not survive the story they have to tell. Moreover, there is a monstrousness placed between us and the main characters: we can and do sympathize with Mary Shelley's monster, and with her character Mathilda, but we can only come so close to them. The monster has committed acts of real violence, murders of the innocent. Mathilda, while certainly

less overtly frightening, is also set apart or pushed away from the reader by the repeated claim that her experience of incest has made her unlike other human beings — she is monstrous in her own eyes.

There are a multitude of ways to approach Mary Shelley's works. We can think of her as a figure of Romanticism. Married to Percy Bysshe Shelley, friends with George Gordon Lord Byron, daughter of radical philosophers Godwin and Wollstonecraft, Mary Shelley carries forward in her works the revolutionary potential of her times and the *sturm und drang* of Romantic discourse. Arguably, we are still in the Romantic mode, still privileging the solitary desires of the individual, caring most about individual subjectivity (albeit within a capitalist frame that very much tends *not* to care about the subjectivity of the poor). Writing a few decades after the French Revolution, and writing during the height of the Industrial Revolution, Shelley reflects the tenor of her times.

But Mary Shelley also steps outside that discourse and critiques it. Her critique is lasting, transcending the time and place in which she wrote, because Shelley broaches questions and problems that go beyond specific historical epoch. Shelley's early works brilliantly and painfully question what makes a moral human being? What is the difference between public perception/reputation and actual ethical goodness? Who is responsible for the young, and what does that responsibility entail? She also deeply searches — in both *Frankenstein* and *Mathilda* — the question of how past acts determine future occurrences. Frankenstein, as a very young man, creates a monster, commits a monstrous act. He is never able to transcend or put away the consequences of this act. Likewise, Mathilda who never committed a crime or a sin but only was the recipient of her father's desire is never able to move beyond this trauma.

Mary Shelley's early works contend with the problem of mortality and its entwinement with morality. She writes characters who struggle with catastrophic fates, who are banned from human society because of these fates. Most of us do not face such extremes. But we all do face our own mortality and with it our own morality. It is the sounding out of this core drive to understand what it means to be mortal and the need to find real morality within that human frame that makes Shelley's early works so hauntingly vivid centuries after she wrote them. We all have monsters that we fight against, because we are all mortal and we all struggle to behave morally. Those who cast off that struggle — that is, who forget they are mortal and forget they are bound to other human beings through moral bonds — are the monsters. Mary Shelley understood that it is precisely such people who often gain public acclaim and social power. Her works are more important now than ever before, because of this insight.

As a teenage girl (writing *Frankenstein*) and a very young woman (writing *Mathilda*), Shelley bravely reached the place, through her writing, where nightmare reveals truth. Shelley's reputation as a writer has never been as high as that of her husband, the poet, or of her mother, the philosopher, and yet one may ask why? It seems to me it is the frightfulness of Shelley's vision that subtly pushes critics to interpret her as a lesser light. If we take her seriously, that changes our lives. Despite the struggle for critical acclaim, Shelley's insightful understanding of human nature and modernity, expressed with the condensed symbolic power of nightmare, conveys to us centuries after the intellectual and artistic movements of Enlightenment and Romanticism the flaws and power of those very movements. If, as I've suggested throughout these notes, we still live in a culture heavily influenced by Enlightenment and Romantic beliefs and values, Shelley's texts tell us about our present-day reality. Hers is a voice meriting all the seriousness of attention we can bring. We, like Woodville, are asked to carry her stories into our lives. ◄

CHAPTER 12

A S I WAS PERPETUALLY HAUNTED by these ideas, you may imagine that the influence of Woodville's words was very temporary; and that although I did not again accuse him of unkindness, yet I soon became as unhappy as before. Soon after this incident we parted. He heard that his mother was ill, and he hastened to her. He came to take leave of me, and we walked together on the heath for the last time. He promised that he would come and see me again; and bade me take cheer, and to encourage what happy thoughts I could, untill time and fortitude should overcome my misery, and I could again mingle in society.

"Above all other admonition on my part," he said, "cherish and follow this one: do not despair. That is the most dangerous gulph on which you perpetually totter; but you must reassure your steps, and take hope to guide you. Hope, and your wounds will be already half healed: but if you obstinately despair, there never more will be comfort for you. Believe me, my dearest friend, that there is a joy that the sun and earth and all its beauties can bestow that you will one day feel. The refreshing bliss of Love will again visit your heart, and undo the spell that binds you to woe, untill you wonder how your eyes could be closed in the long night that burthens you. I dare not hope that I have inspired you with sufficient interest that the thought of me, and the affection that I shall ever bear you, will soften your melancholy and decrease the bitterness of your tears. But if my friendship can make you look on life with less disgust, beware how you injure it with suspicion. Love is a delicate sprite and easily hurt by rough jealousy. Guard, I entreat you, a firm persuasion of my sincerity in the inmost recesses of your heart out of the reach of the casual winds that may disturb its surface. Your temper is made unequal by suffering, and the tenor of your mind is, I fear, sometimes shaken by unworthy causes; but let your confidence in my sympathy and love be deeper far, and incapable of being reached by these agitations that come and go, and if they touch not your affections leave you uninjured."

These were some of Woodville's last lessons. I wept as I listened to him; and after we had taken an affectionate farewell, I followed him far with my eyes until they saw the last of my earthly comforter. I had insisted on accompanying him across the heath towards the town where he dwelt: the sun was yet high when he left me, and I turned my steps towards my cottage. It was at the latter end of the month of September when the nights have become chill. But the weather was serene, and as I walked on I fell into no unpleasing reveries. I thought of Woodville with gratitude and kindness and did not, I know not why, regret his departure with any bitterness. It seemed that after one great shock all other change was trivial to me; and I walked on wondering when the time would come when we should all four, my dearest father restored to me, meet in some sweet Paradise. I pictured to myself a lovely river such as that on whose banks Dante describes Mathilda gathering flowers, which ever flows

— bruna, bruna,   Sotto l'ombra perpetua, che mai   Raggiar non lascia sole ivi, nè Luna.

And then I repeated to myself all that lovely passage that relates the entrance of Dante into the terrestrial Paradise; and thought it would be sweet when I wandered on those lovely banks to see the car of light descend with my long lost parent to be restored to me. As I waited there in expectation of that moment, I thought how, of the lovely flowers that grew there, I would wind myself a chaplet and crown myself for joy: I would sing *sul margine d'un rio,* my father's favourite song, and that my voice gliding through the windless air would announce to him in whatever bower he sat expecting the moment of our union, that his daughter was come. Then the mark of misery would have faded from my brow, and I should raise my eyes fearlessly to meet his, which ever beamed with the soft lustre of innocent love. When I reflected on the magic look of those deep eyes I wept, but gently, lest my sobs should disturb the fairy scene.

I was so entirely wrapt in this reverie that I wandered on, taking no heed of my steps until I actually stooped down to gather a flower for my wreath on that bleak plain where no flower grew, when I awoke from my day dream and found myself I knew not where.

The sun had set and the roseate hue which the clouds had caught from him in his descent had nearly died away. A wind swept across the plain, I looked around me and saw no object that told me where I was; I had lost myself, and in vain attempted to find my path. I wandered on, and the coming darkness made every trace indistinct by which I might be guided. At length all was veiled in the deep obscurity of blackest night; I became weary and knowing that my servant was to sleep that night at the neighbouring village, so that my absence would alarm no one; and that I was safe in this wild spot from every intruder, I resolved to spend the night where I was. Indeed I was too weary to walk further: the air was chill but I was careless of bodily inconvenience, and I thought that I was well inured to the weather during my two years of solitude, when no change of seasons prevented my perpetual wanderings.

I lay upon the grass surrounded by a darkness which not the slightest beam of light penetrated — There was no sound for the deep night had laid to sleep the insects, the only creatures that lived on the lone spot where no tree or shrub could afford shelter to aught else — There was a wondrous silence in the air that calmed my senses yet which enlivened my soul, my mind hurried from image to image and seemed to grasp an eternity. All in my heart was shadowy yet calm, untill my ideas became confused and at length died away in sleep.

When I awoke it rained: I was already quite wet, and my limbs were stiff and my head giddy with the chill of night. It was a drizzling, penetrating shower; as my dank hair clung to my neck and partly covered my face, I had hardly strength to part with my fingers, the long strait locks that fell before my eyes. The darkness was much dissipated and in the east where the clouds were least dense the moon was visible behind the thin grey cloud —

The moon is behind, and at the full   And yet she looks both small and dull.

Its presence gave me a hope that by its means I might find my home. But I was languid and many hours passed before I could reach the cottage, dragging as I did my slow steps, and often resting on the wet earth unable to proceed.

I particularly mark this night, for it was that which has hurried on the last scene of my tragedy, which else might have dwindled on through long years of listless sorrow. I was very ill when I arrived and quite incapable of taking off my wet clothes that clung about me. In the morning, on her return, my servant found me almost lifeless, while possessed by a high fever I was lying on the floor of my room.

I was very ill for a long time, and when I recovered from the immediate danger of fever, every symptom of a rapid consumption declared itself. I was for some time ignorant of this and thought that my excessive weakness was the consequence of the fever; [sic] But my strength became less and less; as winter came on I had a cough; and my sunken cheek, before pale, burned with a hectic fever. One by one these symptoms struck me; & I became convinced that the moment I had so much desired was about to arrive and that I was dying. I was sitting by my fire, the physician who had attended me ever since my fever had just left me, and I looked over his prescription in which digitalis was the prominent medecine. "Yes," I said, "I see how this is, and it is strange that I should have deceived myself so long; I am about to die an innocent death, and it will be sweeter even than that which the opium promised."

I rose and walked slowly to the window; the wide heath was covered by snow which sparkled under the beams of the sun that shone brightly thro' the pure, frosty air: a few birds were pecking some crumbs under my window. I smiled with quiet joy; and in my thoughts, which through long habit would for ever connect themselves into one train, as if I shaped them into words, I thus addressed the scene before me:

"I salute thee, beautiful Sun, and thou, white Earth, fair and cold! Perhaps I shall never see thee again covered with green, and the sweet flowers of the coming spring will blossom on my grave. I am about to leave thee; soon this living spirit which is ever busy among strange shapes and ideas, which belong not to thee, soon it will have flown to other regions and this emaciated body will rest insensate on thy bosom

"Rolled round in earth's diurnal course   With rocks, and stones, and trees.

"For it will be the same with thee, who art called our Universal Mother, when I am gone. I have loved thee; and in my days both of happiness and sorrow I have peopled your solitudes with wild fancies of my own creation. The woods, and lakes, and mountains which I have loved, have for me a thousand associations; and thou, oh, Sun! hast smiled upon, and borne your part in many imaginations that sprung to life in my soul alone, and which will die with me. Your solitudes, sweet land, your trees and waters will still exist, moved by your winds, or still beneath the eye of noon, though [w]hat I have felt about ye, and all my dreams which have often strangely deformed thee, will die with me. You will exist to reflect other images in other minds, and ever will remain the same, although your reflected semblance vary in a thousand ways, changeable as the hearts of those who view thee. One of these fragile mirrors, that ever doted on thine image, is about to be broken, crumbled to dust. But everteeming Nature will create another and another, and thou wilt loose nought by my destruction.

"Thou wilt ever be the same. Receive then the grateful farewell of a fleeting shadow who is about to disappear, who joyfully leaves thee, yet with a last look of affectionate thankfulness. Farewell! Sky, and fields and woods; the lovely flowers that grow on thee; thy mountains & thy rivers; to the balmy air and the strong wind of the north, to all, a last farewell. I shall shed no more tears for my task is almost fulfilled, and I am about to be rewarded for long and most burthensome suffering. Bless thy child even even [sic] in death, as I bless thee; and let me sleep at peace in my quiet grave."

I feel death to be near at hand and I am calm. I no longer despair, but look on all around me with placid affection. I find it sweet to watch the progressive decay of my strength, and to repeat to myself, another day and yet another, but again I shall not see the red leaves of autumn; before that time I shall be with my father. I am glad Woodville is not with me for perhaps he would grieve, and I desire to see smiles alone during the last scene of my life; when I last wrote to him I told him of my ill health but not of its mortal tendency, lest he should conceive it to be his duty to come to me for I fear lest the tears of friendship should destroy the blessed calm of my mind. I take pleasure in arranging all the little details which will occur when I shall no longer be. In truth I am in love with death; no maiden ever took more pleasure in the contemplation of her bridal attire than I in fancying my limbs already enwrapt in their shroud: is it not my marriage dress? Alone it will unite me to my father when in an eternal mental union we shall never part.

I will not dwell on the last changes that I feel in the final decay of nature. It is rapid but without pain: I feel a strange pleasure in it. For long years these are the first days of peace that have visited me. I no longer exhaust my miserable heart by bitter tears and frantic complaints; I no longer the [sic] reproach the sun, the earth, the air, for pain and wretchedness. I wait in quiet expectation for the closing hours of a life which has been to me most sweet & bitter. I do not die not having enjoyed life; for sixteen years I was happy: during the first months of my father's return I had enjoyed ages of pleasure: now indeed I am grown old in grief; my steps are feeble like those of age; I have become peevish and unfit for life; so having passed little more than twenty years upon the earth I am more fit for my narrow grave than many are when they reach the natural term of their lives.

Again and again I have passed over in my remembrance the different scenes of my short life: if the world is a stage and I merely an actor on it my part has been strange, and, alas! tragical. Almost from infancy I was deprived of all the testimonies of affection which children generally receive; I was thrown entirely upon my own resources, and I enjoyed what I may almost call unnatural pleasures, for they were dreams and not realities. The earth was to me a magic lantern and I [a] gazer, and a listener but no actor; but then came the transporting and soul-reviving era of my existence: my father returned and I could pour my warm affections on a human heart; there was a new sun and a new earth created to me; the waters of existence sparkled: joy! joy! but, alas! what grief! My bliss was more rapid than the progress of a sunbeam on a mountain, which discloses its glades & woods, and then leaves it dark & blank; to my happiness followed madness and agony, closed by despair.

This was the drama of my life which I have now depicted upon paper. During three months I have been employed in this task. The memory of sorrow has brought tears; the memory of happiness a warm glow the lively shadow of that joy. Now my tears are dried; the glow has faded from my cheeks, and with a few words of farewell to you, Woodville, I close my work: the last that I shall perform.

Farewell, my only living friend; you are the sole tie that binds me to existence, and now I break it. It gives me no pain to leave you; nor can our seperation give you much. You never regarded me as one of this world, but rather as a being, who for some penance was sent from the Kingdom of Shadows; and she passed a few days weeping on the earth and longing to return to her native soil. You will weep but they will be tears of gentleness. I would, if I thought that it would lessen your regret, tell you to smile and congratulate me on my departure from the misery you beheld me endure. I would say; Woodville, rejoice with your friend, I triumph now and am most happy. But I check these expressions; these may not be the consolations of the living; they weep for their own misery, and not for that of the being they have lost. No; shed a few natural tears due to my memory: and if you ever visit my grave, pluck from thence a flower, and lay it to your heart; for your heart is the only tomb in which my memory will be enterred.

My death is rapidly approaching and you are not near to watch the flitting and vanishing of my spirit. Do no[t] regret this; for death is a too terrible an [sic] object for the living. It is one of those adversities which hurt instead of purifying the heart; for it is so intense a misery that it hardens & dulls the feelings. Dreadful as the time was when I pursued my father towards the ocean, & found their [sic] only his lifeless corpse; yet for my own sake I should prefer that to the watching one by one his senses fade; his pulse weaken — and sleeplessly as it were devour his life in gazing. To see life in his limbs & to know that soon life would no longer be there; to see the warm breath issue from his lips and to know they would soon be chill — I will not continue to trace this frightful picture; you suffered this torture once; I never did. And the remembrance fills your heart sometimes with bitter despair when otherwise your feelings would have melted into soft sorrow.

So day by day I become weaker, and life flickers in my wasting form, as a lamp about to loose it vivifying oil. I now behold the glad sun of May. It was May, four years ago, that I first saw my beloved father; it was in May, three years ago that my folly destroyed the only being I was doomed to love. May is returned, and I die. Three days ago, the anniversary of our meeting; and, alas! of our eternal seperation, after a day of killing emotion, I caused myself to be led once more to behold the face of nature. I caused myself to be carried to some meadows some miles distant from my cottage; the grass was being mowed, and there was the scent of hay in the fields; all the earth look[ed] fresh and its inhabitants happy. Evening approached and I beheld the sun set. Three years ago and on that day and hour it shone through the branches and leaves of the beech wood and its beams flickered upon the countenance of him whom I then beheld for the last time. I now saw that divine orb, gilding all the clouds with unwonted splendour, sink behind the horizon; it disappeared from a world where he whom I would seek exists not; it approached a world where he exists not. Why do I weep so bitterly? Why my [sic] does my heart heave with vain endeavour to cast aside the bitter anguish that covers it "as the waters cover the sea." I go from this world where he is no longer and soon I shall meet him in another.

Farewell, Woodville, the turf will soon be green on my grave; and the violets will bloom on it. There is my hope and my expectation; your's are in this world; may they be fulfilled. ◄

ACKNOWLEDGMENTS

I N CLOSING, A PERSONAL NOTE: I undertook the study of Mary Wollstonecraft Shelley as a doctoral student at The Graduate Center of the City University of New York, studying primarily with Joseph Wittreich. As is obvious from a quick review of my publications, after my first book, *The Posthumous Voice in Women's Writing from Mary Shelley to Sylvia Plath* (Routledge 2006), I developed other scholarly interests and have not, until the present volume, returned to Mary Shelley. My annotations here, then, draw from my memory of classes and private discussion of her oeuvre for which I am forever grateful. I kept no notes from those years, but it would be irresponsible not to make clear here my deep gratitude to Joseph Wittreich for all he taught me about Mary Shelley, her writing, her life, and her world. That education is reflected in countless ways in this book, *Monsters: Mary Shelley's Frankenstein and Mathilda.* ◀

RECOMMENDED FURTHER READING

Note: While all of the resources listed below are excellent representations of scholarship on Mary Shelley, I have listed the texts in order according to what I see as the most immediately relevant and helpful to the reader coming to Shelley's work for the first time. ◄

Mellor, Anne Kostelanetz. *Mary Shelley, Her Life, Her Fiction, Her Monsters.* New York: Methuen, 1988.

Mellor, Anne Kostelanetz. *Romanticism & Gender.* New York: Routledge, 1993.

Mellor, Anne Kostelanetz, and Richard E Matlak. *British Literature, 1780-1830.* Fort Worth: Harcourt Brace College Publishers, 1996.

Sampson, Fiona. *In Search of Mary Shelley: The Girl Who Wrote Frankenstein.* London: Profile Books, 2018.

Seymour, Miranda. *Mary Shelley.* London: John Murray, 2000.

Bennett, Betty T., and Stuart Curran, eds. *Mary Shelley In Her Times.* Baltimore: Johns Hopkins University Press, 2003.

Veeder, William R. *Mary Shelley & Frankenstein: The Fate of Androgyny.* Chicago: University of Chicago Press, 1986.

Spark, Muriel. *Mary Shelley.* London: Constable, 1993.

Britton, Ronald. "Mary Shelley's Frankenstein: What Made the Monster Monstrous?." *Journal of Analytical Psychology* 60, no. 1 (2015): 1-11.

Brennan, Matthew C. "Mary Shelley's Cinematic Progeny: The Fidelity of Young Frankenstein." *South Carolina Review* 48, no. 1 (2015): 195-202.

Holterhoff, Kate. "What Mary Shelley Can Teach STEM Readers." *Science Fiction Studies* 45, no. 2 (2018): 341-344.

Comet, Noah, and Susan J. Wolfson, eds. "New Directions In Romanticism and Gender: Essays In Honor of Anne K. Mellor [Special Issue]." *Studies In Romanticism* 3, no. 3 (2014): 292.

Shelley, Mary Wollstonecraft, and Betty T. Bennett. *Selected Letters of Mary Wollstonecraft Shelley.* Baltimore: Johns Hopkins University Press, 1995.

Buss, Helen M., David Lorne Macdonald and Anne McWhir. *Mary Wollstonecraft and Mary Shelley: Writing Lives.* Waterloo, Ontario, Canada: Wilfrid Laurier University Press, 2001.

Fisch, Audrey A., Anne Kostelanetz Mellor and Esther H. Schor. *The Other Mary Shelley: Beyond Frankenstein.* New York: Oxford University Press, 1993.

Bould, Mark, and Sherryl Vint. "Introduction: Mary Shelley, Frankenstein and Women In Sf." *Science Fiction Film & Television* 11, no. 2 (2018): 153-155.

Morrison, Lucy, and L. Adam Mekler. *Mary Shelley: Her Circle and Her Contemporaries.* Newcastle upon Tyne, UK: Cambridge Scholars Pub, 2010.

Schor, Esther H. *Bearing the Dead: The British Culture of Mourning From the Enlightenment to Victoria.* New Jersey: Princeton University Press, 1994.

Schor, Esther H. *The Cambridge Companion to Mary Shelley.* Cambridge, UK, New York: Cambridge University Press, 2003.

Clark, L. J., "The Letters of Mary Wollstonecraft Shelley, Volume III, 'What Years I Have Spent!', Betty T. Bennett and Mary Wollstonecraft Shelley." *Text* 8 (1995): 435-444.

Gelpi, Barbara Charlesworth. "Mary Shelley In Her Times." *Modern Philology* 102, no. 3 (2005): 438-441.

Bloom, Harold. *Mary Shelley*. New York: Chelsea House, 1985.

Williams, John. *Mary Shelley: A Literary Life*. New York: St. Martin's Press, 2000.

Guernsey-Pitchford, Julia. "Divided Selves of the Social Alien From Milton's Satan and Mary Shelley's Monster to Damien Echols of the West Memphis Three." *Studies In Popular Culture* 40, no. 2 (2018): 51-81.

Vargo, Lisa. "Mary Shelley, 'The Swiss Peasant,' and the Keepsake." *Wordsworth Circle* 48, no. 1 (2017): 46-52.

De Bruin-Molé, Megen. "'Hail, Mary, the Mother of Science Fiction': Popular Fictionalisations of Mary Wollstonecraft Shelley In Film and Television, 1935-2018." *Science Fiction Film & Television* 11, no. 2 (2018): 233-255.

Bowers, Will. "On First Looking Into Mary Shelley's Homer." *Review of English Studies* 69, no. 290 (2018): 510-531.

Solomonescu, Yasmin. "Mary Shelley's Fascinations: The Last Man." *Modern Philology* 114, no. 3 (2017): 702-725.

Bolea Ştefan. "Of Hatred and Solitude In the Works of Mary Shelley and E. M. Cioran." *Philobiblon: Transylvanian Journal of Multidisciplinary Research In Humanities* 22, no. 2 (2017): 105-116.

Moro, Alfredo. "Strange Bedfellows: Cervantes and Mary Wollstonecraft Shelley." *Anales Cervantinos* 49, no. 0 (2017): 325-352.

Raymond, Claire, *The Posthumous Voice in Women's Writing from Mary Shelley to Sylvia Plath*. London & New York: Routledge, 2006. ◄

ABOUT THE EDITOR

PHOTO: Amy Wilton

CLAIRE MILLIKIN RAYMOND grew up in Georgia, North Carolina, and overseas. She received her BA in philosophy from Yale University, MFA in poetry from New York University, and PhD in English literature from the Graduate Center of the City University of New York. She has taught at the University of Virginia, Charlottesville since 2007.

Raymond's academic works include *Substance of Fire: Gender and Race in the College Classroom* (2018), *Witnessing Sadism in Texts of the American South (2017), Francesca Woodman and the Kantian Sublime* (Ashgate, 2010), and *The Posthumous Voice in Women's Writing from Mary Shelley to Sylvia Plath* (Ashgate, 2006). Her academic works have appeared in publications such as the *Emily Dickinson Journal, Puckerbrush Review, Meridiens, Connotations*, and *Feminist Studies.*

Raymond's poetry (published under her maiden name, Millikin) has appeared in numerous literary journals and magazines, including *Crab Orchard Review, Alabama Literary Review, North American Review, Iris: A Journal About*

Women, Willow Review, Ekphrasis, The Southern Poetry Review, North Carolina Literary Review, Cold Mountain Review, Kestrel, the Beloit Poetry Journal, and *Grain.* among others. She has published the poetry collections *Television* (2017) a finalist for the Maine Literary Award in poetry; *Tartessos and Other Cities* (2016), *After Houses: Poetry for the Homeless* (2014), *Motels Where We Lived* (2014), and *Museum of Snow* (2013). Her poem "Atlantic" received the 2015 Lois Prize, from *CALYX*, and earlier poems have been noted for literary distinction by *Stone Voices* (2013).

Raymond participates in numerous conferences, colloquia, presentations, and workshops around the country capturing a wide range of topics, including women's literature, femininity, gender and violence, gothic and ghosts, poverty, and race relations. Her fellowships, honors, and awards include Excellence in Diversity Fellow (Univ. of Virginia, 2011-2012); The Carolyn G. Heilbrun Dissertation Prize (2003); and The Helene Newstead Dissertation Year Fellowship (Graduate Center, CUNY, 2000-2002). www.claireraymond.org. ◄

OTHER BOOKS BY 2LEAF PRESS

2Leaf Press challenges the status quo by publishing alternative fiction, non-fiction, poetry and bilingual works by activists, academics, poets and authors dedicated to diversity and social justice with scholarship that is accessible to the general public. 2Leaf Press produces high quality and beautifully produced hardcover, paperback and ebook formats through our series: 2LP Explorations in Diversity, 2LP University Books, 2LP Classics, 2LP Translations, Nuyorican World Series, and 2LP Current Affairs, Culture & Politics. Below is a selection of 2Leaf Press' published titles.

2LP EXPLORATIONS IN DIVERSITY

Substance of Fire: Gender and Race in the College Classroom
by Claire Millikin
Foreword by R. Joseph Rodríguez, Afterword by Richard Delgado
Contributors Riley Blanks, Blake Calhoun, Rox Trujillo

Black Lives Have Always Mattered
A Collection of Essays, Poems, and Personal Narratives
Edited by Abiodun Oyewole

The Beiging of America:
Personal Narratives about Being Mixed Race in the 21st Century
Edited by Cathy J. Schlund-Vials, Sean Frederick Forbes, Tara Betts
with an Afterword by Heidi Durrow

What Does it Mean to be White in America?
Breaking the White Code of Silence, A Collection of Personal Narratives
Edited by Gabrielle David and Sean Frederick Forbes
Introduction by Debby Irving and Afterword by Tara Betts

2LP UNIVERSITY BOOKS
Designs of Blackness
Mappings in the Literature and Culture of African Americans
by A. Robert Lee
20TH ANNIVERSARY EXPANDED EDITION

2LP CLASSICS
Adventures in Black and White
by Philippa Schuyler
Edited and with a critical introduction by Tara Betts

Monsters: Mary Shelley's Frankenstein and Mathilda
by Mary Shelley, edited by Claire Millikin Raymond

2LP TRANSLATIONS
Birds on the Kiswar Tree
by Odi Gonzales, Translated by Lynn Levin
Bilingual: English/Spanish

Incessant Beauty, A Bilingual Anthology
by Ana Rossetti, Edited and Translated by Carmela Ferradáns
Bilingual: English/Spanish

NUYORICAN WORLD SERIES
Our Nuyorican Thing, The Birth of a Self-Made Identity
by Samuel Carrion Diaz, with an Introduction by Urayoán Noel
Bilingual: English/Spanish

Hey Yo! Yo Soy!, 40 Years of Nuyorican Street Poetry,
The Collected Works of Jesús Papoleto Meléndez
Bilingual: English/Spanish

LITERARY NONFICTION
No Vacancy; Homeless Women in Paradise
by Michael Reid

The Beauty of Being, A Collection of Fables, Short Stories & Essays
by Abiodun Oyewole

WHEREABOUTS: Stepping Out of Place,
An Outside in Literary & Travel Magazine Anthology
Edited by Brandi Dawn Henderson

PLAYS
Rivers of Women, The Play
by Shirley Bradley LeFlore, with photographs by Michael J. Bracey

AUTOBIOGRAPHIES/MEMOIRS/BIOGRAPHIES
Trailblazers, Black Women Who Helped Make America Great
American Firsts/American Icons
by Gabrielle David
Edited by Carolina Fung Feng

Mother of Orphans
The True and Curious Story of Irish Alice, A Colored Man's Widow
by Dedria Humphries Barker

Strength of Soul
by Naomi Raquel Enright

Dream of the Water Children:
Memory and Mourning in the Black Pacific
by Fredrick D. Kakinami Cloyd
Foreword by Velina Hasu Houston, Introduction by Gerald Horne
Edited by Karen Chau

The Fourth Moment: Journeys from the Known to the Unknown, A Memoir
by Carole J. Garrison, Introduction by Sarah Willis

POETRY
PAPOLíTICO, Poems of a Political Persuasion
by Jesús Papoleto Meléndez
with an Introduction by Joel Kovel and DeeDee Halleck

Critics of Mystery Marvel, Collected Poems
by Youssef Alaoui, with an Introduction by Laila Halaby

shrimp
by jason vasser-elong, with an Introduction by Michael Castro

The Revlon Slough, New and Selected Poems
by Ray DiZazzo, with an Introduction by Claire Millikin

Written Eye: Visuals/Verse
by A. Robert Lee

A Country Without Borders: Poems and Stories of Kashmir
by Lalita Pandit Hogan, with an Introduction by Frederick Luis Aldama

Branches of the Tree of Life
The Collected Poems of Abiodun Oyewole 1969-2013
by Abiodun Oyewole, edited by Gabrielle David
with an Introduction by Betty J. Dopson

2Leaf Press Inc. is a nonprofit organization that publishes and promotes multicultural literature.

FLORIDA ■ NEW YORK
www.2leafpress.org